SAPPHIRE DAWN

Also from Christopher Rice and C. Travis Rice

C. Travis Rice
SAPPHIRE SUNSET: A Sapphire Cove Novel
SAPPHIRE SPRING: A Sapphire Cove Novel
SAPPHIRE STORM: A Sapphire Cove Novel
SAPPHIRE DAWN: A Sapphire Cove Novel

Thrillers
A DENSITY OF SOULS
THE SNOW GARDEN
LIGHT BEFORE DAY
BLIND FALL
THE MOONLIT EARTH

Supernatural Thrillers
THE HEAVENS RISE
THE VINES
BONE MUSIC: A Burning Grill Thriller
BLOOD ECHO: A Burning Girl Thriller
BLOOD VICTORY: A Burning Girl Thriller
DECIMATE

Paranormal Romance
THE FLAME: A Desire Exchange Novella
THE SURRENDER GATE: A Desire Exchange Novel
KISS THE FLAME: A Desire Exchange Novella

Contemporary Romance
DANCE OF DESIRE
DESIRE & ICE: A MacKenzie Family Novella

With Anne Rice
RAMSES THE DAMNED: THE PASSION OF CLEOPATRA
RAMSES THE DAMNED: THE REIGN OF OSIRIS

SAPPHIRE
DAWN

Sapphire Cove, Book 4

Christopher Rice
Writing As
C. Travis Rice

BLUE BOX PRESS

Sapphire Dawn
Sapphire Cove, Book 4
By Christopher Rice writing as C. Travis Rice

Copyright 2024 Christopher Rice
ISBN: 978-1-963135-02-2

Published by Blue Box Press, an imprint of Evil Eye Concepts, Incorporated

Author's Note

Dear Reader,

If this is your first time visiting Sapphire Cove, welcome. I'm excited for you to meet Richard and Donnie, and I can assure you these wonderful men find their happily ever after—after some intense drama. (And after Donnie learns to watch his mouth.) I've posted detailed letters about the themes explored in each Sapphire Cove novel, including this one, at the website for the series, www.VisitSapphireCove.com. Please be advised, these letters may contain spoilers about the books. You'll also find a lot more information there about the series in general.

Love,
C. Travis Rice

Jonas Jacobs hadn't seen a two-way mirror in years. He was pretty sure he was seeing one now. He had to squint to see around the edges of the blinding spotlight his captors had trained on him, but it was there, a smooth glossy plane amidst the shadowed concrete walls.

The scene on the other side was easy enough for him to imagine—a little squad of his former colleagues, pacing and sipping bad coffee as they quietly debated his fate. Ordinary-looking folk, for the most part. The kind you'd only glance at on a street corner unless your eye caught on the tell-tale bumps of holstered semiautomatic handguns hiding under their business-casual attire.

Had the bag over his head and the headlong pass into the backseat of an SUV really been necessary? The handcuffs seemed excessive as well. For starters, he was trained to get out of them. Trained to endure hours of interrogation without cracking as well. His captors knew that. They were the ones who'd trained him. So why waste time on the cloak and dagger set up?

Someone was pissed.

This little kidnapping was a charade. A show of force. Designed to punish, but not to break. And he wasn't surprised. You didn't anger the people he used to work for without paying a heavy price. That's why he'd avoided doing it until now. But some things were just too important. Not jobs, past or present. Not love; he'd had that once and lost it. Family was always important, but he'd lost most of his years ago.

Friendships were his family now.

The few friendships he could allow himself given the secrets he was required to keep.

"*A wedding.*" The voice-altering filter made his interrogator sound like a slasher movie villain, but he was pretty sure he recognized his old boss's tendency to put all her emphasis on the first word of each sentence. "*You commandeered a helicopter and strike team for a wedding?*"

"*Take it from a veteran of the hospitality industry, weddings can be dangerous business.*"

In the silence that followed, he was pretty sure they were arguing about whether or not to question him like normal law enforcement professionals—which they most certainly were not.

"*Look, how about I pay a rental fee for the chopper and we call it square?*" he asked the shadows. "*It was a lovely machine and those mountain roads can be quite treacherous.*"

A few seconds later, a door creaked on its hinges. The square of light that fell across the concrete floor was weak. Heels clacked toward him through the dark.

The blinding spotlight gave Carol Lu's crisp pants suit a glowing edge. He could barely make out her face, so he couldn't tell how much she'd aged. If she still rose at four am each morning to run three miles through rain, snow, or sweltering heat, he figured the answer was, well.

"*I thought you wanted a quieter life,*" she finally said.

"*I had one. Up until a few days ago.*"

"*Hardly. In the past three years that hotel of yours had a blackmail scandal involving the entire security department and a sham wedding that destroyed the career of one of the most famous women in the world. Oh, and your accountant was almost thrown off a cliff.*"

"*Technically a hotel's accountant is called a* controller *and they—*"

"*Shut up, Jonas.*"

He sighed. "*The handcuffs are a bit much, Carol. No one died.*"

"*I'm no expert, but weddings are usually held to a higher standard than that.*"

She reached behind her into the shadows and pulled forward a metal chair just like his. When she sat so that she was blocking the blinding spotlight, he realized this was the only small mercy she was willing to grant.

"*We've checked. Neither groom had a criminal history.*"

You didn't check the wedding planners, though, *he thought.*

"*Perhaps if we focused on the potential gift I brought you, Carol, we can—"*

"I'll call it a gift once I see what it's good for and not a second before."

"And you're going to leave me here until you do?"

Carol crossed her legs and folded her hands atop one knee. *"We are going to sit right here until you start telling me why you raided my agency's assets like a college kid returning to his parents' house for Christmas break. Which is not how I'd describe our relationship, by the way. Explain to me why I shouldn't have you disappeared."*

"Because people will miss me. Because unlike most of the folks you deal with, I'm not a monster."

"Are you talking about our targets or my coworkers?"

"Both." Jonas smiled.

"Your eleventh-hour moral objections to our work were well noted during your fiery departure. Let's focus on the business at hand."

"Getting me a pot of Earl Grey?"

Carol bent forward over her knees, her jaw in sharp relief thanks to gritted teeth. *"What happened at Sapphire Cove? I want to know how a wedding that used more flowers than the Rose Parade turned into an international incident."*

Jonas sighed. *"Well, for that we'd have to go back to the beginning."*

"Where's that?"

"Where do all weddings begin?"

"Two people fall in love?"

Jonas tittered and shook his head. *"Oh, no. The perfect wedding always begins in the same place."*

Carol stared at him through the shadows.

"With the wedding planners, my dear. And believe me, these two were a piece of work."

1

Six Months Earlier

Richard Merriweather had only thrown a drink on someone once before in his life, a giant frat boy in college who'd made the mistake of performing a loud, mincing parody of the way he'd greeted his best girlfriends in a crowded bar. If the homophobe in question hadn't started his impression with a slur, he might not have slung a foamy tendril of Stella Artois across the front of the snide bully's shorts and T-shirt with a single flick of the wrist. But the words *Check out this bonesmoker* had simmered in his chest, and suddenly his friends were corralling him out of the bar before fists were raised. "Ballet lessons when I was a kid!" Richard called after him. "They do wonders for your posture. Give 'em a try, Frankenstein."

Years later, he still didn't regret the act. He'd put up with far too many bullies in high school to tolerate them in college. And it wasn't like he'd thrown the bottle itself.

That said, he was a grown man now, and he'd shunned all forms of physical violence since. But if there was ever a time to break such a vow it was with a total stranger who'd just bragged to you about sleeping with your ex-husband—when the man had still been your husband.

To his credit, the obnoxiously handsome IT executive—his name was either Billy or Bradley; Richard couldn't remember and now he had no interest in trying—didn't threaten Richard's physical well-being, but he did stare down at his ice-water soaked crotch with a grimace that suggested at least one testicle had frozen over.

A shame since Richard had aimed for both.

"All I said was you should try to relax about the whole thing," the shithead finally managed. "Jesus!"

"Clearly I disagreed with you."

"Look, it's not like I knew he was married. I mean, we were at a sex party, for God's sake. But when you said Henry Cavill lookalike with a Texas accent who worked in finance I..."

Thought it would be appropriate to loudly blurt out, "Hey, that guy plowed me last spring," Richard thought as his would-be seducer lost his voice to a series of gasping breaths and went back to fruitlessly dabbing ice water from his tailored dress pants with a paper napkin.

Amazing how quickly the worm had turned. In an instant, Richard had gone from studying one of the exhibition's more impressive canvases to being utterly charmed by a handsome stranger who'd stepped forward and introduced himself with a winning smile. Then, for a brief, blush-inducing few moments, they'd been delightedly chatting, an island of flirting and eye contact around which the reception's other guests seemed to fade away. Right up until Richard revealed the broad circumstances of his recent divorce, and his would-be suitor proudly proclaimed himself an unwitting accessory. But if the lewd declaration had been his only response, Richard might have been able to make a quiet and graceful exit from the Laguna Art Museum's opening reception for its new exhibition of California impressionists.

After all, this was hardly the first disclosure of his ex-husband's rampant infidelity. *About once a month for four years,* Mark had finally admitted in a quiet, breathy voice that seared the fateful figure across Richard's memory like a terrible brand. And it wasn't the fact that the man across from him now had gone on to share detail after detail of how he and Mark had done the deed—on the floor in the middle of a suite at the Chateau Marmont crowded with other rutting men who'd been pre-approved by way of naked selfies emailed to the party's organizer; *His cock bends a little to the left, right?*—as if he were bragging about the conquest and heedless of the fact that every awful detail was making Richard feel like his stomach was about to strangle his throat.

No, it was Benji's or Baxter's or Bobby's condescending lecture about it that initiated Richard's first return to physical violence in almost twenty years. The same lecture Richard's husband had given him after he'd caught him doing his trainer doggy-style in their bed.

The *it's just sex* lecture. The *we're gay so we shouldn't have to play by the same rules* lecture. The *most of our friends aren't monogamous, so why are we?* lecture. Complex topics in any relationship, to be sure, but when you failed to raise them with your husband until *after* you slept with many of your mutual friends, the only appropriate response Richard could manage required the intercession of a divorce lawyer. There'd also been the not-so-convenient fact that Mark had stared him dead in the eye on their third date years before and given him the most earnest of lectures about how "you can't build a ship with one man that takes to the open seas if you keep heading back to the pond with a guy you met five minutes ago," as Richard's insides had melted into a puddle of goo.

Did their hot tub with Julio, Fred, and Larry count as a pond? Because that excursion had apparently happened a few months after their wedding, when Richard had been in Paris overseeing a lavish birthday celebration for a Dutch princess inside several rooms of the Musée d'Orsay.

The fact of the matter was that Mark Scottman had gone about his extramarital dalliances in the way he did most everything else—with no thought of the consequences and a firm conviction he could charm or sleep his way out of them when they arrived.

The museum's parking lot was bathed in the orange light of dusk when Richard reached it. Breathless with anger, he slammed himself into the driver's seat of his Mercedes, replaying the conversation in his head against his will.

Jonas. He'd forgotten the douchebag's opening line. The handsome stranger had claimed to be friends with Richard's good friend, Jonas. And hadn't he told Jonas himself earlier that day that he'd be attending the reception solo that evening? Had this been his old friend's idea of a fix up? If so, he planned to send a scorching text message in response, asking what sewer he'd met the guy in.

But that wasn't fair. Jonas Jacobs had been a source of constant support in his life for years, and an absolute prince to him since the divorce. As the newly promoted assistant general manager of one of Southern California's premiere resorts, he'd brought Richard a professional opportunity so exciting it had lured him back to the U.S. after several months of what he'd dubbed his "self-imposed exile"—a fancy term for dealing with his broken marriage by spending obscene amounts of money traveling throughout Europe under the false pretense of supervising the London office of his events firm.

No way would Jonas have set him up with this guy if he'd known. His record as a friend was almost spotless.

As he wound along the Pacific Coast Highway in the direction of Sapphire Cove, his new, temporary home, his pulse returned to normal. The Mercedes he was still getting used to was a loaner from the hotel, typically used for chauffeuring guests to dinner and John Wayne Airport, and as an added perk, they'd removed the decal of the hotel's logo from both front doors.

A gorgeous sunset was setting fire to the Pacific off to his right. The temperature was a perfect seventy-five degrees. The palm trees lining the highway did a seductive, swaying dance in the ocean winds. He was still fighting jet lag, but the forty-eight hours since his arrival had seemed idyllic compared to the months spent aimlessly wandering London streets, fighting tears until the next spot of rain came to wash them away.

When he stepped from the Mercedes and handed the valet his keys, he wasn't confident his feet would touch the ground. The next thing he knew he was in the hotel's bustling, marble-floored lobby, his chin raised defiantly, his old pose for marching down high school hallways past jeers and taunts from the kids who ridiculed him for the fact that he didn't play sports, had once given an elaborate in-class presentation on how to assemble a formal place setting, and walked with spine straight, shoulders back, and chest out.

Ballet, he thought. *It's great for posture, bitches.*

His posture held as he made a beeline for the nearest restroom, thank God. He didn't feel like crying in the elevator on the way up to his suite.

How many times could one man humiliate you in less than half a year?

He seemed destined to find out.

2

I'm getting fired, Donnie Bascombe thought as he sat glumly at the bar in Sapphire Cove's main restaurant.

A weird thing to be thinking given he owned his own company. But the gig he was about to get axed from didn't come with a paycheck. It wasn't professional, it was personal, the result of stupidly agreeing to play best man for his best friend's wedding. Somehow that made the rejection to come seem even worse.

Donnie didn't know crap about weddings, and he'd said as much when Logan first asked him to serve.

"You know about *me,* dude. And I'm fifty percent of this wedding," his best friend had commanded in that former Marine Corps staff sergeant tone that brokered no disagreement. And damn if Donnie hadn't gone soft inside and wiped away a few tears during their bear hug after he'd sputtered out a yes.

But that had been almost a year ago now. Clearly, Logan and his fiancé had come to their senses. His guess was that, after years of vagueness and delays about their big day, his two closest friends had finally decided to get serious about planning and realized their porn star best man needed the boot. That's why they'd summoned him at the last minute to the hotel they both ran for "a discussion about the wedding" before they'd even announced a date.

Not a meeting. A *discussion.*

And could Donnie blame them?

At the last bachelor party he'd attended, his friend Justin had tied his fiancé ass up and buck naked to a lazy Susan and invited all of their groomsmen, Donnie included, to take a turn. Fun for all, especially Jason, but Donnie was pretty sure that if another man so much as laid a finger on Logan's fiancé, Logan would tear off the attached hand. And arm. As far as planning a wedding himself, the closest Donnie had come was a porn film he'd written and directed the year before about two cheating grooms who eventually realize they want an open relationship and decide to celebrate this fact by having an orgy with the minister and all their groomsmen. Some of his studio's best work, for sure. But definitely not Logan and Connor's style. Indeed, Donnie's closest friends were so monogamous and so wildly in love, Donnie thought there was a good chance Connor might change his last name to Murdoch once they were officially hitched.

Fat chance, he thought. The Harcourt name was synonymous with one of the nicest resorts on the West Coast and the crazy rich—if drama-filled—family that had founded it. No way could Connor give it up. It would be bad for business.

And right now, business looked good.

It was almost dinnertime and the hotel was abuzz. Couples and families who'd spent the day baking by the resort's swimming pool or down on its compact crescent of private beach were now dolled up and spritzed with designer fragrances. They gathered under the three-tiered crystal chandelier near the reception desk or took their seats in the restaurant behind him, their excited chatter amplified by the lobby's vast white marble floor.

Whenever he visited, most of the staff recognized him and greeted him with a warm smile, a perk of being best friends with the hotel's security director and his fiancé, the general manager. And even though he'd stepped behind the camera years before, the guests often gave him long, curious looks suggesting they'd enjoyed at least one of his performances as Bo Bonin, the porn star a leading adult industry blog had once hailed as "gay America's favorite perverted football coach." But none of this relaxed him. When he wanted to unwind, he headed to one of the San Diego dive bars close to the harbor where he lived aboard his boat. And if he wanted to get laid, he headed to the gay clubs in Hillcrest where his résumé meant at least one or two or three or four men would throw themselves at him, hoping to check *banged a porn star* off their gay bucket list.

And if he wanted his best friends to tell him they'd basically reconsidered their crazy idea to have him help plan their wedding, he was summoned an hour north to Sapphire Cove.

He should be relieved, shouldn't he?

When the big day came, he could kick back and relax with the other guests. Make a toast that embarrassed Murdoch until he was bright red. Maybe hook up with the cutest cater waiter. But then he remembered the look that had come into Logan's eyes when he'd asked him to serve. The big lug had seemed more vulnerable and full of need than he'd ever seen him, like asking Donnie to be a big part of his most special day was almost as significant as asking Connor to marry him. And maybe Donnie had been flattered. More than flattered, *honored.* Because he was a runaway from a potato farm in Michigan who'd somehow managed to make sex his career after a few years of using it to survive. And if you'd told him when he was sixteen that he'd someday be asked to help plan a fancy gay wedding in California, with a multimillionaire groom no less, he would have laughed in your face.

Fight for yourself. If they've got doubts, take them away. You're not dead on the side of a highway because you picked the wrong trucker. That means you know how to beat the odds.

"Hey buddy," he asked the bartender, "you got any idea how to plan a wedding?"

The guy had returned from delivering two giant martinis to a handsome older couple who'd been cheerfully describing the blizzard they'd fled in Chicago the day before.

"Sorry, man. Weddings aren't my thing. Breakups, though. I got those figured out. Best ones involve a text and a lot of quick packing before they get home from work."

"A text message?" Donnie winced. "That's cold, man. I mean, you could at least write them a note."

"I'm the one who wasn't home from work yet in that scenario. Reason I recommend it is she made off with my good wine glasses. So if you're looking to turn a profit…" The bartender shrugged and wiped down a section of the white marble bar.

But his own words, *write them a note*, had dropped him dead center in the middle of one of his most painful memories, and he was suddenly desperate to get out.

He was already angsted out enough. Zach Loudon, the guy who'd broken his heart fifteen years before, the one who'd vanished from his life with only a weird goodbye note, was the last person he wanted on his mind.

It didn't help that Zach was currently walking through Sapphire Cove's lobby.

For a few seconds, Donnie's heart felt like it was going to explode in his chest.

He sat up so straight it earned him a concerned look from the bartender.

No fucking way, he was thinking as he clocked the same height, the same thick chin-length *run your hands through it while you moan his name* hair. The wrong color—darker, less blond. But it had been over a decade since he'd seen his old flame. God knows, he could have dyed it a hundred times since then. But when Zach looked up suddenly to avoid plowing into a little boy and girl who were running in tight circles around their parents, Donnie saw his eyes were brown, not crystal blue, but they had the same attentive, penetrating, doesn't-miss-a-beat look in them. His chin was more rounded, but this only amplified the fact that he also walked with his jaw up like he was daring someone to block his path. But it was the man's poise that sent tingles up the back of Donnie's neck and desire throbbing to his balls. Erect, elegant, proud. Class meets sass; steel edged with silk.

Ballet, he thought. *If the dude didn't do ballet like Zach, then he took classes, at least.*

If anything, Not Zach looked like a more sophisticated and polished version of the guy who'd broken Donnie's heart fifteen years before. And as Donnie rose from his bar stool, he was already imagining himself wrapped in those long limbs as he made the dude moan his name.

3

Donnie made a beeline for the men's room door as his target disappeared on the other side of it. Logan had placed him under strict orders to keep his antics at Sapphire Cove to a minimum, and for the most part he'd obeyed. But a man who marshaled this combination of lust and memory from every inch of Donnie's bones merited an exception to the rule.

They called him Sex Monster for a reason.

The handsome specimen wasn't at one of the urinals when Donnie entered. He was at the counter, dabbing at his nose with a paper towel. Because the man in question, who'd walked with such pride across the lobby seconds before, was suddenly crying.

Several locks of dirty blond hair draped Not Zach's face. Donnie fought the urge to reach out and lift them off his forehead. He won. By a hair. It was a dangerous thing, Donnie thought, that the guy was still attractive to him even while fighting a losing battle against his tears.

Not Zach was now dabbing at his nose with precision and care, making Donnie wonder what it would feel like to have those same careful fingers gently tracing the hairs on his chest. His desire deepened, boring down into a space in his gut that felt too deep to be vented by a single good nut. Logan liked to joke that Donnie only had two lanes—caretaker and fuckboy, but Not Zach combined soft beauty, elegance, and some kind of heartbreak into a package that might send him careening dangerously back and forth between two lanes, something he'd only done once before in his life.

"What's his name?" Donnie asked.

His target jumped, cleared his throat and brought his clasped hands to the bridge of his nose as if he were simply suffering an allergy attack. "Excuse me." He coughed into his palms.

"Fine. What's his address? I'll go throttle the guy."

Not Zach lowered his hands. "I'm sorry?"

"The guy who made you cry."

His target laughed silently, turned to the marble counter, and began washing his hands.

Donnie took a step closer. "It's a serious offer."

"Well, thank you, but I've engaged in enough physical violence for one day."

"I didn't say you had to come. I can handle him on my own and report back. You know, for my reward."

"How do you know it's a him?" the guy asked, drying his hands carefully with a towel from the nearby basket. So he wasn't going to take the bait and ask what sort of reward Donnie had in mind. No biggie. He'd find another way in.

"Lucky guess. You've got a nice swing in your walk." Now the man looked into his eyes with an intensity that was hard to read. Maybe he was offended by Donnie's assumption, but there was a flare of interest in the way his lips stayed slightly parted, his eyes wide and intense, and the way his breath lifted his chest. "Trust me, it's a good thing. Wouldn't be here otherwise."

"Thank you… I guess."

Now his tone sounded distracted. His hands had to be dry already, and there was only so long the guy could pretend to be toweling them off. Donnie could sense things slipping away. A new line of inquiry was required. "You look pretty good for a guy who roughed somebody up earlier."

"I didn't rough them up, per se." He tossed the hand towel into the receptacle under the counter and turned to face Donnie. "I poured a glass of water on their crotch."

"Dangerous stuff, man. You should probably see a doctor. Get that head checked out just in case."

"I take it you're being sarcastic?" Mr. Luscious Locks asked with his first genuine smile.

"Very."

"Well, you're cheering me up, so thank you."

Score, Donnie thought, and took a step closer, leaving only a few feet between them. The smile left his target's face, as if Donnie's sudden proximity had brought home the seriousness of his intentions.

"I'm real good at cheering people up," Donnie said. "But I'm better at making them forget their name."

"My," the man said, "you're forward." His voice was that particular husky whisper that combined desire and a bit of resistance. Donnie knew that whisper well. It set him on fire. Whenever he found a performer who could emulate it convincingly on set, he signed them as an exclusive on the spot. In a moment like this, it was a promise of good things to come—literally.

"I see something I want, I go for it," he said.

"How *Wolf of Wall Street* of you."

"So what do you say?" Donnie jerked his head in the direction of the nearest bathroom stall.

"To what?"

Since he clearly wasn't getting the picture, Donnie jerked one thumb in the same direction. Finally, the guy looked from Donnie's hand to the nearby bathroom stall as if the distance between the two were a thousand miles. When he looked to Donnie again, all traces of interest had left his expression, replaced by a wide-eyed, horrified grimace. "*Here?*" he asked.

"Don't worry, baby. If you've got somebody waiting for you, I can be quick."

Not Zach took a step back, jaw slackening into the first threat of a sneer. "You mean like a boyfriend?"

Donnie shrugged, trying to affect his best, *don't ask, don't tell* grin. The truth was, in his experience, the boyfriends usually wanted to join or watch.

Ice frosted over his gaze. "Thank you, truly. But I don't have sex in public places with human reptiles. Good evening, sir."

Fuck, Donnie thought, *or lack thereof, it looked like.*

"Aw, come on now." The man's hand was on the door and he was getting ready to disappear into the lobby. "You shouldn't be offended, handsome."

He spun, eyes ablaze. "Oh, really? What should I be?"

"Flattered. It's a nice place. You're worth the risk of getting caught."

"Five minutes in a bathroom stall with a stranger doesn't make me feel flattered. It makes me feel *disposable*. And to be perfectly honest,

I've had enough of that feeling lately."

Lotta information there, Donnie thought, but he needed to ramp up the charm, not launch into an interrogation.

"Five minutes?" Donnie whined. "I can last way longer than that. I mean, ten, fifteen at least."

Not Zach's stunned look turned to amusement, and a second later laughter he was clearly trying to fight shook his shoulders. "What is this?" he finally asked. "What are you?"

Donnie smirked. True, it had been years since he'd performed on camera, but he'd left hundreds of scenes floating around the Internet in the wake of his move behind the camera. "Come on," Donnie finally said. "No offense, but you seem pretty gay and you've been on the Internet at some point, right?" Donnie raised one eyebrow and winked at him. "You know what I do for a living."

"Vice cop?" the guy asked.

"Nah."

"Problematic janitor?"

"What you got against janitors?"

"Nothing. So long as they don't hit on me with all the grace of a St. Bernard."

"Aw, dude, come on. I love St. Bernards."

"A question, Cujo. Are you ever going to let me leave this bathroom?"

Donnie grinned. "I'm not standing in your way."

Blushing furiously, Not Zach sucked in a deep breath through his nose. "Give my best to your wife."

"What? I don't have a wife."

"Lucky her." The door swung shut behind him.

Donnie was no stranger to being shot down. As he liked to say, a good sex life required ten strikes for every home run. But something about this guy had felt different, his rejection harder to play off. A judgy voice in his head told him he'd blown something that could have been interesting, *different,* by moving at his usual pedal to the medal, face to the pillow speed. Although maybe the problem was that bathrooms didn't have pillows, and the only way to get inside this particular beauty was in a bedroom.

He'd been a proud sex worker for years. When it came to getting laid, he didn't care what most people thought, and he rarely minced words. If you wanted someone, try for it. The worst they could say was no. But his moves just now hadn't felt like his typical Sex Monster confidence. They'd felt desperate. Like the guy was a beautiful butterfly and if he didn't cup his hands around him, he'd fly away forever and Donnie would never get a good look at his colorful wings.

That's why he waited a beat before returning to the lobby. Because if he spotted the guy outside, he thought he might have a hard time not approaching him again.

This is about Zach, he thought, *all he did was remind you of Zach.*

And so he pushed the door open and headed back to his stool, relieved to see the guy wasn't seated at any of the tables in the restaurant. But damn if he didn't scan the lobby for him over and over again once he took his seat at the bar.

This time, he ordered a double, hoping it would cool him off and bone him down.

A few minutes later, it hadn't done either.

4

The truth was, Richard hadn't recognized his bathroom intruder. Not at first. Not until the guy had made such a smug show of implying he was the Brad Pitt of the gay porn world. Only then did his strong jawline and scruffy face and sandy blond hair and drowsy blue eyes trigger an image of a football coach laying claim to his star player on a locker room bench, some random Pornhub clip Richard had relieved himself to a few weeks before.

It made sense, he thought as he slipped into the elevator, that the guy did porn. Richard couldn't remember the last time he'd felt targeted by such powerful sexual energy. Those wolfish looks had made him feel like his feet were floating up off the tile floor. And the flutter between his cheeks he felt at the sight of the man's drowsy, inviting grins reminded him of what his old assistant had said one night after too many drinks at the Christmas party for his LA office. *You can be as cisgender as you want, but some guys just make you feel like you've got a pussy down there.*

He'd been right to shoot the guy down. But he was frightened by how close he'd come to inviting him up to his room. He was starving; that was all. Emotionally, physically, psychologically. There'd been no one since the divorce. (The massage therapist he'd hired for a rub and tug in his Amsterdam hotel room didn't count. Especially given he'd cried after the guy had left.) Or maybe he was dealing with the fact that his ex-husband had never made him feel like the desirable one. Mark had been handsome and charming, for sure, but their sex play—while frequent and varied—had always been about Richard worshiping and serving Mark, never the other way around.

And desire was all he'd seen in his bathroom visitor's eyes.

Before marriage, he'd been careful about mixing sex and work, but when your new workplace played host to hundreds of new visitors on a daily basis, maybe there could be an exception. Just this once.

He was entitled, wasn't he? After the last few months, maybe he deserved to be a little bad. A little reckless. And he wasn't a priest. He'd slept around plenty before getting married. But by his late twenties, he'd grown thoroughly bored by sex with strangers ordered up by way of a hook-up app, maybe because so many of them crossed his threshold smelling of either weed or dryer sheets, and when he tried to engage them in conversation they skedaddled out the door before whatever fantasy of Richard they'd dreamed up could be spoiled by the reality.

But a bathroom stall? Out of the question.

When he'd first realized he wasn't alone in front of the mirror, then looked up to see the handsome, brawny visitor with the easy smile, his first thought had been, *I'm about to get bashed.* Hardly logical given the setting, but for so many queer men, including himself, it was a reflexive one that followed them everywhere. Especially for guys like him who found the term "straight acting" as repulsive as the thought of standing sex in a bathroom stall at a bustling hotel. Technically, he'd never been bashed. But he'd been threatened with it plenty, usually by bastards yelling obscenities out the windows of passing cars.

And it made sense, at first, given the porn star in question had looked like a combination of every archetypal gay fantasy he could think of. He had the brawn of a professional athlete, but his hair and scruff were groomed with the conformist precision of a military officer. In addition, the scuffed jeans and leather motocross jacket he'd worn over a heather gray, pecs-hugging T-shirt had screamed repressed, married dad who listened to Joe Rogan podcasts on the way to his CrossFit gym and secretly hooked up with guys on Grindr. All were stock characters in the wild, fantasy world of gay porn that had sustained Richard since his marriage ended, and he was willing to bet the boor who'd offered to penetrate him over a toilet had played all three characters more than once.

But, of course, it was the *someone waiting outside* comment that had killed all hope of creating a fantasy of their own. Like the gallery opening earlier that evening—like the collapse of his marriage—it made him feel like no sexual boundary or relationship was safe from the sexual free-for-all that defined so much of gay life. Like his own inability to be anything other than monogamous with a man he loved made him an Aunt Lydia in a world of June Osbornes, trying to escape his puritanical reign.

Because that's how Mark tried to gaslight you about his lies, he thought as he stepped into his room.

The Pacifica Suite, his new home, was allegedly a mirror image of the Penthouse Suite across the hall, only its view was angled north up the coast. Laughter came from the pool deck below, and he could hear the pianist playing in the hotel's restaurant. His things—meaning the two suitcases he'd fled the country with four months before—were still resting against the wall in the corner. But Connor Harcourt, the hotel's general manager and his new business partner, had made the other accommodations he'd asked for during his contract negotiation. He'd placed lower-wattage bulbs in all the lamps and sprinkled Richard's favorite scent diffusers throughout the room, so that he was kissed by the mingled odors of leather and cognac as he took a seat in front of his laptop now. A gift basket full of his favorite bath products still sat unopened in the spacious marble bathroom. And a veritable tech center had been set up at one corner of the long, eight-top dining table so that he could work out of his suite until his office downstairs was complete.

Richard told himself to put the porn star out of his mind. Prepare for the meeting he had scheduled in twenty minutes. Instead, he went straight to his computer, opened his browser's history, and went looking for the coach-claims-jock clip he'd jerked off to a few weeks before. There was the guy's name down in the metadata.

His professional name, at least.

Bo Bonin, Richard thought, *a sexual compulsive's idea of clever.*

A Google search later, he discovered Bo Bonin's Instagram account was mostly candid shots of other porn stars on sets and in between shoots, some more of them lounging on the deck of a large boat. It looked like he worked behind the camera now and ran a studio named Parker Hunter. It also looked like he called San Diego home, which was an hour's drive south. Had he come up to Sapphire Cove to get away or was Sapphire Cove one of his regular cruising spots? Or did the hotel promise guests a porn star in every bathroom?

There was a knock on the door. Richard snapped the laptop shut and went to answer it.

His old friend Jonas Jacobs gave him a slight smile, his hands folded over his belt buckle, his dark bald dome gleaming. His pocket square always matched his tie, and today they were both the blue of the hotel's logo.

They'd met Richard's freshman year at Georgetown at an on-campus dance for the LGBT Students Association. Terrified to be attending his first event as a newly out gay man, Richard had pre-gamed far too aggressively with a six-pack of hard cider. When Jonas had realized the precocious young freshman he'd started dancing with was in danger of losing his lunch, he'd hurried him to the nearest restroom, then spent the rest of the night taking care of him. He'd also gently poured cold water on Richard's drunken attempts to make out with him, which Richard woke with a mortifying memory of the next, head-throbbing morning. Even though he was only two years older at the time, Jonas had seemed infinitely wiser. He instantly became Richard's mentor in the ways of gay life on and off campus.

Behind his wire-framed glasses, the man's dark brown eyes were unreadable as always. As a friend, he was generous and supportive to a fault, but there were often times when the friendship felt one way. Times when it felt like Jonas preferred being a detached parental figure who seemed to have it all figured out, rather than another friend on the uneven road of life who occasionally fell and skinned his knees. He'd practically dropped off the face of the earth after graduation, staying in touch with Richard by email and mostly to learn details about Richard's life, all without sharing many about his own. Whenever he'd asked Jonas about his post-college professional life, his old friend had given vague answers about "a lot of international travel for some new startups." There were rumors about that part of his life, Richard found, rumors circulated by their mutual college friends, but also by the staff here at Sapphire Cove, rumors that centered around three letters that often loomed frighteningly large in international politics.

Right now, those aspects of his character made it impossible to determine if Jonas knew about the water toss incident.

He followed the invitation of Richard's outstretched arm and stepped inside. "How did it go?"

"So Buddy called you?" Richard asked.

"Bronson. And it was a text, actually. A largely incoherent one, but what I could decipher seemed fairly hostile. So not well, I take it."

"I poured iced water on his crotch."

Jonas swallowed. "Oh, dear. So he said Whistler was a better portrait painter than John Singer Sargent?"

"He bragged about sleeping with Mark. While we were still married. And he kept bragging about it even after I told him we'd still been married at the time."

Jonas went stone still, then walked to the edge of the long dining table, head bowed, deep breaths lifting his broad upper back. "I had no idea," he said quietly. "I'm so sorry, Richard."

"I take it you encouraged him to make an introduction?"

"I barely know him. A friend of mine dated him for a bit and said he had a nice time. He's got quite the résumé. I thought he might make for a nice distraction."

"Well, I appreciate you thinking of me."

"I thought it would make for a nice diversion from recent events, not a party foul. I'm so sorry. Truly."

"It's fine," he said. "Don't worry about it."

The words *a nice diversion* had him imagining what it would have been like to brace his palms against the closed bathroom stall door downstairs while a porn star with a ridiculously slutty name chewed on his neck, prodded at his entrance with several fingers, and whispered words into his ear that made him feel like a meal poised for devourment. As opposed to the four years he'd spent servicing a husband whose dirty talk consisted mainly of references to how good looking you were supposed to think he was.

"Something to drink?" Richard asked as he headed to the wet bar in the kitchenette.

"Still on the clock, I'm afraid. I just wanted to stop by to tell you your meeting with Connor and Logan's been moved out onto the pool deck."

"And to find out how the fix-up went."

Sinking into one of the dining room chairs, Jonas nodded. "And to find out how the fix-up went, true. But to be honest, there's something else I wanted to warn you about."

Turning to face Jonas, Richard sipped from the bottle of club soda he'd pulled from the mini fridge. "Interesting. I do love a good warning."

"The best man they want you to work with on their wedding..." Jonas cleared his throat and studied the rose-colored carpet, seemingly in search of his next words. Or trying to make the ones he wanted to speak sound more diplomatic than they were.

"Logan's friend, you mean."

Jonas nodded. "He's kind of a character."

"How so?"

"He can be a little boundaryless. And ridiculous."

"In what way?"

"In a flirtatious and often inappropriately sexual way. Look, he's harmless, ultimately, but he has a tendency to throw himself at men like us."

"Uptight priss pots who have a panic attack when they have to fly coach?"

Jonas raised his eyebrows. "You've done far better than I have, friend. My last vacation was economy all the way. What I meant was classy, elegant, mature, and sophisticated men who would never ordinarily give this guy the time of day. Wait. Why are you nodding?"

"Does this man ever go by the name Bo Bonin?"

Jonas's face fell. "Oh, dear," he whispered. "I'm too late."

5

"Sorry, pal. No porn stars allowed." Logan Murdoch had a voice like thunder and a grip like a C-clamp. Whenever he squeezed Donnie on the shoulder like he was doing now, Donnie's flesh sealed itself to the man's giant palm, his body going wherever Logan's hand did so he could avoid the threat of crushed bones. The guy's standard work uniform was a blue blazer bearing the hotel's gold logo on the lapel and khaki trousers with a white dress shirt open at the collar.

His engagement had changed him some, but not too much. He was still Donnie's ride or die friend and probably always would be—even if his black hair was thicker than when they'd first met in a San Diego gay bar. Connor had encouraged him to grow it out and try for a side part, so the high and tight fades of his Marine Corps days were only a memory now.

Rising off his barstool, Donnie turned as much as his best friend's grip would allow. "I can do this, man!" he blurted out. Then he had to catch his breath. This slight change in altitude made his head spin. Crap. He'd slugged that last vodka soda way too hard. "I know you guys probably have your doubts, but I'm ready. I've been on YouTube researching like a mofo. Let's go. Let's throw a monster fucking wedding. The wedding to end all weddings. Weddingfuckingpalooza, Logan and Connor style. Fancy and gay and sparkling and all that bullshit. *Let's go!*"

Smiling and nodding in a way Donnie thought seemed tense, Logan patted him on the chest. "Already drunk. That's cool."

"Lightly buzzed, man. Lightly buzzed, is all. But still sharp as a tack. Don't worry."

"You know, I've always wondered about that expression. Like why not sharp as a knife?" Logan started adjusting the shoulders of Donnie's jacket. "Who needs a tack when you can have a knife?"

"Knifing people's a part of wedding planning now?" Donnie asked, looking down as Logan started adjusting his jacket's flaps.

"They didn't cover that on YouTube?" Logan took a step back and studied Donnie's appearance. Was he satisfied? It was hard to tell. And why did he give a damn how he looked in front of his fiancé? They'd all known each other for years. "Not quite. But I need you on your toes. We've got some late breaking news, and I want you to rise to the occasion. Come on."

As he followed Logan toward the open wall to the pool deck, he felt like a puppy chasing his master's heels. "So, Oregon, right? You guys still want to have it at the place in Cannon Beach?"

"Yeah, that's kinda why we wanted to meet."

At least it's a meeting now and not a discussion.

The sun had set, leaving the ocean slate gray under a darkening sky. Standing at the table furthest away, and with a commanding view of the twinkling hillsides plunging toward the Pacific, was Connor Harcourt, Sapphire Cove's general manager and the love of Logan's life. Pretty as an angel and small enough to fit in Logan's back pocket, his shock of bright blond hair danced in the same winds fluttering the tiki torches lining the expansive deck. His nickname for the guy had been Tintin until Logan had told him to fucking quit it because it was disgusting and made Logan sound like a pedophile.

As Donnie neared him, Connor closed the distance, smile tense and forced.

I'm totally getting fired, Donnie thought again.

After a peck on the cheek, Connor began pulling tiny bits of lint only he could see from the zipper of Donnie's leather jacket. "Okay, sweetie, it's like this. There's Bo Bonin and then there's Donnie Bascombe, and tonight I need you to be Donnie Bascombe with a nice, big side of Barack Obama."

"Forgive my fiancé," Logan said. "He's kinda starstruck."

"I thought you guys didn't watch my porn."

"We don't. I'm talking about somebody else. Have a seat, buddy."

Once he complied, Logan and Connor shared a look, as if they were debating who should speak first. There were already drinks on the table in front of both men, and Donnie found himself looking for a waiter so he could get one for himself. A hand came out of nowhere and placed what looked like a vodka soda on the table in front of him. Clearly, they had bad news to break. And at the rate he was going, he wouldn't be able to drive home that night.

"Oregon's out," Logan said. "The wedding's going to be here at Sapphire Cove."

"Here?" Donnie yelped. "That's going to be a lot more people." *Way to sell yourself, dude.* Once he swallowed a hearty slug, he managed, "So what's the move about?"

"It's about the fact that one of the most prominent queer couples in the hospitality industry cannot *not* throw their own wedding at their own resort." The voice was both seductively and frighteningly familiar. Standing over the empty chair next to his was Not Zach, smelling of a fresh spray of some pricey cologne, his hair smoothed out. "Especially when they've hired me to take over their special events office and turn Sapphire Cove into the premiere destination for high-end weddings in Southern California."

Connor shot to his feet. Logan, looking a tad less enthusiastic, followed suit.

"When I was working in event planning in New York, there were two names that commanded almost universal recognition and respect in the business. One was Martha Stewart, and the other was Richard Merriweather." Connor was slightly breathless, gazing at Richard like he was Harry Styles stopping by his table to compliment Sapphire Cove's standard of service. "Donnie Bascombe, meet one of the finest event planners on Earth. His firm is opening an office here now that Jonas has been promoted to AGM. And *you* will have the honor of working with him on our wedding."

Fuck me in the rain with a rake, Donnie thought. He stood and shook Richard's extended hand, bracing himself for Mr. Fancy Pants to huff out some version of *We've already met and oh, by the way, this will never work because he's a filthy horny toad and I want him banned from the property so he can't touch a silky hair on my fancy head.* But Richard Merriweather did nothing of the kind. Instead, he gripped Donnie's hand and nodded, his expression blank save for a knowing glint in his eyes. "It's nice to meet you, Mr. Bascombe," he said quietly, as if their bathroom meeting had never happened. "Sorry for being so blunt. But I figured I should do everyone the favor of cutting right to the chase given how diplomatic they're being about the fact that I've hijacked their wedding."

"Oh, nonsense. You didn't hijack our wedding," Connor said, giving Richard a light tap on the shoulder.

"You kinda did, actually," Logan grumbled.

Under the glass table, Connor gripped one of Logan's hands hard enough to make him wince. "He also tripled our budget by declaring it a promotional expense for the hotel."

Logan grinned at his fiancé. "Oh, you know me, babe. I would've been happy if we eloped in Vegas."

"Actually, you wouldn't have because I would have found a way to make you very, very unhappy."

Logan leaned in, voice husky, eyes full of lust. "And then I'd find a couple ways to make us both happy again."

Connor giggled and blushed. Logan kissed him gently on the cheek.

Donnie did his best not to barf on the table. That's when he saw Richard observing Connor and Logan's display with a tense expression and almost as much pain in his eyes as he'd had while crying in the bathroom. Jealous? Offended? It was impossible to tell. Caught, Richard's eyes cut to Donnie's, and the unguarded emotion left them instantly.

As if suddenly remembering someone other than his fiancé was present, Logan cleared his throat and sat up straight. "All I care about is that this wedding has some *me* in it. You know, not just a bunch of flowers and a lot of string quartets that know every Taylor Swift song. That's where Donnie comes in."

Richard gave Logan a stiff smile, then leveled Donnie with a penetrating stare. "So what is it you do, Mr. Bascombe?" he asked, an edge in his voice.

And suddenly everything got quiet.

Connor's Barack Obama comment rang loudly in Donnie's brain. If he'd been referring to his sense of humor, then fine. He could keep it relatively clean for the evening. But if he expected him to lie about his profession in front of the fancy new events director, they could take their wedding and shove it.

"I make porn. Gay porn. Good porn. The real stuff. Not that OnlyFans crap that looks like two chicken breasts in olive oil rubbing together under a heat lamp in a messy apartment."

Richard raised one eyebrow, as if his slow nod wasn't already condescending enough. He started to speak, but Donnie wasn't done.

"I was a performer for about seven years. Did a couple hundred scenes. Racked up a bunch of awards. Now I run the studio where I got my start. Parker Hunter. Ever heard of it? We were a punchline on *Saturday Night Live* once."

"No offense, but the names all sound the same to me," Richard answered.

"Oh, so you're a porn fan."

"Not sure that's an appropriate question, Donnie," Connor said quietly.

Donnie gave Connor a wink. "Not sure it was a question, Blondie. It was more like an observation."

Blushing, Richard was fighting a smile. Problem was Donnie couldn't tell if the smile was sarcastic or genuine. "Well, now that the wedding isn't happening..." Richard twirled one manicured hand through the air next to him. "...somewhere in Oregon—"

"Cannon Beach," Logan interjected quietly. "One of the most beautiful spots on the West Coast."

"Right," Richard said, nodding. "And now that we're moving it here—"

"*The Goonies* was filmed in Cannon Beach," Logan added. "Great film."

"Let it go, babe," Connor whispered.

"I'm just saying," Logan continued, "it would have been nice to have had an actual holiday at our own wedding. Having it here kinda makes it feel like it's more work."

Richard smiled. "That's why you have me."

"Us," Donnie added.

Richard's smile stiffened as he met Donnie's stare. "So, Mr. Bascombe, how are you feeling about the change of venue? I know it's dramatic, but it sounds like you're early in the planning stages. Are your ideas portable now that we're moving everything here?"

Donnie swallowed. He was supposed to have ideas, plural?

"Well, they haven't set a date yet."

"It's in six months," Richard said. "Invitations go out next week."

Donnie did his best not to fall out of his chair. "That's really soon," he managed.

"I've done bigger events in less time. Trust me, I've got

considerable infrastructure at my disposal. What we need—" The event planner's eyes cut sideways, and Donnie realized he was looking more at Logan than Connor. "—are some ideas and a theme."

Logan was studying his clasped hands, jaw subtly working. Had he been stonewalling their new wedding planner because he was pissed about the location changing? That would only make Donnie's job even more complicated.

His heart raced. Crazy to think the guy could smell the insecurity on him that had led him to down three drinks at the bar inside, but that's how it felt. What he was fairly sure of was that Richard Merriweather had no interest in working with him—not in any real, serious way. This cut to the chase interrogation was probably designed to make him feel like an idiot. Problem was, everything about this process already made him feel like an idiot, so Richard had his work cut out for him.

This was ridiculous. He'd spent most of his professional life naked in front of strangers. Why was he this nervous about sharing his thoughts about the kind of wedding his best friends deserved? Because it was new, that was why. Trying to do a good job of something this far outside his comfort zone made him feel naked in an entirely new way.

And then there was the man across from him, who kept reminding him of the man who'd broken his heart.

"You got a napkin?" he asked Logan, who nodded and handed him one.

Donnie pulled a pen from his inside jacket pocket. When he was done with his sketch, he passed it to Richard. Connor craned his neck to try to get a glimpse. For a few silent seconds that seemed to stretch toward eternity, Richard studied it, then looked up with a completely blank expression.

"This is two squares with a circle in between them," he finally said.

"It's a layout. For the ceremony. Only it's different. The altar's not at the front of the room. It's in the middle."

"Of the aisle?" Richard asked.

Donnie nodded.

"That's decidedly unconventional."

Donnie tried not to wince at the dude's desert dry tone. Richard Merriweather knew how to slide a knife in with a velvet glove.

And who did that remind him of? In the span of an hour, his

memories of Zach Loudon had been knocked out of the bag he tried to keep them in. Now they were rolling all over the place like marbles, threatening to trip him at every turn.

"Look, I make people's fantasies for a living. We do all kinds of different scenes. And I spend a ton of time looking at the metrics and the numbers on how many people watched what and for how long. The numbers don't lie, and they all say the same thing. Every scene needs a point of view. And I'm not talking about where the camera is. I'm talking about the setup. The *scene*. It needs to satisfy someone's *specific* fantasy, and that means it can't be everyone's. I don't shoot three-ways where everyone takes a turn and gets all versatile. If I'm going to shoot a three-way, it's two gruff tops making the bottom the center of the action. Or it's some big daddy being tended to by two bottoms who look like gymnasts. Not everyone will like it. But the ones who identify with whoever's at the center of the action will *really* like it, and they'll watch it over and over again. The alternative's soup. It's only hot boys naked together with no flavor or spark."

Connor cleared his throat. "Donnie, the Ted Talk on porn creation is compelling, but perhaps we could—"

"He's getting there, babe. Give him a sec," Logan said in a low voice.

"The point I'm trying to make," Donnie said, "is that this wedding needs a point of view. It needs a story. A story about *them*. And stealing a bunch of stuff from some ceremony where a dad walks his daughter down the aisle and gives her away like she's property isn't going to cut it. That's not them. And I know we all want to pretend like Connor's the bride just 'cause he's the power bottom and Logan's big as a tree. But that's not the whole story. And it's shallow. That's just trying to make it sound like some story we've all heard before. Somebody else's story."

Was Richard impressed? Or did the tension in his jaw and the slight pucker in his wildly kissable lips mean he was disappointed Donnie hadn't belly flopped what basically amounted to an audition? He had the same half smile as Zach, both patronizing and seductive. The same unflappable poise. The same graceful, long-fingered hands Zach had once used to guide Donnie's as he showed him how to navigate a formal place setting for the first time, prep for a black-tie fundraiser he'd taken him to as his date—Donnie's first.

"I see. What's their story?" Richard asked quietly.

Donnie swallowed.

He'd always feared Zach had abandoned him for someone richer and classier because he hadn't taken enough of his mentoring to heart. Now, here he was, reincarnated, albeit in far more elegant and successful garb, asking him to audition for the role of best man. Zach had thought he was a dumb kid he could use for sex and companionship and then dump; Richard Merriweather clearly thought he was a dumb porn star who had no business planning a complicated, high-profile event. Two men, beautiful in the same intoxicatingly elegant way, both trying to put him in a box. As far as he was concerned, they both deserved to learn a lesson.

"Their story," he finally said, once he'd steadied himself, "is that Logan can't remember what his mom's voice sounded like 'cause she died when he was so young. And his dad took about thirty years to figure out how to be a dad. And Connor, he didn't speak to his father or his grandfather for the last years of their lives 'cause his dirtbag uncle did everything he could to drive him away from this place.

"Their story is that it took them five years to find the right moment after the world tried to keep them apart. And when they finally got together, they both got a complete family for the first time in years. Logan's dad, Connor's mom, me, Connor's best friend Naser. The wedding party's only four people for a reason. If this day's truly gonna be for them, after all they've done for the people around them, then it should *surround* them. It should make them feel supported. Protected. No longer on their own in the world."

When he looked to one side and saw both of his best friends blinking back tears, he felt a swell of pride in his chest. Problem was, he was blinking back tears too and had no choice but to bow his head and hold them at bay before he could see how the speech had landed with Richard Merriweather.

He'd wanted to sound sincere, but for fuck's sake, he didn't want to cry like a little bitch in front of a man who reminded him of the guy who'd broken his heart.

6

As if he'd bared his soul to the entire Pacific Rim, Donnie Bascombe looked down at his lap, a slight quiver in his jaw before he wiped at a cheek with the side of one fist. Richard looked to the couple beside him. Hands linked, they were clearly struggling to steady their breaths. They gazed at their good friend with wide, dewy eyes. Adoring eyes. Clearly, they'd never heard this pitch before.

And to be honest, Richard was a bit moved himself.

The divorce had given him a crash course in how quickly the things you took for granted in life could be yanked away. Despite the luxurious trappings he'd surrounded himself with during his exile, he'd spent the last few months feeling like he'd shipwrecked on a desert island. And given his emotional delivery, Donnie Bascombe knew that feeling too. But while Richard had lost most of his friends in the divorce, Donnie had the men sitting next to him. And wasn't that part of what Jonas had offered when he'd pitched him on the idea of a partnership with Sapphire Cove? A new support network in a place run by queer men who looked out for each other. God knows, his old support network had been blown to smithereens.

The number one rule of Richard's business was to learn as much as he could about his clients. Logan had been resisting his efforts for weeks now, probably because of the resentments he'd expressed, and Connor had been too preoccupied with trying to bring his fiancé around to let loose with any ideas. A window into the happy couple's past was exactly what he needed to build a narrative for the wedding to end all weddings, and one that offered a wider view than the collection of press clippings about the hotel's various scandals his LA office had put together over the past few weeks. Had it just arrived in the form of this gruff, inappropriate horndog?

After the collective sniffles eased, Logan leaned over and gave his best friend a half bear hug that knocked their foreheads together playfully. Then he withdrew, ruffling Donnie's hair like a proud parent.

All hope of relegating the infuriatingly attractive porn person to a purely ornamental role had faded away thanks to one powerful and unexpected speech.

The truth was, he didn't hate the idea—revisiting the fundamentals of a wedding ceremony, building a unique version that felt authentic to the men involved. Most of the gay weddings he'd done had simply opted to have the grooms or brides walk down the aisle together hand in hand. But Donnie wanted to revisit the very concept of the aisle itself.

Which was…*interesting.*

But given the man's lack of experience, the prospect made him feel like Oppenheimer revisiting the structure of the atom with a *Magic Mike* dancer as his lab partner.

The real problem was the stirring he felt in his chest at the sight of the big, beautiful brawn pile getting misty eyed and sincere over the union of his best friends. The Donnie he'd met in the bathroom was one he might jerk off to later and forget about. This Donnie, on the other hand, was proving impossible to look away from, and the more he didn't try to, the more he felt a hungry ache in his chest as well as his loins.

Snap out of it. You're a professional.

He held up the napkin sketch. "Logistically, this could be very challenging. The minister would have their back to somebody the whole time."

Donnie shook his head. "No minister. That's religious. These guys don't go to church. They don't need anybody's blessing to be together. They read their vows to each other after we've all read something about them. The altar's round and it's got two levels. They're on the top one, we're on the lower one."

"Surrounded," Richard said, nodding.

"Protected," Donnie added quietly.

"You're proposing something that's akin to a fashion show catwalk. The seating would most likely have to be elevated or angled in some way. It would require a very large space."

Connor cleared his throat. "Well, the entire hotel's at your disposal."

And that cinched it. He was stuck with Donnie.

Richard nodded.

Another silence fell.

One of the security team signaled to their table from the doorway to the pool deck. Logan must have recognized the signal's meaning because he patted Connor on the shoulder. They both shot to their feet. "We'll be back in a second, gents," he said, and then, just like that, Richard was once again alone with Donnie Bascombe.

"Thank you," Donnie finally said.

"It was a moving speech and the idea is intriguing. It needs to evolve, but it's intriguing."

"That's not what I meant. Thank you for not mentioning, you know…"

"Our bathroom altercation?"

Donnie's drink froze halfway to his mouth. "Okay, *altercation's* kinda extreme, don't you think?"

"Scuffle, then."

"Come on. It's not like things got physical."

"Thanks to my self-esteem," Richard said.

After a hearty slug, Donnie set his glass down with a tad too much force. "Forget I brought it up."

"Sounds like a plan." Richard took his phone from his jacket pocket and began scrolling. "And let's maybe put a pause on the discussion until they get back. I don't want to tackle anything big when they're not here."

"Fine, I just…I want you to know I'll be sure not to do anything like it in the future. Since, we're, you know, working together."

Richard didn't want to voice his agreement that they would be working *together*, technically. Sure, Donnie could advise on Logan's preferences, and his ideas were interesting in theory, but he was already devising ways to silo the preposterous horn ball from the nuts and bolts of the planning so that he was spared getting sprayed by his waterfall of hormones. "I'll also be sure not to compliment you, ever, or say anything flattering. I don't want to lose an eye."

Richard set his phone down on the table and glared at Donnie. "As I've already said, there's nothing flattering about a guy offering to cheat with someone in a bathroom stall."

"Woah, there, Merriweather. I didn't offer to *cheat* with you. I'm single as a hot dog without a bun. And I don't see a ring on your finger."

"Every relationship involves a ring? You didn't seem to care in the slightest that I might have a significant other waiting for me outside."

"*Did* you have someone waiting outside?"

"That's not the point."

Donnie went still, as if he were making a quick calculation in his head. "Is that what he did? The guy who made you cry? He cheated on you?" It felt like he'd been slapped, and it must have looked like it too because Donnie's gaze softened instantly, and his lips parted but nothing came out. And for a while they sat in a tense silence. "Sorry," Donnie finally said, and with more gentleness in his tone than Richard had heard him use before. "That was over the line, I guess."

"Yes, well, you seem to live over the line, so I figure I should get used to it."

"Because we're going to be working together," Donnie said with a smile.

Once again, Richard said nothing.

Smile vanishing, Donnie said, "Just admit we're going to be working together."

"Define together, Mr. Bascombe."

"Look at them. They're gone. They said it'd be a minute. You see them anywhere? This is how it's been with the wedding for two years. They start making a plan and then something with the hotel gets in the way. That's why they need us."

"Let's be honest. It's why they need *me*."

"Yeah, because nothing will make their big day more special than turning it into a soulless commercial for this friggin' hotel which already runs their lives day in and day out."

Richard took the deepest breath he could manage. "Okay, look. The message of this meeting wasn't lost on me. Logan wants you as a bulwark against the fact that Connor and I have the same tastes, and those tastes are a tad too delicate for him. Even though he outright refuses to share his desires for the wedding with me at all. So rest assured, I will make every effort to include design elements that celebrate his more conventional form of gender expression. Perhaps I'll have hot dogs on a grill in one corner. At the reception, we can invite someone's uncle to show a slideshow of their fishing trip so all the masculine-presenting gays in the room don't get too uncomfortable with all the terrible, horrible very gay flowers."

"Damn. That Taylor Swift comment hit you where you lived, huh?"

"Here's the plan. Write me up something. About Logan. The things about him you think are the most special, his history with Connor. Make it as moving and eloquent as the speech you gave and I'll find a way to incorporate some of it into the ceremony."

Donnie shook his head. "Yeah, no. I'm not going to tell my best friend I wrote a book report about him, gave it to the man who hijacked his wedding, and then bowed out."

"I did not *hijack* his wedding."

"Those were your words, Fancy Feather."

"It's Merriweather, and I was being facetious."

"Logan wasn't."

Richard sighed before he could stop himself. "Donnie, with all due respect, I'm one of the best in my field. I don't collaborate with people in your position."

"Tops?"

"No."

"Porn stars?"

"People with no experience."

Donnie leaned forward as if he were about to share a secret that would display his great wisdom. "Look, I know how to shoot a four-way in a boathouse at a public park with no reliable power source and no permit. And a performer who's having a psychotic break because he started intermittent fasting that weekend and all he's got in his system is Hydroxycut and Turbo Tea."

A silence fell before Richard said, "And this skillset is going to help you plan a *wedding?*"

"I get logistics, is what I'm saying."

"These are very different logistics."

Donnie looked down to his clasped hands, started twiddling his fingers. "Okay, fine. I can do my own thing and you can be surprised on the wedding day. But I gotta warn you. Some of Logan's favorite things include that *Vikings* show, horses, and old Metallica songs."

Envisioning Donnie in his best Ragnar costume leading a restless mare by the bridle down the aisle of the ceremony while "Enter

Sandman" blasted from hidden speakers, Richard brought one hand to his brow to halt the threat of a headache.

"What are you asking for here? From me? Specifically?"

Donnie's smirk vanished, and for a while he was silent. But he also looked serious and focused. "Teach me how to do this," he finally said. "Teach me how to do right by the best friend I've ever had. Do that and I'll tell you all the personal stuff you need to know to throw a wedding that'll make 'em both cry for all the right reasons. Maybe you'll even win Logan over. 'Cause you clearly haven't yet."

He was not prepared for what the request did to his body. Again he tried to chalk it up to sexual starvation and emotional isolation. But a man like Donnie Bascombe, a man who combined flashes of boyish innocence and earnestness with dizzying sexual confidence, asking for a lesson from *him* in anything was the stuff secret, late-night fantasies were made of. When he'd watched *My Fair Lady* on repeat with his mother as a child, he'd always secretly identified with Eliza Doolittle. Now, years later, he felt like his own special version of Professor Higgins, and his Eliza had the hard muscle and bedroom eyes of every forbidden jock he'd ever thirsted for in his life.

"This isn't simply another attempt to get me in a bathroom stall?" he heard a voice that sounded more rational than his thoughts ask.

Donnie studied him, as if imagining how things might have gone if Richard had accepted his offer earlier. "I'm sorry I think you're a sexy bitch, Merriweather," he finally said, his voice far too husky for Richard's liking. "I promise not to do anything about it. Believe it or not, I do know how to control myself. Even though most guys prefer it when I lose control completely."

The skin on the back of Richard's neck felt tight and hot, and he could suddenly hear his own strained breath whistling through his nostrils. "Comments like that aren't going to get us off to a fresh start, Mr. Bascombe."

"We'll start now then," he said with a smile that made Richard feel like a vein of heat was shooting straight down his spine and into his ass.

"Sorry, guys." Logan's voice startled them both. "Weird leak down in one of the service corridors. Maintenance wanted us to see, but they're on it."

Suddenly, Connor and Logan were sitting at the table again as if they'd never left.

"Let's talk branding," Richard said brightly, no doubt trying to smile away the lingering tension their exchange had left in the air. "I'm thinking *The Cogan Wedding*. It'll make a great hashtag, and it fits on a napkin."

"Barf," Donnie said.

Richard felt his teeth clench before he could stop them. "I'm sorry. *What* did you say?"

"I said barf. It sounds like the name of some spoiled brat whose parents are going to let him study basket weaving until his trust fund becomes available."

"And you have strong feelings about the basket weaving community, I take it?" Richard asked.

"I have strong feelings about lousy names, and that's a lousy name. What else you got?"

Richard looked to Connor and Logan, who were both staring at him with pained smiles. Connor broke the silence. "Sorry. We aren't fans either."

"We'll discuss branding another time then. Connor, if I may, why isn't *your* best man involved in the planning?"

"Trying to outflank me, are ya?" Donnie asked with an evil-looking grin.

"Naser?" Connor answered. "He's an accountant. I'm not letting him anywhere near my wedding. He'll yell at me about every penny we spend, and we'll end up never speaking to each other again. He's in charge of my bachelor party. And that's it."

There was a soft buzz, and Logan pulled his phone from the pocket of his blazer. "Shit. It's Jonas," he said. "The Tardif wedding's short on banquet tables." To Richard and Donnie he added, "High-maintenance clients. Connor and I need to go tend to this."

"We can pick this up later?" Connor asked.

This time, Richard stood when Connor and Logan did. "That sounds fine. Maybe we can all meet next week—"

"Next week's really tight," Connor said. "But I'll have my assistant get with you. In the meantime, we should have your office done by Friday, and we'll set up a tour. You're going to love it. Promise." Connor raised crossed fingers and then gave Richard a half hug before he quickly departed, Logan on his tail.

7

Once again, Richard had been left alone with a talking ball sack. As the man's grin lit up hairs on the back of his neck, he turned to face him.

"Not to put too fine a point on it, but it's not possible to hijack a wedding from two people who are too busy and distracted to plan it."

Donnie stood. "Just admit Cogan's a barfy name."

"I'm a grown-up. I don't call things *barfy*." Richard extended his hand. "Have a good night, Mr. Bascombe. It was complicated meeting you."

"I'll walk you out," he said.

"That's really not necessary." Richard started moving through the tables toward the wide entrance to the restaurant. Under no circumstances was he going to let Donnie know that he was living at the hotel. Which meant he couldn't give in to temptation and start running for the elevators.

"You hungry?" Donnie asked. "We could get some food."

"Perhaps a cooling off period first."

"From what? God, the bathroom thing. Still?"

"It was less than an hour ago. But I'd also be happy to start the clock from right after you called one of my ideas *barfy*. Let's see how long we can go without you doing that again and then perhaps we can enjoy a pot of tea. With chaperones."

"Oh, come on. You've probably had worse clients than me."

"It seems we're going to find out."

They weaved around the back of the restaurant's bar and entered the lobby.

"Well, you and I should still meet even if they can't," Donnie said, keeping pace with him.

"We'll set up a call."

"Dude," Donnie whined. "Come on. You just said we could work together and now you're blowing me off."

Near the chandelier seemed like a safe place to stop walking. He could bring their conversation to a close with a variety of implied final destinations surrounding them. But now Donnie's pouty face was visible to scores of bystanders as well as the reception and concierge desks. Guests were shooting them curious looks as they weaved around them.

Donnie smiled. "Hey, if it makes it any better, I didn't follow you into the bathroom just 'cause you got a sexy strut and hair I want to run my hands through." Donnie was grinning now. "You also remind me of a guy who broke my heart fifteen years ago." Donnie's grin flickered, maybe because he could hear this proclamation didn't quit merit the cheerful tone he'd given it. "But he was basically a hooker who just wanted to be as classy as you so..." For a few tense seconds, they stared at each other. Finally, he said, "I mean, I was kind of a hooker then too, so it's not like I'm judging him, it's just—"

"Donnie, what in God's name—"

"I know, I know. It sounded like a compliment in my head, then it went off the rails. I'm serious, though. I really do want to learn from you, Fancy Feather."

"Okay, lesson one. Don't call me Fancy Feather again. It's vaguely homophobic and femme-shaming. Two. Don't hit on people in bathrooms. It's not the seventies anymore. Queer men don't need to resort to public cruising to meet each other. God knows I sat through my fair share of boring black-tie dinners so we could get enough mainstream acceptance not to resort to bathrooms for sex."

To Richard's surprise, Donnie was nodding like he was agreeing with every word he was saying. "Alright, well, I was talking about wedding planning. But since you brought it up, I want to be clear. Was it the hitting on you in the bathroom that was the problem? Or was it suggesting we head to Poundtown in the first stall?"

Richard sighed and looked at the floor like he wanted to disappear into its swirls of marble.

"Are you single or not, dude? Because if you are single, I don't know why you have such a problem with guys being hot for you.

Especially guys like me. I'm a top and I look like an auto mechanic who works out a lot. The boys can't get enough of me."

Richard cleared his throat. In order to lower his voice, he needed to close a bit of distance between them, but he didn't want to get so close Donnie might feel comfortable trying to lick his throat. "You were not attracted to *me*. You were attracted to the idea of distracting yourself with a quick, meaningless bang because you were completely nervous about meeting with your best friends about their wedding. Because planning this wedding is going to take you into a realm where your lewd jokes and your aggressive come-ons and your general sexual braggadocio will be of absolutely no use to you. I, on the other hand, have worked all my life to be something more substantial than a thirsty Instagram post who expires at age thirty. And that's why I have no interest in being a five-minute cock sleeve for a boundaryless porn star looking for a quick release for his sexual compulsion. There is a big difference, Mr. Bascombe, between being attracted to a person and being excited by what they can do for you in five, ten, or possibly fifteen minutes."

Donnie looked amused, as if Richard were a small, precocious child who'd performed a semi-competent magic trick. "Let's say twelve minutes and call it even."

For what felt like an eternity, they stood there staring at each other as the crowded lobby pulsed around them. Breathing had never felt like a hostile act to Richard before, but that's what it felt like now—like they were breathing *at* each other.

"Can I ask you something?" Richard finally said.

"Anything. I'm an open book."

An open fly is more like it, he thought.

"Do you believe in cheating?" Richard asked. "Like is it even a thing in your world?"

Donnie furrowed his brow. "What, like it's a religion or something?"

"I'm asking if you're one of the many gay men who thinks I'm a fool to have asked for a monogamous commitment from my husband."

There was no smirk in response, no mischievous glint in Donnie's eyes. The man was suddenly as serious as he'd been when describing the meaning he wanted to give the wedding of his closest friends. Just this sudden shift in his facial expression made Richard feel more seen, more valued, than he'd felt in months.

"Cheating is what a couple decides it is. If your husband did something you agreed he wouldn't do, that's wrong."

Not the answer Richard was expecting. The sober, serious tone was a shock too.

"And if he did it once a month for the entire length of our marriage?"

"Then he's a fucking son of a bitch and my offer to kick his ass still stands. Guess you forgot about that part of our bathroom…powwow or whatever."

"That's the first sensible thing you've said to me."

"Hey, I thought you liked my idea for the wedding."

Finger raised, Richard took a step back. "You have an intriguing *concept* for the wedding. It's not an idea yet. As I said, it needs to evolve. Catwalks are good at fashion shows because the audience's eye is constantly engaged with a target that's moving laterally across their view. If you do that setup for a stationary wedding altar, it won't have the same effect. The guests won't all be focused on Connor and Logan. They'll be looking at each other. And if the ceremony has no officiator at all, that'll put too much work on the grooms to act as hosts, which I can assure you, Connor and Logan will like less and less as the date nears and nerves increase. I'll review your thoughts, get back to you with some ideas, and we can talk next week on the phone. In the meantime, perhaps you can focus on a bachelor party for Logan that doesn't destroy their relationship."

"Already got it covered. We're having it at the The Blast Zone."

Richard glowered at him. "I assume that's an all-male strip club?"

"If you don't know, you don't know."

"Goodnight, Mr. Bascombe."

"So, what's the next event you're doing?" Donnie asked.

Richard's feet froze in place. The request didn't seem like a loaded one, but Donnie's tone was suddenly neutral, restrained. With a guy as expressive as him, that could only be a bad sign. "It's in Bel Air this weekend. Why?"

"Bel Air. What are you, moonlighting? I thought you were working here."

"I have offices in London, New York, LA, and Vegas. This is going to be the fifth. I'm not exclusive to Sapphire Cove by any means. Why are you asking me this?"

Donnie smiled as if he were genuinely impressed. "Can I come? I want to see how you work." Richard sighed. Donnie held up his hands. "No bathrooms involved, I promise."

"Well, it's not a wedding. It's a birthday party for one of the most important men in television. In 1996, anyway. But they're very loyal clients, and they're hugely connected in Hollywood."

"I promise I won't embarrass you. I'll hang back and watch you do your thing. Believe it or not, I know how to be in public without whipping out my di— Sorry, cock."

"Perhaps, but it feels like you learned only recently."

There was that grin again. "Hey, if the money's good."

Richard laughed against his will.

Donnie kept smiling, kept looking into Richard's eyes like he was soaking up the sound of his laughter and didn't want it to stop.

"I'll need you to dress appropriately."

Donnie spread his arms wide. "I know how to dress. I live on a boat, not in a cave."

"Do you have a suit and tie?" Richard asked. "Preferably a dark one."

Donnie's nostrils flared. He licked at his upper lip nervously before he managed a profoundly unconvincing, "Yeah."

Richard nodded.

Donnie nodded.

A baby cried somewhere nearby.

An expensive sports car's engine revved in the motor court outside.

"Are you lying to me right now?" Richard finally asked.

"I'll get a suit and tie. Don't worry."

"It's in two days. It'll need to fit."

"I ran away from home at sixteen and I run a business today. I'm pretty resourceful, okay?" Donnie tapped the side of his head. Richard was tempted to say one's cranium was not where one got alterations done on short notice. But Donnie was trying for something that felt sincere—and possibly professional—and so he decided not to be a bitch about it. Or a bigger bitch than he'd already been. And had Donnie really let drop that he'd been a teenage runaway as if it were no more significant than naming his star sign?

"Okay then. I'll have Connor's office send you all the details and the schedule and the—"

"Or you could give me your cell and I could—"

"Not yet." It came out harsher than he'd planned and he'd raised a finger at the guy as if he'd taken a step toward him. Which he hadn't. Donnie flinched at the bite in his tone, but after a tense second, he nodded and raised his hands in a conciliatory gesture.

"Fine. Fresh start first," Donnie said.

Richard extended his hand again and Donnie shook it. "Until next time. I have to pick up some files before I head out so I'm going to..." The second sentence was already a lie and any end he gave to it would only make the lie seem more extreme, so he headed for the elevators without another word. When he glanced over his shoulder and saw Donnie staring after him, he walked past the elevator bank and toward the conference center. Then he walked up and down the carpeted corridors of the conference center feeling like he was back in high school, trying to avoid the hallway with the most bullies in it.

A few minutes later, he looked around the corner, saw no sign of Donnie underneath the chandelier or on the other side of the glass doors to the motor court, and ducked into the first elevator.

For the second time that evening, he was returning to his room, determined to focus on work only to find himself Googling a porn star. Because he had more information to go on this time, the results came fast and furious compared to his last search.

A quiet, nagging voice in his head told him this was a terrible idea. But a louder voice asserted it was exactly what he needed—to see the arrogant hormone tsunami crash against the rocks of a cheap porn set and its punishing hot lights. To see self-consciousness and awkwardness flit across his facial expression as he barked his way through a boring rotation of emotionless, badly scripted dirty talk.

True, Richard had been using porn as his only sexual outlet since the divorce, but that didn't change the fact that most of it was incredibly stupid. Despite their spectacular bodies, the performers very often looked either uncomfortable or just bored, and he usually turned the volume off so he could imagine his own, more sophisticated—or more forbidden—setup and dialogue.

All that said, it was probably wise to go for one of Bo Bonin's earlier works. To replace the confident sexual powerhouse of earlier with an awkward, fumbling young man who'd made questionable life choices.

On one of his usual clip sites, he did a search for Bo Bonin and found a full-length movie from the mid 2000's that featured a younger, clean-shaven Donnie on its box cover. According to the synopsis and the punctuation-free customer reviews below, *Seed* billed itself as a parody of the 90s thriller *Speed,* only instead of featuring a bomb on a bus that would go off the second it dropped below a certain speed, this story involved a magic spell that would cause a man's giant dick to shrink if he didn't have sex every three hours. The well-endowed victim of said spell was played by none other than Bo Bonin.

There were a few quotes from the industry trade publications of the day. Richard's favorite was, "Bo Bonin shows affable charm and amazing power top skills as Gonnaboneyou Reeves, a performance so hypnotic that you'll easily forget the actor bears little to no resemblance to the famous action star for which his character is named."

The movie opened with the sounds of sex, but no visual sign of it, as a bejeweled fortune teller played by a drag queen who looked vaguely familiar announced to the camera that she was tired of being awakened by the constant rutting of her next door neighbor and had decided to put a spell on him by way of her incredibly cheap-looking and fingerprint-spotted crystal ball. The next morning, she ran into a cheerful and whistling Bo Bonin in the hallway of their building and cackled out his punishment. Bo—looking leaner and more baby faced than the Donnie of today—cried out in alarm and threw his hands over his crotch as if she'd kicked him there. The camera zoomed in on his wide-eyed silent scream that played like a close-up from a Hammer horror film.

The fact that the fortune teller had attempted to cut down on her late-night disturbances by giving the horn dog next door even more reasons to have sex was not adequately explained, and Richard felt like a bit of a spoilsport for getting hung up on this detail. Maybe he should be more forgiving of porn plotting. But he'd never been a big fan of stories that involved magic in general; he much preferred historical fiction. If only Bo's oeuvre had included a smutty take on the life of artists in Belle Époque Paris.

The more salient point was that almost fifteen minutes into this supposed gay porn classic, Richard was distracted, bored, and decidedly unaroused. Then Bo Bonin boarded a suspiciously empty city bus, save for one other male passenger, an absurdly pretty blond who looked like a late nineties boyband member forced into a football jersey and tight jeans. As Bo Bonin walked past him, the boy gave him a look that was supposed to appear lascivious but made him look sleepy and confused.

When Bo Bonin smiled at the passenger, suddenly it was Donnie's smile filling Richard's suite.

The same smile that had done a number on Richard's insides several times that evening.

Utterly convincing. And a warning.

This was a mistake. A big one. He'd wanted to see Donnie's confident swagger ironed out of him by what he imagined was a cold and emotionless process at heart—having sex on camera. He should close his laptop now and walk away.

But he didn't, and when the bus passenger sank to his knees and fished Donnie's—*Jesus H. Christ, that thing should have its own zip code*—cock out of his jeans, Donnie's eyes hooded with what looked like genuine desire, and he began caressing the guy's hair with a convincing mix of tenderness and force. And when he took the twink's turgid cock into his mouth like it was a long-delayed meal, it was as if the bus around them and whatever camera crew they'd jammed onto it had faded from his world, and there was only pleasure. The giving of it, the receiving of it. The performing of it.

If it was a performance, it was a damn good one, and by the time Bo Bonin was claiming his jersey-clad admirer doggie style over the back row of seats, Richard's hand had floated down to his own crotch, and he found himself digging his own cock from his slacks. The dirty talk—which Richard had expected to sound stilted and silly—throbbed with conviction and desire. Everything about Bo Bonin throbbed with conviction and desire.

There was, he was learning, almost no difference between the man he'd sparred with downstairs and the sexual performance artist on screen.

He blamed the stress of his divorce. And the stress of the evening in general. And stress itself. And being a man. And Bo Bonin. And the fact that he'd been satisfying himself mostly with fantasies like these since finding himself suddenly single in his early forties. Anything other than the performance on screen, which somehow made him float out of his skin as a realm of fantasy wrapped around him and the only thing he could feel was his throbbing cock and his stroking hand.

You mean, Donnie's ha—

SHUT UP!

What a stupid, stupid idea this had been. He'd assumed it would be the same as watching a YouTube video of the guy falling on his face in the snow. He'd wanted to see Donnie humiliated and instead he'd found...abandon.

Wildness.

Freedom.

When Donnie bent forward and wrapped his arms around his scene partner's torso while chewing lasciviously on his ear, Richard imagined he and the porn star on screen stumbling into the warmly lit bathroom stall, imagined easing himself back onto the same cock he was watching plunge in and out of the—

He let loose with a barking cry. When he opened his eyes, he was still shuddering and gazing breathlessly at the ceiling.

He could also hear "Memory" from *Cats* and was wondering why it was playing on a city bus while two guys had sex. Also, how could a porn company afford the rights?

Shit.

He'd left the balcony door open before he'd headed downstairs for the meeting. If he could hear the pianist from the restaurant a few stories below this clearly, how many people had heard his movie screening and self-love session? He shot to his feet and closed the door.

As laughter from the pool deck below pierced his post-orgasmic haze, Richard wondered how many more scenes like this he'd have to watch in secret to keep his relationship with Donnie entirely professional.

8

When jet lag snapped Richard awake at two a.m., he was sprawled on the suite's sofa with a half empty bag of potato chips on his chest. Worse, the Sister Wendy marathon he'd dozed off in front of had turned into a blaring infomercial. A bunch of people sat in folding chairs around a sunny swimming pool while someone purporting to be a doctor explained what looked like an absurdly unnecessary modification to a toothbrush.

Since he'd drifted off to sleep before his nightly cocktail, he might as well treat himself to one now, he thought. See if he could manage another few hours of sleep before his early morning run with Jonas.

The ice bucket was empty.

In hotel branded slippers, he headed for the ice room down the hall. White walls, soft white lights, white ceiling. Inlaid paneling and the occasional muted painting of a beach scene. Outside the plush guest rooms, with their marriages of rose-colored carpet, plum-colored drapes and brown marble bathrooms, Sapphire Cove was desperate for some color, but he hadn't been hired to redesign the place.

As soon as the giant, humming machine finished making its thunderous deposit, a gruff voice behind him said, "Howdy, Merriweather."

Richard cried out and spun. Standing in the ice room doorway, as shirtless as he'd been in the scene Richard had watched a few hours before, was Donnie Bascombe. But his bare torso was thicker and scruffier, his shoulders broader, his stomach a tight drum of brawn— more inviting, Richard thought, than a six-pack. And then there were those muscled, hair-dusted thighs emerging from the legs of his boxers.

The kind of legs that gave you plenty to grip as you sank to your knees and—

"Jesus! What are you doing here?" Richard barked, forcing his eyes up from the manicured happy trail that led invitingly to the waistband of Donnie's plain white boxers.

"I heard they were running a sale on high-strung party planners. You should drink less coffee."

"I drink tea. Are you stalking me?"

Donnie raised the ice bucket in his right hand and gave it a shake. "Water. That allowed? I knocked back a few last night. Logan didn't want me driving home, so he got me a room."

Down the hall from mine? Richard thought. *Does he hate me that much?* "Do you usually stroll the hotel in your underwear?"

Donnie shrugged. "Everyone's out cold. Besides, the security guy on tonight used to work for me. Naked." Donnie smiled. "What's the matter? Can't sleep?"

"Jet lag. I was in Europe for a couple months."

"Working?"

"Sort of."

Donnie raised his eyebrows, silently inviting Richard to continue. Meanwhile, Richard was doing his best not to let his eyes travel to the shadowy outline of Donnie's massive cock, which he'd seen in full a few hours before, although at a much greater—and more comfortable—remove.

"I needed time away after the…"

Donnie nodded with surprising reserve. "Gotcha," he said quietly.

Stepping out from the machine, Richard gestured for his unexpected visitor to take his place. He wanted nothing more than to make a quick escape, but that felt suddenly rude. They'd be seeing each other in two days, after all. A polite parting was in order.

"Sorry," Donnie said. "That's gotta be rough. So did you guys divorce or…"

"We're going through the process. Our house is up for sale."

Again, Donnie nodded. He was leaning against the machine instead of using it, but the looks he gave Richard were more wary than the ones he'd slathered him with a few hours before. Maybe he was chastened after their last conversation. Or maybe the cocktails he'd been slugging at their table had made him hornier than usual.

"I'm going to…" Richard said, then nodded at the door.

"See you Saturday."

Richard had one foot in the hallway before he turned. "Okay, I need to say something that's bothering me. In the lobby, I didn't mean to roll past the fact that you ran away from home at sixteen. We were just…the conversation was moving very fast and I should have at least paused to recognize it."

"Don't worry about it. I wasn't looking for pity."

"I could have at least acknowledged it."

Donnie nodded. "What I wanted you to acknowledge is that I might be more competent than you think I am."

"I didn't say you were incompetent. I said you were moving a bit too fast in a lane that's not normally yours. And since you basically asked me to mentor you in wedding planning, I figured it was my right."

"That's fair, I guess." Donnie turned to the ice machine and filled his bucket. The machine made a thunderous roar. Worried the noise might awaken the other guests, Richard stepped back into the room, letting the door drift shut behind him. Finished, Donnie turned, but he was staring down at the bucket, gently shaking it to get the cubes into some alignment that suddenly mattered to him more than anything else. Lost in thought, clearly. Introspective in a way that hadn't seemed his nature a few hours ago.

"A few years back I got the call my dad kicked the bucket and left me the shitty farmhouse he threw me out of when I was sixteen 'cause he caught me making out with another guy behind the barn. Kind of a shock, to be frank. I wasn't expecting to inherit a damn thing from that son of a bitch. So I text Logan and before I know it he's on my boat. Then he's booking plane tickets. For both of us. Then we're on a red-eye to Michigan and we're walking up the steps of that rathole my old man died drunk in, and up comes his methed-out girlfriend of the moment, screaming bloody murder about how I'm a homo whore from the devil who has no right to my family's things. Things I didn't want. Things I didn't expect.

"And I'm getting ready to rip her a new one. Tell her the house isn't worth shit because he had to sell off all the land and the tax bill's through the roof. Probably 'cause he fell in with vampires like her. But worse, I'm getting ready to do something I said I'd never do with anyone from back home. I'm getting ready to *explain* myself. Justify my life. But before any of that can happen, Murdoch looks that woman dead in the eye and in this voice like thunder he says, 'Ma'am, you have mistaken us for two men who don't have a job to do.'"

The memory made him smile. He snapped his fingers. "She just crumbles right there. Like she's got no spine all of a sudden. And then she's gone. And it's me and him going through the checklist. The shitty funeral no one came to. The tax bullshit. Emptying out the house, putting it up for sale. All of it, he was right by my side." Nostrils flaring, upper lip tense with emotion, Donnie looked up at Richard for the first time since starting the story. "I'd walk through fire for Logan Murdoch. Even if I know good and well his fancy fiancé doesn't want some white trash porn star anywhere near their wedding."

Richard was humbled by the story's specificity. By the simple, honest way in which Donnie had told it. By the sudden devastating sound of the man being incredibly cruel to himself. As cruel as Richard had been to himself during these past few months of anger and grief. Donnie Bascombe carried a life's load of pain with confidence and a smile, and this suddenly made Richard feel like a child for crying over his broken marriage. It wasn't like he'd been left homeless and destitute. For Christ's sake, how many cuckolded spouses had the funds to flee to Europe for months to avoid all reminders of their ex?

"I don't know Logan and Connor as well as you do," Richard said softly. "But I have enough experience with weddings to know that Connor Harcourt has all the earmarks of a potential bridezilla. If he didn't want you anywhere near his wedding, you wouldn't be."

"Yeah, well," Donnie muttered. "Connor's only doing it because Logan wants him to."

"That's not nothing. Seeing someone as valuable because the man you love does, that's important. And it's not all that common. Trust me."

There was eagerness in Donnie's eyes when he looked up, eagerness to believe everything Richard was saying. "I guess I wanted to tell you that because...well, you were right. I was really nervous last night, and I knocked back a few more than I should have. So I was probably more inappropriate than usual. I mean, you were really bitchy about it, but you were right."

"Well," Richard said before he could stop himself, "I've been bitchier than usual ever since..."

His vision wobbled and his throat closed up on him, and he heard his own sharp intake of breath through his nostrils.

"You want to talk about it?" Donnie asked. "We could go for a walk." He looked down at himself as if suddenly surprised by his own bare torso. "I could, you know, put some clothes on first."

Richard swallowed once, twice, then three times before he felt like he'd held his tears at bay.

No, he didn't want to go for a walk with this man.

He wanted to fall into his arms, lose himself in the power of what would no doubt be a confident and hungry embrace. He wanted to hear Donnie Bascombe's husky voice whisper dirty things into his ear. And he was afraid those things were as likely to happen on a night-shadowed hotel walkway as they were in one of their rooms. But unlike the man who'd broken his heart, Richard didn't have to do everything he wanted to do. Especially when it seemed like a colossally bad idea. He'd been betrayed by his husband of four years in exchange for a retinue of men who were mostly younger and fitter; he was in no mood to be checked off another guy's list because he reminded the guy of his ex. The few friends he hadn't lost were encouraging him to have some cheap fun, take his mind off things, but Richard had ended up in the strangest and most impossible of places—he wanted to either be loved or left alone.

"Thank you. But I should get some sleep. I've got to head up to LA tomorrow."

As if he were masking genuine disappointment and not just a dented ego, Donnie nodded down at his ice bucket. "Yeah, me too. I'm going to try to get back to San Diego before rush hour."

"Goodnight, Mr. Bascombe."

"Goodnight, Mr. Merriweather."

When he reached the door to his suite, he felt a presence down the hall.

Donnie was at his own door, about three rooms down but on the same side of the hallway.

He nodded at him with a half smile, but his expression was hard to read. Like he'd solved a tough riddle and was trying not to gloat about it.

What's that about? Richard thought as he stepped inside and closed the door behind him.

Then he saw his laptop sitting on the dining table, across from the sliding deck door he'd left open the night before and thought, *Shit shit, shit* more times than he could count.

9

Donnie was enormously proud of himself as he stepped into his room. For once in his life, he'd held his tongue. And this particular revelation had made his tongue more slippery than usual.

When he was almost to the closed balcony door, he allowed himself a cackle he was pretty sure couldn't be heard in the hallway outside.

So Richard Merriweather had run right back to his room after their lobby dust up and jerked it to one of Donnie's old scenes. And Donnie hadn't rubbed the man's pretty little nose in it. True, he was tempted to write a note and slide it under the guy's door right now. **So how'd you like SEED, Merriweather? Are porn parodies your jam?**

Surely, this would earn him points with the guy who now occupied his every thought.

Problem was, if the guy didn't know Donnie knew, how was he going to score points off keeping his mouth shut about it? More importantly, did this catch-22 mean he should bring it up on Saturday when they saw each other again? It might be worth it just to see the guy's cheeks flame red over it. Despite his frosty butler speech patterns, Richard Merriweather blushed easily, and Donnie wanted to know how far those blushes extended down the man's neck, his throat, his chest. Did his nipples get involved?

Why had Fancy Feather picked such a deep cut? That shitty *Speed* rip-off had been his first studio feature after a raft of amateur scenes. And when he'd recognized the stupid theme music as he'd sat on his balcony checking emails on his phone, he'd actually giggled, chest swelling with pride that someone, somewhere was always enjoying his work. If you didn't get off on the idea of getting random people off, sex work wasn't for you. The idea that it might be Fancy Feather himself hadn't occurred to him. Hell, he hadn't even known the guy was staying at Sapphire Cove.

And yeah, okay, he'd ditch the nickname if Fancy Feather wanted him to. But Donnie didn't intend for it to be homophobic. In his mind's eye, it conjured a ball-churning image of the sexy, slender beast running a feather across his bare chest while giving him one of those cocked eyebrow, half smiles he did right before he said something cutting.

He couldn't resist. He stepped onto his balcony, leaned out over the rail so he could peer down the side of the hotel. The building's gently curvilinear shape allowed him to see into a few of the rooms between his and where he thought Richard's must be. They were all dark, their glass reflecting the glowing swimming pool a few stories below.

Enough fooling around. He needed sleep.

He'd awakened earlier with a start, probably when the cocktails finally left his system, and he was still parched. Now he poured himself a glass of Pellegrino over ice, turned off all the lights, and sat in the dark, thinking about Richard and trying not to sprout wood.

The truth was, he loved bitches. He loved the kind of sharp-tongued, mouthy guys that sometimes drove his friends nuts. He loved the sassy ones, the disruptors. Maybe because he was one too. A lot of his buddies bristled when the guys they were sleeping with criticized them. Donnie kinda loved it. And the speech Richard had slammed him with in the lobby the night before had made his head spin in a dozen different directions, and only one or two of them had been nauseating.

Richard had read him to filth, as the young folks liked to say these days.

Yes, he'd been nervous. Yes, he'd been looking for a hot distraction in the men's room. Yes, he'd felt the difference between checking a guy like Richard Merriweather off his list and getting tangled up in his hair in more ways than one. But what mattered was that Richard had seen him, all of him, insecurities and all. Seen him as something other than Bo Bonin. It made his skin tingle and his chest get tight to remember the look on the man's pretty face as he'd cut Donnie down to size under the lobby's three-tiered chandelier. Maybe it was because he'd grown up with a dad who was usually too drunk to know he'd entered the room until a day or so later, but Donnie loved guys who corrected him when he used the wrong word, or stepped forward to wipe a spot of food off his shirt as they *tsked tsked tsked* under their breath. He liked guys who treated him like something they wanted to primp and preen and polish and present to the world.

Guys like Zach, he thought, *and look how well that worked out, genius.*

But the sobering thought left him with another. The real gift Richard had given him that night was the thing he'd said in the ice room about how Connor wouldn't let Donnie anywhere near his wedding if he didn't want him there. Coming from a guy as honest and sharp-tongued as Merriweather, it had the ring of objective truth. And it lifted a weight from Donnie's shoulders he'd been carrying for months.

But when Donnie had returned the favor with the offer of a late-night stroll so Richard could unload his heartbreak, Richard had turned up his pretty little nose at the idea.

Maybe he didn't trust Donnie to keep his hands to himself, or maybe he thought Donnie would have nothing of value to say. The latter thought stung, and the resulting pain made his swell of ego over discovering Richard had watched his porn feel like a distant memory and reminded him of another man for whom he'd never felt quite good enough.

Fifteen Years Ago

The entry door that day bore a small sign for Parker Hunter's parent company, not the website's more recognizable name. When it opened to reveal Zach Loudon in khaki shorts, a pressed white polo, and with a big fancy watch on one wrist, Donnie's first thought was no way could a guy this hot be working behind the camera anywhere, much less a porn studio.

The night before, he'd studied all the scenes on their website for research; if he'd spotted a performer as stunning as Zach—tall and lean, with thick shoulder-length blond hair, crystal blue eyes, and a sculpted jawline—he would have walked in begging to shoot with the guy.

Just then, Zach introduced Donnie to the balding bear of a man sitting behind the front desk in a wreath of cigarette smoke. The studio's owner, Eddie Frye. When he stood to shake Donnie's hand, things started to make more sense.

Later, Donnie would learn that Zach's job was to interview the models while Eddie set up the lights and the cameras. That when it came to making professional decisions, Eddie Frye had a tendency to be blinded by lust, while Zach, whose years working as an escort—or a "true courtesan" as he often called himself—thought himself a good judge of character who could weed out the ticking time bombs who had no business doing sex work. "You'd be surprised how many guys audition for gay porn in the morning and hang with skinheads in the evening, Danger Boy," Zach had told him as they lay in bed together later that day. Zach's job was to make sure those guys never made it onto a set.

Danger Boy.

He'd given Donnie the nickname because he said Donnie made him want to do dangerous things. Like drag a new model back to his place for sex a half hour after screen testing him. And Eddie was the one who got blinded by lust? Donnie hadn't minded, though. Not in the slightest. The fact that he'd been hot enough to inspire someone as pretty and poised as Zach to step out of line had thrilled him.

Over ten years older—his exact age he wouldn't say—and infinitely more experienced, Zach took over his life almost instantly, not just with makeovers and new clothes, but with lessons in everything from culture and art to how to make more money off his body. Donnie was barely of drinking age, a runaway since the age of sixteen. Zach seemed like a man of the world who'd been to tons of places Donnie had only seen in movies.

He gave Donnie more than his body and his bed. He gave him a new home after smoothly negotiating his exit from a messed-up living situation in West Hollywood where Donnie had been trading sex five times a week with both members of a couple in exchange for being able to stay in their tiny guest house. Only after he'd settled in had the happy couple started tightening the noose, asking for more and crazier sex, pushing at Donnie's boundaries around his own backside. When he pushed back, citing their original agreement, they'd lay down new rules. No eating in the backyard where they might smell his dinner. No using the fridge in the main house even though the guest house didn't have one. If they'd yanked the cheap gym membership they'd secured *for him at a 24 Hour Fitness on Santa Monica Boulevard a few blocks away, he would have walked. He needed those mornings spent pumping iron. They were getting him the kind of body that scored you an audition with studios like Parker Hunter.*

But as soon as Zach heard the terms of his first stable living arrangement in the Golden State, he put Donnie in his BMW and drove him north to LA. Ordered Donnie to pack his things while he took the couple aside and fed them a bogus story about Donnie having been involved in something criminal before landing in California a few months before. An investigation was headed their way. Best for the couple to let him clear out before law enforcement knocked on the door.

Nobody had ever stuck up for him like that, and Donnie was dewy eyed and grateful when they drove south later that night. Even better, he'd get to sleep in Zach's soft, silky bed, in his smooth, slender arms.

Problem was, Donnie didn't want to keep escorting no matter how consistently and gently Zach pressured him to, no matter how much Zach claimed he could turn Donnie into a cash machine. He was a fantasy much in demand, as Zach put it, a young, strapping blue-collar power top with a friendly devil-may-care attitude and a giant cock.

Look at what Zach had done for his old friend Ethan Blake back in New York. He'd turned the fallen Southern fraternity boy into one of the Big Apple's most expensive male escorts. After four years of putting Zach's lessons to use, Ethan had earned enough to retire and put himself through culinary school.

Donnie didn't care. His path to California had taken him through countless dirty motel rooms and truck stop bathrooms. Worse, his first few California clients had been far crazier than the men he'd met on the road, hiring him to do things like break into their house late at night and put a knife to their throat while their husband was asleep upstairs. He didn't want to crap on anyone's fantasies, but he also didn't want to cut a guy's throat by accident. The knives on a porn set were sure to be fake.

Besides, he was an exhibitionist at heart. During his first shoot for some low-rent twink studio in Palm Springs, he'd been more turned on by the eyes staring at him from behind the camera than any of his three scene partners. Porn stardom, that's what he was after, no matter how many times Zach lectured him about how porn was just a business card for escorting. He didn't care.

Zach he cared about, however. And sometimes he tempered his resistance so as not to push the man away. Their sex was fire, and Zach was beautiful, one of those surfer-boy types you think they made up for the movies until you get to SoCal and find them everywhere, from working behind gas station counters to staring down at you from billboards with a seductive smirk. And every time they kissed Donnie felt a *tug, tug, tug in the center of his chest he'd never felt with anyone else.*

And Zach's desire to transform him, educate him, mentor him, felt like the truest love he'd ever had.

Sure, there were lessons in fashion and table manners, but there were also lessons in the bedroom that only added to their mutual pleasure. Before Zach, Donnie's sexual vocabulary had been limited to the words grip and thrust. After Zach, he'd added words like stroke, suckle, knead, and devour.

The whole thing made him feel indebted to the guy, the first debt he'd had in a while that he couldn't repay through sex alone. So he put what handyman skills he'd developed on his dad's farm to good use. Fixing whatever he could around the house, even adding a few improvements. In the bedroom, he was king, pounding Zach face first into the pillows. In every other room of the house, he was a puppy nipping at Zach's heels, eager for approval from the man who'd connected him to a world that seemed bigger and more sophisticated than any he'd ever known.

But he noticed things, things that bothered him and made him feel less grateful for all the support and sex Zach was giving him.

Things like Zach's penchant to adopt the speech patterns of whoever he was talking to. Or the fact that while the rest of their tiny rental house in Hillcrest was spare, with no photographs of anyone Zach might have cared about, Zach had plastered the walls of his bathroom with images cut from design magazines—private jets and gilded ballrooms, expensive silver sets and sprawling beachfront villas. Were these images from a life he'd lost or one he aspired to? There was no telling. Every time Donnie asked him about his past, Zach got distant and condescending, with some phrase like, "We're always picking ourselves up and brushing ourselves off on the boulevard of broken dreams, aren't we, Danger Boy?"

There was a vague story about studying to be a ballet dancer before an injury took him out, but the details he coughed up were *spare.*

And after he disappeared, impossible to verify.

But the worst was when Donnie asked about his clients.

In the beginning, he did a good job of hiding his jealousy.

What right did he have, after all?

Donnie was often shooting multiple scenes a week. Some of it was grueling work, but some models he really connected with and the fucks felt real and hot. But those models earned a check and so did he. Zach, on the other hand, slipped away every few nights to spend hours with men who paid big money—and his outfits and BMW suggested it was, indeed, big money—for something they thought only Zach could provide. And Donnie had never prepared for a client the way Zach did. Like he was getting ready to go to prom. An hour in the shower, an hour on his hair, another on his face. Then one night Donnie finally asked Zach to leave him with an address where he was headed. That way, if he didn't come home, Donnie would know where to look.

"This isn't some goddamn truck stop, Donnie. You don't share details about clients out here. That kind of shit could get you killed." Zach had said the words before, but never with that much anger. And he'd never slammed a door in Donnie's face after saying it.

He thought things were over that night. But Zach came back like he always did after a client call, desperate for Donnie's touch. Donnie knew the feeling. Hours of sexual attention from someone you didn't desire could leave you desperate for release at the hands of someone you truly wanted. This, too, had made the client calls easier to take. But the next morning, Zach announced an outing. He'd hoped they were headed over to Coronado Island to ogle hot Navy SEALS running along the shore.

It was far from that but closer to home, a visit to a garage apartment two blocks away owned by the same landlord, a former Parker Hunter model who'd opened a body building gym after retiring from porn.

Once the reality of the exchange had sunk in, Donnie had cried and begged Zach not to throw him out, cried in a way that made embarrassment twist his gut when he remembered it later. But Zach had hugged and comforted him and said it was no big deal. Just a healthy boundary, that's all. Donnie was still his Danger Boy and always would be.

10

Most of the beaches close to Sapphire Cove were cut up by cliffs, so for their morning run Jonas drove them north to Crystal Cove State Park, where a nice long, empty stretch of sand awaited them. While traffic was sparse at this early hour, the bluffs were set back from the surf, offering a nice buffer with Pacific Coast Highway's six lanes. The sun had yet to crest the coastal mountains to the east by the time their sneakered feet hit wet sand.

At first Richard had agreed to this ritual so he could reset his body clock to California time. To his surprise, it had made for a meditative start to his day. Jonas, who always chose his words carefully, wasn't one for early morning chatter. This morning, however, it was like he'd been replaced by a caffeinated doppelgänger.

"It's a pity, really. I adore Logan. Always have." He strained to keep his tone even between heavy breaths. "He's a man of his word. He'd fall on his sword for the hotel, and he treats Connor like a king. But his background was fairly rough. Before the Marines even. Which explains why he met his best friend in a dumpster behind a sex shop."

"Not really?" Richard asked. "The dumpster, I mean."

"Figure of speech. But I don't imagine they met at a meeting of their local arts council."

"Were they ever together?" Richard asked.

"No. They're famously incompatible in that way. Rumor has it they used to raid San Diego gay bars and walk out with power bottoms draped over their shoulders. The Twink Slayers, that was their nickname. But nothing about them being a couple." *Rumor has it* was usually an indication Jonas had conducted a surprisingly thorough investigation into a subject that would escape most people's notice. If he was doing deep background on Logan, it meant he was as protective of Connor Harcourt as he was of his close friends. Made sense. The hotel's GM had recently promoted him. A few years before that, he'd saved Jonas's workplace from ruin.

"Have you two ever…"

After a brief, startled silence, Jonas shot him a look. "Me and Donnie? Christ on his throne, no. I wouldn't touch him with ten pairs of gloves on. He's a pig."

"Is he, though?" Richard asked. "I mean, he's got an inappropriate streak for sure. And he was clearly sired in some porny social universe that puts a premium on dick size over class. But how are we defining pig here?"

"Seems rather philosophical for such an early hour." Jonas's tone pulsed with suspicion.

"Yes, well," Richard said in between breaths. "You're chattier than usual. I figured you'd be up for it." Richard waited for Jonas to come out and ask how the meeting had gone. He didn't. After the silence grew awkward, Richard added, "Don't get me wrong. He's a completely ridiculous person. Just…there's a side to him that's interesting, that's all."

"Oh no." Jonas groaned. "Please tell me you are not being charmed by the man they call Sex Monster."

"I didn't say he was charming. I said he was interesting. Georges Seurat is *interesting*. It doesn't make him a good artist." Jonas, who owned several different household items emblazoned with *A Sunday Afternoon on the Island of La Grande Jatte*, growled predictably at this deliberate dig. "Some of his motivations…they seem sincere, that's all."

"Motivations?"

"He's got some ideas for how to make the wedding ceremony more personal."

Jonas grunted.

"They're not completely terrible."

"Nude bartenders?"

"Jonas."

"Glory holes in all the bathrooms?"

"Some of the things he said in our meeting were actually quite moving."

"Well, which is it? *Not completely terrible* or *actually quite moving?* Because, forgive me, but *not completely terrible* sounds like the kind of faint praise we offer someone who's skirting through life on their looks."

"Trust me. Donnie Bascombe pulls no wool over my eyes. I'm simply making the best of a less than ideal situation. And I'm fairly sure once he shadows me on Saturday, he'll see—"

Jonas came to a dead stop and turned. "After he does *what* on Saturday?"

Sighing, Richard did the same. "He's shadowing me at the Mitchell event in Bel Air. He wants to see how I work so he can make more informed contributions."

Jonas grimaced. "That's absurd. He's not the floral designer, he's the best man."

"And he's trying to do his best."

"He's trying to get in your pants. I'll talk to Connor. Maybe he can dial him down a bit."

"That's really not necessary."

Jonas crossed his arms over his chest and raised one eyebrow.

"Jonas, I appreciate your protectiveness. Truly. I'm having a hard enough time getting Logan to open up about the wedding. I don't want any tension with Connor as well. We should head back. I've got to get up to LA today."

Richard started running in the direction of the parking lot.

"You watched his porn, didn't you?" Jonas called after him.

Grateful for the fact that the exertion of their run would cover up how badly the question made him blush, Richard didn't answer as Jonas caught up to him. But how would he hide his response if Donnie asked him the same thing come Saturday?

He'd jump off that bridge when he came to it.

11

Parker Hunter made the magic happen seven to eight times a week inside a warehouse just south of Miramar Naval Air Station, on a drab industrial street where its neighbors were mostly clueless as to the smutty shenanigans that happened within its four stark walls. Before the cigarettes finally claimed its founder, Eddie Frye, Donnie had helped transform the studio into a profitable outfit that made more than cheap amateur scenes with bogus lead-in interviews in which the models lied about having never banged a dude before. It was also Donnie who'd moved the studio from the dingy downtown offices where he'd first auditioned to an expansive production facility full of standing sets for various elemental fantasies.

As soon as he pulled into the parking lot, he yanked his phone from the cupholder. He was rattling off the list of folks who might help him pick out a good suit on short notice when he saw one of the candidates, his good friend Ethan Blake, had already sent him a text.

> Dearest Sex Monster. Can you meet up this afternoon? There's something I'd like to discuss with you. Preferably over a meal.

Uh oh, Donnie thought. Ethan's days, nights, and later nights were being spent almost entirely on preparations for the opening of his first ever bakery. And the hours he had left over were spent in the arms of his much younger fiancé, Roman Walker. If he needed to carve out time to talk to Donnie during the day, that meant it was serious.

Hopefully, there wasn't trouble in paradise. Ethan and Roman had come together in a manner so scandalous it had made headlines around the world, but they'd been desperately in love ever since, and Donnie hadn't noticed any changes the last time they'd had dinner with him on his boat.

Sure. On one condition. Help me pick out a good suit. I gotta go to a big event this weekend.

Of course. You wanting to dress nice is an event. Scratch that. You wanting to dress at ALL is an event.

They made plans to meet at the Westfield Mall in La Jolla around two p.m.

Then his phone rang. Donnie recognized the outgoing number for the Sapphire Cove switchboard. Stepping from his Dodge Durango, he answered, expecting to hear Logan's voice on the other end of the line. Instead, he'd accidentally taken a call from one of his least favorite people on Earth. "I understand you have an interesting engagement scheduled for this Saturday."

"You know there's a rumor you used to be a spy, right?" Donnie asked.

"For Marriot?"

"No, for, like the government."

Jonas Jacobs grunted. "I prefer the one that had me in a secret relationship with a closeted NFL player for which I had to sign an NDA. So, allow me to ask, Mr. Bascombe. What exactly do you see as your role in this wedding?"

"I see it as not involving you. Any other questions? I've got to get to work."

"No questions. Simply a statement of fact. Richard and I are old friends, so watch your step."

A few paces from the studio's front door, he froze. He and Jonas rarely had a conversation he'd call pleasant, but this level of aggression was new. "Is *old friends* code for *old flames*? You worried I might move in on your turf now that he's single again?"

"Hardly. Unlike you, I don't sexualize all my relationships."

"Yeah, well, unlike you, I don't make assumptions about people just 'cause I went to a fancy school."

"That is *literally* what you just did by accusing me of having feelings for Richard."

"You started it."

There was a brief silence before Jonas said, "Oh, that's your entire comeback, I see."

"And if I don't?"

"Don't what?"

"Watch my *step* with your *old friend.*"

"There will be consequences."

"So you'll disappear me in a foreign country? That's another rumor, by the way. That you used to make people disappear. But you want to know what I think?"

"I'm more interested in what you're not going to do."

Donnie ignored him. "I don't think any of them are true. I think you don't want to talk about what you did after college 'cause you went and got some fancy arts degree and the only job you could get was upper management at some shitty retail outfit like Old Navy or Urban Outfitters."

Jonas cleared his throat. "Donnie, this is your last friendly warning."

"When have you ever been *friendly*?"

"Richard has been a very good friend for a *very* long time. He is heartbroken and going through a divorce and, as it happens, he is now very important to this hotel. The two of you also have markedly different approaches to sex and relationships. Now, I don't know what you think you're up to by *shadowing* him at some—"

"I'm planning a wedding. Which is what my best friend asked me to do. And if you don't like it you can go take it up with him and Connor. Got it? But first I gotta run and go fuck your dad. Stay friendly, James Bond."

Donnie hung up before his growing anger could steal his sense of humor. He'd always known Jonas was a pretentious, condescending snob, which is why he usually made a show of brazenly flirting with the guy in an attempt to throw him off his snotty game. But this took the cake. And he didn't need anyone else telling him he was an idiot for nursing any kind of attraction to the fancy event planner. He'd been saying as much to himself all morning.

A few deep breaths later, he headed inside, grateful to find two of the three models for the morning's three-way shoot were already showered and getting into their soccer player costumes.

12

Gabe Sanchez was one of the best investments Richard had ever made. Three years ago, the young man had come to him with no experience and no fancy connections. Just heartfelt tales of growing up as a lonely gay teen in the Inland Empire, hiding wedding magazines under his bed the way gay men of Richard's generation used to hoard copies of the *International Male* catalog. At seventeen, he'd managed to blunt his family's homophobic dismissals of him by throwing a quinceañera for his baby sister that wowed the entire neighborhood. And required multiple city permits.

A few weeks into an unpaid internship—during which Gabe had risen at four in the morning each day so he could take two buses to get to the office before his new boss—Richard fired his nightmare of an assistant and gave the job to a crying-with-gratitude Gabe. No small sacrifice, given the assistant in question had been the spoiled and insubordinate son of one of Richard's key vendors. But in almost no time at all, Gabe had proved more than worth the headache of finding a new flower wholesaler for all of Merriweather's West Coast events. And during Richard's flight to Europe, he'd essentially taken over the management of Merriweather's LA office, earning a promotion to West Coast Regional Director as a result.

That's why when Gabe texted him to tell him that he'd been subjected to a profanity-laced tirade by the leader of the fire dancer troupe they'd hired to perform at Harry Mitchell's birthday party, Richard rearranged his schedule for the afternoon so he could pick Gabe up from the West Hollywood office and drive them both out to

Will Rogers State Beach, where the fire dancers in question were rehearsing their performance. By the time they pulled into one of the beach's public parking lots, he could feel steam pouring from his ears.

When the two of them reached the edge of the sand, Richard used the young man's shoulder for balance, pulling off his loafers and socks before handing them over to him for safekeeping.

"Are you sure about this?" the young man asked.

"Perfectly. You stay right here. I won't have you subjected to this man's abuse again."

"Richard..."

But he was already striding across the sand. The troupe was six men strong, all of them muscle-bound, barely dressed and Caucasian. Their performance wasn't nearly as impressive as it would be after dark, but the energy and complexity of their choreography was obvious to the small crowd of beachgoers who'd gathered to watch them practice. The fire breather, who used a burning staff to power geysers of flame skyward, performed at the group's center, surrounded by companions who twirled flaming balls on long twine strands. At any second, it looked like the balls might collide, but they never did, and that was what made their display so riveting. Two young women filmed everything with their smartphones.

When the leader saw Richard approaching, he stood suddenly and gestured for the rest of the group to fan out and keep practicing. On Instagram and TikTok, his seven million followers knew him by the name Bya'at'mu, a name Richard's office had not been able to trace to any known language or ethnicity. But he'd signed the contract John Bailey. Chest out, chin raised, he approached Richard with the confidence of a military leader who was there to accept the terms of Richard's surrender.

"Your assistant's energy is disruptive." His tone was somewhere between pretentious guru and those automated broadcasts of tide conditions you sometimes stumbled across on the radio. "I need him to leave if we're going to repair our communication."

"He's not my assistant. He's my West Coast Regional Director. Please ask your friends to put their phones away."

"We include our followers in all discussions of our process. I don't expect you to understand our generosity. It's generational, if you will."

"Lovely. Let's include them in a discussion of the fact that your act is appropriated from a host of cultures none of you belong to."

"Phones away now," the guy shouted.

The women hurriedly complied, and the fire twirlers let their balls sag and began extinguishing them.

"Here's the deal," Richard said quickly. "In your contract, you'll see that it requires you to be dressed to my satisfaction tomorrow night. If you're not, you will not perform. And that constitutes a breach. On your part. If that happens, I will charge *you* a cancellation fee twice what you're being paid to appear. So when my number two calls to tell you that you'll be wearing bike shorts instead of G-strings so that you do not literally expose yourself to five hundred guests, many of whom have won both Oscars and Emmys, that means you politely agree. It does not mean you call him a spineless pussy who represents the conformist, capitalistic, sex-phobic patriarchy. Some of our former clients have been deposed by their own generals, and even they never talked to Gabe the way you did today. With all due respect, which in this particular instance is quite almost none, exactly who in the hell do you think you are, young man?"

Pale, the dancer swallowed, his terror obvious. "I'm passionate about my work," he finally managed.

"So am I. Be passionate in bike shorts."

He nodded and looked to the sand between their feet like the chastened boy he was.

"So we have an understanding?"

He nodded again.

"Good. I will see you tomorrow night. *Before* you go on stage." Richard cleared his throat and addressed the rest of them. "Back to rehearsal, everyone."

Richard stalked back across the sand to where Gabe was waiting for him. He modeled his work attire after Richard, which meant he was in tailored dress slacks and a dress shirt that hugged his husky frame.

"Wow." Gabe handed Richard his shoes. Richard sank onto the stone bench. "I think he's crying."

"Nobody abuses my staff." When he stood, he followed the direction of Gabe's dazzled gaze. The head fire dancer was actually sobbing as both of the young women who'd been filming earlier held him up with half embraces. "What? You think I was too hard on him?"

"I'm not worried about him. He's a jerk," Gabe said. "I just hope you didn't think I told you what happened because I wanted you to…"

"To what? Stick up for you? Well, I did. So there."

Gabe had huge expressive brown eyes. Right now they were hidden behind sunglasses, but Richard was pretty sure they were full of sympathy and concern. "If you want me to handle tomorrow, I can. You know that, right?"

The implication was clear. Richard's anger was spiking higher and harder than usual ever since his marriage ended in disaster. With an event on this scale, where many of the guests would be aware of his ugly divorce, that might prove challenging for all. He turned. Somewhere deep within the canyon-dotted hills behind them was the house he'd shared with Mark for four years. Now up for sale. A place he'd not set foot in since walking in on his husband in bed—*their* bed—with another man. He'd felt its proximity as soon as they'd parked, like a cloud of insects buzzing right behind his neck. Had it made him go even harder on the insulting fire dancing poseur?

"If I'm not ready to come back, you mean."

"If you don't *want* to come back. Yet. Everyone will understand, Richard."

"I've been gone for four months. Vacation's over."

"It's hardly been a vacation."

Richard turned to his number two and clasped him gently on both shoulders. "Gabe, I adore you. I don't know what I'd do without you. You are a combination of competence and kindness I did not believe existed in this world. And that's how I know you're going to forgive me for the conversation we're about to have." Gabe had a soft, cherubic face, but right now it looked tense. "What sort of porn do you watch?"

The young man's lips parted but no sound emerged.

"Trust me. I have a completely professional reason for asking."

"Sure, um, okay… Well, there's this guy on OnlyFans. He sings songs about, like, each of his tattoos and what they mean. But he does it naked."

"Interesting."

"And then five guys who look like Cristiano Ronaldo come in and take turns on him. But it's very artistic. And it totally makes me want to get a tattoo."

"We've talked about making permanent decisions in your twenties."

Gabe nodded somberly.

"Does the name Bo Bonin mean anything to you?"

He shook his head.

"What about Parker Hunter?"

Gabe squinted. "Vaguely. Like I've heard it before. But honestly, studio porn isn't really my thing. It's a little old school. And kinda cheesy."

"Indeed. As opposed to the high art that is musical tattoo group sex."

Gabe smiled. "Just curious. When does this conversation get professional?"

"There will be a gentleman shadowing me tomorrow night. He works in adult films. Gay ones. And he has a penchant for trying to use that to his advantage. Should he attempt to charm you into doing something unwise on his behalf, I need you to stay strong."

"Not possible. I have one boss and it's you."

"Good. For the most part, he's a drooling sex ghoul, but he's also capable of surprising moments of earnestness and charm. One of many strategies he's used to manipulate young men into bed with him over the years, I'm sure. Don't be fooled, Mr. Sanchez. Hold strong. I've already allowed him to push me to my limit. I will go not one inch further."

"So he's into you," Gabe said, nodding.

"He's into anyone who reminds him of his ex, apparently."

"You say that like it's the same as being into tall guys, but it sounds way more specific than—"

"Gabe, I'm serious."

"Your wish is my command, as always. I'm just saying, if I spot you guys sneaking off into the bushes to have a little fun, I'm not going to file an OSHA complaint over it. You deserve to have some fun, Boss Man."

Richard nodded as if he were seriously considering the advice. Which he wasn't. "My dear, Mr. Sanchez. Your youth endows you with many fine qualities. But like many people your age, you are also hopelessly mired in the belief that a single night of good sex is a cure for deep emotional distress, and while the last thing I want to do is deprive you of your innocence and your joy, I fear it falls on me to tell you there are some things in life a little fun won't fix."

Richard started for the car.

"Maybe," Gabe said, "but I think it's worth making sure."

13

The AC in the studio had been set to arctic levels before they'd started shooting, but now, after over three hours of stop and start sex with three models at once, things were getting warm. Donnie's studio manager and lead camera operator, Brutus Paulson, had done a great job prepping the locker room set. The bank of flame-red lockers was still gleaming. He'd even artfully draped some towels over the rim of the rolling laundry bin to make them appear freshly tossed.

The shoot took off like a rocket. Maybe because their top for the day, Harrison Peters, aka David Allen, had been pumped up by the knowledge that his costars, the Apple Pie Twins, had requested another scene with him, specifically with the words, "If you want real moans out of us, let us ride Harrison until the sun comes up, Porn Daddy." It was amazing the results you could get out of building performers up rather than tearing them down, something a lot of directors he'd worked with over the years would have done well to learn.

The Apple Pie Twins weren't actually twins or brothers. They were a real-life couple named Cody and Ken, two blond, smooth-skinned twinks—or *twunks*, given the amount of muscle they'd put on recently—who'd moved from Knoxville to LA to start a career in studio porn after pulling down six figures on OnlyFans in less than a year. For the most part, they were sweet Southern boys who'd been nothing but professional and well-mannered since Donnie had signed them as exclusives. While they had developed an irritating interest in creative input of late, they'd spared him a pitch for an elaborate and unworkable backstory — often involving a portal to another dimension—to go with the traditional coach-nails-star-players locker room scene they'd scheduled for today.

Whatever the case, it was all going along so smoothly his mind started to wander. Instead of his rutting performers, he kept seeing the look on Richard's face as he'd rejected Donnie's offer of a walk the night before. Then he started trying to imagine the kind of suit that would chase that look off his face forever.

He'd said dark, so maybe navy blue.

Or charcoal.

But with a bright tie that really popped.

Maybe the color of Richard's logo.

Did Richard's company have a logo?

He'd have to check.

"Earth to Porn Daddy!" Brutus barked overhead. "Ken's leg's cramping up. We need to switch to missionary."

Embarrassed by his distraction, Donnie slid out from underneath Ken's body where he'd been shooting the penetration shots from below. The models repositioned. "Sorry, guys. Let's do what Brutus says."

In another forty or so minutes they were wrapped, the boys showering up while he and Brutus cleaned the set.

The building's exterior walls had been reinforced and soundproofed so nobody in the parking areas on all sides would be bothered by sex sounds during business hours. In the harsh overhead lights, the other standing sets ringing the vast space looked like a spotless showroom of archetypal queer male fantasies.

Next to the locker room set, there was a gym floor, complete with workout benches and a dumbbell set. The classroom had about six desks and a giant one for the teacher. The generic corporate office next door sported another desk, also big enough to have sex on, and a leather office chair on wheels that had barely visible brakes on them so a model could get blown in it without rolling backward into the false wall. The BDSM dungeon at the studio's far end featured a glistening leather pommel horse, an equipment wall, and a mattress on the floor laced with bondage straps. One of the newer additions was a college dorm room with matching twin beds in front of a fake window. Surrounding the window frame were what looked like posters of rock stars until you got up close and saw they were all hand drawn, the detailed work of one of Parker Hunter's devoted fans, a middle-aged woman who lived in Idaho and ran a fruit canning business on the Internet.

The barnyard set was still empty of hay bales after last Friday's shoot. He'd have to make a note to order a refill.

But his brand-new crowning achievement was the recently installed doctor's exam room set that had required six months of equipment purchases and order delays and some smart budgeting.

He'd built this place. And he'd cleaned up some of the studio's shadier business practices while doing so. Most days he felt a deep sense of pride whenever he surveyed his smutty kingdom. But today he had Richard Merriweather on the brain, and everything seemed like wasted time until he could find a suit that would impress the guy.

"Penny for your thoughts?" Brutus finally asked. He was a fireplug of a man whose dark bushy eyebrows sometimes made it hard to tell if he was angry or focused. He'd spent his early sixties covering his shoulders and neck in tattoos that extended the sleeves he'd sported for years. By the time he turned seventy, his entire scalp would probably be covered. A holdover from the studio's old days, he'd also been one of the cameramen on Donnie's first ever sex scene for Parker Hunter and close friends with the studio's founder. A man of few words and decisive action, he was exactly who Donnie wanted as a number two.

"Just a penny?" Donnie asked. "I've got some kickass thoughts."

"Sometimes, but not all the time."

"I met someone last night."

Threading a cable around his forearm with his outstretched thumb as a hook, Brutus stared at him. "For sex?" he finally asked.

"No. I mean... Almost, but no."

"Did you have a car accident?"

"What, you think I don't meet people for something besides sex?"

"The way you said it is all. It wasn't like you."

"Whatever. The guy said this thing I can't stop thinking about. How there's a difference between actually wanting someone and only wanting what they can do to you for five or ten minutes."

Laughing, Brutus dropped the wound cable into the plastic storage tub nearby then went for the Clorox spray and paper towels. "I love that that's a big revelation for you, Sex Monster."

"What?"

"That you actually have to get to know someone to fall in love. That's, like, romance 101."

"Yeah, well, romance isn't exactly my thing. And who said anything about falling in love? I've never been in love."

"Not even Zach?" Brutus watched Donnie with one eye as he asked the question, always careful on this topic.

Everyone who'd been in his life from those days was careful on the topic of Zach Loudon. Maybe because they'd seen Donnie walking the streets of Hillcrest, posting missing persons flyers to telephone poles while his friend Ethan Blake trailed close behind, gently encouraging him to give up the effort and head home and get on with his life.

"How can you be in love with someone you don't know anything about?"

"Deep," Brutus answered, nodding. "Teddy and I were together ten years before he passed away. Sex wasn't the only thing that kept it going. In the end, it's about who you want to share the remote with. That sound like Zach?"

"Zach always controlled the remote. And I was always supposed to learn something from whatever we watched."

Brutus swiped at the spray of Clorox he'd covered one bench with. "Learn something," he said quietly, tone brimming with contempt. "About what?"

"I don't know. How to be strong. How to make money off sex." Donnie flipped one hand over and stuck his palm out like a white-gloved butler. "How to be elegant and refined."

"Yeah, well, the last one really didn't take."

Donnie shot him the bird then finished removing the lens from the camera he'd been fiddling with absently since the shoot had ended.

"I know where the salad fork is, okay?"

"The *tossed* salad fork, maybe," Brutus grumbled.

"Fuck you, dude."

They both laughed for a few seconds, then the silence returned, and with it, more memories that Donnie didn't want weighing on him.

Brutus smiled and left.

And once again he was alone with Zach's memory, a memory that might as well have been a ghost.

Fifteen Years Ago

Zach proved true to his words. Forcing Donnie to move to an apartment down the street turned out to be a warning shot and not much else. Donnie still ended up spending most of his hours at his house. Except on the nights when he had to prepare for a client. Rules were rules; boundaries were boundaries.

So when Zach announced that his former pupil, that old friend of his from New York, the one he'd taught to escort, the one who'd earned enough from clients to put himself through culinary school, had landed a fancy restaurant gig in La Jolla and would soon be moving into Zach's guest bedroom, Donnie knew better than to speak up or show his jealousy. Make that mistake again and Zach might drive him back to that couple's guest house up in West Hollywood.

But the day Ethan Blake pulled up in his moving truck, Donnie's heart was in his throat. Then Zach's new housemate hopped down out of the cab looking like something out of one of the fashion magazines Zach devoured—Clark Kent good looks, rugby player brawn, big brown eyes—and when he and Zach embraced, they were a vision of masculine perfection. Donnie could suddenly feel the grit of every dirty roadside motel room he'd turned a trick in tattooed across his skin for all to see.

It's over, he'd thought. I've lost him. I should run.

He wouldn't run so far this time, wouldn't have to leave California. He had more friends now, a career. Eddie Frye might take him in. But then Ethan Blake mounted the porch and started for him with nothing but warmth in his eyes. When Donnie extended his hand, Ethan took him into a warm embrace and said, "So this is Danger Boy, huh? Doesn't look so dangerous to me."

Donnie went soft inside, and it wasn't too long before he realized Ethan's arrival wasn't bringing things to an end, it was starting something new, something that would keep Donnie tied to Zach for longer than he might have been otherwise.

Upon their first meeting, Ethan had gifted him with more honesty and attention than Zach ever had. As Donnie had helped him empty out his moving truck, Zach had slipped off to get ready for work, a sign that his rule about Donnie clearing out whenever he had to prepare for a client had been rewritten by Ethan's arrival. As the two of them lugged heavy boxes up the front steps, Donnie found himself bragging to Ethan about his new porn career in a way that made him feel foolish and kinda desperate whenever he took a breath. But Ethan listened patiently and nodded, then he offered to pay him back for his help by cooking a nice meal. More importantly, he laughed at Donnie's jokes, which back then, was almost as important to Donnie as complimenting *his dick. The conversation had flowed. Maybe because unlike Zach, Ethan had given honest answers to Donnie's questions about his past, his life, his loves.*

They'd decided to watch a movie together on Zach's sofa as they awaited Zach's return. When he'd leaned over and rested his head on Ethan's shoulder, he thought the sweet, brawny guy might flinch or pull away. Instead, he'd curved an arm around Donnie's shoulders protectively.

Maybe Donnie had been trying to make Zach jealous.

Or maybe Ethan had melted his heart and he wanted to be touched by someone he thought he could trust.

Whatever the case, when Zach had walked through the front door and saw the two of them snuggling on the sofa, a strange light came into his beautiful blue eyes, and when he'd returned from the shower, he was clad in only a pair of white briefs and a hungry smile.

What followed between the three of them lasted almost a year and was defined by as much white hot, spur of the moment sex as it was by a lack of discussions about its boundaries or rules. Ethan would later call it more of a bubble than a throuple, meaning it had protected them from more than it had given them. Ethan had been saved from entering the dating world with his escorting past nipping at his heels, and Donnie and Zach hadn't been forced to address the one-sided nature of their relationship, which was about to completely fall apart, leaving him with what he really needed. A good friend who understood the realities of sex work and would never judge him for it.

14

If Ethan was demanding they eat at a chain restaurant in the mall before going suit shopping, that meant he was either starving or whatever he wanted to discuss couldn't wait.

The man wasn't a total snob about food. He'd drag Donnie clear across San Diego County to a roadside taco stand if he thought the proprietors had done something amazing with the spices. But whenever he scheduled a meal for the two of them somewhere other than his well-stocked kitchen, he picked a place where he thought the cooks had spent the kind of time and attention on the menu he'd devoted to his pastry over the years—Seasons 52 at the Westfield La Jolla mall hardly fit the bill.

As he crossed the restaurant, Donnie spotted his old friend sitting by himself at a booth. With the only other diners in a cluster about half a room away, it was clear he'd sweet-talked the hostess into giving them some privacy.

Another sign he had something serious to discuss.

Ethan stood when he saw him, his smile as warm and open as the one he'd given Donnie on the day they'd first met. His trimmed mustache was a new addition since he'd returned from Europe the year before, and over the years he'd grown out his hair. It was thick and wavy, and the gray showed. He didn't seem to care. Neither did the love of his life, who called him Daddy whenever he thought no one was listening.

"Slumming it at a chain restaurant with your porn star friend," Donnie said once he'd taken his seat. "What's your life come to,

Blake?"

"Let's have a look at the menu, shall we?"

"No need. Us Michigan boys don't eat anything besides fried dough, you know."

Without looking up from his menu, Ethan said, "I would like to suggest that after twenty some odd years in Southern California, having sex with every male thing that moves, it has been quite a long time since anyone could safely consider you a Michigan boy."

"Fifteen years, but close. And how's that work? You think I lose more of my square state edge every time I hook up with a surfer boy?"

Ethan smiled. "Pick out your food."

In those early days, Donnie had tried hard to fall in love with Ethan Blake.

It had seemed like the right thing to do, the logical thing.

He'd been as wise and experienced as Zach, but he was kinder and more forthright. Handsome in an entirely different way. And he'd been determined to teach Donnie how to do things other than have sex for money. Useful things, like find a good doctor you could trust, stock his kitchen with food that would satisfy his appetites and not stuff his feelings, and keep himself in shape without resorting to dangerous injections. But whenever their mouths had met above Zach's sweaty back, it had felt less like a passionate kiss and more like a fist bump, none of that *tug, tug, tug* feeling in the chest he got whenever he kissed Zach. Whenever they played around one on one, it had felt like time-killing mutual masturbation until their hungry bottom got home.

The server arrived, and they both ordered.

"It's not Roman, is it?" Donnie asked as soon as the woman departed. "Whatever you need to talk about. You and Roman are good?"

"Beyond good. Excellent, in fact. Roman is an undeserved miracle in my life."

Ethan picked up a file folder off the booth. He opened it on the table between them then slid a single piece of paper out of it and toward Donnie.

It was a printout of an email, and as soon as Donnie realized what it was, his heart started hammering.

Mr. Blake,

Wild ride you've been on, old friend! Congrats though. Your new boy's a hottie. Bet you're getting all kinds of crazy messages these days, but this is your old friend Zach Loudon. I'll get right to it. I'm in a bad way and could use some assistance. Send your number and I'll give more details by text?

XO, Zach

The skin on the back of Donnie's neck went cold.

When he slowly lifted up the piece of paper, the tips of his fingers felt numb.

The address was some Hotmail account with Zach's initials followed by a string of numbers that made no sense. But they weren't Zach's initials, not really. After he'd vanished, Donnie and Ethan discovered there was no real evidence a man named Zach Loudon had ever existed, suggesting the very real possibility that he'd used the same alias with Donnie and Ethan that he'd used with his clients. The lease on the house had always been paid in cash.

The more he read the letter, the more he was seeing another in his mind's eye. One he'd discovered on the kitchen table of that tiny house in Hillcrest on a day that had changed his life.

My Dearest Danger Boy,

The Buddhists say, "One clings to life although there is nothing to be called life; another clings to death although there is nothing to be called death. In reality, there is nothing to be born; consequently, there is nothing to perish."

What we had will never perish.

Thanks for making me do dangerous things.

Love,
Zach

P.S. The rent is paid for six months. The clothes and furniture that are left are for you and Ethan. You were always good at sharing. :)

He'd exploded into Zach's room, found the bedside drawers all empty. Half the clothes in the closet had been missing. The BMW had been gone too. Hysterical, he'd called Ethan at his restaurant, who told him to go into his room and see if there was a note there too. There had been and Zach had read it to Ethan over the phone. Basically identical, with the same postscript about rent and clothes. The Buddhist saying had been different, though, but just as infuriatingly opaque.

"You okay?" Ethan finally asked, jerking him back to the present.

Donnie looked up, and the open, patient expression in his good friend's eyes melted something in him.

He'd been a nightmare on the subject of Zach back then. Ethan had put up with all of it. Indeed, it seemed like the only way their friendship had survived was that eventually, once it was clear the man was gone for good, they'd basically stopped talking about Zach altogether. But what other choice did Ethan have? Donnie would turn red faced and start to cry whenever Ethan even suggested a possible explanation Donnie didn't like. Namely that Zach was alive and well and didn't want to be found. Living under his actual name, all ties to his sex worker life effectively cut forever. Back then, it had been too hard for Donnie to hear himself described as a *tie*.

But now, he knew how busy Ethan was with preparations for the bakery, knew how much it had taken for him to carve time out of his day to deliver this shock in person, and it made the torrent of memories a single paper had unleashed easier to deal with.

"You think it's really him?" Donnie asked.

"Anyone in the world can open up a Hotmail account. I take it you haven't gotten anything?"

Donnie shook his head. "I'll check my spam folders later. Did you send your number?"

"Not a chance. Could be some reporter trying to hack my phone. Roman and I are still getting hit with interview requests. Or maybe it's some crank stirred up by the scandal who thinks they can swindle me for some cash. I've written back asking for him to verify details, but I haven't heard anything yet. It's odd."

"How would anyone today know to use Zach to try to get in? It was forever ago, and it wasn't like he was ever in the papers for anything."

"Like I said...odd. But to be honest, the most telling detail is that after I refused to give my phone number I heard nothing back. Maybe that means it isn't him. I can't be sure. But I thought you needed to know right away in case whoever this is makes a run at you too."

"Thank you. Seriously. I know how busy you are and telling me in person is a big deal, so thank you."

"I appreciate that. Now back to my original question. Donnie, are you going to be okay?"

"Of course I'll be okay. It was fifteen years ago."

"True, but it was another five before you gave away his clothes."

"I know I put you through hell."

"You didn't put me through hell. Don't be so hard on yourself. It was a difficult situation."

"I did and I'm sorry. I would yell and scream whenever you said he didn't want to be found."

"Well, it was my penance."

"Penance? What did you do? You were right there with me the whole time. You were a better friend to me than he ever was."

"Penance for not taking you aside the first time I ever saw you look at him with love in your eyes and telling you what I already knew about Zach. That he could never love anyone. Except himself."

"Sweet, but not your job."

"I taught you how to stock your kitchen and open a bank account. I could have at least taught you how to protect your heart."

"Some lessons are harder to learn. Besides, I was too far down that road by the time you moved in."

Ethan shrugged. "I don't know. Perhaps if I hadn't let things go the way they went that first night."

"Oh, whatever, dude. I started the damn thing. You think I put my head on your shoulder because the movie was scary? It was *Jaws 3*. It's, like, the dumbest movie ever."

"The tunnels. Dennis Quaid. I remember."

"It would have happened eventually, Blake. It was what Zach wanted. Two tops in the house to service him on call and keep each other occupied when he was out with a client. In the end, it was always about what Zach wanted."

"I can't argue with that," Ethan said quietly.

The server brought their drinks. Ethan sipped his iced tea.

Donnie studied the paper again, saw the date on the email for the first time.

"This was three weeks ago?" he asked.

"It got sent to a general address at Sapphire Cove, and they forwarded it to me a few days ago. I wrote back immediately, and I still haven't gotten a response. I figured it was time to tell you in case you got one too."

Donnie read the words again.

It wasn't Zach. It couldn't be Zach. The tone was all wrong. Jokey and friendly wasn't Zach's style. Or at least it hadn't been. Back then it had been Zach's MO to adopt the style of whoever he was talking to. And if he was writing to Ethan, he would have written like Ethan talked. Like the pages out of some old novel Donnie could only manage a chapter of.

"I appreciate you looking out for me," Donnie finally said.

"Always."

"Just don't ask me to plan your wedding because I'm already freaking out about Murdoch's."

"Rest assured, Roman and I are thinking about something very small and very private and possibly out of the country. While we'd love for you to be there, the planning in general will be kept to a minimum."

Donnie nodded. Ethan and his fiancé had been brought together by the celebrity wedding of the year turned scandal of the decade. No surprise they'd been left with no appetite for a big ceremony of their own.

"I met the wedding planner last night," Donnie finally said. "He's…interesting."

"Oh, dear. You only call men *interesting* when you want to jump their bones but you think I won't approve."

"Basically true, but he's still interesting."

"In what way?"

"He's, like, a *real* version of who Zach wanted to be."

Ethan's eyes widened, and he nodded slowly. "That is interesting."

"You know what I mean. He's rich and sophisticated and cultured and successful. And he's worked all over the world. And he's got amazing fucking hair. You know how I am about hair. But we're planning a wedding together, so it's hands off." Donnie gestured like he was yanking his fingers back from an unexpectedly hot plate.

Ethan nodded somberly. "So you tried to sleep with him and he shot you down?"

"I always forget how well you know me."

"Do Logan and Connor know about this?"

"*No*. Look, I didn't know he was their wedding planner when I hit on him. So we're readjusting. That's why I need the suit, by the way. I'm shadowing him at one of his events up in LA tomorrow."

Nodding gravely, Ethan said, "That's sweet. And you're going to keep your hands off him while he does it?"

"If that's what he wants. He's very bitchy."

"Oh, God. You're doomed. You love bitchy."

Donnie nodded down at the table.

After a brief, tense silence, Ethan said, "Court him."

"Huh?"

"I said, court him."

"Seems early for a lawsuit."

"Donnie, you simply must watch some better television now and then."

"You always put on shows with a bunch of whispering butlers and violins. How am I supposed to stay awake?"

"Must everything begin with an exploding spaceship?"

"*Game of Thrones* didn't have spaceships."

"It had dragons, which are the spaceships of medieval fantasy." Their lunches arrived. Ethan gave the server a polite smile, then, once they were alone again, he said, "*Courting* means to signal one's romantic interest in someone in a gradual and gentlemanly way. Without taking one's clothes off. The advantage of it here is that you can show that interest without making a firm commitment. And if he doesn't reciprocate, or, more likely, *you* lose interest thanks to some hot, low-maintenance twink you meet on Grindr, you can both move on without a messy entanglement or a misunderstanding."

"There's no such thing as a low-maintenance twink, Blake."

"Donnie, I'm serious. Practice showing an interest in someone that doesn't end in you blowing your load."

"Hey, now. I'm a charitable guy. I've gotten plenty of guys off without finishing myself off too."

"Your medal is in the mail."

"Okay, but what am I allowed to do other than buy him flowers? I mean, what if he's allergic?"

"You are supposed to listen to him and respond. Consistently do things that demonstrate you are hearing what he has to say. If he tells you he's running low on his favorite breath mint, pick up an extra pack at the store and leave it on his desk. If he tells you he has a favorite movie, see if there's a screening at some nice theater you can take him to."

"What about rim jobs?"

"Not before the wedding."

"*I can't eat his ass for six months? That's gay erasure!*"

Ethan glared at him. "Just be careful, whatever you do."

"Trust me. I'm not going to do anything to mess up Logan and Connor's big day."

"That's not entirely what I meant."

Donnie raised one eyebrow.

Ethan finally took it as his cue to elaborate. "This wedding planner, the way you've described him. Rich. Sophisticated. Successful. That's not just who Zach wanted to be. That's a description of the phantom client you've always thought stole Zach away from you. And you've used that description to beat the crap out of yourself for years. You didn't lose Zach because you weren't rich and successful enough, Donnie. You lost him because nobody could keep him. Besides, he only wanted us to believe his clients were fabulous and rich."

"You don't think they were?"

"Not at the end, no."

"Do you think one of them hurt him?"

Ethan stared into his eyes, and Donnie saw traces of all the tantrums he'd thrown in his presence on this very subject over the years. The fact that they could now discuss the subject this calmly felt like a huge leap forward. And it suggested Ethan was preparing to say something he'd never said to Donnie before.

"I was building a career. You were clearly going to take over Parker Hunter. We had our loves, our obsessions. Zach's only purpose in life was to be adored and showered with gifts for being young and beautiful. Problem was, he wasn't young anymore, and he didn't have a next act. I think whatever he decided to do to keep the adoration going, he was ashamed of it. And he didn't want us to know about it, and that's why he left."

"You always said you thought he walked away from the life and wanted to cut all ties, including us."

"I did. And then I got this email."

Their food arrived, but Donnie didn't go for his fork. He was staring at the printout of Zach's alleged message.

"That's your copy, by the way," Ethan said.

"Thanks." Donnie placed several fingers on it and slid it back across the table toward his good friend. "But I'm good."

Ethan nodded, studying him.

Donnie smiled back. It felt a little dishonest, given he'd memorized the email address.

15

A half hour before guests were due to arrive, Richard Merriweather was standing in the command center for Harry Mitchell's birthday party, wondering what in God's name he would say if Donnie brought up the fact that he'd watched his porn the other night at Sapphire Cove. At least he wasn't hot under the collar now. Gabe had pressured him to replace the trailer's AC after the team had almost sweated to death outside the Equality Gala at the Academy Museum the year before. Now they were enjoying the frosty benefits.

But the closer he'd drawn to the event, the more the resolve he'd shown Jonas on the beach yesterday morning had started to crumble. Maybe because he'd watched Donnie's porn again last night. For two hours.

Behind his staff, who'd assembled in military-like formation to deliver their final pre-event checks, a wall of flat screens offered multiple, high-definition views of Harry's lavish Holmby Hills Estate. Ten-top tables filled the center of the terraced gardens. The linens and place settings were being added at a healthy clip. The concert stage was already complete, as evidenced by the blasting sound checks that had been making everyone jump for the past twenty minutes. Even better, as the sky overhead darkened, the precision lights Richard had added to the Georgian mansion's garden façade were revealing themselves to be perfectly, delightfully symmetrical.

As with most of Harry's parties, the theme was an awards ceremony where the only award went to Harry. They were well on track to deliver by seven p.m.

Prep had been crisis free, but still, his staff deserved his full attention.

The attention they were giving him, however, was only adding to his nerves. Straight-backed, wide-eyed and nervous, as if they thought he might fly off the handle at any moment. He was a firm boss, but never an abusive one, having worked for more than his fair share of tyrannical, iced coffee hurling divas on his way up the ladder. But when it came to his team, he'd vanished from their lives almost a half year before, for reasons that were now common knowledge. No wonder they were greeting his return to service as gently as one would nurse an elderly grandparent recovering from a double hip replacement.

"...but if we don't have a ton of requests for the vegan dish, I think we should be fine. And the caterer's confident that bringing the beef Wellington and sauteed salmon on the same plate will mollify everyone except the hard-core vegetarians."

Richard nodded as if he'd heard more of the catering representative's update than he had. "Thank you, John. Lucy, entertainment report."

Lucy Bradford cleared her throat and held her clenched fists out on either side of her as if gathering strength to take an imaginary leap. Never a good sign with her. But it was only a full-on crisis if she started fiddling with one of the hairpins that secured her massive pile of curls, and right now her hands didn't go above chest level. "So the bad news is Elton John's plane was grounded because of weather. So he won't be here in time to sing 'Harry in the Wind.' But after a slight delay at LAX, Ringo Starr is coming direct from the airport and should be able to perform 'Harry in the Sky with Diamonds' on schedule. "

"So we're down one tribute song. What's the plan?"

Lucy raised a hand, giving him a self-satisfied smile. "I've got an amazing Aretha Franklin cover artist on the way, and she's going to sing—wait for it—'Harry the Beautiful.' *And* she's got the Obama inauguration hat."

"The real one or a replica?" he asked.

"I can find out."

"And she's actually a cover artist and not a drag queen who's going to lip sync?"

"Correct. The drag queen would have broken our budget."

"Perfect. Excellent work, Lucy. Security update."

There was a tug on his shoulder. Richard turned to see Gabe right behind him, clipboard pressed to his chest. "Your ghost is here," he whispered. "Just parked."

A few seconds later, he and the young man were moving swiftly down the hedge-lined, pea gravel walkway toward the estate's staff entrance.

"Okay, so here's the plan," Richard said. "The minute, make that the *second,* he's in danger of making an ugly scene, I'll need you to evacuate him. Instantly. The code will be, *That's quite enough, Mr. Bascombe.* As soon as you hear those words in your earpiece, I'll need you to drop whatever you're doing, summon at least two members of the security team, and get to my location immediately." Richard snapped his fingers. "Then once you escort him from the property, don't let him out of your sight until you've seen him drive away."

"Absolutely."

Richard stopped walking so abruptly the pea gravel crunched loudly under his dress shoes. He dug into the inside pocket of his jacket and pulled out a dark blue necktie. "Now put this on."

Gabe frowned. "I'm so sorry. I didn't know you wanted me to wear a tie."

"I didn't. I want you to wear one right *now* because I'm wearing one. And if Donnie shows up without one, I'll have an excuse to send him away."

Gabe handed Richard his clipboard, flipped up his collar, and began tying the tie. "But nobody else on the team's wearing a tie."

"And it won't matter because if Donnie isn't, he won't make it through the back gate, and he'll never lay eyes on the rest of the team." Richard smiled.

"Oh my God, Richard. What did this guy do to you?"

He knows I watched his porn right down the hall from him, and I have no idea what to say if he brings it up, he thought. What he said was, "I am doing everything I can to keep the situation professional as I endure a collaboration I did not ask for."

Except not watch his porn. Because he's so…so…dirty.

Richard smoothed out Gabe's tie with one hand and handed the young man his clipboard. "There. Perfect. And to be honest, the tie's probably irrelevant. I'm sure he'll be dressed like a rodeo clown, demanding entrance based on the fact that he once won an award for a movie called *Bo's Backyard Gang Bang.*"

"Is that a real movie?" Gabe asked as Richard started them forward again. "You know the names of his movies? What's going on?"

"Let's focus."

Load-in had completed hours ago, so the check-in table at the estate's service driveway was mostly being used for staff arrivals. A few members of Harry Mitchell's security team were hanging about, including a handsome new guy in a pricey-looking navy blue suit he didn't recognize. But he didn't see any sign of the porn star in question.

Because, upon a second glance, he realized the porn star in question was the handsome new guy in the navy blue suit.

With a now familiar, drowsy-eyed grin, hands resting easily in his pants pockets, Donnie Bascombe turned to face them. He'd trimmed his dirty blond scruff and styled his hair in a way that brought out its natural curl, a few of which draped his forehead, boyishly offsetting his gentleman's attire. His tie was bright gold with an expensive luster. The suit's rich blue fabric brought out the lighter blue of his eyes, making them twinkle.

Blue and gold, Richard thought suddenly, *the same colors as my logo.* He also thought he saw traces of highlights in Donnie's hair that hadn't been there during his first meeting, but he couldn't be sure.

He didn't want to be sure.

He didn't want to be this excited about the fact that Donnie had followed his instructions.

He didn't want to consider the implications of what else might happen if a guy as brawnily handsome and sexually uninhibited as Donnie Bascombe actually listened to him.

"I see no rodeo clowns," Gabe whispered as Donnie started for them.

And Richard said nothing, because if this had been the moment he'd laid eyes on Donnie Bascombe for the first time—with no knowledge of his professional history—he would have grabbed the elbow of the person nearest him and asked if they had any details about the ruggedly handsome man in the designer suit.

Donnie grinned and raised his arms on either side. "So, what do you think? Do I pass muster?"

"You're fine," Richard said.

Clearly disappointed in Richard's clipped, professional tone, Donnie reached into his jacket pocket and removed what looked like a small ring box. "Brought you a little something."

Before Richard could get a good look at what Donnie was doing, his handsome shadow for the evening had fastened something tiny to Richard's lapel. Having seized the moment of surprise generated by his dashing outfit, the artist known as Bo Bonin had pinned him like they were in high school.

Gabe was beaming.

Richard pulled his lapel out from his jacket and took a good look at the thing. Figuring if the initials DB—or BB—were staring up at him, he'd have a great excuse to remove it. Instead, it was the letter M, a loose, serpentine version of it that roughly mirrored the logo for Merriweather Events, which was the M in Merriweather rendered as wedding arches with billowing fabric forming the letter's three stems, and tiny floral bouquets bursting atop the outside ones.

Tonight was his first night back in the saddle after a personal crisis. His trusted number two was doubting his ability to return to work, and as for the rest of his staff, he'd been greeted not with gifts, but with kid gloves. Until now. Donnie's gift was the first kind gesture someone had done to commemorate his return to regular life. Of course, Donnie probably hadn't figured out—

"It's your first big event back in the States. Might as well do something to celebrate it. Something for you, I mean. Not Mr. Big Deal Birthday Boy with the monster driveway. Looks like he's getting taken care of tonight."

Godammit, he figured it out.

"That's very thoughtful. Thank you."

The word *thoughtful* seemed to make Donnie's brow tense. Maybe he'd been hoping for something more along the lines of, *Take me, Daddy.* "Hey, if you don't like it, I can take it off. Just thought you should see how it looks before you make a call."

"Oh my God, leave it on," Gabe said. "It's precious."

Richard gave his number two a look that was supposed to say, *I hope you won't miss your skin.*

Gabe patted Richard on one shoulder. "You boys have an amazing time together. Guest arrivals start in fifteen, so I need to go make sure valet's in place."

"Donnie, this is Gabe Sanchez. Without him I am nothing. I'm sure you guys will see each other again very soon."

Donnie extended his hand. "Nice to meet you, Gabe."

And then they were alone together.

Richard did what he always did when he was uncomfortable—he

focused on work.

"The command center's inside a trailer over there in those trees. I doubt we'll need it at the wedding since we have most of the hotel at our disposal, but it's got video feeds of everything. Normally that's where I'd monitor the event, but since you're here, I figure we'll stay in circulation so you can get a look at all the different moving parts."

Left unsaid was the fact that the trailer would empty out and become Richard's exclusive domain once the party started. No way was he spending this evening alone with Donnie in a cool, dimly lit space, especially now that Donnie's shiny gift seemed to be pressing a tingly halo against his chest. Not with Donnie looking like a menswear model and smelling of smoky, expensive cologne.

"Is that where the party's going to be?" Donnie was pointing to a two-story stone edifice not too far from where the command center was parked amidst a curtain of tree branches.

"No, that's the guest house."

Donnie swallowed. "Damn," he whispered.

"Come on. I'll give you a tour."

After a minute or two of walking past lit box hedges and under a canopy of oak branches, Donnie said, "Is this a house or a national park?"

"Welcome to Bel Air," he said, just as the path curved up ahead to reveal palatial gardens overtaken by Richard's sparkling vision.

"Welcome to Richard Merriweather is more like it," Donnie said.

And despite himself, Richard turned back at the man behind him and smiled.

16

It wasn't Donnie's first mansion. Tricks and his last few escorting clients had often called him to pricey pads in La Jolla and Rancho Santa Fe. And today there was a constant retinue of rich old gay dudes who enjoyed hosting Donnie and his performers around their expansive swimming pools because they liked adding a dash of porn to their parties. But it was the first time he'd seen a combo of mansion and garden on this staggering scale.

Richard had come to a stop next to a giant, life-sized statue, a robed female goddess that stood on a pedestal in one corner of the intersection of two walkways, her back to the garden's glittering expanse.

"Syndication money," Richard said when he saw Donnie's shock. "Nothing else like it in Hollywood. The way streaming works now, you can't really make it anymore. But when it was good, it was good. His big hit was that show *Helicopter Parents* back in the nineties."

Donnie swallowed. "The one where the ghosts of the cop's mom and dad possess his police helicopter and they all solve crimes together?"

Richard nodded. "Actually, it's a lightning storm that puts them there, I think. But close enough. I can only remember the one where they're chasing some robbery suspects and the mom's spirit forces the helicopter to land at a restaurant because the son skipped breakfast and he's grumpy."

But it wasn't the house that had left Donnie slack-jawed and goggle-eyed. It was the work Richard had done throughout the enormous gardens. He knew the basics of good lighting, but porn lighting was mostly about trying to see every vein in a boner. What Richard had done was amazingly intricate and crazy expensive.

The mansion's massive stone terrace was roped off. A string quartet was tuning up in one corner. Falling rain lights filling the nearby trees gave the terraces around the sunken banquet area an enchanted forest vibe. High-end theatrical lighting, the kind Donnie could barely afford for his studio, was positioned along the house's roofline. It bathed the tables below in rich shades of amber and rouge that made the silver and china place settings shimmer. The concert stage was two stories tall, with the kind of light rigging you'd expect to find at fairgrounds. But the curtains masking the stage's side pillars were covered with twinkling imitations of tree branches that met in a glittering arch high above the stage. It was like Richard and his team had opened a portal to some dazzling, alternate fantasy world in the middle of an already beautiful garden.

"This is incredible," Donnie said quietly.

Richard's eyes widened, as if he thought Donnie might be kidding. Or was braced for him to follow up about how good Richard's ass looked in those pants. They looked fantastic, but Donnie kept that thought to himself. Eventually, Richard nodded. "Thank you."

"Dickie!" A tall, olive-skinned woman came striding up the stone steps toward them. Her ink-black hair was long, straight, and layered. Her flaring gold eye shadow matched the piping on her cherry red cocktail dress. "I'm hearing rumors about Elton's plane."

"They're true, unfortunately, but we have an excellent backup plan that's already in place."

"Oh God, please not the cast of *Stomp* again. There's only so much aspirin one can take, and Vicodin makes me itchy."

They exchanged air kisses, then the woman looked at Donnie and her expression went suddenly blank and still, save for the flash of recognition in her eyes. Donnie knew the look well. He told himself to play it cool.

"Thalia, this is Donnie Bascombe. He's shadowing me this evening because he's consulting on another event I'm working on. Donnie, this is Harry's wife, Thalia. Arguably one of my most important clients. If not *the* most important client."

Donnie heard the undertone of warning in Richard's voice and extended his hand. "It's a pleasure to meet you, Mrs. Mitchell. This is an absolutely lovely home you have." On Ethan's instruction, he'd been watching clips from *Downton Abbey* to get into character for the evening. He'd sounded pretty damn Matthew Crawley, if he did say so himself.

"Oh, please. If he'd wanted me to take his last name he shouldn't have made me sign a prenup. Just Thalia, please. So you're…shadowing. What does that involve?"

"Watching the best at work," Donnie smiled.

"He is, isn't he? Are you in the event planning business, Mr. Bascombe?" A small crook at the corner of her mouth, a raised eyebrow, eyes wide and unblinking as if she was the one trying not to give something away.

Yep, she definitely recognizes me.

Richard spoke up. "Donnie is going to be contributing some—"

"We're working together on my best friend's wedding at Sapphire Cove."

"That should be exciting. I mean, the idea of Dickie working *with* anyone is exciting. He's the only person in the world who can tell my husband what to do. Including me."

"Oh, come now. You convinced him not to buy that villa in Positano."

"And you'd think that when it fell into the sea the next month, I would have earned some credit. Now he's buying a vineyard despite all my warnings about spotted lanternflies. Anyway." She gave Donnie a shrug as if an effective villa-buying strategy was a thing everyone had to worry about. "No *Stomp.* This is confirmation, right?"

"Way better. Ringo Starr. 'Harry in the Sky with Diamonds.'"

"Perfect. He'll go nuts. See you both later, gentlemen." With a look back at him as she departed, she said, "It was nice to meet you, *Donnie.*"

"Speaking of which, where is the man of the hour?" Richard called after her.

"Oh, don't worry. I'm sure he'll turn up," she said with a wave of the hand. The oddness of the response had Richard staring after her, his brow furrowed.

Once they were alone together, Richard turned to face him. Donnie was struggling to measure his next words. He'd been practicing for the part of courtly gentleman, but none of the YouTube videos he'd watched the night before had schooled him in how a courtly gentleman would make the disclosure he was about to make.

He heard a low clamor of voices in the distance, saw arriving guests streaming out onto the terrace. The string quartet had begun to play. The party was underway.

"Listen," Donnie finally said, "I know you said you wanted to circulate, but maybe we hang back a bit. Be more behind the scenes, know what I mean?"

"Not really. I thought you wanted to—"

"She recognized me."

"From what?"

"From my xylophone concert. What do you think, *Dickie*?"

"Please don't call me that. Only they call me that, and I loathe it. And trust me, Thalia is not watching your porn."

"Well, not right now. But trust *me*, some of our biggest fans are women. They get super motherly with the models too. They'll write us the longest emails and be like, *Is Colton Hammer eating enough? He looked really droopy in that group scene.* And I'm like, *of course he wasn't eating, he was the bottom.*"

"Donnie, I realize that in the gay world you might get treated like a major celebrity, as you *abundantly* made clear to me at Sapphire Cove, but there are several Oscar winners on the guest list tonight. So let's keep this in perspective, shall we? I need to check on the kitchen. Come along. I'm sure we can avoid being mobbed by all your adoring fans."

Donnie felt his cheeks flame. He wasn't sure if it was Richard's words that had set him off or the bracingly condescending tone with which he'd delivered them. Richard was halfway down the nearby stone steps when Donnie lost his battle against his tongue.

"*You're* apparently a fan now."

Richard froze and turned.

"Heard you watching the other night at the hotel."

Jaw working, nostrils flaring, cheeks flaming in a way that made Donnie want to pinch, kiss, and nibble them, maybe in that order, Richard mounted the few steps he'd just descended. "What you heard was me doing a bit of Internet research on someone who's advising me on a big event. That's all."

"Yeah, well, your research had the same soundtrack for about fifteen minutes, and then it went dead silent all of a sudden. Probably while you went to get a rag. Hey, I'm not judging you, alright? I'd be upset if you didn't watch it. That's what it's there for. I'm just saying, if you want to avoid a little scene, maybe we lay low. And maybe don't be such a snob about who does or doesn't watch my po…my *work*."

"I'm not a snob. I'm a bitch. There's a difference."

"A tiny one, but trust me. Thalia recognized me."

"She did *not* recognize you."

"Look, this isn't some ego trip, okay? I know tonight's your first night back in the saddle and I'm not here to fu—screw it up. So make whatever call you need to. But I didn't expect you to parade a porn star through your fancy party when I asked you to do this. I expected to, you know…be backstage. Watch the levers move. That kind of thing."

"You're not dressed like someone who wants to be backstage."

"I'm dressed for you."

There it was. Finally. The look he'd been searching for from the awkward moment they'd first met. Disarmed and breathless, thanks to four words that had come out of him unrehearsed.

Richard swallowed. "I appreciate that you would… I appreciate you being concerned about whether or not I would be concerned that…"

Speechless. He'd truly rendered him speechless. And he'd done it by being honest. By being *concerned*.

"I don't care if people recognize you tonight. This is LA, not Vatican City. I care that you behave professionally. Professionally for *my* profession, I mean. Which makes sense given we are apparently going to be working together."

"Finally you say it," Donnie said.

"Yes, well. The suit suits you, so…"

The suit also apparently made Richard blush, but pointing that out wouldn't be considered courtly, he figured. The Matthew Crawley thing would have been to offer him a handkerchief to pat down his cheeks with, but Donnie had forgotten to bring one. Because he didn't own any. He wasn't sure how much one would cost, but it didn't matter because he'd pretty much blown his budget on the suit and the pin. Would two Kleenex in one hand count? He had some balled up in his front pocket.

"Onward. The party begins!"

Feeling lighter, and like he'd finally earned some of the points he'd been shooting for with the gift, Donnie followed Richard toward the terrace where guests were gathering. The house's vast interior rooms were roped off and guarded by hulking security men in black suits. As they skirted the knots of champagne-sipping rich people, he recognized multiple familiar faces from shows he'd watched as a kid, some of them remarkably well-preserved by a surgeon's scalpel and strategic injections.

When they stepped around one of the ropes and into the house, he felt a skip in his step. The excitement that came from getting a private tour of a royal palace. The sparkling, marble-filled kitchen had been overtaken by the caterers, but plates and dishes were being brought in hurriedly through a side door. Through it, Donnie caught glimpses of additional food prep happening in tents outside. He'd seen plenty of backstage activity at Sapphire Cove over the years. This hustle and bustle rivaled the busiest of it.

Richard had begun to explain the menu when Gabe appeared, looking breathless. "He's doing it. The thing we told him not to do. Harry's doing it."

Cursing under his breath, Richard looked to the ceiling. Over the clink of plates and silverware, they could hear an approaching rotary chop. "If that man lands a helicopter in my garden."

"Isn't it *his* garden?" Donnie asked.

Richard's blazing eyes met his. "Not tonight it isn't."

"Valet captain got a call to stop the cars coming up the driveway, so I think it's going to happen out front. Come on." They followed Gabe into the house's massive, empty front hallway and then out the soaring double front doors.

Outside, security and the valets had corralled arriving guests to the borders of a massive motor court, one side of which was packed with some of the most expensive-looking cars Donnie had ever seen. From around one side of the house, guests he'd seen on the terrace earlier were gathering to watch the show. He and Gabe followed closely behind Richard as he fought his way down to the first line of spectators, right to the spot where Thalia was staring up at the halo of night sky visible through the tree branches above.

"You knew," Richard said to her.

"Sorry," she said, when she saw Richard next to her. "Like I said, prenup."

A second later, the branches went nuts. Cries of both awe and alarm went up throughout the crowd. A helicopter's searchlight blasted the motor court with light. Donnie didn't know helicopters, but the one that descended out of the sky looked shiny and new. It touched down a few feet from the giant stone fountain at the motor court's center, then the pilot's door opened and out stepped a man in a Zebra-print jacket, black leather pants, and dark sunglasses. Unlike the hair and outfits of the awaiting crowd, his mop of salt and pepper curls looked perfectly in place.

He raised one arm. The guests erupted with cheers and applause. No one else emerged from the helicopter; the guest of honor had flown himself solo to his own birthday celebration.

Richard started for the birthday boy. And because Gabe followed, Donnie figured he should as well.

"Do I know how to make an entrance or do I know how to make an entrance?" the producer bellowed in a gravelly voice.

"I hope you also know how to wash and detail forty-six Bentleys and a dozen or so Maybachs. Otherwise we'll need to add that to the bill."

There was a loud *thunk* as the stone cherub atop the fountain fell to one side and splashed head first into the basin. "Hey, Thalia, we're going to need a new naked kid!"

"Not how we should phrase that, but okay," Thalia said, approaching.

"Dickie!" Harry Mitchell threw out his arms, then pulled Richard into a big embrace when it became clear Richard wasn't about to initiate one. "You're back! My Dickie's back. My prince of the parties. I've missed you. I've *needed* you. I need gays. I love the gays. The best taste, the best sense of humor. All my hit shows had gays in the writer's rooms. Every single one."

"Yes, but rarely on the shows themselves," Richard added.

"Aw, horseshit. There were plenty on camera. Just nobody knew which ones." Harry shrugged. "Different time. Anyway, *you*."

Donnie jumped when he realized Harry Mitchell was pointing at him.

"You the new boyfriend?"

"No, Harry," Richard said, clearing his throat and attempting to step between them. "This is Donnie Bascombe. He's shadowing me this evening so we can—"

"Yeah, yeah, yeah, outta the way. I don't need the cover story," Harry said, brushing Richard to one side. Then suddenly he was gripping one of Donnie's hands. Maybe he was looking into Donnie's eyes, but his dark glasses made it impossible to tell. "Do me a favor.

Scratch that. Do the *world* a favor. Plow this guy into next week."

"*Harry!*" Thalia screeched.

"I take it back. Plow him into next month. Do whatever it takes to get his mind off that shitbag in a suit he calls his ex." Harry turned to Richard, who'd gone white as a sheet. "We all hated that guy, by the way."

Richard cleared his throat. "I didn't realize you even remembered meeting—"

"Oh, of course, I did. Came to my Christmas party with all this attitude. Called Dickie a *little party planner*. Like it was a friggin' hobby. Dickie was the high-value one in that relationship. What did Marco Douche-oh even do? Some shady shit with money I'm probably going to be pitching a documentary about to Netflix next year. Fuck him. And the way he treated you? Fuck him to *death*."

Thalia stepped forward and seized one of her husband's hands. "Okay, Harry. I think everyone got the point. We're quite invested in Dickie's happiness. Now come on. Your guests await. And some of them haven't heard your Donna Mills stories six hundred times. Get ready to shine."

As his wife slid one of his arms through her own, Harry said, "Love is love, right? I mean you meet people where you meet 'em. Everyone thinks I landed this girl at Soho House. She was a nurse in my foot doctor's office. I showed up late one day, gave her attitude. She tells me, sit your ass down and the doctor will see you when he's ready. I don't care how many Emmys you got. Fell for her on the spot."

Thalia kissed him on the cheek. "That's sweet, babe. But you're going to fall down the stairs one night under mysterious circumstances if you don't learn to watch that mouth."

"It'll be worth every step," he said, and then the couple was moving arm in arm into a crowd of awaiting admirers.

Gabe followed.

Richard was staring after them as Donnie approached.

"I love that guy," Donnie said. "He's like me if I was crazy rich. And straight."

Richard's shoulders shook with silent laughter, but he was still staring after them. Was he stricken by their comments about his ex-husband? Or did he envy their marriage? Donnie thought of the distant, wounded look that had come into his eyes at Sapphire Cove when Connor and Logan had practically nibbled on each other at the table.

Behind them, the valets had started letting arrivals back into the motor court. Headlights bathed them suddenly. Donnie put a hand on the small of Richard's back and nudged him forward to safety.

Richard cleared his throat and turned to Donnie. "The dinner starts in about thirty minutes and the entertainment shortly thereafter. Let's go tour the concert stage before the performers are all over the place."

They were heading up the steps to the front house when Donnie said, "Little party planner? Is that really what he used to call you?"

"Among other things."

"Nothing little about any of this."

This time Richard tried to hide his smile, but he didn't do a good job, and when Donnie saw how genuine it was, there was a skip in his step as they headed back inside.

17

I'm dressed for you.

Throughout their backstage tour—during which he made sure there was nothing but docile obedience in the eyes of the bike short clad fire dancers—and another more complete tour of the kitchen, Donnie's four simple words played on a loop in Richard's mind. It was starting to feel like the slightly nervous, slightly needy tone in which he'd said them, such a departure from his husky confidence, would ring in Richard's head for hours if he didn't create a different noise. So he found himself giving microscopically detailed lectures on everything from the management structure for the event's staff to the breakdown procedures scheduled for the party's end.

He was also trying to prevent a silence from falling, he realized. Trying to prevent Donnie from saying something else unexpected that would end up pulsing inside of him like a second heartbeat.

They were standing on a stone walkway, looking out over the banquet area toward the concert stage. Far enough away to chat without disturbing the party. They weren't alone together. Not technically, anyway. But it was starting to feel that way.

"How about cowboy boots?" Donnie said suddenly into one of Richard's rare breaths.

Looking down at his own shoes, Richard said, "These are more my speed, thank you."

"No, for the centerpieces at the wedding." Donnie turned to face him, propping one elbow on the stone banister they were both leaning against. "I was online the other night and a very wise event planner was telling me how centerpieces at weddings are an..." Donnie looked skyward as he attempted to remember the quote.

Richard fought the urge to finish it for him.

"...often squandered opportunity for personalization."

Don't blush, he told himself. But the heat in his cheeks told him he'd failed. "My YouTube channel, I take it. What's the significance of cowboy boots?"

"Oh, I love this story." He straightened, eyes brightening. "So, Connor went *way* overboard on their first date, rich-kid style. When they met, Logan told him he liked line dancing and he was a freak for anything with chocolate and peanut butter in it, so for their first coffee date, Connor rolls up in this big rented Rolls Royce that's supposed to take them out on the town, and in the back seat he's got this designer pair of cowboy boots stuffed with chocolate and peanut butter cups. Problem is he's got no idea Logan's about to throw cold water on everything 'cause he's afraid of messing up his new job at the hotel. Total cringe, as the kids say. But the plot twist? Logan kept the boots and wore them on their first real date. Five years later. Isn't that something?"

He knew he should smile, or gently laugh, but both urges met a stone wall of resistance inside of him. "A lovely story," he said unconvincingly, "and an interesting idea."

No doubt Donnie mistook Richard's reticence as proof he thought the idea was intrusive or simply bad—and that wasn't it. But whatever Donnie thought, he wasn't giving voice to it. Finally, Richard looked his way, found himself suddenly staring into a questioning gaze.

"I guess this isn't easy for you," Donnie said gently. "I mean planning a wedding right after...you know."

Richard was caught between two contradictory feelings, anxiety over having his real emotions exposed, and a deeply satisfying sense of having been seen. "Envy is a hostile form of self-pity."

"Did you make that up?"

"No, my therapist quoted it to me. It's in a book of affirmations for the Al-Anon program called *Courage to Change*, but I'm not sure if that's the original source."

"Maybe that's for the best."

"You don't agree?"

"Sounds kinda harsh, to be frank."

"It is, but in the end it's about not allowing what Mark did to get in the way of what I love doing, which is my work. The vast majority of which are weddings. And there's another way of looking at it that's less...harsh, as you said." He had Donnie's full attention. "I took one marriage out of the world. Now I get the chance to put another one into it."

"Sounds like Marco Douche-oh's the one who killed your marriage."

"Oh, it was my decision, trust me. Mark was perfectly content to keep going." *Enough,* he thought. *He couldn't talk about this.* "What about you? Have you ever been married? Or close to it?"

Something flashed across Donnie's eyes. He looked away just as Richard noticed it. Some history, some glimmer of heartbreak. "Nah, not really."

"Ever been in love?"

Too intently, Donnie watched the concert stage where the actor and actress who'd played the titular parents in *Helicopter Parents* were making a tribute speech to Harry. "Maybe," he said quietly. "I was young. And I never knew his real name, so..."

Was this nameless lost love, the ex-boyfriend Richard reminded him of? He was hungry to ask. Too hungry. The topic would bring them back to dangerous territory.

Donnie straightened suddenly. "Champagne, Mr. Merriweather?"

"Not while I'm on the clock. You neither, mister. We don't want a repeat of the other night."

"I was only offering to serve." Donnie grinned. "It's nice out here. Thanks for not making us hide out in the command center."

"Well, that was your idea."

"Yeah, but you were afraid to be alone with me." Donnie waited for Richard to dispute this; he didn't. "You shouldn't be, by the way."

"That wasn't it. Entirely."

"Oh yeah? What was the rest of it?"

"The look on your face when you suggested it, it reminded me of how I used to feel when we'd be going out to meet some of Mark's friends and he'd ask me not to be so *extra.* I knew what that was code for. Don't be yourself. Don't be too gay. The worst part is, we'd never be on our way to meet straight friends. Mostly he'd say it before we got together with our gay friends who considered themselves to be"— Richard raised his fingers and made a set of air quotes that could have crushed bugs—"*straight acting.* Whatever the hell that means. And since it turned out he was sleeping with a lot of them behind my back, I guess it makes perfect sense that he would—"

"*Richard?*"

Suddenly, the bottom dropped out of Richard's stomach. He had to grip the edge of the stone banister in front of him to stay standing.

"You okay?" Donnie asked quietly.

"We need to relocate," Richard said, but the two men approaching were closing the distance so fast there'd soon be no chance of escape. "Now."

"Mark?" Donnie asked quietly.

"Worse," Richard said, then suddenly he was face-to-face with Evan Johnson and his much taller husband, Joel. He hadn't seen them in over six months, and by design. They wore matching white tuxedoes and matching buzz cuts. It was impossible to tell if the boozy smell coming off them was their cologne or the fact that they'd been overserved.

"I knew this was your doing," Evan said. "Everything is *perfect*. It's spot on. It's so Richard." And then, to Richard's horror, Evan threw his arms around him and pulled him close, allowing him to see the stunned expression on Joel's face, an expression that said he knew how inappropriate his husband was being given their recent history.

Richard choked back his pride and a bunch of other things as he said, "I hope you enjoy the party, Evan. We've got some things to attend to, so I need to—"

"Oh, don't even. Enough of all this drama. You're coming to dinner. Our place in Montecito. Next week. How's Friday? Maybe Saturday, so you don't have to deal with traffic."

The only thing that could have astonished Richard more than this suggestion would have been devil horns sprouting from Evan's forehead. "Not the right time. Quite busy at the moment, I'm afraid. Have a good evening, gentlemen."

When Richard went to move past them, Evan's hand planted itself in the center of his chest. "Richard, please. This can't go on like this. It's like our lives are all at a standstill. I mean, we've told you our side how many times now and you won't—"

"Easy there, Evan." Donnie's voice was deep and authoritative. The couple looked at him as if they hadn't noticed his presence until now. "Doesn't really seem like the place, know what I mean? Richard's got a full plate tonight. Maybe you guys can hash this out another time."

Evan glared daggers at Donnie. "This doesn't involve the *staff*, thank you." To Richard, Evan said, "Look, we need to move on. All of us."

"All of us?" Richard asked before he could stop himself. "You're still married."

"And you could be too if you would let it go. Richard, he was all over town telling people you guys were opening up. He even said you had a guy in London you were seeing."

Richard could feel heat in the sides of his neck. His mouth opened. But it was Donnie's voice he heard next.

"And so you two decided to hop in the sack with him before fact checking that story with his husband? Not your best plan."

Hearing a total stranger describe what they'd done turned Evan and Joel as stiff as rods. Joel swallowed and looked to his feet. Evan, Richard knew, would not be so easily deterred.

"I didn't ask for your advice, sir," Evan said.

"That's okay. I'm a nice guy. When I see someone making a total ass of themselves, I give it for free." Donnie grinned.

Eyes blazing, nostrils-flaring, Evan Johnson was as angry as he'd been when they'd all arrived in Monaco the summer before to discover they'd been downgraded to junior suites. "I'm not sure the tone is your best choice here. We happen to be friends with the hosts, *porn star*."

"Oh yeah? Well, it sounds like you're better friends with Mark. And last time I talked to Harry he called the guy a shitbag in a suit who should literally be put to death for what he did to Richard here. So go ahead. Make a play, Bowtie. We'll see how it turns out. In the meantime, get out of Richard's way and leave him alone. He's got a job to do, and it's not to deal with some jackass friend of his who screwed him over and wants to be let off the hook without doing any work to redeem himself." Donnie winked. "Good to know you're a fan, though."

Donnie's cool and confident voice sounded like something he could fall into, something that would carry him if he let it. But to Evan it must have sounded like something else. A brick wall, perhaps. Nodding dumbly, his former friend backed up, turned, and took his husband by the hand. The two men's arms went taut. Joel was trying to return to their table; Evan had another destination in mind and after another second or two he won their game of tug of war. The two men were heading in the direction of the main house. They were leaving the party. Thanks to Donnie.

"Sorry if that was out of line."

"No, that was…" The tears were right there, a lump in his throat that became a hard ball at the roof of his mouth the second he tried to talk. Sniffing it away only made his eyes water. "Thank you… They are…"

"How about we head to the command center? Catch our breath for a bit? What do you say?"

He didn't have the strength to argue.

Of course it was the one moment out of the night when the trailer wasn't empty. Gabe was there with some member of the stage crew Richard barely recognized. Bent over the master control laptop, both men stood at the sound of Donnie pulling the door closed behind him.

"Hey," Gabe said quickly. "The stage manager's kinda worried about the trigger for the balloon drop after the gospel choir sings "Happy Birthday," so we set up a redundant system here in case the one backstage doesn't…" His words trailed off when he saw the expression on Richard's face, the tears he was trying, and failing, to fight. "Is everything okay?"

When his eyes cut to Donnie, Richard realized he needed to speak up quickly, lest Gabe mistakenly summon security and have Donnie escorted off the property. "Something must be blooming and we got a whiff. Donne's going to give me a Claritin. He's being a prince."

Gabe studied Richard's smile, gauging its sincerity. "Great," the young man said, but it sounded like he hadn't bought the cover story one bit. "Well, I think we're all good here. I'll come back to check on things before the cake reveal."

Richard nodded. Gabe ushered the guy from the stage crew out ahead of him. The only sounds in the trailer were the audio from the stage feed where Ringo Starr was wrapping up his performance to a burst of applause. Then the lights on stage went dark. Energetic drum beats pumped from the stage's speakers. The fire dancer troupe was taking to the stage. Richard glimpsed bike shorts, but it didn't relax him any.

Suddenly, despite all his best efforts that evening, he and Donnie were alone.

"Damn," Donnie finally said, "This place is cool. I feel like we should be meeting with the generals about how to defeat Godzilla."

Richard wanted to laugh, but now that he had some privacy, he felt like he couldn't breathe.

"You want to talk about it?" Donnie asked softly.

"How did you figure it out? With Evan and Joel, I mean?"

"I could tell by how hurt you looked when they walked up."

Richard nodded. "I appreciate you noticing that."

"Yeah, well, it sounds like you've got the right to be hurt."

He could tell he wasn't going to recover quickly from this. If he wanted to leave the trailer, he had to attempt some sort of purge. On the feed from the stage, the fire dancer's blossoms of orange flame twirled and spun and erupted from the center of the group.

"It was like something out of a movie," he finally said. "I got home early from a work trip and there he was in our bed with Chad, this trainer slash terrible artist who was staying in our friend's guest house. Suddenly it made sense why he was so invested in Chad's art career. I mean, the guy's water colors all looked like lab accidents. But there's a lot of that in our world, you know. Pretending some cute young guy is more talented than he is because he has a bubble butt and a six pack. Anyway, I should have seen it as a red flag, but I didn't. And there I was. All I could think to do was pack a bag and go to a hotel. I was in shock. Not two hours later, the emails started to come in."

"From Mark?"

"No, from our friends. At first I thought they were trying to console me, and they were, sort of. And I thought, well, that's fast, and why would Mark want to run off and tell everyone what he'd done. Why would Chad, for that matter? And then I started reading them all the way through and I realized what they really were. They weren't condolence letters. They were cover stories. They were justifications."

"Because they'd all slept with him?"

Richard nodded. "And when they heard Mark had been caught with one, they were afraid he'd confess to all of them. And the ones who didn't sleep with him knew what he was up to and didn't tell me anything. And it's hard not to believe they picked Mark's side because he looks like a superhero and runs a hedge fund. Meanwhile, I'm a little party planner who needs to not be so *extra*." He had Donnie's full attention. That made it easier to continue. "I didn't just run to Europe because I lost my husband. I ran to Europe because I lost all my friends except for Jonas. And I know it's childish, but the whole thing made me feel like I was in high school again. I mean, for Christ's sake, he was slipping out of bed with me on vacation and going into the bedrooms of our friends and we were all having breakfast together the next morning and I had no clue. Like all around me there'd been this secret world of sex parties and hookups and I wasn't hot enough to be invited. He'd never said one word to me about opening up. Not one. But when I found out about it everyone told me to get over it. Because they didn't want the party to stop. And they could have given two shits about my marriage. Or what I needed my marriage to be. I'm sorry if I've been a bitch to you, but…"

"But what?" Donnie asked.

Richard sucked in a deep breath through his nose. "I look at someone like you and I see them."

Only once the words were out of his mouth, he could feel what a shitty thing it was to say. Meaner, perhaps, than the comments he'd pelted the guy with since their bathroom exchange went south, maybe because he'd said it with sincerity. Because he'd meant it sincerely. But the fact was, he'd called the guy a cheater and a homewrecker without much evidence that he was either. True, there'd been his snarky comment in the bathroom about not wasting time if someone was waiting outside, but Richard hadn't worn a ring on his finger and he hadn't been traipsing through the lobby moments earlier with a boyfriend on his arm, and Donnie Bascombe said a lot of things about sex that sounded like performance and role play.

To his relief, Donnie didn't seem all that offended. Maybe it took more than snap judgments to wound a guy who'd run away from home at sixteen. Turning down a late-night walk with him at Sapphire Cove had hurt him far worse. That much was clear.

"Your ex and his friends, they're all about lying about sex. My life's the opposite. When it comes to sex, I tell no lies."

Richard nodded.

"Also, those queens clearly did vampire facials or something. I'd rather grow out my beard to cover up my laugh lines, know what I mean?"

Richard laughed. "I'm sorry if I've said some hurtful things since I met you. But the truth is, this whole thing's made me feel so invisible. I've had some days where I think no one hears a word I say."

"Well that's crazy," Donnie said.

Richard was surprised by the guy's easy smile.

"Because I don't live in a world where a man as amazing as you could be invisible."

Suddenly Richard's vision wobbled, and he bowed his head to hide his tears. He heard Donnie closing the distance, felt powerful arms curving around his back, felt his cheek come to rest against Donnie's chest. He'd assumed his first touch of Donnie Bascombe, if it ever came, would bring with it dozens of images from his porn performances, pulsing through his memory one after the other. But that wasn't the case. This Donnie was real and here. And still. Not some bouncing image on a screen. The solidness of him, his smoky cologne, enveloped Richard, making him feel rooted in place, more inside of his skin than he'd been for months. He'd watched him plow, lick, and rim his scene partners. But he hadn't seen him hold them, and that's what he was doing to Richard now.

"You're too mean to yourself, Merriweather," he said after a while. One of his hands kneaded the back of Richard's neck, and Richard's sob turned into a gentle sigh. "Too damn mean to yourself."

Don't look up, he told himself. If he did, this tenderness and support would spin dangerously out of control. He didn't listen. The tension in Donnie's expression, the struggle of a man trying to retain control over himself despite the fact that their bodies were pressed together, the distance between their lips reduced to inches—the sight of these things melted something inside of Richard Merriweather he assumed had iced over forever when he found his husband in bed with another man.

As he blinked back tears, he realized what he was doing and felt a stinging burst of shame. He thought if he stayed locked in Donnie's gaze, Donnie would crumble first and lean in. Then everything that came after could be his fault.

But Donnie stayed strong, a faint smile coming to his face.

So Richard cupped Donnie's face in his hands and brought their mouths together.

18

For fifteen years Donnie had waited for the return of this feeling at the moment his lips met another man's, the *tug, tug, tug* in the center of his chest he'd felt whenever he'd kissed Zach.

Here it was, the instant Richard's hands had caressed his face and pulled him in.

The instant the man's arms encircled his back and he tilted his head to one side.

The instant his mouth met Richard's.

Everything else about the man since they'd first met had been resistance, but this kiss, this yielding, open-mouthed kiss, was pure hunger. Pure need.

When was the last time he'd kissed a man who'd bared his soul? Maybe never. There'd been plenty of lip locks—professional and non—throughout his life, but they weren't always a given when the clothes came off. For years he'd lived by the swipe and click based rhythm of app-driven sex. Mostly it brought boys to the yard who wanted to dive right into the deep end without checking the temperature of the water first.

This was altogether different. Richard Merriweather had offered up his pain and his inviting lips in almost the same instant, making Donnie feel desired and needed in ways he never had before. He had a crazy, paranoid thought that Logan or Connor would walk in right then and start wailing on him for kissing their wedding planner. But it wasn't strong enough to make him gently push the event planner away. Maybe because Richard's lips were soft and tasted like spearmint, but his kisses were hard and determined. And the man's hair. It was so close. Right there. He could touch it if he wanted to. He'd just have to move one hand up off his neck and into…

Don't do it, Bascombe. You touch his hair and you're done for. Touch his hair and this turns into a helluva lot more than a kiss.

Donnie touched his hair. Ran one hand through it gently enough to let its thick locks fill the gaps between his fingers, not so rough that he'd pull the roots. The last thing he wanted to do was cause Richard Merriweather pain. He was in so much of it already. He needed warmth. He needed pleasure. He needed his every fantasy fulfilled. He needed all the things Donnie had learned to give an audience and countless cheap tricks. And he needed them now apparently because his embrace was vise-grip tight, so tight it was pulling Donnie forward off his feet. But Donnie didn't care. Nothing seemed more important than keeping his lips sealed to Richard's, and if it meant they both went over sideways and—

He ignored the sound at first. A weird double beep. Like a phone alert. Only it wasn't coming from his phone. Richard ignored it too.

Then came a *pop, pop, pop* that sounded like gunfire.

Next came the sound of screaming and breaking glass, so loud it distorted the concert stage's audio feed.

In a flash Richard pulled away. Donnie—stunned and blinking— was still trying to get his bearings back, taking in the sight of Richard frantically tapping keys on the laptop Gabe had been working on moments earlier. The laptop they'd apparently knocked into during their fierce kiss. He'd only felt the edge of the table against his hip, but apparently they'd hit the keys somehow. He prayed it hadn't been him.

"Bring the lights up to full!" Donnie realized Richard was shouting into his almost invisible earpiece, hand inside his jacket, pressing something hidden at his waist. "It's the balloon drop! Bring the lights up to full so they can see it's just balloons."

With growing horror, Donnie realized what had happened. They'd triggered the drop on a darkened stage full of fire. Tumbling balloons popped by swirling flames had sounded like gunshots to the guests.

On screen, the concert stage was blasted with light. And that's when they saw all of the banquet tables were empty. A few of them had been overturned. Outside the trailer he heard screams and gravel being punched by dozens of footsteps. The guests were fleeing the garden in all directions.

Like fish swimming against the tide, he and Richard raced toward the garden. When they entered it, the scene before them was chaos. A whooshing sound brought his attention to the stage. A crew member was using a fire extinguisher on a curtain that had clearly been touched by the flames of one of the fleeing fire dancers. Across the garden on the terrace, he saw Harry holding Thalia in his arms as they both surveyed the ruins of their garden in horror. The whole thing reminded him of that movie *The Poseidon Adventure* only right side up.

The other major difference was that he might have caused this disaster.

"I need you to go," Richard finally said.

"Let me help. I can—"

"*Please.*" Richard spun. There were tears in his eyes. "Please go, Donnie."

But Donnie wasn't seeing Richard. He was seeing something else that was wrong about the garden. Given the widespread destruction, it had been easy to miss. The robed goddess statue was facing the wrong direction. Her back was to the spot where Richard stood and she was staring down one of the walkways and not at the intersection.

Fleeing guests had probably clawed their way up the stone railing and knocked the thing off its base. Which was why it wasn't level. Which was why it was tilting.

"Donnie, please, just let me—"

Donnie reached out, yanked Richard forward and off his feet. He lost his balance in the process, slamming back first to the stone, the breath huffing out of him in a painful woosh as Richard's face became a mask of rage above his.

"What the *hell* are you—"

Then came the thunderous crash of the goddess hitting the walkway behind him. Richard went silent. Gasping for breath, he sat up, turning. Donnie let him, then struggled to sit up himself, wondering how sore the impact with stone would leave him in the morning.

As they sat together on the walkway, legs spread and looking like they'd both been dropped from a great height, which wasn't far off, Richard gazed at the ruined statue, which had landed across the spot where he'd been standing. The anger wiped from his expression, he turned to Donnie.

"Dickie?" They turned. Thalia was walking up the steps toward them, her face a mask of polite shock. When she saw she had their attention, she stopped. "If you're both alive, perhaps we should discuss."

There was another belch from the fire extinguisher. Sirens wailed in the distance.

19

The mansion's great room had drapes so high it looked like they had to be cleaned with a cherry picker. The furniture below was all cream and gold with intricate wood detailing. At first, Donnie assumed the old-timey-looking paintings on the wall were Harry's rich, long dead ancestors. But after a couple minutes of standing next to Richard before Thalia's piercing glare, he realized the paintings were all of her in various historical costumes. The one of her in cowgirl garb was the weirdest, maybe because her expression in it was as serious and scary as the one the real Thalia was wearing now.

Her high-backed chair looked kind of like a throne, which was fitting, Donnie thought. But on one end of the adjacent sofa, her king looked distinctly uninterested in the proceedings. Harry was scrolling on his phone, dark glasses pushed up onto his curls.

In the motor court outside, the idling fire engine gave off a steady whooshing sound, its bridge lights flickering through the front windows. The tiny fire on the concert stage was long out, but the firefighters were inspecting the entire garden just to be safe. Every now and then a burst from one of their radios made the staff members and security guards who filled the great room's six doorways—Donnie had counted—jump. To his astonishment, a surprising number of guests had abandoned their cars in the motor court and fled on foot. But a group of cheerful holdouts had gathered on the garden terrace where everyone had first met for cocktails, and their occasional ripples of laughter made for a jarring counterpoint to the serious faces in the great room.

One by one, various members of the household staff had come in to deliver verdicts. No injuries. The damage to the garden looked physical. Better yet, the news vans massed at the subdivision's front gate were all local—for now.

"Well!" Thalia finally said. "A fatality report is not how I usually like to end a party."

Richard took a step forward. "It's my fault. We had some issues with the balloon drop trigger backstage. One of my staff set up a redundancy on the master computer, and I should have been more careful of it when we were in the command center."

"So you were *both* in the command center?" Thalia asked.

Donnie stepped forward. "It's actually my fault, Mrs....Thalia, ma'am."

"So I'm supposed to pick which one of you to kill at random?"

"Sure," Donnie said. "But you should pick me 'cause Richard was only doing his job."

"And what were you doing?" the woman asked.

"Getting in the way. Look, I asked if I could shadow him tonight. He had reservations. Told me what an important and amazing client you were. But I pressured him, and that's on me. So this is my fault. How about I pay for the statue?"

"It was rehabbed from a three-hundred-year-old villa in Naples. Do you happen to have two hundred-k lying around?"

Donnie grinned and tried not to swallow his tongue. "I can check the sofa cushions."

Thalia didn't smile.

A long silence followed.

"When Harry said plow him into next week, I don't think he wanted you to do it *at* the party," she finally said.

Harry finally looked up. "Alright, babe. Let's not go crazy. Nobody got hurt. We're insured. Dickie's insured. Let's enjoy being filthy rich here. No reason we should deal with this like normal people."

"Makes sense. Wasn't exactly a normal person's birthday party," Donnie grumbled before he could stop himself. The hard sting on his shoulder came so fast it took him a second to realize it was the back of Richard's hand.

"Trust me," Richard said. "I will do absolutely everything in my power to make this right."

"It's fine," Harry said with a wave of the hand, then, when he saw his wife's stunned glare, he turned his phone around and held it up where she could see. "Check this out."

Thalia leaned toward the phone, read what was on the screen, and then sank back into her chair, eyes wider than before. "*TMZ* says there was a shooting at our house. How is this *fine*, Harry?"

"You have any idea how many fake fights I've had with valets to try to get me on this damn website? I haven't had a hit in eight years, babe. They've put me in the In Memoriam segment at the Emmys twice. And newsflash, I wasn't dead either time." He started scrolling through his phone. "I mean, look. We're on CNN, *Hollywood Reporter*. My picture's in *Variety*. My picture hasn't been in *Variety* since I had that mole removed." He turned to Donnie and Richard with a thousand-watt grin. "I'm *back*, baby!"

"It was too soon." Richard's voice was so clear and distinct it brought the room to a halt, silencing whatever Thalia had been about to say to her husband. "I apologize. I should have given someone else oversight of tonight's event. The truth is, I had a challenging interaction with a guest at the party. It raised the subject of my divorce in a painful way. And I allowed this interaction to make me emotional when I should have been paying more attention to the event."

Which meant Richard had only kissed Donnie because he was so upset over his run-in with his shitty ex-friends. Donnie winced and looked to his shoes.

"Which guest?" There was protectiveness in Thalia's voice.

"I'd rather not say," Richard answered, head bowed.

"Some douchebag named Evan," Donnie said.

Thalia's eyebrows went up. "Evan Gregory from Artist Empire?"

Richard's answer was in his silence.

"Jesus. Did he sleep with Mark?"

Instead of nodding vociferously like he wanted to, Donnie raised one eyebrow and made a show of looking out the window. Thalia and Harry exchanged a meaningful look that said Evan's dalliance would have consequences. Professional ones. *Good*, Donnie thought.

"In tribute to what loyal and wonderful clients you have always been, I owe you the most honest explanation possible. But it should also go without saying that I'm willing to do just about anything to make this right."

"Are *you*?"

It took Donnie a second to realize Thalia was talking to him. There was a pleading look in Richard's eyes. Donnie nodded as enthusiastically as he could.

Thalia sighed, then turned in her chair, eyes traveling over all the staff standing guard in the surrounding doorways. "Could you all give us the room please?"

When Gabe's eyes met Richard's, Richard gave him a small nod granting him permission to leave. The other staff members dispersed, trying not to let their suspicions show. But as soon as some of them were a few paces away, they started speculating in harsh whispers about Thalia's sudden need for privacy. Donnie leaned over and whispered into Richard's ear. "You ready to drop trou and put on a little show? 'Cause this is starting to have a weird group vibe, if you know what I mean."

"I'm ready for you to be quiet unless she asks you a direct question."

When the departing footsteps finally faded, Thalia's eyes met Donnie's. "Some women have book clubs," she said quietly. "I've got a...movie club. We're called the Smutty Sisters. The sisters and I would like a tour of the studio."

"The studio?" Donnie asked.

"The *Parker Hunter* studio."

Donnie cackled before he could stop himself. He also spun and whacked Richard lightly on the shoulder the way he'd done earlier. "See! I told you she recognized me."

"You couldn't have waited five minutes to gloat about this?" Richard asked through clenched teeth.

Donnie turned to face Thalia again. "Absolutely, ma'am. We love our female fans. A lot of women say gay porn is the best strike against the patriarchy because men get screwed."

Thalia shook her head. "Yeah, I don't know about all that political stuff. I just like all the spitting and the extra dick. And I don't just want a tour. I want a reception for me and my fellow sisters. And I want to meet the models. Especially Stone Spencer."

Donnie winced. "That last one might be tough. Stone dropped out of porn a few years ago to go splatter paint abandoned cars in the desert. He's also thinks birds are drones now so... I'm just saying there's a lot of meth happening there."

"Harrison Peters? The guy who's always plowing his assistants because they can't type?"

Wow, she was a fan.

Donnie smiled. "Just signed him as an exclusive."

"Great. I want to meet all the exclusives. And I want desserts, a champagne fountain, flowers, the works. Dickie, you'll put it all together, of course. How's two weeks from now?"

Richard swallowed. "Perfect."

"Can I come?" Harry asked.

"No. Girls only."

Harry made a wounded child's face. "Yeah, but it was my party that got ruined."

"Your press event, you mean?" she fired back.

"Oh, one thing," Donnie said. "I don't know what kind of marriages you and the sisters have, but no sex with the models. I mean, not at the studio. 'Cause we'd have to get you set up as performers, and then there's testing protocols and releases and it's a whole thing, is what I'm saying."

Cheerfully, Richard asked, "Would anyone mind if I ran screaming through a plate glass window real quick?"

"That's it," Harry said. "I'm coming."

Thalia flashed a *stop right there* palm at her husband. "You're not coming. There will be no sex. It's just a reception, a meet and greet. No different than a bunch of guys going to a strip club." Her eyes cut to Harry as soon as his mouth opened. "I'm sorry, how many friggin' parties did you attend at the Playboy Mansion again?"

"I brought you with me every time," Harry whined.

"Against my will."

Harry sighed and rose to his feet. "Glad we got this figured out." He crossed to Richard and extended his hand.

Head bowed, Richard accepted the handshake.

"Relax, kid. Even the star player strikes out now and then."

If his words were meant to console, it looked like they did the opposite. Richard's shoulders sagged, and his eyes fluttered closed.

A minute or two later, there were drunken, boisterous shouts on the garden terrace as Harry was greeted by his few remaining guests.

20

"Well, dammit," Richard whispered once they reached the staff entrance. Donnie thought it was a general comment on the night in general, then he saw a black Mercedes trapped in one corner of the driveway by other parked cars and figured it was Richard's.

"Let me see if I can find those people," Gabe said. "Folks mostly took off running and grabbed Ubers at the bottom of the hill."

The Mercedes looked like a chauffeur car from Sapphire Cove, but without the logo on the side. Weird. Why did Richard need a hotel car? Surely he had his own wheels somewhere in California.

For the past few hours, Donnie had stayed close while Richard supervised tear down, figuring the best he could do was wait until he was brusquely dismissed. But he hadn't been asked to leave, and Gabe's constant presence had helped ease the tension. Now it was almost two in the morning and they were all bone tired to the point of being dazed.

Richard sighed. "Don't worry about it. I'll get a room somewhere."

Donnie looked to his right. His blue Dodge Durango wasn't trapped, probably because he'd arrived later than most of the other staff. "I'll take you back. It's on my way."

Richard's expression looked weary and blank, but apparently Gabe saw agreement in it because he gave his boss a half hug and Donnie a brief handshake and then he was gone. Suddenly the two of them were alone together for the first time since they'd hit the chaos button inside the command center.

"I don't think we should pick up where we left off," Richard finally said.

"It's just a ride, that's all." Donnie started for his SUV, hoping he'd cleaned off the passenger seat. He had, but the interior still smelled faintly of the drive-through cheeseburger he'd eaten on the way there, so he lowered the windows. And quickly stuffed the bottle of Listerine he'd gargled with earlier further down into the pocket on the driver's side door.

A minute later they were winding their way down Bel Air's woodsy, mansion-lined streets. They sailed past the guard house. The news vans they'd been told about earlier were all gone, thank God. Then they were heading west, Sunset Boulevard rising and falling like ocean waves.

"You sure you're alright to drive?" Richard finally asked. "You want to stop and get a coffee or something?'

"I'm good. Why don't you put the seat back and take a nap?"

Richard nodded as if he thought it might be a good idea. But he didn't do it. He was still piano wire tense. A moment later they entered the 405 freeway, blessedly free of traffic at this late hour.

"Any reason you wouldn't let me take the blame back there?" Donnie asked.

"Well, for one it wasn't yours to take. I'm the one who hit the computer when I put my hand out to brace myself." Richard winced at the memory, rubbing the bridge of his nose between his thumb and forefinger. "Besides, it wouldn't have mattered. It's my event. I was responsible for you." Richard sucked in a deep breath and looked out the window. "Listen, your studio, this reception. I'm going to need everyone on their best behavior. Thalia's friends are rich and entitled, and their husbands are worse."

"My models do public appearances all the time. They know the drill."

"Yes, well, they need to do this one sober."

"I'll tell them the champagne fountains are for guests only."

"Other substances need to be off the table too."

"Other substances?"

"I've seen their work. They look…altered."

Donnie felt his blood boil and did his best to take a deep breath. It ended up sounding like a dog's growl.

"What?" Richard asked.

"How about you take that nap I recommended, Merriweather?"

After a tense silence, Richard said, "Obviously I've touched a nerve."

"Let me be real clear about something. Every model who shoots with me has to attest on paper and on camera that they were sober and they weren't coerced. I've got an entire file room at my studio to prove it. It's a government regulation that applies to my perfectly legal, legitimate industry. And I support it. So maybe you're implying my boys are hard partiers. But it sounds like you're saying I drug up my models before I put them on camera to have sex. And I'd never do that in a million years.

"For one, it's illegal. It's also unethical, and in my case a straight up lie. If my boys look high to you in their scenes, it's 'cause you're not watching sex. You're watching them *perform* sex. It's different. You're watching guys spend three hours under hot lights, trying to keep their enthusiasm up as they twist themselves into pretzels so they can hit the right angle to get you off at home. Porn is not a sex party where you hit the record button on a camera and yell go. It's hard work and one scene can take all day, and I can't do it with guys who are high. Also, newsflash. Drugs kill boners, which are kind of the lifeblood of my industry. That's why the only pills you'll find on my sets are Viagra and Cialis."

As he stared dead ahead, he felt Richard's eyes burning a hole in the side of his face. He risked a glance to his right, saw his passenger was wearing a half smile. Prepared himself for a bitchy remark.

"I apologize for making assumptions about your business," he said instead.

Maybe his slight smile had meant he was impressed with the pride Donnie took in his job. "And me," he added.

"And you," Richard said with a nod.

Which surprised Donnie so much he quickly said, "Apology accepted."

"But we're going to need to have your studio cleaned."

"My studio's not *dirty*."

"That may well be the case. But if one of the Smutty Sisters goes home with a sniffle or a rash and decides to blame it on you, however wrongly, I need to be able to say we brought in a cleaning crew beforehand."

"Fine. We'll figure it out."

Richard nodded.

Donnie managed a deep breath, but it was hard. He hated when people threw him in league with human traffickers and mafiosos and drug runners just because he made perfectly legal porn—especially when the accuser in question also consumed the product he was selling. "We'll have a meeting this week. You, me, the models. You can come in and get a sense of the space and we can run through everything beforehand."

"Sounds good."

Another silence fell.

"Look, I'm sorry about the drug comment," Richard finally said.

"And I'm sorry if I went too far," Donnie finally said. "Comforting you, I mean. In the trailer."

"Yeah, well," Richard said, "I'm sorry I kissed you."

The tone had been all gentle and conciliatory, but the words landed on Donnie like a slap. He stared dead ahead, trying to hide how much they stung. Trying to hide how very *not* sorry he was that Richard had kissed him. It felt like the heat their kiss had brought to his face still hadn't left.

This was insane. He'd lived sex for most of his life, gone to bed—and bathrooms and back seats and the rocky parts of nude beaches—with more guys than he could ever count, and here he was, a grown man undone by a single kiss.

"It was a pretty good kiss, though, right?" Donnie asked before he could stop himself.

"I didn't say it wasn't." Richard's response was so quiet the words had almost been lost to the woosh of speeding tires.

"Well, I'm sorry I touched your hair," Donnie said.

Richard nodded.

"I'm sorry I let you pull me in real close so I could feel your heart beating in your chest. I'm sorry your lips tasted like spearmint and heaven—"

"Donnie."

He was staring out the window so Donnie couldn't see his face, but it sounded like there was a hint of laughter in his voice. And what he was trying to hide was a smile. Maybe teasing a guy about how hard he was fighting his desire for you qualified as courting. So long as he left it there.

The silence between them grew so long Donnie thought his weary passenger might have fallen asleep with his forehead resting against the window.

"I need this to work," Richard finally said.

For a startled second, Donnie thought he might be talking about their relationship prospects.

"The reception. At your studio. I need it to work."

"It will," he said. "And it sounds like you've halfway smoothed things over with them anyway."

"I haven't," Richard said, turning his face to him. "Harry's right. His career's been on ice for years, but they have a ton of money and Thalia's used it to become a charity goddess in Hollywood. If she poisons the well for me, I could lose a huge amount of business. Hell, I could lose the town. And it's a big fucking town."

"Don't worry. We'll show her the time of her life. You know...legally."

Richard nodded and looked back out the window. But he didn't seem convinced.

"They like you, Richard. Doesn't that count for something?"

"Clients only like you when you can deliver."

"Maybe, but the look on their faces when I told them that douchebag Evan slept with Mark. That was not a client look. That was, like, a mom and dad look. You know, a good mom and dad. The kind that give a shit. I'm just saying, maybe there's more people around that care about you than you realize."

He seemed too tired to disagree. "Thank you. But I'm in uncharted waters here. I've never fucked up this big before."

"You've also never gotten divorced before. Or walked in on your husband with another guy before. Or been forced to plan a wedding with a loudmouth porn star before."

Richard's shoulders shook with silent laughter, and even though he'd bowed his head, when Donnie glanced to the right he saw the man was smiling.

"A couple bumps on re-entry sounds normal, don't you think? Kiss or no kiss, I stand by what I said back in that trailer. You're too mean to yourself, Merriweather."

There was a long silence. He was learning to like long silences when it came to Richard Merriweather. The guy was usually so quick with a response it meant he was seriously considering whatever Donnie had said.

For a while there was just the woosh of tires and an endless parade of sodium vapor lights flashing past the sides of the freeway and Donnie's quiet amazement over how much ground you could cover in SoCal when you weren't dealing with the usual rivers of traffic.

Finally, Richard broke the silence as if they'd never stopped speaking at all. "My brother, Paul. Sweet guy, but a complete mess. You wouldn't know it, though. He's got this perfect life in Greenwich. Perfect wife, perfect kids. On the Christmas card, at least. And he's got it because my parents bankrolled all of it. Because everything he tried, everything he touched, turned to crap. I mean, I hate talking about him like this because he's always been kind to me, but he's never willing to do the work. It's all get-rich-quick schemes and dodgy investment stuff. He always wants to fast forward to the results. And my father, when he was still alive, used to make that happen because he didn't want to see him screw up again. Now my mother does it in his place. But it's been like this my whole life. I'd be ten years old and recreating the place settings for a state banquet at Buckingham Palace on the living room table. I'd go to show my mother and all she'd say was, 'That's nice, darling, but I have to go talk to Paul about his grades.'

"And I knew why they were doing it even then. Because Paul was the straight one. Paul was going to have a *normal* family and he was going to have kids the *normal* way. I could dance on the ceiling and impress all their friends by the time I was thirteen. But he was still going to get all the investment and attention. Which is a really long way of saying Mark is not the first person who's made me feel invisible. And my work was my way out of that." As if snapping himself out of memory, Richard looked to Donnie. "And yes, I realize I'm complaining about my childhood in Oyster Bay to a man who was kicked out of the house at sixteen for being himself, so I apologize."

The final thought had been the last one on Donnie's mind. He'd been too enamored by the sight of Richard letting his guard down for the second time that evening. It was like he was finally taking advantage of that late-night stroll Donnie had offered him two days after turning it down.

"Your story's your story," Donnie said. "Mine's mine. Thing about mine is, when the people who're supposed to care for you throw you out, it really takes the idea of being perfect off the table. You never have to worry about it again."

"That's what you think? That I'm trying to be perfect to get my mother's attention?" There was soft curiosity in his tone, as if Donnie's opinion truly mattered to him.

"A lot of gays have best little boy in the world syndrome. I got spared, I guess. I got to be my own boy. My own dirty boy."

Then he remembered following Zach Loudon around like a puppy in those early years and wondered if being his own dirty boy just meant switching to a different form of approval seeking.

"So you don't regret it?" Richard asked.

"The porn? Hell, no. Loved every minute of it."

"Why did you quit performing?"

"'Cause I like mashed potatoes." Donnie flashed the same grin he always gave with this stock response.

Richard smiled back, but it looked like he was searching Donnie's face for more of an answer.

"I was burning out. It wasn't fun anymore. I used to always get a thrill whenever I stripped down on a set. Like I was about to do something exciting and rebellious. And I was way more of an exhibitionist when I was younger. It was like I was shining all this daylight on parts of my life assholes had tried to beat out of me. Then after a few years, the thrill left and the whole thing felt like a drudge. Then I inherited the studio and I had the chance to turn it into the kind of place I'd wanted it to be when I was new to the biz."

"That can't be all of it. I mean, to do what you do, you've got to love *porn*."

Donnie gave Richard as long a look as he could without swerving out of his lane. "What I love is giving people something they've been told they're not supposed to have."

He hadn't meant it as a comment on the dynamic between them, but that's suddenly how it felt. Richard's unblinking stare and slow, careful swallow suggested that's how he'd interpreted it too.

"I've never met anyone like you, Donnie Bascombe."

There was no anger in the way he'd said it, no hint of sarcasm or even weariness. And Donnie couldn't help but hear it as a retraction of what he'd confessed in the command center earlier that night, that every time he looked at Donnie he saw his lying ex and the entitled men he'd cheated with. And Donnie wasn't sure what to say in response. So he smiled, pride blossoming in his chest.

Richard gave him a smile then looked back toward the road.

The next time Donnie looked over, he saw the man had nodded off. This seemed like a compliment too. Maybe he'd put Richard

Merriweather so at ease after a shitty night that the tension had finally left him, and he was breathing deeply and evenly as they sped through the early morning hours.

He wasn't used to seeing the motor court at Sapphire Cove this abandoned. No sign of doormen or a valet, just the gentle classical music coming from hidden speakers that was almost impossible to hear during the clamor of a regular day. Save for the few luxury sports cars parked up front for display and the canopy of morning glory vines threaded through the pergola overhead, blossoms rustlings in the ocean breezes, his idling Durango was alone.

Richard stirred, blinking like a little boy.

"You have arrived at your destination," Donnie said in his best imitation of a GPS voice. It wasn't very good, but his passenger smiled anyway.

"It's late. You're not going to get a room like last time?"

"Nah, I gotta do that through Logan, and I don't want to wake him up."

Richard nodded, looked to the lobby doors and the empty expanse of brightly lit marble floor beyond. "My suite's got a sofa in the sitting room," he said, mouth so close to the passenger side window his breath fogged the glass.

Donnie nodded.

Slowly, Richard turned his attention to him again.

"Not sure that's such a good idea," Donnie heard himself say.

"I'm capable of keeping my hands off you. Promise."

That put the ball back in Donnie's court, for sure. He imagined the look on Logan's face if he found out he'd slept with their wedding planner before the wedding. Then he imagined Connor's, which would make Logan's scowl seem tame and probably be accompanied by a thrown pillow. He thought of Ethan tsking and shaking his head in that superior way of his when he found out Donnie had managed to court Richard for a whole four hours before ending up in bed with him like a Grindr trick. Imagined another phone call with Jonas that would make him want to drop ice down the front of the guy's pants. Then he thought of all the other things he used to suppress a boner, mostly visuals of various foods that made it impossible to perform an hour or two after eating them. Doughy bread, in particular. A giant, sizzling T-bone steak.

And suddenly not sleeping with Richard Merriweather on a night when the guy was exhausted and drained and hurting seemed as important as being able to help plan his best friend's wedding, a way of stepping outside the box he'd lived in for years and seeing what might be waiting for him beyond its borders. He couldn't remember the last time he'd shut down even a potential offer from a man he was this attracted to—with the exception of his exclusive models, who were always off limits, no matter how flirty some of them got. But he also couldn't remember spending this much time in someone's presence before sex became a real possibility. For years now, the dates in his life had mostly been after the fact, casual post-sex meals with Internet hookups who turned out to have halfway decent personalities and senses of humor. And even those were few and far between.

"What do you want me to do?" Donnie heard himself ask.

Richard's eyes met his.

The valet on duty finally emerged from the lobby. Donnie held up one hand, telling the man to wait.

"I've caused enough disasters for one night. I don't want to think of you hurt or dying on the side of the road because you had to drive me home. Come upstairs. We'll be grown-ups about this."

Donnie nodded, heart racing, then gestured to the valet.

He turned down Richard's offer of private bathroom time. He wasn't rank, but he never made a serious move on someone unless he was feeling minty fresh. Down one of his daily showers, he was even more likely to keep his hands to himself.

As Richard disappeared into the bedroom, Donnie kicked off his shoes, slung his suit jacket over the back of one of the dining room chairs, then started closing the suite's heavy, plum-colored blackout drapes. A short while later, his host, still fully dressed, brought him a blanket and bed pillow under a primly folded pair of pajama pants and plain white tee, all stacked in a neat pile on his outstretched arms. Then, eyes averted, he bid him goodnight, and closed the door to the suite's bedroom firmly. For a while, Donnie sat on the sofa, heart hammering, trying not to remember their kiss.

And failing.

So he got busy. Turned off most of the lights, changed into the pajamas in the deeper darkness of the kitchenette, settled down onto the plush sofa. He was lying on his back, staring at the dark ceiling before he realized what he was really doing—waiting for the tempting sounds of shower spray hitting tile. They didn't come. Maybe Richard was too tired to bother. A good thing. For Donnie. Now he'd be less inclined to imagine the guy naked, a few feet away. Then he realized he was in the very room where the beautiful son of a bitch had pleasured himself to the sight of Donnie's past work a few nights earlier. A jolt went through him. He rolled over onto his stomach, pressing his growing, throbbing cock into the cushions like some oversexed teen.

Grown-ups, he reminded himself, *we are being* grown-ups.

But he was pretty sure the door next to the entry was for a guest bath. Relieving himself inside of it felt like going right up to the line and dancing a two-step on it. Donnie believed in the power of fantasy. Hell, he'd made his career of it, so in the end, it was fantasy that got him to sleep. A fantasy of Richard reaching out through the shadows, gently caressing the back of his neck, tugging him to his feet and through the shadows and into his bed. And most importantly, and maybe most shockingly, not blowing him or stroking him or talking dirty to him. Holding him. Holding him the way he had in that trailer, as if Donnie were both his foundation and his source. A fantasy that rid him of the burning urge to jerk himself off by spreading his desire throughout his skin, his limbs, his bones.

When he woke, a fierce sliver of late morning sunlight pierced drapes he apparently hadn't managed to pull all the way shut the night before. His phone was on the glass coffee table next to him. It was 11 a.m. His pride surged. He'd done it. Made it through the night without throwing himself at the man in the other room.

And vice versa, which was kind of disappointing, but they were being grown-ups, goddammit.

A shower felt like a safer endeavor now that the sun was out and chipper voices were traveling up and down the hallway outside and housekeeping was vacuuming some of the nearby rooms. When he pressed the bedroom door open a few inches, he expected to find Richard awake, maybe tapping through emails on his phone or having whispered phone calls. He was out cold instead, jaw agape, hair coming loose of the manbun he'd apparently tied it into before hitting the sack. Donnie tiptoed into the bathroom. Once showered, he wrapped himself in not one, but two towels. One draped over his shoulders, the other tied tightly around his waist. As soon as he was relatively dry, he poked his head out, expecting to find Richard awake and blinking at the bedroom. But he was snoring lightly. Probably a combo of jet leg and emotional fatigue.

In the living room, he put his suit pants back on, found some hotel branded slippers and donned the T-shirt Richard had given him to sleep in the night before, which he hadn't used. He was almost out the door when a thought occurred to him. He ducked back inside, dashed off a quick note telling Richard he'd stepped out for a few and would be back shortly. Because it seemed like the right thing to do.

The grown-up thing.

21

Richard woke from a deep and dreamless sleep, immediately astonished that he'd managed any at all. As he'd tried to drift off the night before—*morning* before, he corrected himself—he'd kept hearing the sounds of popping balloons mingled with screams and shattering glass. And then he'd imagined Donnie's embrace in the trailer and everything in his head had gone quiet enough for exhaustion to finally claim him.

Was it possible the nearness of Donnie had helped too? Knowing he was close by, that for the first time in almost half a year he wasn't sleeping alone. Technically.

He grabbed for his cell phone on the nightstand, saw the home screen clotted with texts from Gabe, mostly links to spreading news articles about the disaster. But there was one text that stood out, and it wasn't from Mr. Sanchez.

Call me.

Determined to ignore the blunt summons for as long as he could, he swung his legs to the floor.

He peered his head into the living room, expecting to see Donnie futzing with his phone or maybe raiding the snack bar. His overnight guest had folded and stacked his blanket atop his pillow at one corner of the sofa. Richard felt a tug in his chest.

He'd wanted them to act like grown-ups, but maybe not that grown up. They could have at least had breakfast or a pot of tea or… Then he saw the slip of paper resting on the coffee table and rushed to it.

Back in a few. You were too peaceful to wake up. X, D

The hesitation marks around the *e* in peaceful had him bringing the paper closer to his face. It looked like Donnie had gone to write another letter and changed his mind at the last minute. Maybe an *r* instead of an *e?*

Pretty, Richard wondered, *had he started to say he was too pretty to wake up?*

He enjoyed this prospect way more than he should. He enjoyed being called pretty far more than he enjoyed being called some of the other supposedly complimentary things Donnie had called him. A sexy bitch, for starters. What he liked most about the *p* word in question was that he hadn't heard it much on Donnie's lips. If he'd gone to use it with Richard, maybe it meant he was seeing Richard differently than he saw most of the other men he wanted to cross off his list.

For too long, he stared down at the note. So long, he realized what he was really doing—delaying a prospect that filled him with more dread than the calls with attorneys and insurance agents that were sure to fill his afternoon.

His mother had texted him first thing that morning, and if he didn't return the call her second attempt at communication would prove far more invasive.

Evelyn Merriweather answered Richard's call after the first ring. She didn't bother to say hello. She didn't ask him how he was doing. Instead, she launched swiftly into a cold and methodical description of all the calls, text messages, and emails she'd received that morning from members of her bridge club detailing what they'd seen about the Harry Mitchell disaster on the news. She recounted these details as if they were as urgent as the events of the disaster itself. A spin-off of sorts, set entirely in one of the wealthiest sections of Long Island and starring only affluent widows with nothing but time on their hands.

Richard kept his mouth shut, knowing full well that any attempt to interject would result in a new flurry of details about what his mother had been drinking or trying to watch on television as the aftermath of Richard's professional crisis had invaded her otherwise peaceful morning.

As he listened, he wondered, for what must have been the

millionth time in his life, why he and his mother weren't better friends. On paper, it would have made sense.

Richard was his mother's version of sophisticated, with joint degrees in business administration and art history from a prestigious university. His clients included major celebrities and actual royalty. His mother, on the other hand, had partied with Gloria Vanderbilt and attended Truman Capote's Black and White Ball before marrying a promising young finance guy who'd made a small fortune later in life. Today, the hosts at fancy Upper East Side eateries in Manhattan swiftly ushered her to her favorite table. But the constant crisis that was his only brother's life had always stolen her focus. If anything, she seemed to regard the similarities between Richard and herself as a kind of irritating redundancy. His father hadn't exactly showered him with attention, but with the exception of the bail out checks he'd written Paul over the years, the blessing when it came to Joseph Merriweather was that he'd ignored everyone in their family equally.

Perhaps in appealing to his mother's love of fine and beautiful things from a young age, he'd overshot the mark and turned himself into her competition. But as he sat struggling to pay attention to her long, winding account of how his latest professional travail had impacted her otherwise peaceful Sunday, he thought it was no wonder his family history had made him suddenly vulnerable to a man who combined warmth and wildness the way Donnie Bascombe did.

"So what's your plan, Richard?" she asked suddenly.

"Well, we have insurance for these sorts of things, and luckily no one was hurt. And I had a long meeting with the clients last night to address their concerns. They're having me throw another event for them free of charge, which is the least I can do. It's much smaller so it won't exactly break my budget. It sounds like everyone's moving on. But I appreciate your concern."

The last line felt like swallowing a bitter pill; she hadn't expressed any concern.

"The press, Richard. What's your plan for the *press*?"

"I'm sure we'll come up with one this afternoon, but to be frank, Harry is enjoying the publicity, so I imagine he's going to let this play out for a while."

"Which is not good for you and your reputation, so what's your plan?"

"Well, I'm not about to do a bunch of interviews that draw more attention to it."

"What about social media? Are you on this Twit Tok or whatever it's called? The kids are all dancing on it. Maybe you could do a dance saying you're sorry. Or hire some children to do one for you."

"I'm sure there are child labor laws against that, mother. Don't worry, the firm has a social media presence. We'll put out a statement soon as Harry's publicist approves it."

"Well, that'll have to do then." It's what she always said when she disapproved of his choices, and the words set his teeth on edge. She sighed. "Listen, your brother and I are going to do some traveling."

"Oh? What about Susan?"

"Susan is also traveling. But not with us."

His mother and brother both went on trips all the time without informing him first. Why was this journey different?

"Where are you going?" Richard asked.

"Oh, I don't know. Italy, maybe. Polly and Fred said we could use their villa in Tuscany. But there's also Vienna. It's been years since I've been there."

"And where is Susan going?"

"Scarsdale. With her parents."

"Not sure a twenty-minute drive from Greenwich is considered traveling, mother. Are the kids with her?"

"Yes, they're having problems. You don't need to sound so satisfied. Your brother adores you," his mother said quietly. "It's not easy, you know. Having both of you going through this at the same time."

"I didn't realize my divorce was weighing so heavily on you."

Which was the kindest way of saying she'd only called him once since getting the news. And her response to finding out Mark had cheated had been to ask Richard if he'd been doing everything he could to keep his cheating husband happy in the bedroom. Paul, on the other hand, was apparently getting an international tour to soothe his wounds.

"What really happened at that party, Richard? Mayhem isn't exactly your brand."

"It was a computer error," he muttered, feeling nine years old again.

"What kind of *computer* error?"

"I made a mistake, mother. I hit a button at the wrong time. What do you want me to say?"

"Maybe you should talk to Mark."

Richard was so stunned, the pen he'd been doodling with fell out of his hand. "About what?"

"Look, he's willing to try again. He says if you all could sit down without lawyers, he'd—"

"Woah, wait. Just wait. I'm sorry. You've been talking to Mark? Behind my back?"

"He called me first. He was devastated."

"You've called *me* once since I moved out. How many times have you talked to my cheating ex?"

"It's not a game, Richard. No one's keeping score."

She was, though, and on the scorecard that mattered to her most, Mark had all the points—hedge fund manager, gorgeous mansion, rich friends, movie star good looks—and her son had none, apparently, no matter how far and wide his business grew.

"Mother, it's been a rough twenty-four hours, and I'm not prepared to have this conversation right now, so I'm going to end this call. Why don't we—"

"Oh, don't be such a drama queen! Now listen—"

He hung up rather than give voice to the words on the tip of his tongue.

I'll stop being a drama queen when you start being a mother.

For about thirty seconds he fought the urge to throw the phone across the room.

He won, but the effort turned his knuckles white.

22

Three years ago Sapphire Cove had been hit with a scandal that almost closed its doors for good. After everyone in the security department except for Logan was arrested in the course of a single morning, Donnie and a few of his former models had stepped in as security agents. During those crazy days, he'd spent plenty of time in the hotel behind the hotel and had learned its hidden map well.

The first floor, known as the administrative wing, lay on the other side of a nondescript, unmarked door across from the entrance to the health spa, not too far from the lobby. It was a long, labyrinthine warren of offices, none of them as opulently furnished as the hotel's guest areas. One floor below, buried inside the promontory on which Sapphire Cove sat, lay a virtual small town consisting of a staff commissary as large as Donnie's high school cafeteria, break rooms, two connected kitchens—one for special events, the other for room service and the hotel's two restaurants—and a cavernous laundry center mostly devoted to cleaning employee uniforms. Contrary to certain depictions on popular television dramas, a hotel's real nerve center was never out front and center and visible to the guests.

In the room service kitchen, he found Chloe Simmons, Sapphire Cove's head chef and a good friend of his buddy Ethan. Before Ethan had dramatically resigned as the hotel's pastry chef in defense of the man he loved, Ethan and Chloe had worked side by side and become fast friends, which was how Donnie had gotten to know her and why he felt comfortable interrogating her about Richard's favorite items from the room service menu and how they could spruce them up. After some back and forth, she agreed to switch out the shredded salmon they used for the salmon benedict—Richard's favorite—with pieces from more formidable filets. Then, with a skip in his step, he was heading back toward the elevator that would take him up to the administrative wing.

In the second before the doors closed, Jonas Jacobs stepped through them, placed one hand against the center of Donnie's chest, and pushed his back against the wall.

"I warned you, Sex Monster," he growled.

"And I hung up on you," Donnie fired back.

"Please tell me you did not spend the night in Richard's suite."

"On the sofa. I was helping him out. He had a bad night."

"Which you were also present for." Jonas yanked his phone from his pants pocket with his free hand and held it up where Donnie could see. His browser was open to the *TMZ* article on Harry's birthday meltdown. Probably the same one Harry had showed Thalia the night before. Donnie hoped so. The prospect of there being more than one article about it on the same website made his stomach cold.

"Nothing happened. Stop being all CIA on me. I drove him back. His car was trapped at the party, and he needed a ride. He said I could sleep on his sofa so I didn't have to drive all the way to San Diego. We were good boys. Promise."

Jonas cocked his head to one side and raised an eyebrow. "Porn star, please." He pocketed his phone. "Connor and Logan saw this."

"Oh, no. Put them off, please. He doesn't need anybody else breathing down his neck right now."

Jonas furrowed his brow. "I'm not in the habit of telling my boss not to come into his own hotel."

"Well, come up then. Richard could use your support."

"Don't worry. He's getting it. You, on the other hand, are entirely on your own."

They rode in silence to the first floor, then Jonas exploded out of the elevator ahead of him. Donnie had to jog to keep up.

Richard figured Donnie had delivered the sharp knock on the suite's door, but when he opened it, he saw he was only half right. Jonas pushed his way inside, Donnie hurrying in after him as if they were being chased. Their general sense of alarm encouraged Richard to close the door behind them quickly.

"Purge the room of all traces of Donnie," Jonas said quickly. "Immediately."

"And the actual Donnie?" Richard asked.

Jonas shook his head. "He followed me. Donnie, go away!"

"Bite me. My shoes are here." Glowering at the floor and Jonas in equal measures, he started a search for them.

"What's going on?" Richard asked.

Jonas said, "Connor and Logan are on their way over. They saw the story about the party on the news, and they're very concerned about you."

"And you think it's a problem that Donnie slept on my sofa?"

Jonas smiled. "I think Donnie's a problem wherever he goes."

Donnie hit the sofa like a ton of bricks and began putting on his shoes. "And I think you let people spread rumors you were in the CIA to cover up the fact that you used to work at Souplantation."

"And I think you're a penis in search of a soul," Jonas fired back.

Shoes on, Donnie shot to his feet. "There's no point in me running now. Everyone's going to tell them I was here. I've been all over the hotel."

Jonas sighed. "Okay, well, can we at least get you some normal clothes so it doesn't look like you just rolled out of his bed?"

"Come on," Richard said, gesturing for Donnie to follow him into his bedroom.

A second later, he and Donnie were both sliding hangers along the single rack in the shallow closet.

"Do you have any jeans or anything?" Donnie asked.

"Of course not. I don't work in construction."

"Jesus, princess. Okay, do you have any non-snob clothes? If I wear any of this, they're going to think I turned into a Log Cabin Republican."

"I am *not* a Log Cabin Republican!" When he saw Donnie's eyes widen in shock, he hastily added, "Sorry. I talked to my mother. Our calls last ten minutes but they take me a week to get over."

"You want to talk about it?" Donnie asked, but the speed with which he was sliding blazers, suit jackets, and dress shirts along the rack made his request seem halfhearted.

"Maybe later… Here." Richard spotted a pair of khaki shorts

resting under a pile of polo shirts. He handed Donnie the shorts then tossed a hunter green polo on top. "Go change in the bathroom."

Donnie complied, revealing Jonas standing in the open bedroom door, arms crossed over his chest, expression grave.

"It's fine," Richard said.

"It's not fine."

"Is this really about what Connor and Logan will think?"

Jonas shook his head. "I had a bad feeling about Mark from the moment I met him, but I never spoke up. Because he was who you picked. I can't keep my mouth shut now."

"There's no...*picking* going on. He slept on the sofa, Jonas."

"Good. Because Donnie Bascombe is not the man to mend a broken heart with."

"Trust me," Richard whispered. "He slept on the sofa."

The bathroom door swung open and out stepped Donnie, looking entirely too attractive in shorts that were a tad too tight for him, and a polo shirt that hugged his muscular torso. It looked like he'd also swiped some product and run it through his hair. He opened his arms and turned in both of their directions so they could get a good look. Richard nodded as gravely as he could, trying to hide the fact that Donnie in a pair of khaki shorts and a clean, ironed polo had a similar effect on him as the designer suit had the night before.

The suite's doorbell rang.

"That could be breakfast," Donnie said.

"Or it could be them," Jonas said.

23

Feeling like he was about to split Richard's shorts with every step, Donnie followed Jonas into the suite's sitting room.

Richard was in the lead, and the second he opened the entry door, a room service table jangled its way across the threshold, pushed by a uniformed waiter who was also wearing a beaming smile—the breakfast order Donnie had put in with Chloe. Donnie was about to heave a sigh of relief when, barely a few seconds letter, another room service table followed it, this one driven by an out-of-uniform Logan Murdoch, wearing a polo that wasn't quite as tight as the one Donnie had tugged on a few seconds earlier. Right on his tail was Connor, clearly so desperate to see inside the room he was practically crawling up his fiancé's back.

The waiter went through his standard ritual, lifting silver domes to reveal the salmon eggs benedict Donnie had ordered. Two plates of it. On Logan's table was one of the hotel's signature high tea services, only instead of finger sandwiches, the accompaniments were all sweets. Extra sugar intended to soothe Richard's wounded ego, he figured. Without asking anyone to sign a check, the waiter departed, a sign Richard's meals were probably on the house.

To cut the tension, Donnie said, "Cookies and eggs. A Sapphire Cove tradition."

"An odd pairing, for sure," Connor said.

"It's a morning for those, apparently," Jonas grumbled.

"If we'd known you'd ordered breakfast..." Connor said, eyes traveling across the three of them. "For two."

"We're talking wedding stuff." Donnie grinned. "Didn't want to meet on an empty stomach."

"Today?" Connor asked. "I mean, not that I mind, but I figured you'd be distracted. I understand it's been quite a weekend." There was concern in his voice as he turned his attention to Richard. "We thought some caffeine and sugar might help. How are you holding up, Mr. Merriweather?"

"It's mostly in the hands of our representatives now. The good news is no one was injured and the property damage was…limited." During that brief pause, Donnie figured Richard had imagined almost getting crushed to death by a falling statue of Venus. "At any rate, this is very thoughtful. Thank you."

Connor nodded, but he was suddenly looking at Donnie. Was that why his face was tingling? No, he realized. That was thanks to a different, more powerful force. A glare from his best friend that had the force of a thousand suns and years of history behind it. Logan Murdoch looked like he was trying to hide a knowing smirk. "Hey, D Man. Why don't we step outside so these gents can talk?" he asked.

"Sure thing, *L Dude*."

The next thing he knew, he was following Logan down the long, carpeted hallway, past guests tugging suitcases behind them and others being tailed by bellmen with fully loaded carts, the usual Sunday check out rush. Suddenly Logan turned, arms folded across his broad chest. "*L Dude*?" he asked.

"Since when do you call me D Man?"

"Just trying to cut the tension in there. Did you hook up with him?"

"No, I told you. It was a meeting about the wedding."

"At three in the morning?"

Donnie tried to think of something to say in his defense, but he felt too stupid to make words.

"You two rolled up at three a.m. and you left your car with valet. It's still there."

"Christ, man. How come you're always watching the security camera footage here?"

"Because I'm the security director, genius."

"Okay, point taken, but we did not hook up."

Logan nodded, but he kept his arms crossed. "Why not?"

"'Cause it's a bad idea."

Logan shrugged. Donnie looked over both shoulders for hidden cameras, wondering if he was being punked. At the mention of Donnie potentially having sex with their famous, high-strung wedding planner, a man his fiancé treated as if he were the King of England, Logan offered a casual shrug. What the hell was going on here?

"Does Connor know I slept here?" Donnie asked.

Logan shook his head, chewed his lower lip, and looked at the floor.

"What's going on right now?"

"I need you to hook up with him," Logan said quietly.

"*What?*"

"Come on. Why do you think I put your room down the hall from his the other night? The sexual tension was coming off you guys in waves."

"He's your wedding planner."

"I know," Logan said in a low growl. "And he's driving me nuts. I need you to throw him down and take him so I don't throw him out a window."

"Well, excuse me, sir. My dick might be a lot of things, but it's not Xanax."

"You're right. It's way easier to get so I'd say it's more like aspirin. Look, I can barely take this guy. He wants to meet eight times a day about a wedding that's six months off."

"Six months is actually, like, almost no time to plan a—"

"He's a maniacal, obsessive control freak and he—"

"And he moved your wedding here."

"That's not it."

"That's totally it, L Dude."

Logan's defiant head shake slowly turned into a nod accompanied by a telltale sag of his shoulders. He sucked in a long breath that ended up sounding like a growl, like his body was resisting this acceptance of the truth even though it was so obvious he was wearing it like clothes.

"I don't want to have the wedding here, okay?" Logan finally whispered. "It's not about Oregon or *The Goonies*, it's… This place kept us apart longer than it's kept us together. Yeah, they're good memories here. But they're bad memories too, and they're around every corner. And they're all scandal and drama, and I don't want the most important day of my life in the middle of all that."

"Did you tell Connor this?"

"There was no point. They ganged up on me."

"Which is it, dude? You didn't say anything or you did and they ganged up on you?"

Logan's embarrassed answer was in his silence and the way he stared down at the carpet.

"Okay, don't hit me, but I gotta say some things. You've clearly got some deep feelings about this wedding but you're not saying them out loud, and it's making everyone's job difficult. And the Taylor Swift and flowers jokes are kinda making you sound like an ass. To Richard, anyway."

Logan's eyes flared.

"I probably shouldn't have said that part. Anyway, you need to tell Connor what you want this wedding to be."

"Well, it's too late to move it now. And he's right about Richard tripling the budget. It's no small thing. I mean, it's not like I don't see the *logic* of it, I just…"

"We don't have to move it to make it what you want. Look, I've seen this guy in action. He is the best at what he does."

"Yeah, especially if you want to add a shooting to your big day."

"There was no shooting. I was there."

Logan closed one eye and pointed a finger at him. "Sounds like something the shooter might say."

"I was shadowing him. For research. What I'm saying is he can turn any room here into any place you want it to be. But you've got to be honest, and you gotta be yourself."

"I'm being myself."

Donnie shook his head. "Trying to get me in your wedding planner's pants with no thought of the long-term consequences? That's not you, Sergeant Responsible. But it's a sign you need to talk through this wedding stuff with the one who matters."

"Jesus?"

"Connor."

Logan sighed and rested one shoulder against the wall next to him. They fell silent as a group of departing guests hurried past, trailed by two little girls who were doing spins down the hallway to make the trip home more interesting. "There might be some truth in what you're saying," Logan said.

Donnie shrugged.

Logan sighed, suddenly looking more relaxed. "You gotta admit, he's crazy obsessive. And kinda bitchy too."

"Richard?"

Logan nodded.

"He's obsessive because he's good. And he's a bitch because his heart has been broken."

Logan looked genuinely confused.

"Do you know why he took the gig here? Why he was in Europe? Why he wants to stay here and not go back to LA?"

Logan shook his head.

"His husband cheated on him with all their friends. For, like, four years. His life right now, it's like someone pulled the rug out from under him and then hit him over the head with it. He's hurt. Bad. And he's trying to put his life back together but he's going too fast and he's being too hard on himself. Way too hard on himself. And he's not someone... He's not someone you play around with. He's a serious person. He's...he's really something, is what I'm saying."

Donnie felt the sides of his face flush, felt the tingly memory of Richard's lips meeting his. Felt his best friend's sudden, wide-eyed stare jerking him back to the present.

"I said hook up with him," Logan whispered. "I didn't say fall for him, Sex Monster."

"You said plan your wedding with him, and that's what I'm trying to do. But I thought you guys were putting this off because you were too busy, and now I realize you were avoiding it because you're not being honest about what you want and it's freaking Connor out. So he brought Richard in for reinforcement."

But Logan was nodding slowly, eyes wide, as if Donnie had changed shape before him in an instant. "Well, this isn't you either. Going all soft and googly eyes for someone you've never seen naked. This is not the Donnie Bascombe who made me do belly button shots off a go-go boy the night we met. Maybe I've been a good influence on you over the years."

"Be a better influence now. Talk to your fiancé about what you want."

Logan groaned and nodded and straightened himself off the wall.

Behind Donnie, the door to the Pacifica Suite opened. He turned in time to see Jonas step from the room, followed closely by Connor.

"We'll let you get back to your meeting now," Connor said stiffly. "I love this look for you, by the way. A tad snug, but still...a nice choice."

Donnie nodded and gave him a thumbs-up. "Great. I'll wear it to your wedding."

"No, you won't," Connor said with a smile.

Logan walked up to his fiancé and curved an arm around his shoulders. Donnie stood his ground, watching closely as they departed, relieved to see them lean into each other tenderly as they rounded the corner for the elevators.

For a second, he thought Jonas would follow them. Instead, once the engaged couple was out of sight, Jonas turned to face him. "If you hurt him, I will cut off your balls, turn them into a purse, and fill them with your teeth."

Donnie returned the alleged former spy's penetrating stare.

"Do *not* make a joke about being turned on right now."

"Trust me. Nothing shrinks my dick faster than a trip to the dentist."

Jonas turned and walked off down the hallway.

24

Donnie returned to the suite, feeling twice as stressed out as when he'd left it, expecting to find Richard collapsed on the sofa with one hand pressed to his forehead. Instead, the place was tidied up. Even better, both room service tables had been pushed next to a now open sliding door where the taffeta drapes fluttered in the ocean breeze. Laughter from the pool deck below made for pleasant music. Even better, the table with the breakfast plates on it had been set for two.

Between his conversation with Jonas and Logan, he felt like he should run screaming from the hotel at the idea of ever laying so much as a finger on Richard again. But the effort put into the scene before him—the invitation offered by the second chair he'd carried from the long dining table to the room service table with a view—was too seductive to turn down.

He could hear the room's resident talking in a business-like tone in the bedroom. On the phone, no doubt. Damage control, or the first stirrings of it. When he shut the entry door behind him, Richard ducked his head in at the sound, pulled his phone from his ear, and whispered, "Eat. It's getting cold."

From a shameful secret to a welcome guest in an instant. Another head-spinning reversal offered up by this crazy morning. The gorgeous view helped. Beyond the sparkling swimming pool, its deck crowded with guests rushing to get a last meal in before checkout, coastal mountains plunged toward the bright blue Pacific.

By the time Richard took a seat across from him, he had more than halfway finished his eggs. "So, it looks like Harry's going with the shooter storyline."

Donnie swallowed his bite. "What does that mean?"

"It means they rewrote my social media statement. My firm's no longer apologizing or offering free mental health services to guests, we are…" Richard reached for his phone and began to read aloud from it. "Extending our heartfelt thanks for the messages of support and concern we've received following the disturbing incident at Harry Mitchell's birthday party last night in Bel Air. We are grateful to announce that all of our staff is safe and unharmed." Richard swallowed. "Like so many of you, we hope for a sensible and common-sense solution to the epidemic of gun violence in this country." Richard set the phone aside and sighed. "All the footage online is too dark for anyone to tell what happened, so Harry's going to let illusion be reality and milk it for all it's worth. Also, heads up. Apparently Thalia's going to have a security detail with her at the reception. But ten bucks says she finds a way to lose them before then. If she doesn't divorce Harry first."

"Hollywood, man. Craziest people I ever met. Back when I was escorting, guys who used to play America's favorite dads would hire me to do stuff that made the Mormon boys on meth look sane. Trust me, nothing ruins classic TV faster than working as a hooker in Southern California."

Richard laughed so hard he almost spat up a bite of food. Quickly, he brought a napkin to his mouth.

Donnie reached over and filled the man's water glass from the sweating pitcher. A second later, Richard took a grateful drink.

"Well, were you technically a hooker?" Richard finally asked. "I mean, am I even allowed to use that word?"

"No, but I am," Donnie said with a grin.

Richard nodded.

"I didn't like it, to be honest. Not the word. The job, I mean. It wasn't like porn. Mostly, when I did it, it was to survive. Trust me. It was the better option. I could have ended up flipping burgers at Mickey D's. That would have been a real nightmare."

"No shame in fast food work. My dad worked at two different McDonald's in college."

"I know. The shame's in McDonald's. Their shit's terrible. Have you had Jack in the Box tacos? They're the bomb."

Richard laughed.

"Look, it wasn't the worst thing. It wasn't *my* thing. I had friends who were real good at it. They could give high-level clients whatever they wanted. Me, though, I was always me no matter what, and some clients didn't like that when I showed up. They're just different, porn and escorting, I mean. An audience of one is harder."

The searching look on Richard's face made him suddenly uncomfortable, but before he could explain further, Richard said, "How's one p.m. tomorrow for a walk-through at your studio? I figure there'll be less traffic then."

"Can we do same time Wednesday? I've only got shoots in the morning, and the afternoon's all model auditions I can move."

Richard's brow tensed. "That could work. Are you sure you can be wrapped with the shoots by one?"

"Yeah, but it's not an issue if you want to come sooner. I mean, you could watch a shoot if you want. Only fair. I've seen how you work."

Richard went very still, clearly stunned by the offer. "I don't know about that, Donnie. I don't want to embarrass the models."

"*Embarrass* the porn models? That's not possible. Trust me. These were the last boys to put their clothes on at the swimming hole. I wouldn't put 'em on camera if they weren't. Look, no pressure. It's just…offer stands if you're ever interested."

"Thank you," Richard said. "But one sounds good."

More silence, more laughter from the pool deck below. More cool winds blowing in through the open deck door that felt like kisses along his neck, kisses he wanted Richard to be leaving. But his face was flushed, he could feel it.

Richard probably thought the offer to let him watch a shoot was casual, meant to make things between them strictly platonic. The opposite was true. Donnie only invited guys to watch him shoot if he was seriously interested in them and trying to prove his job wasn't something to be jealous of, that he didn't spend his time on set getting turned on. Literally nothing was less sexy than the behind-the-scenes vibe on a porn set. He spent it focused on lighting and camera angles and making sure the models didn't get exhausted from being in one position for too long.

"So is it true what you said about not having a bunch of meetings today, or were you trying to calm Connor down?" Donnie finally asked.

"Gabe's coming down in a few hours with the car, and we're going to meet about some things. It's a loaner from Sapphire Cove, so I don't want it to be missing for too long. That's about it."

Donnie nodded, his suspicion about the car confirmed.

"What did you and Logan talk about out in the hall?"

"You first. How'd the call with your mom go?"

As this stalemate settled over them, Donnie smiled, figuring Richard would shut things down swiftly rather than add his family drama to his marital stuff.

"How about a walk?" Richard asked quietly, his face settling into an expression Donnie wasn't used to seeing it make. Expectant, cautious, hopeful. Surely, he recognized the significance of the ask, extending the very invite he'd turned down from Donnie two nights before. And if this had been yesterday or the day before, Donnie would have been thrilled. But words like *turn your balls into a purse* were circling in his head like buzzards.

"Sounds good," he said before he could stop himself. "There's something I want to show you. You know, wedding stuff."

A short while later, they'd reached the band of lawn outside the conference center's soaring, ocean-facing windows. A long stone balustrade kept guests from wandering too far out onto the crumbling edge of the bluff. Plenty of guests were gathered along it now. It offered a stunning view of the horizon, and the wooden steps leading to the resort's private crescent of beach were nearby.

"This is where they first met. Or had their first real conversation, I guess," Donnie said.

"Connor and Logan?"

"Right. See, it was Logan's first night working at the hotel, and Connor was having his college graduation party. Technically, the party was where they saw each other first. But out here was where Connor kinda made his first move. Logan was doing rounds, and Connor brought him a gift bag."

Richard laughed under his breath. "His college graduation party had gift bags? That man and I are birds of a feather."

Donnie smiled, but he was suddenly nervous. He thought this little tour—walking in the footsteps of the grooms-to-be—would focus them on work. Then he remembered how the story ended, and he had to take a deep breath and work harder to forget Richard's kiss from the night before.

"So, they're talking and Logan gets kind of nervous and he starts to shut down. And Connor thinks he's coming on too strong, so he backs off, says goodnight and heads for the door over there. And then Logan starts to freak out inside. 'Cause he already knows Connor's, like, his ideal guy. But it's risky because he really needs this job bad and if he screws it up... So anyway, he calls out to him and Connor comes back..."

And they went down to the beach and then the sea caves, and that's where they had their first kiss. But if he included that part, then Richard might ask to see those places too. The caves were accessed by a small boardwalk from the beach that hugged the cliff's base. They weren't always empty during daylight hours, but if they were... Those deep, concealing shadows, the surf breaking against the rocks outside, drowning out the outside world, all that damp, cold stone driving them closer together in need of heat... No way. Donnie needed to cut this tour short right now.

"I know you want to do a wedding that kinda showcases the resort," he said quickly. "Well, this spot is where it all started for them. So maybe there's a way to bring the outside in. Know what I mean?"

He was looking at Donnie again, but his designer sunglasses hid the emotion in his eyes. "That's very intriguing. From a design perspective. But I won't lie. Outdoor weddings are the bane of my existence. I'd much rather be able to control the elements. But the idea of recreating the coastline in one of the ballrooms as a way of amplifying the overall setting..." Richard scanned the extent of the vista Donnie had brought to life with memory. "Very interesting. Is this what you and Logan talked about in the hallway? Wedding ideas?"

"No." Donnie looked out to the sea.

"Sounds serious, whatever it was."

"I told him to cut the crap. I told him to stop making cracks about flowers and Taylor Swift that were making you feel bad and him sound like some macho asshole. I told him to get honest about what he wanted out of this wedding so we could all do our jobs. Because I realized I was wrong. They haven't delayed the wedding because they're busy. They've put it off 'cause they're scared. Logan's scared of not doing the perfect wedding, and Connor's afraid of setting him off."

"You don't think Logan's having second thoughts about the marriage in general?" Richard asked. "That was my worry when I first met him."

Donnie shook his head. "No, Logan's ex-military. Ex-military folks, they learn how to live inside chaos. But I know from living on the road, chaos can make you superstitious. He's afraid having the wedding here's going to jinx it. They love this place, but not all their memories here are good." Richard nodded, and damn, Donnie wished he could take those sunglasses off and see what was happening in his companion's eyes. "I'm sorry if I'm making it more complicated."

"You're not." Richard leaned one elbow against the balustrade and turned to him. "You're doing exactly what I'd hoped you do."

"Seriously?"

"The night we met, I didn't want to tell you this. I mean, we were at odds, so I didn't want to give you something that felt like an advantage. But the first rule of thumb in my business is this—learn as much about the client as humanly possible, and Logan was as locked up as a bank vault. And you're right, Connor was hiding in the shadows, trying to read his mind. He probably brought me in to say the things he was afraid to say."

"That kinda sucks. For you, I mean."

"Well, it wasn't like I didn't have anything to go on. I know their story. I followed the news about the place. I admired them. Standing up to the world in defense of their relationship. It was moving. It was part of the appeal of setting up an office here, to be frank."

"Was that the only appeal?" Donnie asked.

"No, not at all. I mean, it's beautiful here."

"Yeah, but, you could have gone anywhere. I mean, you've got offices all over, right? And I'm sure most of them are a lot further away from Mark and his shitbag brigade. Is it 'cause Jonas was right downstairs?"

"Part of it, I think. But he sold me on the community here."

Friends, Donnie realized. That's what Richard Merriweather needed. That's why he'd come to Sapphire Cove. Because one of his oldest friends had promised him new ones to replace the ones who'd betrayed him. Friends. Not a roll in the hay with some hit-it-and-quit-it horn dog that might mess up his chance to find a new community made up of folks who showed him respect. They'd already kissed once and it had damn near destroyed the dude's career. Donnie needed to slow his roll, and fast.

"So one p.m. on Wednesday."

Richard nodded. "Sounds good."

"Alright, well, listen, I should probably go…" *Before I rip those sunglasses off and kiss you on the mouth.*

Richard nodded. "I'll see you this week. Maybe not a hug yet given…you know…"

"Sure, yeah. Totally."

He was almost to the conference center door when he heard Richard call out to him. "Where's the studio?"

"Oh, I'll text you." Donnie went to leave again.

"You don't have my number," Richard added.

Because Richard had denied it to him the night they met. Donnie reached for his pocket, found it was empty. "My phone's in your room."

"We should get it then," Richard said thoughtfully, hesitantly, as if they were debating whether or not to parachute off the cliff nearby.

Donnie nodded.

Richard nodded.

Then they were walking together through hotel hallways gone quieter now that the Sunday exodus was underway, feet swishing over carpeted corridors. Both of them looked in different directions inside the elevator as it ascended to Richard's floor. At the threshold to the suite, Donnie considered staying in the hallway, figured that would make him seem like a total wuss, so he followed Richard a few steps inside, but left the door open behind him.

His phone was sitting on an end table next to the sofa where he'd slept. Richard picked it up, turned to face him. But he still had those fucking sunglasses on, and now it felt like a deliberate attempt to hide what he was feeling. He was also holding the phone to his chest, like he didn't want to let it go yet. Not until…not until what, Donnie wondered. Heart racing.

"There's something else I need to say."

"Sure," Donnie whispered.

"I'd like to apologize for watching your porn. Not because it was bad. And not because you're bad. And not because *porn* is bad. Because I was the one insisting we keep things professional. Then I went and engaged in behavior that sexualized you. That's both hypocritical and irrational of me. And I think it set the stage for everything that happened last night."

The speech sounded rehearsed. Had he been practicing it since the kiss? Or since that morning?

"I don't know if it's possible to sexualize me more than I sexualize myself, but I kinda get what you're saying." And he hated it. So he decided to give voice to it, hoping against hope that Richard would tell him he was wrong. "You only kissed me last night 'cause you got worked up watching an old version of me that doesn't exist anymore."

Richard flinched and looked to the floor between them. "No," he finally whispered. "Obviously that's not the only reason I…"

"You were upset. About Evan."

"Not just that either." Richard shook his head, then managed to meet Donnie's gaze. "I meant what I said in the car. I've never met anyone like you." Only he said it like it was as scary and dangerous as it was thrilling and new.

"I really need to go," Donnie finally said, afraid of the sequence his words had taken. But maybe the tone said it all. If he didn't leave, and soon, he'd start something else. Something fast and hard and hot. And there was no balloon drop to stop them this time.

Nodding, Richard handed Donnie his phone, gave him a beat to unlock it, and then hurriedly dictated his phone number.

"See you Wednesday, Merriweather. Don't worry. We got this."

And then he was hurrying down the hallway for the elevators as if the smell of Richard's cologne would consume him and draw him back inside the Pacifica Suite if he didn't get away fast enough. And he wasn't sure what his final words had been referring to exactly—the reception for Thalia, Connor and Logan's wedding, or their ability to keep their hands off each other.

25

Butt. Butt. Butt. Dick. Butt. Pouty face. Dick. Twink in a unicorn costume. Big butt, small butt, a butt covered in glitter paint. A butt with a TRUMP sticker on it. He couldn't tell if it was a commentary on the former president or one guy's weird way of announcing his political views.

The photos filling Donnie's direct messages offered up the usual fleshy previews of potential hookups.

And they were boring the life out of him.

The dancer impressed him. Mainly because he stood out. Or jumped out. Literally. The leotard-clad pretty boy had somehow captured himself mid-leap in the middle of a sun-drenched park. But even this novel approach failed to arouse him for more than a second or two. Maybe because the guy didn't have Richard's hair.

Indeed, he'd been scrolling for over an hour, desperate for some blast of quick lust to drive all thoughts of Richard from his mind. Nothing stirred down below.

Because the truth was, the swipe and click world of Internet hookups had been boring him for a while. Maybe because he was nearing forty and had enjoyed pretty much every type of sex there was. But whenever the prospect of nailing an Internet stranger failed to turn him on, he pushed back against the absence of desire the way he would a difficult set at the gym. Dig deep, dive hard. As an old workout buddy had once admonished him, *create the enthusiasm, don't wait for the enthusiasm.* At his age, if he gave in to a lack of libido, the problem would only spread, he was sure.

But was not being able to bang Internet randos really a *problem?* Call him crazy, but if he wasn't getting paid, he wasn't sure sex should feel like a brutal set at the gym.

Truth was, the older he got, the more he preferred regular NSA buddies he could actually have some chit chat with before and after. But his regulars weren't always available on demand. Right now, he was desperate for a distraction.

He had a few unread DMs from a couple over in La Jolla he'd been visiting for about a year now. Two high-powered doctors who brought him in whenever they both wanted to throw their ankles skyward in the bedroom. They usually liked to schedule in advance. But the last time he'd dropped by, they'd asked him to walk their dog after they'd finished up, and even though he had a soft spot for their slobbery Frenchie, the request had bothered him. He'd complied, though, and it made him feel less like a fun plaything and more like an unpaid houseboy. When he thought of both men now, he didn't think of fun, he thought of being *disposable.* He'd never used the word before in terms of sex. In the course of one weekend, Richard had given it a new meaning.

As more and more naughty pictures slid by, they started to look less like actual body parts and more like abstract paintings in the museums Ethan had dragged him to after he first moved in.

Finally, he settled on a baby-faced twunk whose profile photos showed him wearing athletic uniforms in which he'd probably never played an actual sport. A short while later, there was a knock on the side of his boat. When the guy stepped inside the kitchenette, the usual Grindr/Scruff/Jack'd greeting ritual ensued: a brief flare of eye contact followed by a relieved head nod as they both realized they hadn't been catfished.

"Drink?" Donnie asked.

"Nah, I'm good," the guy answered in a gruff, masculine tone that sounded forced.

Ritual complete, Donnie went to pull the guy in for a kiss, only to be pushed back onto the banquette sofa with one hand on the center of his chest as the guy sank to his knees, eyes averted. Kiss denied. Real target acquired.

Okay, fine. Donnie knew how to be a dick on demand. Less work for him.

He could close his eyes, roll his head back. Imagine he was

somewhere else. Like Richard Merriweather's arms. Under a canopy of tree branches wrapped in glittering lights. While Harry Mitchell flew a helicopter overhead, a searchlight trained on them, shouting "More tongue!" into a loudspeaker.

Wow. That was weird. Had he started to fall asleep?

"You okay?" the twunk asked.

He wasn't sure how much time had passed, but when he looked down, blinking, he saw he was noodle limp in the guy's hand, and the guy was staring up at him with a look of strained patience that suggested yeah, he'd actually nodded off and started dreaming.

"You ever heard the expression envy is a hostile form of self-pity?" Donnie asked.

Rolling his eyes, the guy sat back on his haunches, letting Donnie's limp dick slap to his stomach. "No offense, but therapist role-play doesn't really do it for me. Are you feeling this or should I…?"

"How about a drink for the road?"

"No thanks, I'm good. Maybe some coffee for you, though." The guy was on deck and scaling the ladder before he'd finished speaking. He'd probably have his phone out and the app open before he reached the end of the dock. Because Donnie was that replaceable.

Disposable.

But at least he was free of distractions now.

In the bedroom, thoughts of Richard and his right hand finally brought him the relief he needed.

26

In the end, the only way for Donnie to get all his exclusives to the studio for Richard's walk-through was to promise them each half their regular scene rate. It seemed fair, all things considered. Two of them were missing class, another was delaying a trip out of town. But the number of text messages it had taken to hammer out this compromise had been so high, he'd expected to breathe easier once all five of his boys were finally on site Wednesday morning. Unfortunately, as he tried to talk over the day's agenda with Brutus, his palms felt sweaty and his lungs starved. Maybe it was the noise level. On the other side of his office door, the models were changing into their assigned costumes with the raucousness of a winning sports team.

"Shall we anoint him with lavender oil before or after he walks a path of rose petals into the studio?" Brutus finally asked, clearly sick of Donnie's lecture on the meeting's schedule.

"Alright, don't be a dick. I'm just saying, we need to be on our best behavior. He's a classy guy, and he's got a full schedule."

"And you like him."

"I like a lot of people."

"Yeah, but you like *like* him."

"What are you, six years old?"

"No, but you're acting like a teenager on prom night. Did you get him a corsage too?"

Before Donnie could describe what he was about to give Brutus in the center of his face, there was a harsh knock. A second later, the office door flew open to reveal the studio's most popular power bottom, Matthew Martinez, aka Colton Hammer. At five foot six, he'd squeezed his muscular gymnast body into a bright red wrestling singlet that left nothing to the imagination. His shorn cap of bleach-blond hair popped against his brown skin. "Cup or no cup?"

Donnie's eyes found the waistband and support pouch dangling from the young man's right hand and realized he was talking about a jock strap. "Cup," Donnie said. "Meeting's PG-13 all the way. Make that PG."

"Why am I wearing this again?" he asked, arms out, turning in place so they could see his flawless ass.

"I told you, everyone's wearing the costume from their most popular scene."

Matthew grunted and rolled his eyes. "*No*. Please tell me *Wrestling Bros* is not my most popular scene. It's so boring. And we didn't even wrestle. Why not *Highway Roads*? It was so much better, and we drove all the way out to the desert to shoot it."

"Well, it got kinda arty in the end." He shot Brutus a look. "Someone's final cut had a lot of drone shots in it."

Brutus hung his head. He was in a love affair with their new drone camera.

Donnie understood the appeal, but in a business driven by close-ups of penetrations, it was best not to get too excited about a device that was designed to send the camera further and further away from the guys fucking down below.

"It was literally one of the best things this studio has ever done," Matthew whined.

"Okay, let's not go crazy. You got railed by a truck driver on the front bumper of his cab. It wasn't *Hamlet*."

When Matthew went to leave, Brutus gave Donnie a pointed look, a reminder of a remark he'd made to him earlier that morning. In two quick strides, Donnie reached the door and stopped Matthew in his tracks with a hand on his shoulder. "What am I hearing about you and nursing school?" he asked.

Their star performer glared at Brutus over Donnie's shoulder. "It's hard. It's a lot of math," he said quietly.

"Yeah, well, it's not going to be *all* math. Focus on the parts you're good at and work on the others."

"How would you know what parts I'm good at? You've never been to nursing school."

"I know you're the only model I've ever had whose eyes light up when he talks about how kidneys work."

Matthew nodded at his feet. "The loop of Henle is an amazing piece of machinery. Tell me something, though. You're not pushing me to do this 'cause I'm not young and hot anymore, are you?"

"You're twenty-five, Matty. What do you mean, you're not young?"

The guy looked to the floor.

"You're still one of my most popular models. If I didn't have a soul in this old body, I'd hang on to you for as long as I could. But you're burning out. It happens. And there's nothing wrong with it. After a while, some of us can't do it anymore, and we need to move on. And I always help my boys move on when it's time. You know that."

"Okay, well, can you drive up to Sapphire Cove and get me a security job there like you did Scott, Brandon and J.T.? 'Cause that place is nice."

"You'll make a shit ton more money in nursing if you stick it out. And you'll make it after your ass falls." At Matthew's frightened look, Donnie gripped one of the young man's shoulders. "Which is a long way off, so don't worry."

Donnie rubbed the bristle-short, bleach-blonde hairs on Matthew's head and patted him on the shoulder to dismiss him.

Then he turned to face Brutus. "Happy?"

"I'll be happy when he stops biting the heads off his scene partners because he doesn't like their body wash. Anyway, back to your crush."

"I'm gonna crush your face if you don't stop. Okay. So once we have everyone in costume and on the floor, I want you to go into storage and get that backdrop we used for the step and repeat at that charity event at Rich's. Then—"

Brutus's eyes went wide at the sight of something behind him. Something frightening. When Donnie spun, it took him a second to recognize the two feathered, bejeweled figures with dark circles painted around their eyes and their hair slicked in a dozen different spiky directions. Bedazzled, animal-print kilts covered their private parts, but their furry, feathered vests revealed their tight, muscular white torsos. It was the Apple Pie Twins, Cody and Ken. They proudly extended arms encased in more fur and gave him beaming smiles.

"What in the name of… Are you guys *birds*?"

They dropped their arms and started pouting. "We're dragon hunters," Ken whined.

"You look like owls on meth."

Still smiling, Cody said, "We went to this amazing ren fair this weekend and we met this woman who makes these and she's so cool and she gave us all healing crystals that can—"

Donnie spun to Brutus. "What's a ren fair?"

"Renaissance fair," Brutus grumbled. "It's like Spring Break for hippies and nerds."

"Okay," Ken said, one furry arm raised, "that's not *exactly* true. Let's not be—"

"Enough," Donnie said firmly. "You're both supposed to be Mormon missionaries."

"But we'd rather be dragon hunters," Ken said, smiling and batting his eyelashes in a manner that would have seemed seductive if he hadn't been dressed up like something from a horror movie.

"As I said before, maybe about ten times, everyone is wearing the costume from their most popular scene. The metrics are guiding us here. Not the renaissance fair. We've never done a dragon hunter scene. And I'm sorry, boys, but we never will."

Cody and Ken started jumping up and down and fake crying in unnerving unison.

Donnie brought his palms to his skull to keep it from flying apart.

"Why not?" Ken whined. "We did a *Game of Thrones* parody."

"And it practically bankrupted us. Makeup off. Now. White dress shirt, black pants, black shoes, and narrow black tie. They're all in the costume closet. I checked." Pouting, heads bowed, both boys went to leave. After them, Donnie added, "And comb your hair down or something. Christ."

Once they were alone, Brutus said, "You need to chill, Donnie."

"I'll chill when the meeting's over."

"This isn't about the meeting. It's about this guy. Maybe you all should bang it out just once. You know, get it out of your system."

"I don't know if one time with this guy would get it out of my system."

Brutus's eyes widened. "Seriously?"

Before Donnie could answer for the momentous implications of what he'd just said, there was another knock on his office door. This time it swung all the way open to reveal Joe Coughlin, aka Caden Pounder. The former forklift operator stood about six foot four and had barbarian-level muscles thanks to injections Donnie had been trying to get him off of for months now. If the guy didn't quit soon, his head was going to end up looking like a thumb. But he was wearing a cowboy hat, cowboy boots, scuffed Levi's with gaping holes that revealed his thick quads, and a red handkerchief tied around his thick neck.

"Finally!" Donnie gladly exclaimed. "Someone who's in the right costume."

Joe gave him a double thumbs-up, then stepped inside the office. "So the wife's been selling these herbal supplement things that are really taking off online. She was thinking maybe I could give some samples to the producer lady when she comes and—"

"Tell you what. Put some on my desk and I'll check 'em out and see what they're made of and we'll go from there."

"Oh, they're a hundred percent natural. I mean, they've got a little bit of cannabis oil in them so you probably don't want to drive after you do the immune booster one. But the rumor about the heroin's bullshit. Some bitch competitor started it. Now her ass is in jail for tax fraud so we can—"

"All good, sir. All good. Drop 'em on my desk before you leave and I'll take a look."

Then he and Brutus were alone again.

"Has everyone here lost their damn minds?" Donnie whispered.

"Maybe they're following your lead," Brutus said. "What? Joe's fine. I mean, you always tell your boys to have a side hustle."

"No, I tell them this *is* the side hustle."

"Oh, right. They should all go to school. Like you."

"I had a career here. I run the place, remember?"

"Exactly. So give yourself some credit and calm down, alright? I don't care how fancy this guy is. We're not a low-rent operation that makes their models blow some rich queen so we can shoot at their house all day. We're professionals, thanks to you. You got nothing to be ashamed of. So relax."

Donnie felt like he was about to do exactly that when he heard squeaking wheels rolling across the concrete floor just outside of his office door. "What the hell's that—"

When he threw his office door open, it took him a second to make sense of the scene before him. The first thing he noticed was that Harrison Peters, aka David Allen, was in his assigned costume, the tailored sharkskin suit of a high-powered executive who had plowed more than one mouthy assistant over his desk. That was good. But he was pushing a costume rack packed full of various bright green dresses. The rack's top shelf was crowned by three different bright green wigs, one of them a beehive so tall it was close to scraping the hallway's ceiling. That was very not good.

David turned, lowering both hands in front of him as if Donnie were a difficult child he was trying to hold in place. "I just want to have them on hand in case she shows up today."

"The producer's wife is not coming to this meeting. And when she comes to the reception, she wants to meet Harrison Peters. Not Vagina Listerine."

Jaw tense, taking a step protectively in front of the costume rack while gesturing to his dresses as if they were royal robes, David said, "Her *name* is Diphtheria Mysteria. And what happened to always helping your boys find their next act?"

"No offense, dude, but if you're trying to leave porn I'm not sure a song called "Put Your Balls On My Face" is going to do the trick."

"It's a summer song. It's a joke about beach balls. And it tests my vocal range."

Donnie nodded. The truth was, David's singing voice wasn't his problem. His mind-numbingly stupid songs were. And the videos he'd shot to go with them, which combined all the cheapest elements of a porn film but without the full frontal nudity or penetration sex that made porn popular.

"Everyone on the floor now!" Donnie shouted. The shouting in costume and shower room continued. "*Now!*"

A satisfying burst of silence was followed by the clamor of the footfalls as his exclusives rushed to comply.

When they all reached the main studio, they fell silent and let Donnie arrange them into a receiving line. Then Matthew figured out they were being lined up shortest to tallest and started making the case that he was technically taller than Cody. But he fell tombstone silent when he saw the look on Donnie's face. Once he spaced them out from each other by a few feet, he moved the entire line a little to the left. That way the complete expanse of standing sets was visible from the minute you set foot in the studio.

"Alright. Question. Am I the best director you all have ever worked with?"

All five men nodded.

"Louder, please."

They all uttered versions of yes containing various levels of enthusiasm.

"Is this the best studio you all have ever worked with?"

More nods, more yeses, except for one. Cody was staring at the floor and chewing his bottom lip. When his boyfriend noticed, he chucked him lightly on the shoulder. Cody met Donnie's stare and said, "Falcon bought us Krispy Kreme when we were done with a shoot once."

"Fine, I'll start bringing doughnuts. The point is, I've been good to you boys so now I need you to be good to me." When all five of them started sputtering with laughter, Donnie realized he'd unintentionally made the line sound like porn dialogue.

"I thought you didn't hook up with your exclusives," David said.

"I don't, and that's not what I meant."

"Well, if you ever change your mind, I'm down, daddy," Matthew said with a smile and a wink.

"Enough. Okay, here's the deal. This is an important event. We've never hosted a mixed crowd like this in the studio, so I need you guys to treat it like a public appearance. And what is the number one rule when Parker Hunter boys do a public appearance?"

In grudging unison, all five men said, "No nudity, even if they ask."

"And what's the second rule?"

Again, all five answered, "No nudity, even if they pay."

"Correct. Now hands might get wandery. We know from experience women can be as aggressive as men, especially when booze is involved. The first time they touch something they shouldn't, politely move their hand away. The second time, do the same thing, then come to me and I'll handle it for you and I'll make sure there isn't a third. Alright, item three. There will be booze at this event. It will not be for you. It will be for the guests only. Now there's probably going to be some picture taking, but I'm not sure—"

A delicious smell came from behind him. Suddenly, his boys were standing up straighter at the presence of a new guest. "Tacos," Donnie whispered before he could stop himself.

Richard was behind him. And alone. Dressed in a black tailored suit with a gold pocket square and white silk dress shirt unbuttoned at the collar. In one hand he held a grease-spotted bag, and when Donnie realized what it was his heart surged.

27

Richard's first thought was that the studio smelled far better than he thought it would. His second thought was that it was about three times the size he was expecting. A good thing, since it gave him more room to work with. The models looked spiffy and well-groomed and there was something almost touching about the straight-backed deference they'd showed their head honcho during his pep talk. Either they were exceedingly well paid or they respected Donnie down to their core.

"Greetings, everyone," he said brightly. Donnie's wide eyes had fixed on the Jack in the Box bag in Richard's right hand. "These are the right kind, I hope."

"They smell like the right kind. I'll put them out so everyone can have one."

"If you want," Richard said, "but they're for you."

"I don't want to stink up my breath."

On cue, Richard swung his leather messenger bag in front of him, unzipped the outside pocket, and removed a plastic Ziploc bag containing an unopened toothbrush, a miniature tube of toothpaste, and a tiny bottle of Listerine.

"This is really...cool. Thank you."

Richard smiled. "Well, they're tacos. I've got better things on my résumé. But I'm glad you're pleased."

The next thing Richard knew, the stocky, tattooed fireplug he figured was Donnie's assistant was introducing himself as Brutus and curving an arm around Donnie's back. "Let's take these back to the office."

Donnie said, "We need to introduce Richard to the—"

"We will," Brutus said, using his arm to drive Donnie toward the door to the hallway.

It was an abrupt departure, but he figured they had something to discuss. Richard was a few minutes early.

Regardless, he didn't want to waste any time, so he started working his way down the line, shaking each model's hand and introducing himself. He figured they were giving him their professional names and not their given ones. That was fine. In his other hand, he held his phone and kept glancing at the list Thalia had e-mailed him the day before. A list of performers whose presence at the reception she was specifically requesting, i.e. demanding. At the end of the line was a handsome, toweringly tall Black man in a designer suit who introduced himself as Harrison Peters. Excellent. This was the guy Thalia most wanted to meet. And he was already dressed the part of the domineering executive who punished naughty assistants across his desk. Perfect. If anything about this completely insane situation could be called perfect.

Suddenly, Donnie's voice erupted behind him. He and Brutus had returned to the studio. That was a quick meeting, he thought.

"We've already gone over some ground rules, so maybe you could give them more of a sense of who the guests are gonna be. I mean, I'm not asking for names or anything. Just, you know, a sense of what to expect. Will our guests want pictures?"

"Tons. I spoke to her this morning, and she asked for all the exclusives by name. She's bringing about ten of her friends in a limo bus, and she says they're all going to want lots of selfies. And champagne."

"Gotcha covered."

Richard heard squeaking wheels nearby, turned and saw Brutus wheeling out a step and repeat covered with the studio's green and yellow logo.

"Maybe this will work. We use it for conventions and club appearances."

"Great," Richard said. "But no telling how far and wide they'll post the photos, all things considered. It might not be the best use of your PR materials."

"Oh, no. That's fine. I thought if they didn't want the sets in the background."

"But they can take pictures on the sets? It's not some sort of rights issue?

"Of course they can. The studio's yours."

Richard smiled. "It does look pretty clean."

"If it's out on the floor, it's clean," Donnie said. "Also, hey, boys?" He called more loudly. "Any of you guys high right now?"

Richard glared at Donnie with his best attempt at a smile, hoping the models didn't notice the tension between them.

After a startled silence, Harrison Peters said, "Um, I've been sober six years."

Then Colton Hammer added, "And if I had good drugs, I wouldn't be *here*."

"I guess I deserved that," Richard said quietly.

"Maybe," Donnie answered with a boyish grin.

"Service entrance? I'm thinking of bringing in some big standing candelabras and clustering roses around their bases. The LA office has a bunch in storage."

"This way," Donnie said.

Through a fire door and behind the studio's back wall lay a long and narrow storage space that included a fairly large set of glass double doors it looked like they used for load ins. Being suddenly alone with Donnie in a shadowy corridor gave Richard a sharp jolt that made him feel like they were back inside the command center. He saw the bright outline of double glass doors that had been covered with blackout paper and headed straight for it, pulling a tape measure from his jacket pocket as he went.

"No crew today?" Donnie asked. He stepped forward and took the tape measure's end in one hand as Richard backed up, letting it unspool.

"No offense, but I'm going to be selective about who I get to work this. Can you measure the height please?" Donnie complied, angling the measure until it met the edge of the door frame on top. "If ever there was a special event, it's this one. I want to make sure everyone's comfortable before I bring them in."

"I get it, but I already gave the boys some strict ground rules. We do public appearances all the time. No nudity. Even if it's requested."

Richard adjusted his stance so they could measure the full height of the doors. "I appreciate that. Especially since none of the guests are bringing spouses. I want to make sure nobody they leave at home has something to call and yell at me about later. Especially Harry." Measurement taken, Richard nodded at Donnie. He released the end of the tape "So did they give me their real names? No need. Just curious."

"Depends. Did they all sound like combos of prep school kids and things you'd find on a construction site?"

Laughing, Richard nodded.

"Then no, they didn't."

Now they were standing together in the shadows. Far too close. Far too alone.

"Thank you," Richard said. "I heard some of your speech when I first walked in. I appreciate the seriousness you're giving this, Donnie. Truly."

"Sure. Let's get back out there. See if the boys have any questions."

But there was a skip in his step. It made him positively giddy that Donnie had put this much effort and attention into this meeting. He'd expected the man to act with the best of intentions, but he hadn't expected the studio to be spotless and all of his exclusive performers to be standing at military attention when he arrived.

But when they re-entered the studio, they found it completely empty, save for an equipment table that had been cleared of cables and wires and moved to the center of the space. The Jack in the Box bag sat atop it like an offering to the porn gods.

28

Donnie's phone buzzed in his pocket. He pulled it out and saw a text from Brutus.

> Took the boys to lunch. Bang him on the dungeon set or I quit.

Jaw aching from where he was grinding his teeth, Donnie put his phone back in his pocket.

"Taco time," Richard said brightly.

He was still getting over the fact that Brutus had been forced to escort him out of the studio right after Richard's arrival because he'd noticed that Richard's unexpected gift had given Donnie a raging boner. Though that was technically true, it wasn't the smell of the tacos that had done it. It was the thoughtfulness of it. And when you added the toothbrush into the mix…well, Richard Merriweather might as well have kissed him on the neck while playing with his nipples.

Wondering if he should run over his studio manager later with his own car or the official Parker Hunter van, Donnie pulled two folding chairs up to the table and gestured for Richard to take a seat. His beautifully dressed guest declined with a polite smile, strolling the vast space instead. Donnie was relieved. Being suddenly alone with him would be easier if they weren't forced to look into each other's eyes.

Donnie ate. Richard explored, snapping the occasional photo of an electrical outlet on his phone.

"This is impressive," Richard finally said. "My instinct was to cover up the bones of the place as much as I could, maybe conceal the light rigging with a translucent material we could illuminate from above, creating a sort of sky effect. But since our guests are such big fans of your product, it makes sense to highlight the function of the space, not hide it. So I'm thinking additional lighting to accent the support columns and emphasize the height of the ceiling. Do you have the capacity for that?"

After swallowing a bite of taco that was way too big, Donnie said, "We've got the wiring to support three simultaneous shoots. I mean, we never do that for sound reasons, but every time I added a new standing set, I beefed things up. We should be fine."

"Great," Richard said, then gave Donnie a smile that seemed easier, more relaxed, than any he'd given him before. "Your performers were very well-mannered."

"My exclusives are…carefully selected."

"Really. How so?" Richard started approaching the empty chair.

"I treat my models the way I wanted to be treated then. And I give all my auditions the same speech every time. The one nobody gave me when I started."

"Which is?" Richard asked.

"I tell them it never goes away. Ever. The days of it being on a few VHS tapes in the bad part of town are long over. The Internet changed all that. So if you're not comfortable being recognized for it anywhere in the world, if you're not comfortable with your *grandmother* finding out, do not, under any circumstances, do this.

"I tell 'em the pay isn't great. Per scene rates are lower than they've ever been, way lower than when I started. But if they get their social media and a fans platform going, they could start to see a return. I warn them, you don't just throw up an OnlyFans account and make a bunch of money. It's a content beast. You've got to feed it every damn day, and the guys who make bank are turning their bedrooms into mini studios. They're not shooting a bunch of shaky solo videos in the bathroom each morning."

"And what do most guys do when they hear this speech?" Richard asked, taking a seat.

"Some walk out. Which is good. And some of them move to the audition. It's a solo. Them on a bed, with either me or Brutus on camera. You can tell right away who's cut out for it and who isn't. If they can't perform, if they can't get comfortable, we call it quits and the tape gets trashed. And even if they can, I give them about a week to think about it before committing them to anything further. If they've got regrets after seven days, tape gets trashed then too. It's been a pretty good system so far."

Richard crossed his legs and smoothed out the already perfectly pressed front of his shirt. "Well, they seem to look up to you. They're also quite adorable. In their various Village People-esque ways."

"They're also off limits."

Richard raised one eyebrow. "I wasn't considering asking any of them out."

Donnie felt his cheeks get hot. "I meant for me."

"Oh. I see."

"What, you're surprised I can keep my hands off them?"

"I'm officially getting out of the making assumptions about porn business."

"Eddie, the guy who started this place, he was a good guy, but he wasn't perfect. He was mostly a voyeur, but he went to bed with a few of his models early on. A couple broke his heart. After a while, the performers turned into the enemy in his head. You know, like mean girls he was forced to work with every day. I do my best to stay on the other side of that line, help my guys find their next act when it's time for them to move on. Build a community that doesn't make them feel disposable."

It wasn't intentional, using the same word Richard had used with him during their first meeting. And if Richard noticed it, he was letting it slide by. Maybe it was part of his effort to listen and not judge.

"Your best, huh?" Richard finally asked.

"I made a few mistakes when I first took the reins, but never with a guy who had another shoot on the books. And never with an exclusive. The exclusives are my family. That's how I work."

It felt suddenly like he was pitching himself as boyfriend material. The only solution was more taco. From his chair, Richard studied the space around them. He was studying the individual standing sets. This filled Donnie with an instant, burning desire to ask him which one was his favorite. A seemingly innocuous question, but it would give him an instant peek into Richard's intimate fantasies. Did he want to be strapped down to the bondage mattress by a leather daddy? Seduced by way of a mutual JO session with his oversexed college roommate? Disciplined by his coach? Manhandled by his doctor? The more he thought about it, the answer seemed as dangerous as another kiss.

"You a subscriber?" *Well, shit,* Donnie thought once the words left him. How was that any different from the question he'd been too afraid to ask a second before? "I mean, the more recent stuff…the stuff we shoot here." Not the scenes with *me* in them, he might as well have said.

Richard gave him a sheepish smile. "I don't want to say something offensive again."

"Hey, I've got thick skin."

"Not always." But he said it warmly, comfortingly. Like someone who was getting to know him. And liking him.

"I'll toughen up. Fire away."

"I don't really have any memberships. I mostly do clip sites. And I usually turn the sound off."

"Not the other night." The words were out before he could stop them.

"*Usually.*"

"What's that about?"

"I'm imagining a different scene in my head and sort of writing my own dialogue for it. I mean, I don't want to offend you. I'm sure the basics work for most people, and that's where your memberships come from, but…"

"But you've got different tastes?"

Blushing, Richard uncrossed his legs and rolled his shoulders a few times. "I have an interest in seeing the bottom be the object of desire. Not just an endless parade of guys trying to hide the fact that they're gay while they worship tall, straight-acting white tops who won't kiss them on the mouth. I realize it's a very popular fantasy, but it's not mine."

"It's not mine either."

But Donnie couldn't help but hear the real disclosure hiding in Richard's opinions of porn. His fantasy was to be desired. Was worshiping a straight-acting guy who wouldn't kiss you on the mouth an uncomfortable reminder of his failed marriage? Another dangerous question, so in an effort to avoid it, he said the next thing that popped into his mind.

"I'll take that under advisement," Donnie said.

"I haven't offended you again, have I?"

"Not at all. I'm always looking for new scene ideas."

And lately all of them have starred you, he thought.

"Do you have a floorplan you can send me?" Richard asked quickly.

Donnie nodded.

"Great. That'll save me from having to measure the whole space."

"Lunch?" Donnie asked.

"You just ate."

"Yeah, but you didn't. You hungry?"

'Cause I'd really love to get us the hell out of here and around some other people. And further away from my palace of sex toys. But I don't want to see you go. Not yet.

"I ate before, but thank you. And I've got to get the van back."

Donnie set the remnants of his last taco down. "The *van?*"

Rolling his eyes, Richard nodded. "The hotel's knocking itself out to keep me with a set of wheels. There's a big conference this week, so they needed all the hire cars for airport runs. Today I had to use a maintenance van."

"I gotta ask, then. Where's *your* car?"

Richard sighed, shoulders sagging as if his spine had been drawn out of him. "It's at the house. In LA."

"Mark's getting it in the divorce?"

"No, he's under orders from a judge to give me the keys if I come to get them, but..."

"You don't want to be alone with him."

"Especially now that I found out he's been talking to my mother behind my back."

Donnie wiped his fingers with the paper napkins that had been in the bag with the tacos.

"Let's do it," he said before he could second-guess himself. "Let's go get your car."

"Are you serious?"

"I'll drive you up so you can drive back, and I'll get the keys from him so you don't even have to see his face."

"I can't ask you to do that."

"You didn't ask. It was my idea." Donnie grinned.

"That's a lot of driving. You have the time?"

"Wouldn't have suggested it if I didn't."

And it'll be time spent with you, he thought. *On the road, in motion, possibly around other people. Not here. Alone. Talking about sex and fantasy.*

He wasn't sure how to describe the look in Richard's eyes. Pain or relief or fear or a mix of all three. Had he not had a single conversation with his ex-husband since he'd filed for divorce? Was he afraid of losing his temper, or was he afraid of being drawn back into the man's orbit? Either way, Donnie was determined to protect him from both.

Unless Richard thought it was a terrible idea.

"That's an incredibly generous offer," he finally said.

"Meh, it's nothing. Running my mouth on long drives comes easy."

Slowly, Richard rose to his feet. "He works from home, but I might not be able to set it up on short notice. I'll have to call my lawyer, and my lawyer will have to call his."

Donnie stood. "Alright. Make the call and start back for the hotel. I'll meet you there. If it doesn't work out, shoot me a text and I'll turn around."

"You're sure about this?"

"Go," he said, "call your lawyer."

29

If the last-minute rescue plan for his car didn't come together before rush hour, Richard figured he'd ask Donnie to come to the hotel anyway so they could enjoy a meal together, maybe talk through some of his ideas about the wedding. Their breakfast hadn't been so bad. Lovely, actually. Their stroll along the cliffs hadn't been so bad either. Lovelier, actually. Especially Donnie's disclosure that he'd told Logan to stop beating around the bush about his hopes for his wedding. While it was true that their kiss—Richard's kiss, really, since he'd foolishly initiated it—still felt like a puddle of something sticky around their feet, his visit to Donnie's studio proved that they could step carefully.

For an hour, at least.

There was no denying it. Donnie was afraid to be alone with him. Or alone with him in the shadows of his sex-charged studio. Maybe Saturday's disaster had stolen some of his flirty fire, or maybe it was something Jonas had said to him Sunday morning. Or maybe he was having second thoughts about letting his smutty workplace get invaded by outsiders. Whatever the case, it was Richard's lapse in self-control, not Donnie's, that had caused so much trouble, and he was starting to feel fairly confident that he'd placed his dangerous desires back in the bottle.

Hell, he hadn't watched any of Donnie's old scenes in the three days since they'd last seen each other. Of course, he'd furiously relieved himself to the memory of their kiss on more than one occasion. But each time, as he'd laid there spent and alone, he'd heard his good friend's voice saying, *Donnie Bascombe is not the man to mend a broken heart with.* Perhaps this was a case of closing the barn door after the horse had gotten out. But it was the best he could do.

He was starting to suspect he wasn't the only one hearing Jonas's voice on the topic of their newfound proximity. The fact was, if there was one event that had made Donnie more subdued than he'd been since they'd first met, it was his run-in with Jonas somewhere in the hotel Sunday morning. What had the two men said to each other? He was suddenly curious.

The call from his lawyer came when he was still twenty minutes from Sapphire Cove. Mark would be home until seven that evening and had agreed to turn over the keys to Richard's Porsche any time before then. He'd apparently raised no objections to the fact that a third party would act as intermediary. But there were many steps yet to go, and of late, Mark had proved himself to be nothing if not full of surprises.

At the hotel, he sped up to his room, freshened up quickly, then headed down to the motor court where he found Donnie's Durango next to the valet stand, the driver's side window rolled down as Donnie chatted with a valet he was clearly friendly with. A few seconds later, they were leaving the hotel behind. He felt a sudden pressure on his hands and realized he was clasping them between his knees, something he always did when he was nervous. Fine. So he was nervous. But not nearly as much as he would have been if Donnie hadn't been sitting next to him, offering to do the hardest parts of what was to come.

"He knows you're the one getting the keys, but he still might give you some trouble. He's not a man who's used to being told what to do."

"I can handle him. Don't worry." They were approaching the onramp for a toll road that crowned the coastal hills rising behind Orange County's wealthiest beach communities. "So, where we going?"

"Lord. I didn't even give you the address. Sorry. Give me your phone."

Donnie gestured to the cupholder.

Richard swiped his way to Google Maps and plugged in the address of what had once been his home. Staring at it on a screen after having entered it like it was a strange destination made his vision narrow and his breaths grow shallow.

"So he's been talking to your mom?" Donnie asked, jerking him back to the present.

"My mother was always a fan of his. I'm worried she's still a fan of his." He stared out the window, lost in dark thoughts. "She wants us to work it out. And apparently Mark does too."

"Do you?"

"One trainer I could have forgiven. But when the emails started rolling in, that's when I knew it was over."

"Do you love him?"

"It's like something I can't remember anymore. You want to know the crazy thing? If he'd come to me and asked for an open relationship, I don't know if I would have said no. If we'd had agreements and ground rules."

"And what would your first ground rule have been?"

"Not our mutual friends."

Donnie smiled. He'd known the answer before he asked the question. "There you go."

Richard sighed. "He was so desperate to sleep with people we both knew that he had to go behind my back? I mean, that seems psychotic to me."

"Insecure guys can't live off one vote. They've gotta have a general election. But there was probably something he could only get from you, something special, that he knew he couldn't get from anyone else. That's why he didn't want to risk losing you by asking to open up."

"You're not saying I should give him another chance, are you?"

"Hell, no," Donnie barked, so loudly Richard jerked against his seatbelt. "I'll tie you to that seat if you try."

A delicious chill shot up Richard's spine. He turned his face to the window to hide the smile Donnie's words brought to his mouth, the fact that he was suddenly chewing his bottom lip.

"You're very wise about these things. Are you sure you were never married?" Richard asked.

"I've been a guest star in a lot of bedrooms, a lot of relationships. I know how guys work. Especially guys who sleep with other guys."

No mention of the guy who'd broken his heart fifteen years ago, the guy who reminded him of Richard. "How do I work, then?" Richard asked, studying Donnie's profile.

"Simple. You're either all in or all out. Nothing wrong with it."

"Not as exciting as guys like you and Mark."

"Woah, hold up. How did Mark and I end up in the same camp?"

"I'm not saying you're a liar or a cheater. I'm just saying, I mean… Come on. Are you a big monogamy guy?"

Donnie's face went still as he studied the road. "I don't know," he finally said, and with a confusion that sounded genuine. "Nobody's ever asked me to try. People don't come to me for that. They come to me for fun."

"And that's fun for *you*?"

"Sure." He sounded barely enthusiastic. "Or it was. I don't know." He was clearly struggling with his next words. Finally, he blurted out, "I fell asleep during a blow job the other night."

Richard burst out laughing.

"It's not funny. It means I'm getting old."

"And less impressed by the simple mechanics of meaningless sex."

"Maybe. I mean, the guy was…" Donnie's eyes met Richard's. "Nobody. He was nobody." But his eyes were searching Richard's face as if Richard were, indeed, somebody.

And dangerous as it was, that made Richard feel better than he'd felt in a while.

30

It wasn't Donnie's first visit to LA. He'd headed north plenty over the years, mostly to dance on West Hollywood bar tops for tips back when he was a performer. He'd also been the hired eye candy at some Malibu pool parties back then, and over the years he and Logan had done fun, touristy things in Santa Monica. But he'd never visited the hilly enclave in between—Pacific Palisades, a name he'd first heard on the soap operas his aunt used to watch when he was a little boy.

From the top of the sloping driveway that approached it, Richard's former home looked like several planes of concrete hovering above the steep hillside. But the spaces between were filled by spotless walls of glass and vast open rooms studded with spare, modern furniture, allowing for stunning views of mansion-filled canyons rolling toward a Pacific Ocean splashed with the orange light of dusk. Then Donnie pulled level with the hedge wall framing the front gate and the FOR SALE sign attached to it, and his view of the place was lost.

He drove past a garage door big enough to admit a tank, parking his Durango with its nose pointed up the private drive, angled in the direction of the quickest escape and with enough room on one side for him to pull Richard's car out of the garage.

Donnie put the car in park but kept the engine running, figuring it would make Richard more comfortable. His anxious passenger was staring straight forward, as if relieved not to have to look straight on at his old home, chest rising and falling with breaths he was working to control.

"It's rush hour, so I'd rather not hit the road right away," Richard finally said. "Maybe once I've got the car we can go eat or something."

"Sure," Donnie said. "I'll pull out, hand you the keys, then we can jet. Maybe park at the lookout we passed on the way up. Figure out our next move."

Which they sure as hell didn't want to do here, a stone's throw from his ex and whatever bullshit the jerk might try to pull to drag out this handoff.

Richard nodded and stared down at his knees. Donnie reached over and squeezed his shoulder gently, and when he looked up, the mixture of fear and gratitude in his eyes made Donnie's chest tighten. Reminded him of how he'd looked in those few dizzying seconds before their mouths had met on Saturday night.

Time to get moving.

The gate opened when Donnie was several paces from it, suddenly filled by the imposing shadow of a broad-shouldered, muscular figure who was taller than Donnie by a few inches. Once he stepped forward out of the shadows, Donnie saw the guy was startlingly handsome, with perfectly carved facial features tweaked here and there by a skilled plastic surgeon. He figured there was some human growth hormone in the mix too. The wavy salt and pepper hair looked natural, but on a guy with this much obvious cash there was no telling. He was exactly the type of husband Donnie would have expected a man like Richard to have. On paper, at least. And in his presence, Donnie suddenly felt like he was spoiling for a fight.

"I need to see him," Mark Scottman said without introducing himself.

"Not on the menu, sorry."

"That's not for you to say."

"Correct. It's for him to say, and he's said it. It's why I'm here. How 'bout we get those keys so you can get on with your night?"

For a few tense seconds, Mark didn't move, studying the parked Durango and Richard's shadow in the passenger seat. Then he jerked his head in the direction of the house. On the other side of the hedges lay a gurgling, manicured Zen garden and million-dollar views. Then they were inside, their footsteps echoing over stark white floors. The kitchen counter was devoid of personal effects save for a single Porsche key that at first was camouflaged by the black marble.

"So you're my replacement?" Mark crossed his arms over his broad chest and rested his back against the enormous fridge.

Donnie scooped the key off the counter and put it in his pocket.

"Not bad. He's not bad either. If you learn how to press the right buttons. He's got a real filthy side to him, even though he's spent the last few months acting like an injured saint."

"I'm his friend."

Mark gave him a seductive smile. "Oh. Well, then…"

Was this prick actually hitting on him? With the ex-husband he'd cucked sitting in the car outside? "Yeah, that's what he needs right now. Friends *you* aren't sleeping with." The twitch in Mark's brow and the sudden tightening of his crossed arms suggested he truly had been hitting on him. Without meaning to, Donnie had landed a double blow.

Mark turned and started down a hallway that led to a laundry room. Donnie followed. The more he saw of the house, the more he wondered how a man who created enchanted forests for a living could be happy here. Maybe he hadn't been. Maybe the house had always been Mark's domain. Maybe when you were this rich, this handsome, and this in shape, you got to boss a man like Richard around without really appreciating him—for four years, at least.

Two vehicles were parked in the spotless garage—a silver Lamborghini Urus that Donnie knew had a sticker price of around two hundred grand, and another one, presumably Richard's Porsche, that was shrouded in a dust cover. Mark made no move to take it off, so Donnie went to work. As the Porsche Macan underneath came into view, Donnie smiled when he saw it was ruby metallic. Leave it to Richard to add some color to this sterile place, he thought.

"I heard about you," Mark finally said as he stood by, refusing to help.

"From your buddy Evan?"

"He's in a lot of hot water because of what you said to Harry Mitchell. One of his big clients is threatening to leave him."

Once he had the cover in his arms, Donnie stepped back, checking the car for scratches and cracks, some of them possibly left by an angry ex, as he gathered it into a ball.

"I'm just saying, you might want to be careful. Evan's a powerful guy in this town."

Donnie gave the cheating enthusiast the same look he used to give tricks on the road who tried to get rough with him. "Thanks for the warning, but if he were that powerful, he wouldn't be in hot water 'cause of some loud mouth porn star." He closed the distance between them then pressed the dust cover to Mark's chest, staring into the man's eyes, waiting for him to raise his hands and take the damn thing. Donnie wasn't counting, but the wait felt close to five seconds at least.

"Oh, I'd give yourself more credit than that." He stuffed the wadded-up cover under one arm. "I think a guy like you is pretty admirable."

"Really?" Donnie asked, even as he told himself not to.

"Absolutely. I'm a capitalist. I admire people who try to shoot above their station."

"Yeah, well maybe I'll just try to shoot above yours. It'll be a lot less work." Donnie walked toward the Porsche's driver's side door and held up the key. "You might want to back up. I wouldn't want to run over your foot, *Mark.*"

Eyes blazing, Mark Scottman took a few careful steps back, then he pulled his phone out of one pocket and used an app to open the garage.

Throughout the simple, fast moves that followed, Donnie watched Mark like a hawk and did everything to make clear that what he was doing was precisely that. That if the guy so much as made any kind of move to engage Richard, he'd be out and between them in a split second. Maybe it worked. When Richard popped from the Durango and hurried to the Porsche, head down, Mark's mouth opened, but no sound came out. Donnie lingered as Richard backed up, found enough space to turn around before speeding up the driveway. And for a second, the sadness in Mark Scottman's eyes, the clear sign that he'd lost something he'd actually valued, almost made Donnie feel bad for the guy.

Almost.

Richard's Porsche was waiting for him at the lookout, which Donnie now saw was the entrance to a trail that snaked its way down a mansion-dotted canyon. "Thank you," he said once they were a few feet from each other. "I missed my car."

"So, harder or easier than you thought?"

"Easier. Because you were there."

Like so much of what they'd said to each other on the drive up, the words seemed to pulse with double meaning. If Richard sensed it, he was too relaxed by relief to feel self-conscious.

"What are you in the mood for?" Donnie asked.

"I don't know. There are a couple places up in Palisades Village that are pretty nice."

"Yeah, but do they have funnel cakes?"

Richard cocked his head to one side.

"Funnel cakes. You just did something hard. You deserve a reward. And trust me, there's no better reward than a funnel cake."

"I don't think I've ever had one."

"Oh, then we're definitely having one."

"For *dinner*?"

"You're a grown man. You ate lunch. You can have whatever you want for dinner. Especially since you deserve a reward."

Richard's smile melted Donnie's heart. "Well, okay, then. Where are we going to find these mysterious and fabled cakes of which you speak?"

"Only one place I can think of. The Santa Monica Pier."

"Oh." Richard was nodding, but Donnie could tell his resistance to the idea was fighting a battle with his desire to appear grateful. "I've never been to the Santa Monica Pier."

"It's a night for firsts, apparently. Follow me, Merriweather."

Donnie started for the car, fully expecting Richard to call out that he'd changed his mind. But he didn't do anything of the kind, and when he saw the Porsche fall into an almost perfect alignment with his Durango, he found himself smiling at the rearview mirror.

31

On any other evening, and with any other person, Richard might have turned up his nose at a visit to the Santa Monica Pier. Too many tourists, for one. Too chilly once the sun went down. But this was Donnie asking, the man who'd relieved him of another weight while desiring nothing in return except for his company. The happy throngs gathered around the amusement park rides weren't too overwhelming, their joy proving infectious as he and Donnie approached the sweet-smelling funnel cake booth. As the ocean horizon darkened, the iconic Ferris wheel blazed against the night sky, a reminder of movies and TV shows he'd seen about LA as a child. A reminder of a more hopeful time in his life.

Or maybe, having cut one more tie to a failed marriage, his hope was genuine. And unique to this moment.

Donnie ordered for the two of them, then waited for their number to be called. Richard snagged a metal table so bolted to the boards below it looked like a tsunami would have had trouble making off with it.

A short while later, Donnie arrived with a boyish, beaming smile, carrying two paper plates. Allegedly there was something called a funnel cake underneath both piles of powdered sugar and cherry topping. "Dig in."

"I still think we could have shared one," Richard said as he raised his plastic fork and knife.

"See if you still think that once you're done."

He took a bite. Bliss must have filled his expression because

Donnie smiled eagerly then went about attacking his own. "This is quite delicious."

"Toldja."

For a while they ate in contented silence, save for the occasional screams coming from the roller coaster zipping by overhead. "I don't know if I can thank you enough for this. Truly. I mean, all of it. The drive up here. Dealing with Mark."

"My pleasure. I mean, not pleasure. It doesn't give me pleasure to see you stressed out. But to see the stress go away…" He made an airplane motion with a bite of sugary cake before forking it into his mouth. "Can I ask you something, though?"

Richard nodded.

"What about the rest of your stuff?"

"He trucked most of the essentials over to my office in West Hollywood when I was overseas. He was punishing me for leaving the country, I think. What I needed I took to Sapphire Cove, and the rest is in storage in my warehouse. Anything else can wait until the house goes into escrow. That's the agreement, anyway."

"Call me crazy, but I don't think you care a lot about that house."

"I care about the money I'll get from the sale. But no, it was always his place, really. His style." Donnie nodded.

"Serial killer's lair from a 90's thriller?" Donnie asked. "I kinda felt like Ashley Judd was going to burst out of a back room asking me to save her life."

Richard sputtered with laughter, then, once he caught his breath, he asked, "Do I even want to know what he said to you?"

Donnie looked down at his cake. "Nothing important."

"Liar."

"Your old friend Evan's in some deep shit because of my big mouth."

"I'm devastated," Richard said quietly before taking another bite. "That's enough Mark for one day. Or perhaps ever. Let's talk about something else. *Your* relationship history, perhaps."

"Short convo. I don't really have one."

"What about the guy who broke your heart all those years ago?" Richard asked. *The one I remind you of,* he didn't add. Maybe because Donnie had flinched in response and was now attacking the remains of his funnel cake with renewed vigor. "Oh, come on. Don't be embarrassed. I've laid out my horrible marriage for you on a surgeon's table. It's only fair."

"It's weird that my most significant relationship was fifteen years ago."

"Well, surely, there's been somebody else since then."

Donnie shrugged and chewed. "I mean, there was one guy...a few years ago. I could sort of see it happening with him. He was a dentist, and we hung out for a few months. He wouldn't introduce me to any of his friends. We hooked up online and had crazy chemistry, so we started having meals after. My version of dating, I guess. Anyway, one night we ran into some friends of his at a restaurant and he wouldn't even introduce me to them. I didn't want to freak out about it but I asked him why. And he said they probably already knew who I was, so what was the point? That's when I realized what the problem was."

Donnie took a bite of funnel cake that was almost too big for his mouth.

"The porn," Richard finally said.

"There've been a couple like that, you know. Where you realize there's a cap on anything that might happen. So why bother?"

Why bother. It was, in some sense, a more heartbreaking thing to say about one's love life than *My husband cheated.* Between this comment and the one he'd made on the drive up about monogamy, Richard was starting to wonder if Donnie had turned himself into a hook-up guy solely to protect himself from rejection over his career.

"Maybe a relationship with someone in the industry would make sense," Richard said quickly, eyes on his cake. It felt like the right thing to say, the most *logical* thing to say, but it twisted his gut to say it.

"Even that gets tricky. I mean, most performers are only in it for a year, if that. So they play around because they're not thinking long term. With me, there could be consequences. This is my life. It's what I do." Donnie's eyes met his. "And I'm never changing that fact."

Even for you, the look in his eyes seemed to say. And no, Richard hadn't asked him the question directly, but maybe Donnie was the one who needed the answer. Maybe that's what he was looking for as he searched Richard's face.

"Wow," Richard finally said.

"What? You thought I might go into boat repair for the right guy?"

"No. I'm surprised by how much you don't want to talk about this guy from fifteen years ago. You took us pretty far afield there."

Donnie sighed and took another bite of cake. He only had a few left. "It's not a great story. He worked at the studio but he never did anything on camera. He was in charge of interviewing new models. You know, to make sure they weren't dangerous. He took me home after my first screen test. The sex was fire. So I basically lived with him for two years. I mean, he threw me out after I got too possessive, but all he did was move me down the street. I was still sleeping there almost every night. Then an old friend of his moved in and it turned into kind of a three-way thing. And then..." Donnie took too much time wiping his hands with a wadded-up paper napkin. "One day he vanished. Left us both these Buddhist goodbye notes that didn't really say anything about why he was going. Or where. Told us whatever he'd left behind was ours. That the lease had been paid in cash for six months. And that's when we found out we didn't even know his real name."

"That sounds hard."

"Or for the best. I was young. We were always fighting. He really wanted me to escort like him, and I was all about porn. He was also older. Not by much, but you know, enough for me to look up to him. He taught me how to do stuff. He and Ethan."

"Ethan was the third?"

Donnie nodded, making short work of the last few bites. "We didn't have the same chemistry. It became more of a friend thing with us. Honestly, most of the stuff I *really* needed to know about life I learned from Ethan. But Zach, he taught me stuff too."

"Like what?"

"You know, how to dress. How to talk smart. He took me to this black-tie fundraiser downtown once with all these rich old gays and gave me, like, this whole makeover first. I remember we sat at the kitchen table before we went and he taught me how to use a formal place setting." Donnie smiled wistfully. "Nobody had ever done anything like that for me before."

Richard told himself to stay quiet, that the combined swells of protectiveness and jealousy rising inside of him were childish and best ignored. But there was something he was hearing that Donnie wasn't. "How did he know the older men at the fundraiser?" he asked before he could stop himself.

"I don't know. I always figured one of them was a client. But if I ever asked him for details about his clients, he took my head off so..."

"Did he take you to a lot of fancy events?"

"No."

"He was trying to pimp you out, Donnie." He couldn't tell if Donnie's sudden stare meant he was wounded or surprised. Streetwise as he was, surely he'd suspected this before now. But love is blind, and most people develop vision problems as they age. "How old was he?"

"Closing in on thirty," Donnie said quickly. He didn't seem offended; he seemed intrigued by the amount of passion in Richard's voice.

"I don't imagine that's an ideal age for an escort. It's probably a fine time to find a replacement. Especially if he's going to earn a commission. Your ex sounds like a dishonest snake. He tricked you into believing he was taking care of you when he was really trying to manipulate you into being his income stream." Donnie's eyebrows arched, and Richard heard how angry he sounded. "Sorry. Given recent events, I'm a bit sensitive when it comes to duplicitous men."

"I appreciate you being so protective of me," Donnie said softly.

And to Richard, it felt like high praise. Maybe the highest the guy could give him in this awkward moment. Richard smiled and ate the last of his cake. The brisk and frigid ocean winds threatened to upend their now empty paper plates. With the arrival of full-on darkness, the temperature had dropped. Richard shivered.

Donnie said, "Time to head out?"

Richard nodded. Because it was a weeknight, they'd scored parking spaces in the lot right next to the pier. The shadows were deep enough that they could give each other a tender goodbye hug without worrying about gay bashers. When he stepped into Donnie's arms, Donnie's warmth surged through him and for what felt like a minute, Richard couldn't move.

"Drive safe, Merriweather."

Head bowed to avoid another reckless kiss, Richard took a step back.

"Thanks for getting my car back, Bascombe."

When he caught himself smiling at Donnie like a lovesick teen, he hurried toward the car in question.

32

After finishing up some deferred maintenance on his boat, Donnie spent Thursday afternoon shooting the studio's first ever rugby-themed scene, a bold choice since most Parker Hunter subscribers were American and didn't know the first thing about rugby aside from the fact that its players were huge, hot, and often bleeding from the face. But one of Matty's escorting clients had recently flown him to London where he'd watched a game on television for the first time, an experience he'd described as "like losing my virginity all over again."

As soon as he'd closed the studio down for the day, Donnie headed for the parking lot.

"Hey, buddy. You got a minute?" Ethan startled him so badly the keys to his Durango hit the asphalt with a loud clatter. When he looked up, his old friend was a few feet away, blue BMW glinting in the light of the afternoon sun.

"You okay?" Donnie asked.

"I've got some news. It's not terrible. But it's not great either."

"Roman?"

"No, Roman's fine. Hop in."

He gestured to his BMW, and that's when Donnie saw there was someone sitting in the back seat.

Jonas Jacobs. Which meant whatever this news was, it was serious. The three of them had only met in secret once before, and the stakes in that moment had been incredibly high. For Ethan.

"What's going on?" Donnie said once he'd slid into the front passenger seat.

"I'm going to head someplace quiet then we can all talk there," Ethan said.

Baffled, Donnie turned around and looked to Jonas, who placed a finger against his closed lips then gestured all around him. *Bugged?* Was he saying Ethan's car might be bugged? If that was the case, why the hell were they all riding in it?

"How's wedding prep?" Jonas asked with a polite tone he'd never used with Donnie before once in his life.

"Great." What else was he supposed to say given someone he didn't like very much had implied that Ethan's car might be full of surveillance equipment. Was he allowed to grimace? Had someone put hidden cameras in the car too? Had he fallen down somewhere and hit his head? What the hell was going on?

They rode in silence.

It had always been a point of pride for him that his smut palace stood right down the road from big box stores, red-tile roofed apartment buildings, and Marine Corps Air Station Miramar. As if porn—even the gay kind—was as woven through the fabric of everyday America as 99 Cent Stores, Starbucks, and the *Top Gun* movies. But a little way's west of his studio lay rugged, rolling hills slowly being taken over by cookie-cutter subdivisions. Ethan was driving into them. A few minutes later, they pulled into a mostly empty parking lot for the Tierrasanta Recreation Center, a manicured, open park space serving the surrounding neighborhood. The eucalyptus branches were shifting in the warm, inland winds, causing dusk's orange sunlight to shimmer. The tennis courts were mostly abandoned, save for one game. The community pool looked closed.

They made their way to some picnic benches. Jonas set a file folder on the scored, wooden table between them.

"What did the man you knew as Zach Loudon tell you about his past?" Jonas asked.

"Zach?" Donnie asked breathlessly. "*You* want to talk about Zach?"

And he hadn't wanted to talk about him in Ethan's car. Donnie's gut went cold.

"Nothing much and nothing we could verify," Ethan answered. "There was a story about a ballet injury being the reason he started escorting."

Jonas shook his head as if he thought it was bullshit, then he opened the folder carefully and began spreading its contents out on the table—scans of old documents, some of them handwritten.

When Donnie glimpsed what had to be a driver's license for a sixteen-year-old version of Zach followed by pages of old yearbook photos on which Zach's younger image was circled, his heart skipped several beats. He would have killed for documents like these fifteen years ago. Now he couldn't bring himself to touch them. His heart was racing, his thoughts struggling to keep pace. *Now?* Why now?

"His real name is Greg Raleigh. His father was an evangelical minister in St. Louis. Friends and neighbors say he was no longer seen with the family or living in the house around the time he turned seventeen. He never showed up for senior year of high school but nobody reported him missing. The mother told people he'd had an affair with one of his male teachers and she'd asked him to leave."

"An *affair?*" Ethan said. "He was a high school student. Most people would call that abuse. What happened to the teacher?"

"Nothing was filed, apparently. At any rate, the parents are both deceased now. The rumor was he ran off to New York with an older man he met at a hotel bar in downtown St. Louis. New York is where he pops up working as an escort about two years later."

"Pops up for who?" Donnie asked. "What is this? What are you doing, Jonas?"

Jonas looked him dead in the eye. "I initiated a background check on you."

"Why?" Donnie asked. "Everything about me's on Google if you turn off Safe Search."

"Not Bo Bonin. You."

"Threatening to cut my balls off wasn't enough? Fucking hell, Jonas. Really?"

Ethan's hand was on his thigh. "Okay, okay Donnie. Let's just see what he has to say." To Jonas, Ethan added, "I warned you this would be a sensitive subject."

Jonas looked Donnie in the eye. "Rest assured, my search turned up nothing on you that concerned me. But it turned up a goddamn novel about the artist formerly known as Zach Loudon. It's all recent, it's all bad, and it could be headed this way. So please, listen to me now and be mad at me later if you have to be."

Donnie managed a deep breath, then a nod.

"After he abandoned you two," Jonas began, "the man you knew as Zach became the kept boy of one of the leading organized crime figures in Eastern Europe. This individual, Victor Morozov, had a vacation home in La Jolla. He sold it right around the time your old friend flew the coop. He had some business concerns in town, attempts to organize in some of the immigrant communities. They didn't work due to some lower-level busts, so he pulled up stakes and left, and he wanted your friend to come with him. But let me be clear. When it comes to Morozov, we're not talking about someone who shook down drug store owners for cash. This was a very bad guy, believed responsible for multiple, fatal hits on his rivals. And he didn't care about collateral damage."

Donnie remembered how Zach had exploded that night when he asked him even the smallest details of his client meetings. This tracked. Hard.

Ethan said, "You're talking about him in the past tense."

"He died last year. Natural causes, presumably. A stroke. According to my sources, Mr. Raleigh expected to be remembered in the will. He wasn't. When the family showed up to take over the palazzo in Cyprus where he'd been living, he had no legal recourse. But he was smart enough to see it coming, apparently, because he helped himself to some party favors on the way out. The compensation he felt he was owed, no doubt."

"What sort of party favors?" Donnie asked.

"Art," Jonas answered. "Specifically, several statues of Buddha from the Yongle period of the Ming Dynasty. Morozov was a collector."

"So the murderer and the con artist were both into Zen."

"Hardly. They're incredibly valuable. Their design is impeccable, and they come from a period of native Chinese rule in between the Mongols and the Manchu. Today, Chinese collectors are very eager to bring them home for obvious reasons."

"So our old friend is planning to sell them on the black market?" Ethan asked. "Is that his retirement plan?"

"Possibly," Jonas answered, "but if it is, the plan's already gone south. He managed to sell one to another unsavory character, a more traditional mafioso, if you will. Stefano Niro. This guy works in the drug trade in Naples, Italy. Some of the organized crime elements there invest in fine art, both for the purposes of resale, or they use it to negotiate a reduced sentence if they get caught for something worse.

Niro paid five million for the statue. Cash. No middleman. My sources think your old friend was trying to buy some time and buy his way out of Europe and away from the Morozovs, and that he thinks his collection's got more valuable pieces in it he can sell down the road. There's just one problem."

Ethan sighed. "It's a fake."

Nodding, Jonas continued. "They're *all* fake. Morozov's heirs figured it out when they did an appraisal of the estate. The man was just buying junk to keep his kept boy happy."

"So, our old friend, whatever he's called now, has pissed off *two* organized crime families in different parts of the world," Ethan said.

"Sort of. The Morozovs have no interest in recovering a bunch of fake statues, so they simply alerted Mr. Niro to their suspicions. But my sources say Niro had the statue appraised and now he's confident he was defrauded. He's actively pursuing repayment, which means his minions are tracking your old friend comprehensively and aggressively. All the way to Mexico."

"*Mexico*," Donnie said, as if he couldn't believe it. Zach, Greg, whoever the hell he really was, the man he'd imagined rotting away in a dozen different shallow graves or living high on the hog with some classy master of the universe, was just over the border in Mexico. In hiding. After crisscrossing the world on a trail of lies. Donnie shook his head to stop it from swimming. It barely helped.

"So when he emailed me a few weeks ago," Ethan said, "he thought I'd write him a check for five million to pay back a Neapolitan mobster?"

"Maybe. Or maybe it's about raising living expenses."

"He's got five million cash," Donnie blurted out. "Where the fuck is he living? The Four Seasons?"

"My sources know he flew from Rome to Mexico City about six months ago. He's dropped off the radar since."

Ethan asked, "Is there anything in that file to suggest that the man we knew as Zach Loudon would be any good at outwitting international criminals?"

Jonas swallowed. "Well, just the fact that he shacked up with one for about fifteen years. And it's possible he was a witness or an accessory to crimes that include human trafficking, international drug smuggling, and gun running. Those were all Morozov staples. Needless to say, my old friends will be very eager to talk to him if he attempts to enter the U.S."

A silence fell. Donnie felt an unasked question itching at the back of his throat. "What if Zach doesn't pay this Niro guy?"

"He'll eventually end up in a grave of Mr. Niro's choosing. Five million wouldn't have meant much to his old sugar daddy. Victor Morozov went everywhere in a private plane. But it's a fortune to a lower-level guy like Niro. Not to mention the fact he's been humiliated in front of a crime family that dwarfs his."

Donnie finally broke the tense silence. "Fifteen years ago, how hard would it have been for Zach to find out his new sugar daddy was a killer?"

Jonas shook his head. "A couple Internet searches for his name would have done the trick."

Donnie stood, turned his back on them and walked a few paces from the table. It felt like the horrible story Jonas had told them was a raging campfire, and he needed to turn his back on it before his cheeks got scorched.

Finally, Jonas said, "I am strongly encouraging you all to have no contact with him whatsoever. And if he approaches you in person, call me immediately or notify the authorities. This is a very wanted man."

Donnie turned to Ethan. "It was all about that shit on his bathroom wall, remember? Designer clothes, ballrooms. Fine silver. Watches. I mean, you and I, we did what we did to survive, to build a life we wanted. But Zach, Greg, whatever the hell his name was, he turned his ass up for a psychopath so he could fly private. I got nothing for him. *Nothing.* Everything he got from me he took fifteen years ago. That's it. That's all he gets. End of story."

Jonas began sliding the file's contents back into the folder.

"Maybe give us a minute, Jonas," Ethan said.

Standing, Jonas nodded, then started back in the direction of the car.

"He's checking my car for bugs," Ethan said. "Again. He thinks since...*Greg* emailed me, I might be under surveillance. That's why he didn't want to talk until we got here."

Donnie nodded. It was all he had the energy for.

"You alright?"

"Did you know about any of this? I mean before Jonas's file."

"No."

Donnie felt a pressure against his back.

Ethan was standing next to him, supporting him, comforting him the way he had all those years ago. "Maybe this is what you need to finally let him go for good."

"I've already let him go," Donnie finally managed. "But this shit makes my blood boil. How many flyers did I put all over Hillcrest? How many times did I tell you it was a serial killer and the notes were fake? And meanwhile he was jetting off to the Mediterranean in a Gulfstream with some psycho mafioso. I mean, Jonas says this Morozov guy didn't care about collateral damage. What's that mean? Wives, kids, car bombs? *Fuck.*"

"You were young and you were in love."

"How could I love him? I didn't know him. I only knew his body."

"Yeah, well, that's what a lot of people fall in love with when they're young. And if he emails you too?"

"I'll say I've got nothing for you and I wish you the best and please don't write me again. *Greggers.*"

"Or don't say anything at all and forward it to Jonas." Ethan slid his arms around him for a full-sized hug. "When Jonas called me I tried to think of ways to make this easier. But I couldn't."

"This was easier. You, here. I didn't have to remember all of it alone. And honestly, I might have punched Jonas if you hadn't come." For a while, they hugged. "You were right. He didn't have an exit plan."

"And he picked the worst one possible," Ethan said.

A few seconds later they started back for the car.

As hard as it had been, his steps felt lighter. Maybe Ethan was right. Maybe this was what he'd needed to finally let the man he'd once known as Zach Loudon go.

Ethan slid behind the wheel, but Jonas was standing next to the passenger door in back. At first, Donnie thought the man was offering him a handshake, then he looked down and saw he was extending the file toward him. Heart thundering, Donnie stared down at it. A thick invitation to return to the obsession that had almost taken over his life years before.

He shook his head. If he refused it aloud, he was afraid his voice would shake.

"You sure?" Jonas asked.

Donnie looked into his eyes. "What did you think you'd find?"

"I had no idea. That's why I did it." Jonas seemed less confident—

less *smug*—than usual. Sliding the folder under one arm, he sucked in a deep, strained breath.

"You were that afraid Richard and I would hook up?"

"I'm protective of my friends. Especially the ones who've been hurt." Jonas looked into Donnie's eyes again. "I wasn't prepared for how badly *you'd* been hurt."

It was the first time Donnie had seen the man look vulnerable.

"I know what it's like to be abandoned and not know why."

"Looks like we both have a complicated past," Donnie said quietly.

"We do," Jonas said.

Donnie watched him get into the back seat, wondering if his last few statements were the biggest admission Jonas had ever made to anyone about the years before he came to Sapphire Cove. Wondering if the dynamic between them had been shifted by this meeting forever.

33

When his cell phone chimed with a text alert at four o'clock on Saturday afternoon, Richard cried out as if he'd been startled in the dark. But the suite's drapes were open along with both sliding deck doors, the living room flooded with light.

The message was from Donnie.

> Meet me in the lobby at 7 PM. I've got a surprise for you.

> How should I dress for this surprise?

> The same way you always do. Like a bougie maître d'.

> That's a big word for a porn star.

> It's actually two words, Fancy Pants.

> I was talking about bougie. What should I wear?

Fancy Pants is cool, right? I know feather's out.

I'm going to ask this question one more time...

Dress like you always do. You always look like a million bucks.

You're too kind to me.

It had felt like a stock response as he'd typed it, but now that it was on screen, the truth of it was harder to ignore. For a week now, Donnie Bascombe had been exceedingly kind and generous. Whatever debt might have existed after their awkward meeting had been more than repaid, Richard was sure. If anything, the ledger had shifted in the other direction after Harry's party. And yet Donnie would be on the way there in a few hours with a surprise in tow.

Last Saturday had left him feeling uncomfortable and nervous in Donnie's presence, but Wednesday had left him with an altogether different feeling—safe. Better yet, now he wouldn't be spending Saturday night alone in his room, pretending he was recovering from a stressful work week when really he was avoiding unstructured, non-work life and all the uncomfortable feelings it might draw to the surface.

He set the phone aside, returning his attention to his laptop. One end of the dining table was surrounded by rolling corkboards. Connor had sent them up as compensation for the fact that Richard's office still wasn't ready. They were covered with images of Sapphire Cove's shoreline, a growing concept board inspired by the tour Donnie had given him on Sunday. He was preparing three different pitch decks for possible wedding themes, dreading the thought that Logan might shoot all of them down. Maybe Donnie's surprise was that he'd finally convinced his best friend to crack.

At seven on the dot, he was crossing the crowded lobby. Donnie wasn't wearing his designer suit but he was wearing a tie and dress shirt under his leather motocross jacket. And his jeans looked like the nicest pair he owned. No holes, no bleach stains, pronounced stitching.

"Fancy meeting you here," he said when Richard was a few paces away.

"It helps if you tell me where to meet you."

"So what do you say?" Donnie jerked one thumb in the direction of the men's room where they'd first met. "Looks pretty quiet."

"As you well know, I prefer surprises that don't involve toilet paper."

"Let's go."

One hand gently on his upper back, Donnie steered him in the direction of the conference center. Richard tried to remember the events schedule for the weekend, wondering if they were about to crash some poor girl's bat mitzvah.

They stopped short, and it took Richard a second to realize that they were standing outside the doorway to Richard's supposedly unfinished office. His logo was now hanging on it. Like a proud valet, Donnie opened the door. The plastic sheeting and drop cloths that had greeted him on his last visit were gone. From gleaming, newly installed wall sconces, warm, amber light filled the space, falling across the knots of well-dressed people smiling back at him, many of them strangers. At the sight of him, everyone started to applaud. He spotted Jonas, Connor, and Logan standing next to the wine bar.

Donnie drew him into the center of the room. His eyes roamed the space. The crown molding had been installed. The antique furniture he'd been storing at the LA office had been put in place exactly according to the layout he'd drawn up a few weeks ago. Gabe must have worked in secret to bring the pieces down. The second window they'd added, which had been covered over in butcher paper on his last visit, doubled the view of the lawn outside and the wall of Draco palms standing between the lawn's edge and the first row of villas. Before the renovation, this space had included Jonas's old office, a small corridor that had led to a largely unused employee bathroom, and a windowless cubbyhole of a room that had served various purposes over the years, including the temporary office for Connor's best friend, Naser Kazemi, the resort's chief accountant. Now they'd all been incorporated into a space expansive enough for this impromptu reception.

Slowly, he turned in place. In a gilt frame, his logo covered the wall behind his desk. On the opposite wall, above a sofa and matching swivel barrel chairs designed for receiving potential clients, was a gorgeous framed aerial shot of the entire property. He'd opened offices all over the world, but he hadn't been this affected by the sight of a finished one since his very first. Maybe because this one was a new start in more ways than one. And everyone in it had applauded his entrance.

"I thought it'd be creepy to have a room full of strangers shout surprise at you, so we went with applause instead," Donnie said.

"A wise and most appropriate choice," Connor said, stepping forward and taking Richard's hand. "Okay, I admit, it is a *bit* strategic, debuting your finished office when it's full of people. This way you'll be less likely to fuss at me if something's off. But it looks like you're pleased."

There was a lump in Richard's throat, and he was suddenly worried he might cry. "It's wonderful. And the art's a lovely touch."

"Excellent." Connor beamed. "Welcome to the family, Richard."

"And better friends," Donnie said quietly.

That both men said these things casually only made the words pulse through him with greater force. Before he knew it, Connor wobbled and bent, and Donnie had laid a hand on Richard's right shoulder to hold him in place.

"Napkin," he heard Connor say quietly.

And that confirmed it. Richard was crying. Richard, who'd never shed a tear at the office or a work event, who'd always vowed never to be as emotional or unstable as the event planners who'd given him his start, was bringing the napkin Connor had handed him to his mouth. It was like some knot of hot, fiery tension he'd been holding in his gut for months now had dissolved in an instant, allowing a wave of cooling relief to sweep through him.

"What did you do?" he heard Jonas ask close to him.

"Told him you were in charge of the snacks," Donnie answered.

"We call them hors d'oeuvres," Jonas said.

"We did until the snacks you ordered showed up. Cool Ranch Doritos. Really, Jonas? You had everyone convinced you were classy."

Suddenly, everyone around them was laughing. "This is truly a lovely surprise," Richard finally managed. "I'm sorry, but it's just… This is lovely."

He turned to Donnie, whose smile had a boyish eagerness to it. Before he could think twice, he bent forward and gave Donnie a kiss on the cheek. As he withdrew, he watched his eager smile turn almost bashful. Felt the sudden jolt of silence that went through both Connor and Jonas at the sight of this brief flash of intimacy.

Then—to cut the awkwardness, no doubt—Jonas took him by the hand. "We've got some senior staff here you haven't met yet. And honestly, I think the dewy-eyed look will make a nice impression given how starstruck they already are." And they were off into the thicket of guests. Rounds of introductions and handshakes followed as he worked to put names to faces in his head when all he wanted to do was track Donnie's movements around the room.

Eventually, he found himself standing before a familiar face, Naser Kazemi, Connor's best friend and the hotel's chief accountant. About Connor's height, with ink-black, 1950s matinee idol hair and enormously expressive brown eyes. But it was his first time meeting the man's Nordic-looking fiancé, Mason, one of the few guests in the room nursing a soft drink. Standing directly behind him, he towered over Naser as he rested one hand protectively on his fiance's shoulder. Which made sense given their history. Richard had glimpsed the story on the news at the time, and Jonas had filled in the details after Richard met Naser for the first time. Mason had almost lost his life defending his true love from an old high school bully. Given the way they stood now, it looked like any man who wanted to get between them would have to bring an army.

"I guess I should be jealous of you given my old office now makes up about a quarter of your new one. But I'm sure anyone who has to work with Donnie day in and day out needs a lot of space to scream in. Has he stopped flirting with you yet?"

Mason cleared his throat and placed his hands firmly on Naser's shoulders. "So Donnie's a flirt, huh? You know this from experience?"

"Before you, babe," Naser answered.

"We met in high school. There is no one before me."

Naser reached up and patted the side of Mason's jaw. "There was a pretty long gap period, if I remember correctly."

Mason gave Richard a sheepish grin. "Can't argue with that."

"Seriously, though," Naser said. "We can put a shock collar on Donnie if he's giving you too much trouble."

"He's actually been wonderful."

A silence fell. Naser seemed genuinely stumped. "*Wonderful?*"

"Well, he's very committed to this wedding and..." Describing their Wednesday evening excursion suddenly felt too intimate, like sharing details of a bedtime tussle. A ridiculous comparison when it came to Donnie, but still. Could he share in a general way? "I'm going through a divorce. He helped me deal with some of the logistics so that I can focus more on work. He's been a great help. Truly. Across the board."

"Wow," Naser finally said. "That doesn't sound like his usual…routine. You seem to be a good influence on him."

"He's a wonderful resource. He gave me a tour of the night Connor and Logan met here at the hotel. I'm working up a design scheme inspired by it."

"Fun. What did you think of the sea caves?"

Richard's puzzled look earned a furrowed brow from Naser.

"That's where they had their first kiss."

"I thought they met outside the Dolphin Ballroom."

"They did, but then Logan suggested they go down to the sea caves right there on the beach. They're locked after dark, but he had a key. I can't believe Donnie left that part out. Sexy times are totally his vibe."

Why *had* he left it out, Richard wondered. They'd been standing right there. They could have kicked their shoes off and gone down to take a peek. A cave meant darkness and privacy. Secrecy. Had Donnie been afraid to be alone with him while surrounded by those things, afraid Richard would lose control again? Or had Donnie been the one afraid of losing control?

When he looked across the room, his eyes met Donnie's. He was staring back at him while listening to whatever Logan was saying. He even lifted his glass.

He'd thought, perhaps, that Donnie had truly managed to convert his initial attraction to friendship, or at least some form of camaraderie. How else to explain the fact that someone as sexually prolific as him had managed to stay on the sofa the entire night he'd spent in Richard's room? He'd thought that the more he revealed about himself, the less sexy Donnie would find him. And not because his life was currently a mess. Because Donnie seemed like the type of guy who had trouble putting people ahead of sex. Or maybe that's just what Richard had been telling himself to make the situation less awkward.

But it was Donnie who'd confessed just the other day that his version of dating consisted of post-sex meals with Grindr hookups, and only if the sex was good. Not exactly an accurate description of the time they'd spent together this week.

While Donnie Bascombe's motives suddenly seemed shrouded in mystery, Richard was fairly confident about his own. He was trying his best to get his bearings back after the worst professional mistake of his career, plan the best wedding for Connor and Logan that he could, all while stuffing down his reckless fantasies about Donnie before they got him into more trouble. Because that's what grown-ups did.

But what was *Donnie* doing? Were his acts of generosity and kindness solely about the wedding? Was he playing the long game, hoping to eventually turn Richard into a notch on his belt buckle? If that was the case, why not set Richard—who'd already kissed him once—up for failure by escorting him down to a shadowy, semi-secret grotto a day after he'd already planted one on him?

The question consumed him suddenly.

But Naser's invite to have dinner with him and Mason at their home sometime soon snapped him back to the present, and suddenly the two of them were trading numbers.

As Richard excused himself, he thought of the perfect way to gain some insight into Donnie's motives. But as soon as he took his first steps toward implementing the plan, an ample-framed woman with a dramatic tumble of thick salt-and-pepper locks curved an arm around his lower back. Her perfume smelled both enchanting and expensive, and her outfit was an artfully casual patchwork combo of expensive designer labels and thrift store pieces. She also had Connor's prim little nose and mouth, which meant she must have been the hotel's fabled matriarch, the wife of one of the men who'd founded the place. According to Jonas, she spent most of her time traveling the world, spending money on philanthropic projects that spanned the globe. Her relationship to the hotel didn't extend much beyond her love for her son, as—also according to Jonas—she had complicated feelings about what the hotel had asked of her family over the years.

"It's like this, Mr. Merriweather," Janice Harcourt began. "I realize the etiquette for the mother of one of the grooms in a gay wedding might not be as established as some of our other more widely recognized wedding traditions. So I've decided to write a script for us both. You know. Just to make it easier." Her smile was big and genuine.

"I'm all ears, Mrs. Harcourt."

"Please. Call me Janice. Here it is. You"—she pointed to his chest with one manicured index finger—"are obligated to attend a total of three lunches with me between now and the wedding. Only the two of us, mind you. No Connor, no Logan. During those lunches, you will sit quietly and pretend to listen to everything that I say. You might even indulge me by taking a few notes. This will, in turn, make me feel far more included than my son has ever made me feel in this. But here's the catch."

She brought her nose within an inch of his, peering at him from behind her librarian-style glasses. "When it comes to me you have one job," she whispered. "If my darling, adorable, talented son so much as considers making me wear anything orange, yellow, or puke green, you are to inform me immediately so that I may act with the fire of a thousand suns over desert sand. I've restrained myself admirably when it comes to this wedding. But even a good mother has her limits. And lest you leap to the defense of my son's taste, I speak from experience when I say he has a tendency to sublimate his use of color to an overall design narrative that cares little for how the participants involved must dress."

Richard adored this woman. And he was instantly, wildly jealous that this was the mother Connor had grown up with. It was also clear she had no idea how vague and conflicted her son and his fiancé had been about their wedding plans so far. Maybe that's why they'd kept her out of it. Not to conceal their plans, but to conceal their absence of them.

"You have my word, Janice. On one condition."

She reared back slightly, stirring her drink with too much vigor. "I'm listening."

"It'll have to be six lunches at least. You're far too charming for just three."

Blushing, Janice Harcourt bowed her head and slapped him lightly in the center of the chest. "You're a charmer yourself. But trust me. The minute I hear the word orange, I'll be terrible company, I assure you." She kissed him on the cheek. "Oh, and lace," she added quickly. "Nothing with lace. I had to stand as a bridesmaid in a Southern friend's wedding when I was a young woman. I almost clubbed her to death with the parasol when she came down the aisle."

Richard dragged a finger across his throat in agreement. "No lace," he whispered.

"Back to your fans," she ordered him with a wave of her hand.

He found Donnie standing at the bar. "How's the man of the hour doing?" Donnie asked.

"He's quite impressed with his surprise."

"Drink?" Donnie asked.

"Chardonnay sounds perfect."

The bartender handed him a glass. He clinked it with Donnie's freshly poured cocktail. "So this was all your idea?"

Before Donnie could answer, Jonas was at Richard's shoulder. "Not to turn your reception into a networking event, but we have some vendors here who are eager to meet you." He dropped his voice to a conspiratorial whisper. "And it's possible they may have upped their commitment to the hotel based on your new presence here. But let them share that with you if they feel like it."

As Jonas guided him away, Richard looked back over one shoulder at Donnie and said, "Don't leave before I talk to you."

"Wouldn't dream of it." Donnie toasted him as he departed.

34

Donnie figured Richard had at least another half hour of introductions to go, so he asked Logan for some face time on the lawn outside the conference center. The guests were still in view through the newly updated windows, but the party sounds were muffled, allowing them to hear the whisper of ocean breezes moving through the palm fronds and the occasional peal of laughter from a guest room balcony overhead.

With the same intensity he'd probably given to flight paths and mission plans back when he was in the Marines, Logan studied the photograph of Mark Scottman Donnie had texted him a few seconds earlier. It was a society page shot he'd found on the Internet from some Santa Barbara lifestyle magazine. In it, Richard's ex wore a powder-blue blazer and white dress shirt, precisely unbuttoned to reveal a glimpse of his smooth, sculpted chest. "You think the guy's dangerous?" Logan asked.

"I don't know. Maybe just a nuisance, but we should play it safe. He's not used to hearing the word *no*, and there's gonna be more of it in his future. He wants Richard back, and Richard's been shutting him down pretty hard."

Logan looked up from the phone, one eyebrow arched. "You didn't happen to provoke him during this meeting, did you?"

"It wasn't a *meeting*. We were getting Richard's car back and he had it. I made sure it went quick."

"I'll have everyone keep an eye out. I'll post his picture in back."

"Not where Richard might see, please. I don't want him to know I'm being this protective."

Logan raised an eyebrow. "You don't?"

His tone was full of implications and a reminder that their conversation from last Sunday felt unfinished. He'd been all about Donnie hooking up with Richard when he assumed it would be casual. Now that he knew Donnie had feelings for the guy, where did he stand? Donnie didn't want to know, so he deflected. "You talk to your fiancé about your wedding yet?"

Logan looked to the grass at their feet. "I'm working up to it." When he saw Donnie's look, he added, "What? I'm not a wedding person. I gotta find the right words."

"*What. I. Want. Is. This,*" Donnie enunciated, slowly and carefully. "It's not that hard."

Donnie's phone chimed. With a jolt, he realized it was still in Logan's hand, and he was reading the message on screen. "It's *Riiiiiichard,*" Logan said with a leering grin.

Donnie yanked the phone out of his hand. Thankfully, he'd set his alerts not to reveal the contents of his texts, only the names of the senders.

> Meet me at the balustrade in fifteen mins.

The balustrade. Far from the party and most of the hotel's other public spaces.

The same spot they'd visited on Sunday.

Maybe he'd had a bolt of inspiration about the wedding.

"Never seen anyone look at you the way he looked at you in there," Logan said.

He was desperate for specifics, but asking for them would make him feel like a thirsty teen. Instead, he screwed on his best cocky grin. "Yeah, well, I can handle it. I've been looked at a lot in my life."

"*Bo Bonin* has been looked at a lot in his life. That guy in there was looking at Donnie."

"Boys!" Connor's voice came from behind them. He was approaching across the grass. And he was alone. He patted Donnie on the back. "Well, I'd say that was a roaring success, and possibly the best mood I've ever seen Richard in, so you are definitely to be commended, Donnie. It was a wonderful idea."

Logan curved an arm around Connor's waist, pulling him into a half embrace. "Yes, Donnie seems very committed to making our wedding planner happy."

As he rested his head against his fiancé's chest, the exhaustion of Connor's day seemed to catch up with him. "Well, he's more than our wedding planner, babe." It was a casual, offhand remark, but it lanced through Donnie like a hot sword.

"Let's head home." Logan gave his fiancé a little shake.

Connor nodded, then gave Donnie a kiss on the cheek before starting for the exit door through which he'd just come.

A minute or two later, he reached the balustrade and its stunning view. There was no sign of Richard, just a big starry sky and stronger ocean winds mingling the sounds of surf with the jazz combo playing over on the pool deck.

After a while, footsteps crunched the grass behind him. He was hit by a waft of Richard's cologne.

He expected him to launch into some detailed idea about the wedding. Instead, he took up a spot about a foot from where Donnie stood, staring out at the moon-rippling ocean. In the silence that followed, Donnie's heart started to race. Richard, rarely at a loss for words, seemed to be considering his next ones deeply. And that was a sign something unexpected was about to happen, Donnie was sure.

"Well," he finally said, "Janice Harcourt and I are having lunch next week. And Naser and Mason are hosting me for dinner at their house in the next few weeks. Also, Logan was relatively civil to me, so..."

Donnie grinned. "My work here's complete."

"Hardly."

Donnie straightened.

"The tour you gave me on Sunday was anything but." Richard studied his face through the shadows. "Connor and Logan didn't stop here the night they met. They ended up down in the sea caves."

Donnie swallowed, heart racing.

"If we're going to come up with a design scheme that's inspired by the coastline, we should probably study the entire thing, right?"

"Yeah, well, it's locked up after dark, so..."

Richard reached into his pocket, then he placed a small silver key on the stone between them.

Blood pulsed in Donnie's temples. The sides of his neck felt tight. The quiet clink of the key hitting stone felt like a thunderous, echoing sound, a doorway to exciting new possibilities swinging open or a big iron gate between him and good sense falling shut.

"I told Connor I wanted to take a look," Richard added. "What do you say, Mr. Bascombe? Should we finish the tour?"

"What are you doing, Merriweather?"

"I'm trying to find out why you didn't take me down there Sunday. Were you afraid I'd lose control again?"

"Or I would."

Richard looked at him, eyes alight. "Wouldn't be *again* in your case. You've been a pretty good boy since you found out we're going to be working together."

"I haven't wanted to be. I kissed you back, remember?"

"I have most certainly not forgotten that," he said quietly. Then, as if snapping himself out of a briefly overwhelming memory, he added, "What did Jonas say to you on Sunday?"

"You're heartbroken. He's protective of you."

Richard looked to him with such sudden intensity Donnie was worried he'd somehow said the wrong thing.

"I wasn't heartbroken." But the quiver in his voice belied his words, and Donnie sensed more revelations to come. "My heart wasn't broken. My *pride* was. I didn't love him, Donnie." As if this were an embarrassment, he looked out to the sea again. "I thought we made sense. On paper. I thought he was the type of husband I could take to a high school reunion and have everyone say, 'Oh, wow. Look who Twinkletoes got.' That's what they used to call me, by the way.

"My motives were bad and so was my husband, to be frank. He was never a good friend, never a good companion. The sex was hot for about a year, and then it was nothing but request lists and Yelp reviews after and desperate experimentation to try to keep the spark alive. But our marriage was…presentational. According to my therapist, I picked Mark because I thought he would impress a mother who's barely paid any attention to me. The more she takes his side now, the more I'm inclined to believe Dr. Seeger. I mean, don't get me wrong. I was faithful. I gave it my all. But I treated it like any other job, and in the end, it wasn't a very good one."

"For Christ's sake, Merriweather. Are you ever going to give yourself a break? There's nothing wrong with having a hot husband who blows your doors off for a while."

"I've got a lot of doors, Donnie. And in a week you've blown off more of them then he ever did."

The words startled him, then stunned him, then made him feel like he was floating above the grass. And he'd blown Richard's doors off with his clothes on, he thought. A first for him when it came to guys who made his stomach do a flip whenever they walked into the room.

"I was courting you." He'd practically whispered the words.

"What was that?" Richard asked.

"*Courting* you. You know, it's like from the Middle Ages when you liked someone but you had to keep your distance 'cause they might have Black Plague or something."

"I'm not sure that's the definition, but I think I get your meaning."

"Yeah, I gotta stop learning stuff from YouTube. But you know, all I've got is a GED. Anyway, I was courting you. Thinking maybe after the wedding, there'd be less risk if there was still chemistry. I should have stopped but I didn't. I couldn't."

Richard nodded, considering this. "What would it have looked like if you'd stopped?"

"Me being afraid to be alone with you, I guess."

"The guy I met in the bathroom didn't seem afraid of anything."

"The guy you met in the bathroom was trying to be what everybody else always wants. The guy I've been since then is me trying to be what *you* want."

"You're doing an excellent job. So if this conversation's making you uncomfortable, you should probably work harder on being a selfish jerk."

"It's not the conversation that's making me uncomfortable, it's…"

"What, Donnie?"

Donnie's hands were quivering, and he stared out to sea to hide the fact that he might be on the verge of losing it. "I'm not in your league, okay. If I thought you and I could just bang this out of our system, I would have made the pitch more than once. But what's making me uncomfortable is that when you looked me in the eye the first time, the world started moving in a new direction, and it's never gone back to its original course. But I'm old enough to know what my game is. I don't play the big leagues when it comes to this kind of stuff. I scrimmage with the guys who are always hanging out by the field."

"Donnie, I really appreciate how you're opening up right now, but I don't know enough about sports to follow these metaphors."

"I fuck around and hook up. It's predictable. It's safe. It's what I know. But it never brings me a guy like you. I mean, maybe it does, but he never sticks around long enough for me to know. I didn't just fall asleep when I hooked up with that guy the other night. I was dreaming of you. I mean, it was a weird dream 'cause Harry was there and he was shouting 'More tongue!' into a megaphone—"

Richard's explosion of laughter silenced Donnie, maybe because his Harry Mitchell impersonation had been spot-on, and this in turn inspired laughter of his own. Once they'd finished, Richard sighed.

"I don't do *leagues,* Donnie. I don't do A-lists and B-lists unless a client hands me one and they've paid all their bills. I might be successful and I might have celebrity clients, and I might come from money, but my entire life I've been told there's too much skip in my step and I should cut my hair to look more like a real boy. The only club I would ever belong to is one that makes competence and intelligence a requirement for membership. And the number of clubs that fit that criteria are very small."

"I don't know. You seem like an airport lounge kinda guy."

"Well, if I can afford it. I mean, who wants to wait in the terminal if they don't have to?"

Donnie tried to keep his laughter in his throat, but it didn't work.

Another silence fell. This time, Donnie's sigh broke it. "What are we doing, Merriweather?"

"Crazy thought," he said, "but maybe whatever we want to." Richard turned, eyes meeting his. "Maybe we take my shitbag ex-husband and your terrible father and that terrible ex of yours who tried to pimp you out to pay his rent and we put them all in a back room and let them fight it out with each other, and meanwhile you and I do whatever the hell we want. Now. Today."

Richard had turned to face him, and Donnie hoped his expression wasn't betraying the deep quivers of fear and desire that were coursing through his entire body.

"You're hurting," he finally managed. "I don't want to add to that. Actually, I want to make it go away. But I can't tell if that's a reason to start something with you or keep my hands to myself."

"Well," Richard said, "why don't you leave that decision up to me then?"

He reached out and pushed the key an inch closer to Donnie.

Pulse pounding in his ears, Donnie stared down at it, fighting the urge to reach out and pull Richard's body against his, taking stock of how many guest room balconies were overhead and the fact that he knew of at least two security cameras trained on this very spot.

He closed his hand around the key, and trying to keep the desire from quaking in his words, he said, "Alright, Merriweather. Let's finish your tour."

35

The beach was empty and windswept. By day, the wooden loungers along the sand wore bright white and blue cushions and umbrellas. At night, they were stripped bare and folded flat, like shipping pallets washed ashore. Off to their right, at the base of the craggy wall of rock that shot skyward, the boardwalk's tall, silver gate glimmered in the security lights that dotted the surrounding cliffs and sent bright halos down onto the sand.

Donnie unlocked the gate, looked back and saw Richard a few feet behind him, the wind blowing that thick, gorgeous hair across his face. When he pushed it away with one hand, he revealed a mischievous light in his eyes. He pulled the gate open wide, like he'd done the door to Richard's new office earlier that night. The hinges whined, and then he closed it behind both of them. And locked it. As he started forward, Richard had paused a few paces ahead of him, having watched his last move with a satisfied smile.

"Right here." Donnie pointed to a row of informational placards that lined the short, ocean-facing stretch of the boardwalk. "That's about the marine life offshore. Connor's mom had all that put in years ago. She's a former school teacher."

"I did not know that. Very interesting. And up there?"

The boardwalk hugged the base of the cliff for several yards before making a hard right and disappearing inside the cave's mouth.

"Afraid of the dark?" Donnie asked.

"Should I be?" Richard asked.

Right behind him now, gently gripping his hips, Donnie brought his mouth to Richard's ear. "Not with me."

He could feel him shiver. "Excellent!" He started forward, turned right and disappeared.

"So the caves are old, obviously. And go back hella far." He turned right into a shadowy darkness faintly lit by golden foot-level lighting along the boards. "When Connor was a kid he crawled all over them. He says they go back really—" He never finished the sentence. In an instant, he was pressed against the rock wall behind him as if the darkness had materialized. Richard's breath was at his lips, his hands tugging at his tie, his kiss as firm and powerful and full of hunger as it had been on Saturday night. A moment that had started seven days ago and been on torturous pause ever since hurtled forward again.

The *tug, tug, tug* feeling in the center of his chest returned. Thank God. He'd worried it had been a one-time thing fueled by recklessness and the thrill of the forbidden. But here in the dark, it was back. And with the shadows to conceal them and a locked gate to keep them safe, Richard attacked Donnie's body—his lips, his cheeks, the sides of his neck, and now his nipples through his unbuttoned dress shirt—with feline grace and force.

His hair, Donnie thought. Richard Merriweather's hair had been such a forbidden temptation back in that trailer. Now he could touch it to his heart's content. And that's what he did, running his fingers through it, groaning like it was the softest bedding to ever grace his skin.

"If you ever even *think* about cutting this hair..." Donnie growled.

Richard's lips were inches from his, but he saw the man's smile in his eyes. "You'll what?"

Richard's fingers pried at the button of his jeans, unzipping them, freeing his cock. The weight of it in Richard's hand filled his eyes with lust. He stroked, watching it fill, lips parted with hunger. He'd meant to answer the question with a dozen filthy possibilities, but Richard's hand moved with too much experience and skill. Then he looked up into Donnie's eyes while he did it, his other hand working one of Donnie's nipples, and suddenly Donnie was letting out a raw, authentic version of the kind of groan he'd had to fake on a thousand sets.

Was it true what Logan had said earlier? Had nobody ever looked at him the way Richard Merriweather did? It felt true now.

When he went to go to his knees, Donnie stopped him with a brusque *no* that came out like a fearful bark.

Looking frightened, Richard's eyes met his

"Stay here. With me." Donnie brought their mouths together. "Kissing me. It's what I want. It's what I need."

A few whispered words, but they'd revealed so much. About what Richard was doing to him. Something so few men had ever done. He'd had more sex than most people would ever have in their lives, but kisses like this had rarely been part of it. Deep, forceful, connected, and *close*. They'd brought him to a place of hunger and vulnerability he'd rarely visited. He'd always been the dom top, flipping boys onto their backs, roughing them up if they asked for it. But this—noses touching, Richard's hair caressing the sides of their faces, breaking only briefly to catch their breath—was different. This was eye to eye and on fire.

"Oh, my," Richard said quietly.

That's when Donnie realized his shaft had gone slick with precum.

Richard seemed to appreciate suddenly that it was his kisses that had brought Donnie this close to the edge, and in such a short time, so he went back to work.

Cupping the back of Richard's head, Donnie tried to draw more passion from him while holding him in place. And that's when he heard himself say, "Oh, fuck. I'm gonna... *Fuck.*"

Richard deftly stepped to one side, but he kept stroking, kept kissing him. Then Donnie erupted. His lips exploded open against Richard's as he struggled for breath. Devilish laughter rumbled up out of Richard's chest as Donnie's stuttering groans echoed through the cave, drowning out the sounds of the surf. Then he was recovering, Richard caressing the back of his neck. The man—his *tiger*, he thought of him now—had remained in almost constant, sinuous motion since their first kiss. Stroking, kissing, tweaking. It wasn't manic or frenzied, but when he was tending to the body of someone he wanted he didn't pause his pleasure giving. As if Donnie were someone worthy of his constant attention. Of polishing and preening.

"Sorry to change positions at the last minute, but these are nice pants," he finally whispered. Richard kissed him on the lips, the cheek, the side of his neck. "I wonder if that key of yours opens the cabana outside. I could get us a towel or something."

"What the hell for? We're not done."

Before Richard could protest, Donnie straightened, then with both hands on the man's hips, he turned toward the guardrail. On the other side, the incoming surf bubbled and pushed its way deeper back into the cave, white foam bright enough to pop in the dark.

"Pants, Sex Monster," Richard said, clearly afraid Donnie was about to push his still half hard and cum-slick cock against their silky, designer seat.

"Yeah, yeah. I know you love your clothes, but if you want to get the most out of life, they gotta come off now and then. Trust me." Donnie unbuttoned the garment in question, then went for the belt, yanking it from the loops and tossing it to one side. "You really thought I'd let you get me off and not return the favor? I hope that's not the kind of treatment you're used to because *that*"—he bent forward and suckled Richard's earlobe, heard him groan, felt a shudder course through his body— "is not how I roll."

Donnie dipped one hand into the front of Richard's briefs, gently caressing his balls. Servicing Donnie had left him rock hard and his balls tight. He tugged his briefs down to his thighs and started stroking the man's cock when it sprang into the air. They'd never had a conversation about bedroom roles, and Donnie didn't want to make assumptions based on dress and manner, but the tell was when he sat his half hard cock into the crevice between Richard's bare cheeks, sliding it back and forth teasingly, and the man's back arched like a cat, and a hungry, trembling moan issued from him. At Richard's ear, he whispered, "Tell me what you want. Tell me what you thought about when you watched my scenes." He could see Richard's knuckles whitening as he gripped the rail in front of him. "Come on. You've already seen what does me in."

"My charm?" Richard managed, but his sarcasm was fighting a losing battle with the pleasure Donnie was giving him. Stroking in front, teasing in back, filthy mouth at his ear.

"Your kiss."

The answer must have surprised him because he bowed his head and let out a low, rumbling groan. "You..." Richard finally managed. "You telling me what you want to do to me. In detail."

"Oh, I see." Donnie stroked. "So you want to hear about how I had to get you out of my studio on Wednesday 'cause if I didn't, I was going to fuck you right there on the floor. Is that what you want to hear?"

Richard's answer was in a long, stuttering sigh and the throbbing in his cock.

"You want to hear about how I couldn't stand to sit there anymore because I was going to ask you which set was your favorite? Dorm room, doctor's exam room, dungeon. But I knew if you gave me the answer, I'd throw you down and give you whatever fantasy you wanted right there. Fuck you like a dumb horny college boy, or a dirty doctor or a leather daddy ready to give you the punishment you deserve."

Richard was gasping rapidly. The end was near. Donnie could feel it.

"You think I didn't see the look in your eyes the night we met, you sexy bitch?" Donnie asked. "You think I don't know there's a part of you that wanted to go into that bathroom stall with me so fucking bad?" His hand was slick with Richard's precum. "You think I don't know how bad you wanted to stop being *good* and *professional* and let me turn you into the dirty, cock hungry slut you want to be? Right there in that stall. Put my hand over your mouth so nobody could hear you groan as I fucked you hard and raw in the middle of the hotel."

Richard bellowed.

Donnie stroked, his hand feeling weightless.

Richard emptied himself onto the boards. A few gasping breaths later, he straightened in Donnie's reverse embrace, reached behind him and gripped the back of Donnie's head as he lavished the side of his neck with kisses.

"Dinner?" The question was out of him before he could stop it. And it sounded too abrupt, too rushed. Maybe he should have given them another minute or two to catch their breath. Did he sound needy? He felt needy. Because this was the moment when a guy would usually jet. And now that he'd made Richard come, maybe he'd turn out to be no different. No different from the scores of other men who'd only been interested in one of Donnie's skills. But those men hadn't made him come while gazing deep into his eyes, and he hadn't brought those men over the edge of bliss while holding them upright in a tangled, hot embrace.

"My hair's a mess," Richard said into Donnie's chest.

And inside that chest, Donnie's heart dropped, figuring this was the beginning of the retreat, the withdrawal. The cooling off.

"So it'll have to be room service. Care to join me?"

Rescued from heartbreak in the course of a single sentence, Donnie felt himself sigh. "Love to. But we should be careful on the way up."

"I don't suppose you know a way around the security cameras here."

"There really isn't one. Logan reviews the footage more than anyone, and he won't be much of an issue. Jonas, on the other hand…"

"I'll handle Jonas," Richard said.

"You sure?"

Richard lifted his head. "What I'm sure of is that you're coming up to my room."

36

After several minutes of scrolling, Donnie said, "This is hot."

The tub's generous size had been a painful reminder of Richard's singlehood when he'd first moved in. He hadn't used it until tonight. Now, in the sudsy water's warm embrace, he rested his upper back against Donnie's broad, scruffy chest as he held his phone out to the side with one hand, scrolling through the work of Richard's favorite artist.

"So the dude was into gondoliers, huh? Those are those guys in Venice who steer the boats around the canals, right?"

"Yes. But not just gondoliers. The nudes are from throughout his lifetime. They were a secret until after his death. The first exhibition wasn't until nineteen ninety-nine, I think."

"What's his name again?"

"John Singer Sargent, arguably one of the greatest portrait painters who ever lived. Jonas doesn't agree, and the ensuing argument was the only time I've ever been asked to leave a Starbucks. At any rate, his most famous painting is a portrait called Madame X. It scandalized Paris at the time. Back then an off the shoulder dress on a woman with a wedding ring could nearly cause a riot."

"Damn. If they saw my site, they'd burn down Paris. This is hot, tiger. You've got good taste."

Another kiss, then Donnie laced his fingers through Richard's under the water. Donnie had only stopped kissing him and nibbling on him for a minute or two since they'd entered the tub together. Like Richard was a tasty treat and he couldn't help himself.

Suddenly hearing the echo of the word Donnie had used with him seconds before, Richard asked, "Tiger?"

"It's your new nickname. You like it?"

"Possibly. What's the inspiration?"

"You. Down in the caves. You came at me like a tiger. And I loved it."

Sloshing water, Richard repositioned himself until they were facing each other, lips almost touching, Donnie's arm curving around his back now. "Time to get out." Richard brought their lips together, then caught the bottom one gently in his teeth as they went to part. "Time for me to towel you off," he whispered.

He hoisted himself out of the tub, then toweled off in a rush so he could turn his attention to Donnie as the man rose to his feet. A second later he stepped clear of the water and into the open towel Richard held up in both hands. Richard wrapped his torso in it, patting down his chest, his stomach, before slowly sinking to his knees and drying those deliciously thick, tree-trunk legs that had driven him quietly crazy when they'd bumped into each other in front of the ice machine a little over a week ago.

With a relaxed, inviting half smile, Donnie watched his every move. So Richard let the towel drop to the floor, ran his hands up his hair-dusted thighs, kissed the inside of one, then the other. Then he reached up and caressed Donnie's balls, gently gripping the base of his thickening cock.

"It really is absurd," Richard said.

Donnie cocked one eyebrow. "What's that, tiger?"

"Your cock is fucking absurd." Richard brought the head to his mouth and swabbed it with the tip of his tongue, stroking the shaft before popping it between his lips. He came up for air after a minute or two of making Donnie grunt through clenched teeth. "I try to be a mature and sophisticated adult…" He went all the way down on it. Donnie gripped the back of his head with one hand. "But deep down," Richard said when he came up for air, "I'm a hopeless size queen. And you're hung like a bull. And I'm sure this is going to result in me being…decidedly unsophisticated."

"Yeah, well, I've wanted to make you a dirty mess since the night we met."

That did it. He went to work, felt the white-hot heat that always lit up the length of his spine whenever his mouth was full of a man he desired. Only this man gripped his head, stroking long hair he would never pressure him to cut or trim. This man went wild for the very parts of Richard other men had tried to silence and dismiss. Not an hour after emptying himself down in the cave, Donnie was rock hard again. And yes, he'd be lying if he didn't admit that Donnie's groans thrilled him, lying if he didn't accept that it made him mad with lust to realize he could deliver a blow job that made a man with Donnie's experience struggle for breath.

"Fuck, he's right," Donnie said. "You are a filthy boy."

His words took a few seconds to register. "Wait." Richard stopped stroking, gripping Donnie's cock at its base as if suddenly taking it and the beautiful son of a bitch it was attached to prisoner. "*Who's* right?"

"Oh, God. Forget I said it. Please."

"Who told you I'm a filthy boy? Jonas?"

Donnie's grimace suggested much worse.

"*Mark?*"

"Please don't stop. I didn't want to bring him up. I'm sorry. It was dumb, he was trying to one up me."

"What do you mean *one up you*?"

"He asked if I was his replacement and when I wouldn't answer he told me you could be a filthy boy. It pissed me off."

"Why?" Richard rewarded his candor with one stroke, then another.

"Why do you think?" Donnie was pouting. "'Cause he'd had you and I hadn't. And I wanted you."

"Well." This time, Richard rewarded him with a long, slow swallow of half the shaft before letting his cock pop free again. "He's never getting me again. And you're going to get me a lot more."

Donnie growled with delight, gripping the back of Richard's head with both hands now. Richard went back to work, which in another few seconds, had Donnie slowly and skillfully fucking his mouth. Even though he'd been turned into a slobbery, hungry mess, Richard's hunger expanded beyond the boundaries of Donnie's cock, his mouth traveling to his full, low-hanging balls. Donnie smiled, but it clearly wasn't his most sensitive spot, and Richard was pretty sure he could find one if he searched—and licked—hard enough. His tongue met Donnie's taint. He jerked as if Richard had sparked a live wire. But he also held Richard's head firmly in place, his legs flexing so he could stand his ground, signs he didn't want Richard to be deterred by the first flare of nerves, so Richard kept going. Kept going until he'd turned Donnie to face the marble counter.

Then he parted the muscular cheeks of Donnie's ass and dove in tongue first.

It was like he'd sent a stuttering cascade of electrical pulses up the man's spine. Like so many tops, he didn't seem used to having his ass played with. But Donnie, master of pleasure that he claimed to be, seemed determined to absorb every overpowering wave. The tiger inside of Richard became a feasting lion. The next thing he knew, Donnie had bent forward over the marble counter, muscular back heaving as Richard unleashed a wet, slick assault on Donnie's hole and crack, then down his taint to his balls and back up again.

Richard never understood the people who thought oral sex degraded them. He never felt so powerful as when he was reducing a man to pure pleasure with his lips and tongue. It could be worship, but it could also be laying claim.

The moans and gasps coming from Donnie sounded like nothing he'd ever heard him make on film. They sounded unrehearsed and pure, and soon Donnie's cock was spasming in his hand. Bellowing, Donnie pressed his face to the marble. He'd turned the strapping cocky porn star into a puddle. This knowledge made him erupt in his own stroking fist only seconds later.

Once they'd both finished, he gave one of Donnie's muscular ass cheeks a tender kiss and fell backward onto his haunches, knees aching from the effort he'd just expended. When he was finally able to stand, Donnie was still bent forward over the counter. But his one open eye was trained on Richard through the mirror. Bending forward, Richard embraced Donnie from behind, nuzzling his lips against the back of his thick neck. "Not used to having your ass played with, top man?"

"Not by a tiger."

Richard pulled him to his feet.

"Am I a tiger or a filthy boy?"

"Why choose?" Donnie asked with a drowsy, contended smile.

When Donnie saw Richard stepping into the shower for a final rinse, he joined him, sudsing down his body with powerful kneading hands that turned Richard to jelly against the tile. Then they stumbled together into the bedroom. Under the covers, with Donnie's arms wrapped around him, he realized he was being held by another man in bed for the first time since leaving Mark. The pleasure of this realization rivaled all the others he'd been blessed with that evening.

"Can I stay?" Donnie asked, a whisper in Richard's ear.

"Yes. In my bed this time," Richard answered, and Donnie's arms enfolded him together in response.

After four months of solitary slumber, Richard would have expected at least a moment of disorientation the first time he woke up in another man's arms. Maybe a painful flashback of his ex. But he knew right away it was Donnie next to him. Mark had never held him this close, never hooked one powerful leg over both of his to draw him closer while they slept. Never gathered his hair gently in one fist so he could plant light, good morning kisses on the back of his neck.

"Glad or sad?" Donnie's breath sent gooseflesh down his spine. When he rolled over, his bedhead and sleepy grin made him look half his age.

"Are you asking me if I'm having regrets?"

"I'm a simple porn person. I don't use fancy words like regrets."

"Simple is not how I'd describe any of this." Richard kissed him gently, quickly, conscious of morning breath but unable to keep his distance. "Breakfast?"

"I guess that means you're glad."

He crawled up onto the man's brawn until their noses were almost touching. He gripped Donnie's hands, pressing them into the pillows on either side of his head. "Been a while since you woke up in someone's arms?"

"Excuse me. But you woke up in *my* arms."

Richard kissed him on the forehead. "You didn't answer the question."

"Because you still haven't answered mine."

"Glad," Richard finally said. "Very glad. My jaw is sore, but I'm glad." He grinned.

"Good," Donnie said, also grinning. "Me too."

"Now answer my question. How long since you've had a sleepover?"

"Two years."

"You're kidding."

Donnie pouted. "Oh my God. You're making me feel like a leper."

"I'm just surprised. It sounds like your boat's had a lot of visitors."

"It has, but they rarely stay the night."

"Well, I feel special then." And he did. His cheeks were hot. He was also fighting the urge not to proudly raise his chin and hum the "Battle Hymn of the Republic."

"You haven't spent the night on my boat yet."

"Will I?" Richard asked.

"I don't know if the accommodations are going to be up to your standards."

"Well, send me some pictures and I'll do a thorough review. Then throw in one of your cock and I'll probably forget about all the others and be on my way there in five minutes."

Donnie looked shocked. "Are you really asking me for a dick pic? After all the grief you gave me for hitting on you somewhere other than a perfumed boudoir."

"No. I've got a very good memory."

"That's a shame. 'Cause I was hoping you were gonna need another look pretty soon."

"I will. And trust me. There's a lot more I'd like to do with it."

Donnie growled and grinned, a combo that was starting to send goosebumps down Richard's spine. "Now?" he asked with a hopeful look.

"No. Later. For sure."

"Later today or, like, later another time?"

"I've got plans today."

"Well, that's good to know, 'cause I was concerned. Last night in the bathroom you were throwing off some top vibes. Once I was done coming, that is."

"Trust me. My days of pretending to be versatile to impress a man are long over. The last guy I tried to top got mad when I started reading a magazine. I mean if I hadn't dropped it onto his back he never would have known, but alas."

"That's a relief 'cause I..." Donnie reached down and gripped Richard's bare ass cheeks with such force and determination Richard thought he'd melt. "But I'll need to get in there real soon to make sure you're sure," he whispered, nibbling on one of Richard's ear lobes.

"You will." Richard kissed the side of the man's neck. Then he planted a finger in the dead center of Donnie's pecs. "With a condom, though. I know it's bareback central out there with all the young people these days, but you and I are hardly virgins, so…"

"Not a problem," Donnie said with a grin. "So what you got going on today? Work stuff?"

"Yes, unfortunately. Some garden party in Newport Beach for a prospective client. What about you?"

"Nothing much. I might head home, spend the rest of the day cleaning the boat from top to bottom to get it ready for your eventual visit. You know, pour lavender oil all over the place. Hang eucalyptus everywhere. Maybe a bowl full of dried rose petals here and there."

"That sounds lovely. And labor intensive."

"Yeah, well," Donnie said with a lazy grin. "You're a lot of work."

A silence fell.

Richard broke it. "Now's the part where you say I'm worth it."

"Ask me once I've dried all the rose petals." But to make up for his jab, he pulled Richard close, and suddenly Richard was smelling the delicious masculine blend of scents coming from Donnie's neck.

"You want to come?"

"To your garden party?" Donnie sounded genuinely surprised.

"Yeah."

"I don't know. The last time we went to an event together it didn't turn out so well."

"Well, I'm not working this one. I'm meeting a prospective client. I don't even know her. She sent an email to the office and invited me to drop by today."

"How kind of you," Donnie said. "So how rich is she?"

"One of the richest people in Orange County. I did some research."

After a long silence, Donnie reached up and caressed Richard's hair. "You going to dress me? It's Sunday. If I go home, it might take me hours to get back."

"Sure. I like dressing you."

"Good."

But in the silence that followed, it felt like they were both mulling over the potential implications of what they'd just agreed to.

Was this their first official date?

"Also, you don't actively *dry* rose petals," Richard said because he couldn't help himself. "You just put them out in the sun. But you don't apply anything to them or put them through the dryer or you just—"

"Relax, Tiger. I'm not doing a damn thing with rose petals. I've got way too many plans for your ass."

37

The Newport Beach home of Greta Muntz and her husband Keith was a Spanish Mission style palace surrounded by acres of arid landscaping. When Richard stepped through the giant, double front doors ahead of Donnie, he encountered a bifurcated staircase that rivaled the Titanic's. Or James Cameron's version of it, anyway. The tiled foyer that lay before it could have accommodated several parked cars. Even so, the party's guests were processing through it quickly, bound for the clamor of conversation and string music inside the nearby great room, which, given what he could see of it through the soaring doorway, promised to be ten times the foyer's size.

"What do these people do again?" Donnie asked. Richard's white dress shirt looked a tad snug on him, but they'd found a pair of baggy khaki pants that fit nicely.

"Greta's husband supplies all the beef to two different fast food chains," Richard answered in a whisper.

"Explains why you could land a plane in here," Donnie answered. "And I thought *Connor* was rich."

The great room's glass walls were pushed open to a terraced garden with an ocean view that rivaled that of Sapphire Cove. On the sweeping stone patio, an ice sculpture surrounded by a raw bar had drawn guests like hummingbirds to a feeder. Liveried waiters circulated with trays of champagne and wine. A few glances around the room confirmed the crowd was uniformly white, over fifty, and in vigorous good health. It felt like a glimpse back in time to an older version of Orange County, the one that had only recognized the sovereign authority of John Wayne. Greta's emails had suggested that her pet charity's current event planner wasn't the best, and she thought Richard could level things up—a subtle request for a pitch she hadn't asked for yet, but one which would require some homework. So he studied their opulent surroundings. No evidence of subpar planning leapt out at him—the catering spreads were lavish, the wet bars well placed—but he resolved to keep an eye out. He'd have to inquire as to which elements of the design were native to the house and which had been carted in.

"Doubt I'll be recognized at this shindig," Donnie said quietly. "This crew looks like they just came from the golf course."

Out of the crowd stepped Greta Muntz, a dead ringer for the headshot he'd found of her on the website for the Youth Protection Alliance, which listed all their wealthy board members and included their extensive bios. Her strand of white pearls matched her sleek long bob. Her Nehru jacket shimmered. Raw silk, he figured.

"Richard, I'm so glad you were able to come." She gave him a gentle, regal handshake. "Who's your handsome friend?"

"Greta, this is Donnie Bascombe. We're planning a wedding together out of my new office at Sapphire Cove."

"Wonderful. It's lovely to meet you, Mr. Bascombe." She extended her hand.

"And your home is quite wonderful, Ms. Muntz."

"Please. Call me Greta. We'll have remarks in a few minutes out in the garden. Help yourself to some food in the meantime. We can connect after, and I'll get your thoughts." She raised one eyebrow before she departed as if to imply some quiet conspiracy between them, then she was replaced by a waiter bearing a tray of champagne flutes.

"Can I?" Donnie asked.

"Of course. I'm driving and you're not on the clock."

"Thanks, tiger." Once the waiter departed, Donnie lowered his voice. "Who'd you say this was a fundraiser for again?"

"The Youth Protection Alliance. They run shelters all over the country."

Donnie nodded slowly, eyes draining of emotion. Before Richard could ask him why, the sound of a fork clinking against glass drew everyone's attention. Greta was approaching a microphone and portable speaker that had been set up on the lawn one level below, a few paces from the sparkling rectangular pool. The patio and bistro tables were all taken by earlier arrivals, so Donnie led them to the far corner where they rested their shoulders against the wall and began eating one-handed from their china plates.

At the mic, Greta welcomed everyone. Then what followed was a series of fundraising pitches for a chain of youth shelters that crossed the country, a series of pitches that seemed to make Donnie increasingly stiff and uncomfortable. Maybe it was the executive director's mention of "saving at-risk youth from the dangers of sex trafficking" that had done it.

"You okay?" Richard finally whispered.

Donnie nodded and took too much time to swallow a bite of crab dip.

"Did you recognize the name? Of the organization, I mean."

Donnie nodded again, but this time his eyes were downcast.

"Did you ever…"

"Stay in one of their shelters?" Donnie nodded, fighting a muffled, chesty laugh. "I tried. It didn't work out. Most places have a rule. You can't just hang out during the day. You've got to go to their classes or meet with their counselors. They were different. You had to go to their church every morning. If you didn't, they showed you the door."

"What kind of church?"

"Fire and brimstone kinda stuff. Hardcore Christian." Donnie locked eyes with him. "Guess she didn't say anything about that in her email?"

Richard shook his head. "Or on the website. I'm sorry I brought you here. I had no idea."

"Don't worry about it. Work is work. I'll follow your lead."

Richard wanted to lead them right back to the valet stand, but he was torn. And by the time he saw Greta Muntz making a beeline for them across the patio, he was still struggling to come to a decision.

"So what do you think?" she asked with oozing sweetness.

"It sounds like a worthy cause. So how do these shelters—"

"No, no. I meant the party. I'm sure you can do much better for us than this. Honestly, the ice sculpture's practically melted already, and the champagne isn't even Veuve." She looked around as if she was afraid she'd been overheard. "There's room to grow is what I'm saying. I think the board would be very open to a pitch. And we've got an incredibly busy calendar this coming season." She turned her attention to Donnie with sudden force. "I think it's so brave that you came today."

Donnie stopped mid chew, staring at her wide-eyed. He swallowed. "Brave?"

"It's always inspiring to see someone on the path of redemption. I'm not the only one here who thinks so."

Donnie nodded slowly, swallowing the bite he'd almost choked on.

"Redemption for *what* exactly?" Richard asked.

Greta's smile flickered. "I apologize. One of the other guests here recognized you. Randy Sloane." She gestured to the crowd where a handsome blond man whose muscles were about to split his dress shirt waved and smiled. The young, equally blonde woman on his arm followed the direction of his gaze with an intensity that said she monitored her companion's actions very closely. "He has a very popular podcast about moving on. From the life."

"Randy used to work for me," Donnie said quietly.

Moving on from the life. A former porn star. Redemption. Mandatory church services. In the stultifying silence that followed, the pieces started to fall into place. Worse, Donnie wasn't speaking up in his own defense because he didn't want to spoil a work opportunity for Richard.

"Donnie doesn't have anything to redeem himself for," Richard said. "He runs a perfectly legal business, and he's a good man."

Greta met his stare. "Clearly I've offended you. That wasn't my intention." It also wasn't her intention to apologize, apparently. "I assumed there was no way you'd feel comfortable here if you weren't... Well, let's move on, shall we?"

"I'd like to know more about how these shelters work," Richard asked.

"What questions do you have? The remarks were pretty thorough, I thought."

"I understand church service is mandatory."

"Some sort of spiritual focus is essential for our youth, we've found."

"Are there options or is it all one denomination?"

"We are a member of the World Evangelical Alliance."

Richard felt his blood run cold. "What sort of resources do you have for queer youth?"

"Queer?" Greta's eyebrows arched, and her mouth curled into the threat of a snarl. "Is that the word they're using now?"

"It's the word *we're* using."

Greta exhaled. "We would inform them we think they're entirely too young to be making such a choice."

He felt Donnie bristle.

"A *choice?*" Richard finally said. "I see. Well, sometimes making the choice not to lie about who they are is the reason they end up in your shelters to begin with. What would be your response to that?"

"This was a mistake," Greta said quietly. "I thought you were a professional. But apparently you're some sort of activist who thinks it's appropriate to interrogate people you just met."

"You thought I'd be so impressed by the mansion and the crab dip that I wouldn't pick up on the fact that you operate a front for converting people to your extreme religion while pretending to offer services for at-risk youth."

"And *you* apparently have no need of my business."

"Oh, it's far worse than that, Ms. Muntz. I don't *want* your business. And the Supreme Court recently said I don't have to take it. Donnie?"

Eyes wide and full of delight, Donnie said, "Yes, tiger?"

"Give Greta your plate." Before the woman could react, they'd both extended their hors d'oeuvre plates toward her. Probably in hopes of avoiding an even bigger scene, she accepted them both, eyes blazing with quiet rage. Richard took Donnie's hand and led him out.

He'd just given the valet his ticket when Donnie grabbed him by one hand and pulled him close. Were they about to kiss?

"You sure about this?" Donnie asked.

"Why didn't you say anything back to her?"

"Didn't want to mess up your business opportunity. I mean, you and Thalia are still on the rocks until we pull off this reception, so I figured you needed to fill some gaps."

"That's what I thought." Richard kissed him on the cheek. "And that's why *I* said something. Let's go get a real meal. Without the side of bigots."

But Donnie didn't release his hand. He pulled him in closer. "You're leaving a lot money on the table in there."

"Donnie Bascombe, are you suggesting I go back in that house and patch things up with that awful woman?"

"Hell, no. I just want to stand here for a bit and savor the fact that you set her back on her Gucci heels while defending my honor."

"Stop playing around then and give me a kiss."

"Here?" Donnie asked.

He'd managed to shock Sex Monster with an offer of intimacy, which satisfied him as much as a good kiss might. He should make sure, though. He pulled Donnie in for a long, deep one. When they parted, the valet was gawking at them from a few feet away, standing next to Richard's Porsche. But the young man was perfectly civil as he handed over the keys, then when he closed the driver's side door behind Richard he cheerfully added, "My cousin's gay."

"That's lovely," Richard said. "Don't tell him you worked this event."

The valet nodded but he looked confused, then he gave the giant house a fearful look as Richard drove away.

38

They were halfway through their late lunch when Donnie asked, "Are we traitors for eating here?"

At first, Richard wanted to laugh, but the question seemed sincere.

Calling the Surf and Sand Resort one of Sapphire Cove's competitors was a stretch, he thought. It was less than a quarter of the size, for one, and well inside the limits of the artists' colony turned tourist mecca of Laguna Beach, only a twenty-minute walk from the town's main throughfares of galleries and gift shops. The place had opened as a motel in the years after World War II before blossoming into one of the tallest buildings in town at a whopping nine stories of ocean-facing rooms. Further south, both the Montage and the Ritz Carlton in Laguna Niguel—with their sprawling grounds and large conference facilities—gave Sapphire Cove a run for its money. By comparison, Surf and Sand felt intimate. Small town, even. Better yet, they had a restaurant that sat right above the rocky surf line.

"I don't think Connor would be that upset if he found out there was one meal we didn't get from room service."

"You know what I mean." Donnie leaned forward over his beer, waggling his eyebrows. "Are we sneaking around?" His smile vanished instantly. "Sorry. Maybe not the best joke considering…"

"It was perfectly fine. I'm not willing to give Mark all jokes. And yes. We are kind of sneaking around."

"Jonas threatened to turn my balls into a purse if I hurt you."

"I'm sure he doesn't know how."

"Are you? Dude has a past, apparently."

"As do we all," Richard said. "I'd love to hear more about yours. If you're open to that."

"Ask away."

"Where did you go first after your dad threw you out?"

"My aunt's first, in South Bend. She tried to broker a peace. Dad said I could come back if I went to church with him every Sunday and never laid a hand on another man again. I told him I'd think about it if he never touched another whiskey bottle. I figured that would be the end of the convo, and it was. Then I reached out to my mom, who'd walked out on us years before and she said, thanks, but no thanks. Her new beau wasn't going to be cool with a bonesmoker stepson in the house. So I stayed with my aunt for about a month. Until my dad told her he'd stop sending her money every month if she didn't kick me out. She was sweet, but she wasn't the most together person, and I didn't want to mess up her life, so I hit the road."

"Your aunt let you run away again?"

"Nah, I told her I was going back to dad's. By the time she realized I was lying, I was in Chicago. I used my fake ID to get a job as a barback at a gay club in Boystown."

"How old were you?"

"Sixteen. I was like a kid in a candy store."

"You *were* a kid. Where were you living?"

"I hopped around a bit."

Richard fell silent. He felt foolish for not having seen this coming, the prospect that Donnie might have started turning tricks when he was still a minor. Nodding, he wasn't sure what to say. The last thing he wanted to do was make Donnie feel ashamed or embarrassed. And he certainly couldn't speak from some mountain of experience when it came to being a homeless teenager.

"It wasn't like that, tiger."

"Like what?"

"It wasn't creepy old men trying to play with little boys. That wasn't the vibe. I was already this tall. I'd played football. I never told people how old I was. But yeah, I did a lot of bed hopping, and then this older guy got his hooks in me. He didn't want sex, though. Which was a shame. Would've been easier to manage him if he had. He used to always drink at the bar but he never got messy, and he saw the guys I was running around with and gave me his guest bed to live on. Problem was he wanted to lay down some ground rules. Quit my bar job. Go back to school. No hooking up with guys every night of the week that didn't know how old I really was. That sort of thing. I told him to bite me. I regret it, but I did. He was just trying to help. But I wasn't just a runaway, tiger. I was a rebel."

"Hard to tell which one came first, though, right?"

Donnie studied him. "Maybe."

"I take it you didn't go back to school."

"Are you kidding? I'd gone from a potato farm in Shelbyville, Michigan, to nothing but hot gay guys in Boystown. I thought I had it made. But the old man, he could see the future and he thought it wasn't good. I called his bluff, told him I'd already gotten rid of one asshole dad, and I'd be happy to lose another." Donnie shook his head at this vivid memory of his youthful arrogance. "Stupid. He went and told the club I was underage. Drama ensued. Bye bye, Boystown. So I took my trusty fake ID to North Dakota. Figured I'd make some easy money in the oil fields. Williston was booming up there then. Once I had enough cash, I'd head to sunny So Cal. I was almost eighteen by then, and I already had dreams of porn stardom. Then my ID got found out. And that's when the road to California got *a lot* longer."

A silence fell. Richard sensed they'd reached the most difficult part of the story. Donnie stared down into his beer.

"And harder?" Richard finally asked, as gently as he could.

Donnie's nod turned into a shrug, but he was having trouble looking Richard in the eye.

"I'm sorry," Richard said. "We don't have to…"

"Nah, it's fine. I just…it wasn't as bad as it sounds, but it was…I mean…"

Donnie's typical confidence had left him; Richard didn't think he'd ever seen the man this rattled and paralyzed.

"Most of the time it wasn't official, you know? Like, some older guy would hire me to do yard work and then he'd ask me if I needed a place to stay and I'd say yes. But I knew how it was going to go down. One night he'd slip into bed with me and I needed to be ready to go to town on him. Sometimes it would go on for a while. Sometimes a wife he hadn't mentioned would come back or he'd make a play for my ass and I'd have to go on and find a new arrangement."

"Did you always find one?"

"No. Truck stops were where I made a quick buck when things were desperate. Other times I'd find some legit gig for a short while.

You know, manual labor. Construction. That kind of thing. I kept moving west whenever I could. But it was slow. Wherever the weather's better, life gets pricier. So I was always falling back on my moneymaker to keep things moving, if you know what I mean." Donnie lifted his beer. "And now I'm here."

Richard smiled.

Donnie didn't. "You get real quiet when we talk about this stuff. So does Logan. He'll turn white and grit his teeth. You kinda look like I hurt your dog."

"For people who care about you, it's hard to hear," Richard said.

"That I was such a slut?"

"That you were that young and crossing paths with grown-ups who thought you only deserved a roof over your head if you gave them sex. People should have taken better care of you, Donnie." Donnie's eyes flashed to his, as if this was the last thing he'd expected to hear. Was there a moist sheen in them? Richard wasn't sure. What he was sure of was that Donnie Bascombe had grown used to being naked, but he wasn't used to being this exposed. "I hope that doesn't bother you, me saying that. Me wanting that for you."

"It doesn't. Just as long as you don't judge me for how I took care of myself."

"I would never."

Donnie nodded, but his expression still looked vulnerable. "Good," he said quietly.

"But you better not judge me for being a rich, prissy, spoiled—"

"Filthy," Donnie added with a grin.

A grin that filled Richard with relief because it meant they'd moved on from their dark moment. "That too."

"I would never," Donnie said.

"Good. We're walking to get dessert in town. There's an ice cream shop I found that I love. And ice cream is my funnel cake."

"I thought funnel cakes were your funnel cakes now."

"Sorry. Ice cream got there first."

As they walked down Pacific Coast Highway toward the center of town, Richard could tell something had shifted inside of Donnie. He was slower to respond to Richard's questions. His eyes kept wandering. He was more pensive than was his nature. And suddenly Richard was wondering if they'd moved on from their dark moment after all.

On a bench looking out over Main Beach, they were halfway

through their ice cream when Donnie suddenly said, "Well, I don't want to take up your whole day. Maybe we should—"

"No."

Startled, Donnie looked up from the last of his rocky road.

"No, Donnie. You're not rushing out of here so you can get on the road and spend the whole drive back to San Diego wondering if you said something at that table about your past that's going to make me not want to see where this is going. Because nothing you said back there will." Richard scooted closer to him. "So instead you're going to stay here with me and we're going to wander around town like a happy couple, and maybe we'll even watch the sunset together, and the whole time you're going to hear my voice in your head saying these words, and not the voices in your head that tell you you're not good enough for me or for anyone because of where you've been and what you've been through."

Donnie blinked, and for a second Richard thought he was imagining it, the wet sheen that appeared in the tough, former runaway's eyes. Then he felt pressure on his hand and realized Donnie had gripped it. And without regard for who might have an opinion about two men expressing physical affection for each other in public.

"I don't usually talk about *all* of it, you know," he said quietly, voice thick with the threat of tears. "Just pieces. With different people. But you, I kinda told you all of it, and that's new for me."

"Well, then I'm grateful. And honored." Richard leaned forward and pecked him on the cheek. "Now eat the rest of your ice cream or I will. It looks good."

Text me when you get home.

Those were the words that followed Donnie home.

Nobody had ever asked him to do it before. He was the one who usually kept tabs on everyone else—his boys at Parker Hunter, Logan, Ethan. But now there was someone who cared if *he* got home safely.

But by the time he parked in the marina, the past twenty-four hours started to feel like a dream, and when he entered the *Golden Boy*'s main cabin, out of habit his hand drifted to his pocket and pulled out his phone. Instead of texting Richard he tapped the folder containing all the icons for the apps he usually used for quick sex.

He froze.

What was he doing?

Suddenly, he was rationalizing a choice he hadn't made yet. They were dating, that was all. Nobody had said anything about being exclusive. He was Sex Monster, after all. But these thoughts didn't feel like putting the cart before the horse; they felt like he'd dropped the cart onto the horse's back.

He wasn't even horny. As if he could be. The night before—and again that morning in the shower—had left him satisfied at a level he had only experienced a few times in his life. It was habit, routine, what he'd done with his phone, and he hadn't done it out of a hunger for contact, touch, or even a desire to come. He'd done it because he was uncomfortable. Because halfway home, despite Richard's directive in Laguna, the voices of self-doubt had started to drown out Richard's gentle, comforting words. He'd revealed too much. As soon as Richard had time to sit and think about Donnie's past, he'd realize this whole thing was pointless, that there was no future. That Donnie was tainted. Put back together by pluck and porn but still broken in a bunch of places inside.

Worse, these thoughts made him feel like a hypocrite. How many times had he lectured the other sex workers in his life about how they shouldn't see themselves as damaged goods? Yeah, well, it was easier to talk big when you'd never once taken a real swing at something with a guy who didn't share your fucked-up history. A guy you actually cared about. It was easy to hold principles that were never tested.

Now, standing frozen in the middle of his boat, harbor water lapping gently at the hull and several doorways to quick, meaningless sex staring up at him from his phone's screen, he wondered how many times in his adult life he'd done exactly this. Reached for sex not because he was horny, not because he had an itch to scratch. Because there was something he wanted to avoid, to forget, to stuff down. He'd always told himself his hookups made him feel like a free spirit, but now it felt like they were more of a crutch.

You're running.

And he realized what he was running from. He could imagine it. Texting Richard that he'd made it home safely only to sit there waiting for a response. Waiting and waiting as Richard sat alone in the hotel suite realizing he'd given his body to a whore. He could see it as clear as a movie on a screen. The regret furrowing Richard's brow as he stared out at the nighttime view from his balcony, phone in his hand, wondering how to step back from their night of passion.

He set the phone on the table, staring at it for a while like it was a coiled snake.

Then it lit up with a text. From Richard.

> Don't answer this if you're still driving. But if you're not, let me know you're safe and sound.

Donnie was startled by the sound that came next.

It took him a second or two to realize he'd made it.

A choked, pathetic-sounding sob had welled up out of him with astonishing force. The tears he'd almost shed twice at lunch that day came roaring to the surface, determined to have their way with him now that he was all alone. In an afternoon's time, he'd finally had a moment he'd been putting off for over fifteen years. Not just sharing his whole history with one person, sharing it with someone he'd started to care about deeply. Someone who could hurt him badly if they threw him away.

Let me know you're safe and sound. Years of living on the road, not knowing where his next bed or meal would come from, only knowing what he'd have to do to get it. Not once had anyone ever said those words to him. *Let me know you're safe and sound.* But godammit, if he could survive those years, he could survive his fear of trying to make a go of something with a guy who drove him wild.

He reached for the phone. Richard answered after the first ring.

"I'm good," Donnie croaked out.

"Really? You don't sound good."

"Well, you know…"

"Donnie?"

"You were right. About the ride home. You know, like, how I'd think maybe I said too much."

"You didn't say too much."

"So you don't care that I was a whore?"

"The term is sex worker."

Donnie laughed, savoring the easing of tension that spread through him. "You know what I mean."

"I care that your father was criminally negligent as a parent. I care that your aunt didn't stand up to him. I have questions about the men in Chicago you met and what they knew and what they chose not to know. But they're not mine to ask. Not today. Because what's more important to me than any of that is that you know those feelings are not indictments of you. Or judgments."

"I might need you to say that more than once. If we're gonna keep, you know..."

"I'll be happy to. Because I'd like to keep, you know..."

Donnie felt the weight in his chest lighten. "That's not the only reason I'm calling. Friday night I want you to come down and spend the night with me on my boat. That way you'll be here in the morning on the day of the reception."

"Is that the only reason?"

"No. I'm going to take you out on the boat and fuck your brains out under the stars. So, you know, get ready and skip dinner. I'll cook you something after. I know how it goes."

"So romantic." But it sounded like Richard was smiling.

"I'm Sex Monster. You want romance go to a high tea or something."

"I feel a high tea is in our future. As payback for that remark."

"Sounds good to me. So do you accept or not?"

"Absolutely."

"Alright, excellent. Goodnight, tiger."

"Goodnight, Donnie."

Donnie hung up, feeling like he'd been purged of years' worth of shame in a single phone call. Then he turned in place and realized he'd done something far more dangerous than revealing his entire past.

Richard would be spending the night there in only a few days.

Jesus. He had some cleaning to do.

39

Richard had come to love Monday nights at Sapphire Cove. Sunday evenings were often eerily quiet after a wave of checkouts, but the first night of the week offered up a happy medium between desolate and thronged, the sprawling grounds taking on the more relaxed feel of a private club before the next tide of conference goers washed in. That's why Richard had suggested he and Jonas make a Monday evening dinner a regular tradition. To his pleasure, Jonas had agreed. After that awkward Sunday, Jonas had gone strangely quiet on the subject of Donnie Bascombe, and he thought it a good idea to take his old friend's temperature now that he and Donnie were all over the late-night security footage together.

There was no jazz combo on the deck tonight, but the pianist inside Camilla's could be heard through the restaurant's open glass walls. The song was "Some Enchanted Evening," one of Richard's favorites. The sky over the Pacific was post-dusk purple, the temperature a perfect seventy degrees, the breeze light enough not to blow the cocktail napkins from the glass table. Better yet, in his jacket pocket, his phone was bursting with more of the text messages he and Donnie had been sending each other all day like lovesick teens. And so far his conversation with Jonas had been pleasant despite their last tense exchange.

He felt fully relaxed for the first time since his arrival at Sapphire Cove.

Jonas caught Richard smiling and smiled back.

"You seem in remarkably good spirits," Jonas said.

"I am, as a matter of fact."

"So Donnie's plowing you into the bed pillows, I take it."

"Jonas Jacobs!"

"Sorry. I've gone as long as I can without saying anything."

"And *that's* what you're going to say. Honestly."

"Honestly, I was going to keep my mouth shut. I felt like I might have overstepped the other day. Proceed with your eyes open, that's all."

"He certainly is now that you threatened him."

"You're not someone he should be careless with." Jonas studied him. "Is he? Being careless?"

"He is not the man I thought he was the night we met."

Jonas set his fork down. "Our deal from college still applies, Richard. We're perfectly allowed to date dumb hot fuckboys provided we don't pretend they're something they're not. No describing men who don't read books with the words *still waters run deep*. No pretending a guy who majored in steroids possesses *a certain stoicism*. Have fun, but don't call it something else. That was our credo. Remember?"

"In the past two weeks, he's been kinder to me than Mark was in four years of marriage."

"Well, that's a fairly low bar. You deserved better than Mark too."

"I can't argue with that."

"Look, I'll admit that some of my reaction to Donnie is personal. And irrational. The fact is, he's the product of an ecosystem I don't like. Call me idealistic, but when I went off to college I thought perhaps I'd have a shot at a partnership with a man of similar intellect and achievement, only to discover that what those men wanted was the boy in the Speedo dancing on the bar. I prefer it when one advances based on their intellect and contributions, not their abs."

He wanted to tell Jonas that while the two of them were cabbing it to gay clubs in D.C. and arguing about John Singer Sargent in posh Georgetown coffee houses, Donnie didn't know where his next meal was coming from. When they'd been worrying about AP test scores, Donnie had been a homeless runaway. He also thought of adding that Donnie hadn't stripped or slept his way into Sapphire Cove. He'd become a member of the community by being an incredibly good friend to one of the men who'd saved the place from ruin. But he'd promised Jonas a safe space to unload. And maybe it was more important that he recognize these things than Jonas.

"Yes, well, if planning this wedding is what you call advancement, he's earned the spot by being an incredible friend to Logan. I mean, you're the one who told me they'd never been an item, right?"

Jonas arched an eyebrow. "You came prepared."

"I'm not saying I'm going to marry him. We're just…seeing each other, I guess. It's just…maybe…"

"Maybe what?" he asked softly.

"Maybe don't threaten violence against a man whose father beat him up so badly when he was a teenager he ran away from home. That's all I'm saying. Given the rumors about your past, he took it literally."

Sighing, Jonas went back to work on his meal. "Oh, let's not go there again," he muttered before shoveling a forkful of seabass into his mouth.

"We don't have to, but I just want to say Donnie is convinced you were an international assassin. So when you threaten to castrate him, he takes it seriously."

"Point taken." Jonas nodded.

For a while they sat in silence.

"If I could talk about it, I would."

There was a softness to Jonas's tone suddenly that startled Richard stiff. He looked up into his old friend's eyes and saw an intent look there he couldn't describe. They weren't talking about Donnie anymore. They were talking about Jonas's missing years, as Richard had come to think of them.

"I won't make you."

"You *can't* make me." Jonas's word choice was gruff, but his tone wasn't. It was matter of fact. Resigned, even. It implied that no pressure from a friend, even one for whom he cared deeply, was strong enough to overpower the larger forces that would keep Jonas Jacobs quiet about how he'd spent the years following college.

"I'll say this," Jonas finally added. "Sometimes you have to do something for a good while to find out you're not cut out for it."

Richard nodded and held his friend's gaze, but even that simple statement was an insight into that long ago period of Jonas's life more profound than any he'd been given before. *Not cut out for it.* And *it* was something that was either formally classified by the government or rendered off limits by contracts with a corporation so powerful it could frighten Jonas out of discussing it with even his closest friends. This was also the first time he'd described his own emotion about that time in his life as one of disappointment. And possibly failure.

"Makes sense," Richard finally said.

"At any rate, I have no idea how to turn someone's balls into a purse." Jonas shoveled his last bite of fish into his mouth and chewed. "But if he treats you badly, I'm more than willing to learn. And that makes me a very good and resourceful friend."

Richard couldn't disagree.

40

"Wait," Ethan Blake said, "he's sleeping over? What happened to courting?"

Donnie ignored his good friend, the same one who'd prepared a gourmet dinner for him to serve Richard that night aboard the *Golden Boy*, and kept wiping the galley's hardwood floor with a rag he'd sprayed down with Bona. Meanwhile, Roman Walker, Ethan's much younger fiancé, grimaced when he realized he'd given away Donnie's game by announcing he'd just stuffed some lavender scented sachets under the pillows of Donnie's freshly made bed in the primary stateroom. Roman was a fitfluencer turned budding fashion model whose outfits always looked like they were pulled right out of the pages of a style magazine then run through the dryer ten times in a row so they'd cling to every muscular curve in his body. But when he saw Donnie glaring at him, he grimaced and hung his head like a chastened child.

Yes, Donnie had been less than forthright with Ethan about the schedule for tonight's event, but there'd been no hiding it from Roman. They'd hit the mall together while Ethan cooked, Donnie bearing a shopping list intended to make his boat comfortable, pleasant smelling, and inviting to an overnight guest. He'd sworn Roman to secrecy as soon as the guy had gotten wise to him, but because he was both youthful and emotional, Roman apparently didn't stop to think that their vow of silence also covered glaringly obvious facial expressions and bedroom prep.

Ethan folded his arms across his chest, the insulated cooler in which he'd brought tonight's menu resting on the banquette table next to him.

"Donnie, no!" Roman cried suddenly. He raced toward the sink where Donnie had hung from the faucet one of the eucalyptus branches they'd bought at the art supply store. "This goes on the shower head."

Donnie kept wiping. "In the TikTok she hung it on the sink."

"Oh, no." Roman reached down and cupped Donnie's cheek in one hand. "You're so nervous you're forgetting TikToks." To Ethan, he said, "Isn't it cute, babe? He's obsessed." His beaming smile went unreturned.

"I repeat," Ethan said. "What happened to courting?"

"Well, dude." Donnie hopped to his feet, taking the eucalyptus branch from the hand Roman wasn't using to pat him on the shoulder like he was a lost puppy. "Thanks to your advice, I did such a good job of it he threw his panties at me after a week."

"Gross, Donnie. That's not how we talk about boyfriends," Roman whined.

"*Boyfriends?*" Ethan's voice had dropped to a menacing decibel. His dark eyebrows formed a straight line.

Donnie avoided his glare, heading into the primary stateroom, where he'd scrubbed the bathroom to a gleaming shine earlier that day. He hung the eucalyptus branch from the showerhead using the loop of string Roman had threaded through it. When he returned to the galley, Ethan was glaring at him and Roman was looking back and forth between the two older men as if he thought they were about to brawl.

"I didn't realize I'd been enlisted to prepare the meal for an ill-advised sleepover."

"You're the one who told me to court him, Blake."

"With your clothes on. For once."

"Go easy on him, babe," Roman said, stepping forward and taking Ethan's hand in his. "You should have seen him in the mall today. He was like a little kid, he was so nervous." He looked to Donnie. "So is this like an exclusive thing with you guys?"

"So much for that vow of silence, huh, Romy?" Donnie said.

"Donnie doesn't do exclusive," Ethan said.

"He also doesn't buy lavender bed sachets and cognac and leather scent diffusers, and yet here we are," Roman said. "I, for one, think it's great."

Ethan returned his focus to Donnie. "Have you hooked up with anyone else since you and Richard decided to turn courting into a game of pickup basketball?"

"I haven't had time," Donnie answered.

"Oh my God. They're exclusive," Roman proclaimed joyously.

"Why are you saying that?" Donnie asked, but he was distracted by his vibrating phone. He spotted it next to the sink.

"Because you make time for hookups the way other people make time for coffee," Ethan answered. "If you haven't been with anyone since sleeping with Richard, guy's got his hooks in you."

Expecting a text from the guest of honor, Donnie unlocked his phone. Instead, the message was from Brutus. Richard and his crew had finished loading everything into the studio for the reception tomorrow. Which meant Richard was on his way there. And had been for a half hour, apparently. Donnie had been too busy cleaning to notice the alert.

"*The scent diffusers!*" Donnie bellowed so loudly Roman's hands shot to his ears. They were all still in their boxes.

He went for them before Ethan blocked his path. "Roman will put out the scent diffusers. You stay right here."

Commanded by the deep note of authority in his fiancé's voice, the younger man silently went to work in the salon while Ethan gestured for Donnie to stand next to him at the galley's cramped counter as he unloaded the insulated cooler. Avoiding eye contact, Ethan said, "Low heat, around two fifty, maybe two seventy, for about ten to fifteen minutes. Then take the foil off to crisp it up for another six to seven. You might want to bump up the temperature a bit during the last part."

"You're pissed at me."

"Not pissed. I'm *perturbed* that my fiancé knew about this before I did given I've known you over a decade longer. But hearing you cry out *the scent diffusers* like an actor in a Shakespearian tragedy more than compensates." Ethan placed the foil-covered china plates inside the fridge. "That's my best china, so please be careful with it. As careful as I assume you're going to be with your most important friendship and Sapphire Cove's wedding of the century."

"Look, Logan wanted me to bang him because apparently he was driving Logan nuts and he thought it would chill Richard out. You know, me banging him."

"A genius idea that does not sound remotely lifted from a bad high school comedy. Was Connor in on that plan?"

"Yeah, that'd be a no."

"Then that so-called plan sounds more like a recipe for disaster. I would buy a helmet to prepare."

"I'm working on Logan. He's being weird about the wedding 'cause he's afraid he's going to jinx it. He's not good at asking for what he wants. I'm trying to get him to open up."

"And you thought you'd start by opening Richard's fly?"

"I really tried not to have sex with him, Blake. I did. Seriously."

"Yes, well, to be perfectly honest, I didn't expect you to last until after the wedding." Ethan pulled a bottle of sparkling water from the fridge and opened it. "How long *did* you last, by the way?"

"A week."

Ethan sighed. "I guess that's growth." For a while they glared at each other. "*Is* it exclusive?" he asked in a whisper.

"We haven't said anything. But my hand freezes every time I open Grindr."

Ethan raised one eyebrow. "Have you tried Scruff?"

"Same deal, smart ass."

"Donnie, my dear, I don't know if you've heard, but a recently divorced man is not the best person to fall for when you decide to finally fall."

"You can be kinda condescending, you know that?"

Ethan stuck out his bottom lip and cocked his head to one side. He gently patted Donnie's right cheek. "Oh, darling. It only sounds that way because I'm so much smarter than you."

Donnie reached up and grabbed his old friend's wrist, and suddenly they were skittering across the floor as they pretend wrestled their way into the salon where Roman had finished setting diffusers next to every orchid Donnie had put out earlier. He'd pushed the club chairs to the walls to make the sitting room seem bigger, but it was pretty spacious to begin with.

"Guys, act your old age," Roman barked.

Donnie's phone buzzed in his pocket. This time the text was from Richard. He was fifteen minutes out, according to GPS. "Shit. You all gotta go. Now."

"Worst thank you I've ever heard," Ethan huffed as he headed for the door.

"I'll thank you if we don't get food poisoning."

"I'm so excited for you, Donnie," Roman said, then followed his fiancé onto the dock. "It's about time you settled down."

"Do I look settled down? Get!"

A minute later, Donnie was on the fly bridge, turning on the string lights he'd laced the boat with earlier that day. The glowing orange bulbs webbing the sun deck's roof were still in perfect working order. Now that night had fallen, they looked even better than when he'd first run them. He showered in a frenzy. By the time he'd gone out onto the sun deck to see if he could spy Richard, the man was walking down the dock toward his boat, a plastic-wrapped suit that looked fresh from the dry cleaners draped over one shoulder. It was hard to tell from a distance, but Donnie was pretty sure the bulky backpack was a stylish carry-on. Once Richard came close, he realized he was right.

He hopped down onto the dock, took the suit from his hand, and helped him aboard. "This is lovely," Richard said. "You talked about it like it was some fishing scow."

"Yeah, well…"

Once they were inside, Richard spun in place, eyes brightening when he smelled his favorite scent pulsing through the air. "Leather and cognac?"

"Same as in your room. At Sapphire Cove."

"Donnie…" But instead of finishing the sentence, Richard pulled him in close, gave him a kiss that lit up the nerves on the back of his neck and made his hands want to paw and claw in equal measure.

When they finally broke, Donnie asked, "How was load in?"

"Brutus was both charming and helpful, despite having a dog's name."

"First time I've heard the charming part."

"My crew will be there first thing in the morning. They should be mostly done by the time we get there, and I can finish everything off."

More kisses. "So we have all the time in the world to—"

"I could use a shower."

"Alone?"

"For now, yes. No rush. You've got me all night."

Another kiss, and then Donnie escorted Richard the few steps to the bathroom, which seemed to impress Richard a second time with its space. When he pulled the tiny door shut behind him, Donnie went to hang up the gorgeous suit, heart hammering. He felt as nervous as he'd been before he'd lost his virginity. Because maybe, despite all the sex he'd had since, tonight would be a true first. Planned in advance with a man who'd stay the night. A man who had somehow stolen his desire for other men.

41

They left the bright blaze of downtown San Diego in their wake as Donnie captained the *Golden Boy* around Point Loma. Then the dark sea lay before them as they cruised north up the twinkling coast.

Seated on the edge of the cushioned banquette sofa next to Donnie's captain's chair, Richard gazed intently at the black horizon. His billowy, lightweight pants could have doubled as PJ's. His soft linen popover shirt had a band collar, its three buttons undone. By day, he carried himself like something regal. At sea, the wind blowing in his hair, he looked to Donnie like an angel who didn't quite belong on Earth.

"You afraid of the water?" Donnie asked.

"Not at all, and I would have said so before now, believe me."

"You're kinda far away, is all."

Smiling, Richard rose to his feet, stood behind Donnie's chair and slid his arms down his chest. "Close enough?"

"Closer."

He rested his chin on Donnie's shoulder. "I was trying not to distract you."

"I'm an old hand. I've got good radar."

Richard kissed him on the cheek. "I do love a man with good radar."

"So what *are* you afraid of? You know, so I don't come up with any bad surprises."

"You mean, like phobias?" Donnie nodded. "Not big on heights. And I have an irrational fear of bears given I've never been camping or spent much time in the woods."

"Sounds like you might have a fear of camping."

"Perhaps. But I'm open on that one."

"Define open."

"If I'm sharing a sleeping bag with you, I might be more amenable to the idea."

"Good to know. I'm a pretty good camper."

"Also, there'd need to be a very clean bathroom with some sort of private shower and ample counter space."

"Okay, camping's out then."

"Yeah, I was just trying to be a good sport."

A short while later, they were passing the lights of La Jolla's village, then the wide, dark opening to its mansion-lined cove. As they pulled parallel with Black's Beach, Donnie slowed the engines. It was a rugged, isolated stretch of sand accessible by steep hiking trails that laced its towering bluffs, which were a solid wall of black against the starry sky. He'd spent plenty of time on the nude beach there in daylight. He cut the engine and the *Golden Boy* drifted, the hum of its engines replaced by the soft gurgle of its collapsing, spreading wake. He turned to Richard. They were bathed in the golden glow of the string lights overhead. Floating free from the trappings of their everyday lives, their kiss felt more powerful and unhurried than any they'd shared before.

"You really love the water, I can tell," Richard said.

"It's like the opposite of my old life, water and sky. Before California, everything was either winter or mud." He gathered a fist full of Richard's hair, holding it gently against the back of his head. "And out here we can fuck as loud as we want."

"I'm a little nervous about that part." Richard bowed his head, placing his hands against Donnie's chest. "I mean, I'm hardly a virgin. But you're quite gifted down there, as you well know."

Donnie kissed his forehead. "I'll go slow," he whispered.

"Just *start* slow. Then we'll both decide how hard you should go."

"Deal." Donnie kissed Richard gently on the lips. But when the man went to unzip his jeans, he gently gripped his wrist. "No. You've done enough servicing. Time for you to be the center of attention."

Then it was down to the sundeck where two cushioned banquette sofas awaited them, lined with oversized throw pillows. There was a roof over their heads, but the walls were open to the sea, and in the quiet that had fallen they could hear the rush of surf meeting the nearby shore. It was too deep to drop anchor, but they were well outside any shipping lane. Even so, the radar alarm was on and wired to a speaker in every room.

Garment by garment, he stripped Richard bare, until his delicious conquest was standing fully naked, back pressed to Donnie's chest. The sudden exposure to open air made his cock rise instantly, a sign there was a streak of exhibitionist in him. He found the man's nipples with both hands—wildly sensitive nipples, he'd learned—and worked them tenderly while gently rubbing his denim encased cock against the crack of Richard's bare ass.

"Why aren't you naked?" Richard asked in a whisper.

"I've been naked plenty. It's your turn to be the star."

He steered Richard toward the sofa, turned him, laid him down on his back as he sank to his own knees, bringing their mouths together, stroking Richard's cock as they kissed. He'd made a map of Richard Merriweather's most sensitive spots discovered these past few days, and now he traveled it with skill. His cock was the final destination, and it thrilled him to feel Richard's fingers grip his scalp as he went to work sucking him with long, smooth strokes while swirling his tongue over the head. Gently, he caressed Richard's smooth balls, which he knew drove the guy wild.

"If you're going to fuck the come out of me, you shouldn't make me come this soon." The confidence in Richard's voice rang through the night air like a bell, sending shivers of delight up Donnie's spine. His body seemed defenseless, but inside was a man who challenged and thrilled him. A mature man who knew what he wanted. So often in his life, Donnie was expected to predict someone else's fantasy, but Richard Merriweather knew what he wanted, and what he wanted was Donnie.

The second he stood and unzipped his jeans, Richard reached for his cock. Donnie batted his hand away. "Tonight I do the work."

Eyes glazed, Richard wilted back against the sofa cushions, his own cock so hard it jerked against his stomach. Donnie tugged, yanked, and then pulled his clothes off. He wasn't performing, wasn't trying to tease. He needed to resume the work of opening Richard up so he could finally lay claim.

On his knees again, he reached for the cabinet in the bottom of the end table nearby and pulled out the bag he'd loaded with condoms and lube. Watching his every move, Richard gently stroked himself, and Donnie wondered if seeing the trouble he'd gone to offered Richard a lusty thrill. The bag close to him now, Donnie reached out and gently spread Richard's bent knees further apart with both hands. But it was the look on his face that did Donnie in. Not dazed or frightened or hesitant, but hungry and intent and even mischievous.

"Tell me what you want."

"I want you to fuck me, Donnie Bascombe." His full name. No man had ever made his cock throb by saying his full name. Not the name that had been plastered on box covers and websites. His birth name. His given name. The name he'd sometimes worked to hide in the business that had become his life. "Fuck me like you wanted to fuck me the night we met. Then I want you to fuck me like someone who's earned my ass."

"You dirty boy." Donnie struggled to breathe. If he put the condom on right there, he might risk blowing across the teak between his knees. Instead he covered his middle three fingers with lube and went to work on Richard's hole. "You beautiful, fancy, hungry, dirty boy."

He found Richard's spot, pressed gently, then hard. Richard pushed his head back into the halo his hair made against the sofa cushions. He was absently stroking at his cock. Donnie batted his hand away. "Cut that out. Only one thing's going to make you come tonight. My cock."

But it was looking like Donnie's fingers would bring Richard to the edge too soon if he didn't stop. So he went to work, tore the condom open, slicked his shaft with lube and sheathed himself. Then his head was pressing against the warmth of Richard's hole. And he was suddenly dizzy. When his eyes met Donnie's, something inside of Donnie broke. Dangerous, reckless words rose inside of him, too fast for him to stuff them down.

He wanted to tell him that he'd tried to hook up with other guys after their first time. That he'd tried to get Richard out of his mind because he was so afraid he wouldn't want him after he'd shared everything about his past. But that was too much, too far.

"You're all I fucking want, Richard Merriweather." It wasn't as reckless as his thoughts had sounded to him, but Richard was staring up at him intently now, lips parted as his bare chest heaved with breaths. "I know you think I can probably get this hard for any man, but with you, it's different. It's an ache. And I feel it everywhere." He started pressing gently against Richard's entrance. "I don't just want you." Their lips were inches apart. "I need you."

Richard's eyes went wide. His mouth became a perfect O. For a second, Donnie thought his stupid speech had terrified the guy and he was about to jump overboard. Then he felt the warm embrace below and realized, to his astonishment, what had caused Richard's wide-eyed shock.

He was inside him.

All the way inside him.

No struggle, no resistance, no deep breathing. No need for the other tricks of the trade he'd planned to open Richard up if he'd struggled. Instead, Richard had taken him almost to the hilt on the first stroke. Astonishment washed over them both, rendered them suddenly silent except for their gasps. They were, Donnie realized, sharing a common realization. A bottom's switch didn't reside in their back side. It was in their mind, their soul. Their heart. And Richard's switch had flipped, no doubt thanks to Donnie's words.

"Oh God," Richard moaned. "All of you...*all* of you." There was stunned disbelief in his voice. Donnie held steady but stayed still, giving him a moment to adjust, to settle. To breathe. But Richard wasn't gritting his teeth or gasping. He was clutching Donnie instead, staring up into his eyes as if he'd somehow become more real above him. He was holding on to him like a life raft, wrapping his legs slowly around Donnie's lower back. He felt no resistance anywhere in the man's bones.

Slowly, noses touching, Donnie went to work. Long, steady strokes. Richard's groan was pure pleasure, a sign that Donnie's shaft was grinding along his special spot.

"Like a bull. You're hung like a fucking *bull*."

Richard's filthy words delighted him, helped him settle in to a slow, steady grinding fuck. He wanted Richard to memorize the river of pleasure Donnie's shaft made as it slid inside of him, prepare himself for the bursts of sensations his cock brought on each inward and outward stroke so that he could tune himself to maximum pleasure.

"Oh God...Fuck, Donnie...you're going to make me..."

"Come?" Donnie said tauntingly as he continued his deep and steady work. "Is that what you're trying to say? My cock's going to make you come?" Donnie increased his thrusts. "Well, then you better control yourself. Can you do that? Can you control yourself? 'Cause I know I can't. Not when I'm turning a fancy boy like you into a cock hungry slut."

When Richard opened his eyes, it looked like it was a struggle. Like pleasure and surrender had turned his eyelids to ten-pound weights. His grin was drowsy, but it was also satisfied. "You pig. You're a pig, Donnie Bascombe." But he said it like it was a badge of honor he'd just taped to Donnie's sweaty chest, so Donnie fucked harder. And faster.

"I thought I was a bull," he growled, mouth inches from Richard's.

"You're both," Richard whispered. "And you're going to fuck the come out of me if you don't stop."

"You really don't know how to make a man stop wanting you, do you, Merriweather?"

"Donnie!"

Jets. Three of them. Thick and ropey and shooting across Richard's stomach. It took Donnie a second to realize Richard's hands were both gripping Donnie's shoulders. He hadn't jerked himself off. Donnie's thrusts had driven his seed from him. The sounds ripping from Richard combined bliss and astonishment into something that sounded like a plea for more. More pleasure. More thrusts. More Donnie.

Gripping the back of Richard's head, he held it in place so he could watch his face contort with bliss as his orgasm roared through him.

Once he caught his breath, he gazed into Donnie's eyes. "Paint me."

"What?"

"Pull out and paint me with your come."

He'd never wanted to comply with an order so much in his life. He slid free, yanking the condom off. Within frenzied seconds, he was exploding across Richard's chest. When he managed to breathe again, he watched Richard gently running his fingers through one of the slick strands. For a second, the man studied the moistened tip of his fingers with a dazed look.

He's not, is he? Donnie thought.

Then, to Donnie's astonishment, Richard placed the dollop of Donnie's come in between his lips and sucked it off. "Sorry," he whispered.

Laughing, Donnie brought their faces together again. "What are you sorry for, baby?"

Richard was pouting and smiling at the same time. "Maybe I got a little carried away."

"With what?"

Richard's eyes met his. "Your come." He bit his lower lip. "I kind of have a come thing."

Amazing that he'd be embarrassed to reveal a kink after all they'd shared. Donnie could think of only one response. He ran his fingers through a puddle he'd left on Richard's stomach and brought them to Richard's lips. "Prove it, tiger."

Richard grabbed Donnie's wrist to hold it steady, then sucked his fingers with force and suction.

Donnie wilted into him. Then Richard was tugging on him and Donnie realized he wanted them to lie together on the cushions. After a few seconds of maneuvering, they were spooning with Richard on the outside.

"If I tell you that was the best sex of my life, will you accuse me of lying?" Donnie finally asked.

Richard turned himself around, no easy feat given the narrow sofa, but it meant they were face to face again. "Not to your face," he said quietly. "I mean, I'll *want* to believe you, but I'll doubt it like I doubt everything."

"Don't doubt this," Donnie whispered, gently pushing his locks back from his forehead.

Donnie's words seemed to hover over them both.

You're all I fucking want, Richard Merriweather.

The words felt true, but they also sounded like a promise. A big one, one they might not be ready for.

"You're beautiful, you know that?" Donnie whispered.

Richard's eyes betrayed doubt. "You're the first man to make me feel that way. The first man who doesn't act like I should be grateful to have him. And you know what?"

"What?"

"That makes me grateful to…"

For a second, Donnie thought he'd finish the sentence with the words *have you*, and if he did, maybe, just maybe, Donnie could give voice to what he'd really wanted to say before Richard had taken him.

But Richard averted his eyes quickly as if he thought the complete sentence would be too much, too soon. "For you," he said instead.

Donnie told himself to let the moment pass, let Richard's words settle over them both. But he couldn't leave it lying there. Maybe it was too soon for promises or commitments. But he'd never gotten ahead in life by holding his tongue.

"You make me want to do things I've never done before."

Richard's eyes flashed to his. For a while, they were silent and still. Then Richard pulled them closer and snuggled his head against Donnie's scruffy chest.

"Please don't say bottoming," Richard finally whispered. "Not after that performance."

"Hey. It wasn't a performance. Believe me. I know the difference."

He felt better for having said it, but he also felt like they'd come to the edge of a precipice as high as the crown of the bluffs a short distance away. Maybe it wasn't everything he wanted to say, but what he'd said was true, and he'd wanted to say it, and for now, maybe that was enough.

They returned to the harbor. This time Richard sat on Donnie's lap as he drove the boat. Dinner was such a hit, he was tempted to lie and say he'd made the food himself. But he'd never been a very good liar. So instead, he spent most of their meal on the sun deck trying to get details of how Richard was transforming the studio for tomorrow's reception. Details Richard was determined to keep secret. Which made him realize that part of tomorrow's festivities wasn't just a surprise for Thalia, but for Donnie as well.

At around four a.m., he woke in Richard's arms, the call of nature drawing him out of some of the deepest sleep he'd ever known. The boat was dark, and he extricated himself from Richard's embrace as gently as he could.

A minute later, he emerged from the bathroom and stopped at the sight of an alert flashing on his phone.

The subject line on the email made his heart drop.

I miss you, Danger Boy.

He told himself to delete it without reading it, but he opened it instead.

Even though I left you, I never truly left you in my heart. I know you might not believe it but you've been with me always, and the time we shared together was the greatest gift I've ever received. I need to see you. Write me, Danger Boy. There's so much to say,

so much to catch up on.

Love,
Zach

Donnie felt as if he'd never experienced rage before that moment.

He told himself to forward the email to Jonas, and maybe Ethan too, and be done with it.

But after everything he'd learned, the oily deception running through Greg Raleigh's words left a sticky film on his skin. And it burned. And the difference in tone between this and the email he'd sent Ethan weeks before was a reminder of what a lying chameleon the guy was, adjusting his word choices and tone and mannerisms to mirror whoever he was talking to.

He sank into one of the sitting room chairs. Typically, he was terrible at typing out long messages on his phone, but when anger focused him, the typos were few.

I have nothing to say to you. It's been too long. I understand from the email you sent Ethan that you're in a bad way and need help. Needless to say, neither one of us is the one to offer it to you, and it's not really appropriate for you to be asking us. I don't wish you ill, but I have no place for you in my life.

Take care of yourself, Greg.

He hit send.

It felt like an enormous weight had left his shoulders.

He returned to the bed, took Richard into his arms, savoring his heat and his distinctive smell, the fading musky scent of his cologne mingled with earthier scents of their sex.

He'd done what he needed to do to protect both Richard and himself, their new relationship, from a demonic force out of his past. He slept deeper than he had in weeks.

42

A few steps through the door to the main studio, Donnie's jaw went slack and his feet froze in place.

Richard had switched out the lights angled on each standing set, giving all of Parker Hunter's staple fantasies the same soft, subtle glow as the banquet tables at Harry Mitchell's birthday party. The studio's expanse was studded with life-size male statues—either Roman or Greek, he wasn't sure—and each one held a silver candelabra the size of a coffee table. Gabe was directing the crew as they methodically lit candles. The ones already aflame made the silver shimmer. There were also small seating areas made out of elegant furniture pieces Donnie didn't recognize—love seats and armchairs, all with button-tufted black leather, probably from Richard's warehouse. They would have been lost to the shadows if not for their bright silver wooden trim. He almost missed the columnar planters full of red roses, roses so big and with petals so red they didn't seem real. He touched a few to be sure. The petals were soft but fibrous, and they left a sweet smell on his fingers.

In the end, Donnie had expected to encounter false walls covering up the sexier elements of the dungeon set and doctor's exam room, but Richard had stayed true to his word and embraced the functionality of the space. He'd taken Donnie's smutty fantasy factory and gussied it up with his signature class.

Hanging from the rigging on invisible wires were giant blowups of the exclusives in gilt frames. Not naked, but barely clothed. It took Donnie a second to realize he was up there too. Only his picture was an almost corporate-looking three-quarter shot he'd taken for an industry trade mag after he'd transitioned behind the camera. Which meant, unlike the exclusives hanging on all sides of him, he had a shirt on. He liked that. Liked that he was the only fully clothed man on display. It suggested Richard was laying claim to him in a subtle way.

There was no sign of chocolate-covered strawberries on the food table just yet, but the tablecloth was down and the champagne tower was being assembled.

A loud parade of voices, all of them male, thundered down the office corridor.

The models had arrived.

"I should probably go corral those boys into their costumes," Donnie said.

Richard was moving between the planters, adjusting those blossoms that seemed in danger of sliding out of view. "That sounds great. Honestly, I'm not exactly sure what I should do at this point other than tweak. It's my first reception in a porn studio, so there hasn't exactly been a style book for me to consult."

"Looks like you wrote one."

"Thank you."

"If I kiss you right now in front of everyone, you're never going to hear the end of it. But I totally want to kiss you right now in front of everyone."

"Slap me on the ass instead," Richard said quietly. "It'll look convivial, but I'll get almost as turned on. Promise."

Donnie complied, then used his hand to pull Richard close so he could plant a brief, hard peck on the back of his neck.

The boys were mostly well-behaved during dress-up, but a few of them made a last-minute play for ridiculous costume changes. By the time Richard knocked on the shower room door and told them the limo bus was ten minutes out, they were all dressed and ready to hit their marks.

A few minutes later, he assembled the performers into the receiving line Richard had sketched out on a paper diagram last week, then he took his position at its head. Next to Richard, who was stiff as a board. When he looked back, he saw his exclusives standing proudly at attention in their various costumes, all of them holding a sparkling champagne flute in each hand, ready to distribute them to the ladies on their arrival. They were all smiling.

Gabe went to the parking lot to await the guests of honor.

"Nervous?" Donnie asked.

"For as long as I've known her, Thalia has always said goodbye with a kiss on the cheek. The night of the party, no kiss. If she does it today, I figure we're in the clear. If not, this whole thing might have been a complete waste of time."

Female laughter powered down the office corridor. A wall of expensive-smelling perfume followed. Seven well-dressed women, most of them middle-aged, were filing into Donnie's smut palace, led by Thalia herself. Flanking her were two black-suited men with conspicuous earpieces, military-style haircuts, and shoulders so broad they looked poised to split their jackets down the back. Her new security detail, no doubt. Behind him, he heard a few of his boys twittering over the handsome new arrivals. He shot them a warning look over one shoulder and they fell silent.

Richard approached the guest of honor. He was obviously trying to make himself available for a half hug, maybe that kiss on the cheek he was after. She gave him neither. Offering a half smile instead, she surveyed their surroundings like a prospective buyer studying a new real estate listing.

Hand extended, she approached Donnie. Accepting the gesture, Donnie bent forward and gave her a princely kiss on her knuckles. "Welcome to Parker Hunter, Thalia."

There was a tense few seconds, then Thalia started to nod in appreciation, and her smile got bigger. "This is very nice," she said, then she looked back over one shoulder and added, "Let's meet the boys, ladies." The ladies pushed forward in an eager, smiling tide.

Somewhere in the shadows, Brutus turned on the sound system. Ambient techno pulsed through the candlelit space, and suddenly Donnie was shaking hands and getting kisses on the cheek from their guests, all of whom were bubbling over with excitement now that their ringleader had given them permission to fangirl.

Right when he was hoping to step off to the side with Richard, Donnie was swept away by admirers. To his surprise, they were as excited to meet him as they were his current exclusives, and this made his ego swell. Porn could be an out of sight, out of mind kind of business, and the fact that these women knew his directing work meant they were hardcore fans. But he had to work to keep his focus on them. He kept shooting glances Richard's way, and each time he caught him observing them all from the shadows, occasionally engaging in low, whispered exchanges with Gabe.

After a while, and once the champagne fountain was half empty, the attendees broke off into little groups, each clumped around their favorite model, and Donnie found himself free at last. He headed for Richard, who was alone now and several paces from the barnyard set.

"She give you that peck on the cheek yet?"

"Maybe at the end. She's enjoying herself. That's good. It's interesting, though. I expected the vibe to be a bit rowdier, to be frank. It's kind of sweet that everyone's just talking. Maybe since they've already seen every inch of them, the mystery's in what they have to say."

"Which scares the crap out of me. Joe over there's got some iffy politics, and Matthew sometimes acts like he's visiting the rest of us from some other planet where everything's figured out and he's king. Honestly, I'd prefer it if they were whipping their dicks around. It's more predictable."

Richard shook his head. "Clothes stay on. That was the agreement. He might have acted cool at the party, but Harry called me about all this maybe ten thousand times. And he wasn't concerned about the food."

"Gotcha."

Richard nodded, fighting a bigger smile than he was allowing himself, it looked like, and for a few moments they watched the action unfold without incident.

"I didn't want to talk wedding stuff last night," Richard said quietly. "Buuuuttt…"

"Sure."

"I keep asking Connor for any kind of direction or insight into a theme, and he keeps saying he'll ask Logan and then I don't hear anything back. They're gridlocked. It's still early and I don't want to pressure you, but…"

"I'll lean on Logan again. Don't worry about it."

"I appreciate that. I mean, the alternative is you and I sit down and bang out a presentation deck on our own, but then we run the risk of them hating everything and all that work going down the drain. And to be perfectly honest, I'm afraid that's exactly what Logan's going to do. This headspace he's in, it's not about aesthetics."

"Logan's afraid. He's not having second thoughts. Trust me. I'll work on him. He's a complicated guy."

"How so?"

"He's great at stepping up when he thinks it's for some greater good, but when it's for *himself*...he gets wobbly. Marines are ultimately rule followers. When you ask them to make the rules, things get weird."

He curved an arm around Richard's waist and pulled their hips together.

Several piercing screams made them jump. Matthew was standing proudly in the middle of a group of frenzied women, slowly pulling the straps of his wrestling singlet down over his shoulders strip-tease style. Only this was Matthew, so there was bound to be almost no teasing involved. Donnie snapped his fingers three times in quick succession. Their resident power bottom responded by glaring daggers at him and quickly yanking the top half of his singlet down—to his waist. Then he gave Donnie a leering, defiant grin as he flexed both biceps. The screams turned to squeals.

"I better go rein that one in," Donnie said.

"You do that, captain."

Donnie turned. "Is that my new nickname?"

"Maybe. You like it?"

"Yeah." Donnie leaned in close until his mouth was at Richard's ear. "You know what I'm going to like more? After everybody leaves, you're going to tell me which set's your favorite, and then I'm going to show you some of my other talents."

When he stepped back, Richard was wide-eyed, nostrils flaring. He took too long to swallow, and even then it didn't look like his Adam's apple had fully complied. Donnie waggled his eyebrows then headed off. With the champagne flowing more copiously now, his attempt to pull up the top half of Matthew's singlet resulted in various suggestions from the increasingly tipsy women of all the other things he could do to Matthew's body as well. Blood alcohol levels were up. It was time to stick close to his boys.

The next thing he knew he'd been pulled into a corner by the Apple Pie Twins, who were flanking one of the guests, a tall, mature woman in a Pepto pink pants suit who handed him a business card that looked pricier than Donnie's shoes. She was willing to make a significant investment in the dragon-slayer themed scene the twins had apparently been chatting her up about for an hour. When Donnie asked her how much, she mentioned a figure so astronomically high he swallowed three times in a row. She clearly had no idea how threadbare most scene budgets were. If he'd been a bad guy, he would have simply pocketed the difference and shot it in his usual manner. But as they shook hands, he thought that if she was serious, Cody and Ken's dream project might end up being the first ever Parker Hunter scene that farmed out special effects to a CGI studio. Or maybe they'd fly to Morocco to shoot it. Or both.

After what turned out to be about two hours that felt more to Donnie like thirty minutes, Thalia took to the center of the studio, raised one arm and gave them a ten-minute warning. The boys hurried off to the shower room where they quickly changed out of their costumes and into outfits matching the dress code California formal, meaning black jeans or slacks and shirts that had some sort of collar and sleeves. Then they each paired up with a different guest they'd be escorting to dinner at a fancy seafood restaurant in La Jolla.

As the couples assembled, Donnie noticed Richard in a huddle with Thalia in one corner of the room. Brutus approached. Before he could speak, Donnie silenced him with a warning finger. "Wait for it," he whispered.

Thalia Mitchell leaned in to Richard and gave him a kiss on the cheek before heading off down the office corridor.

"Score!" Donnie whispered.

Then Thalia gave them all a big goodbye wave, and the procession filed out toward the limo bus waiting outside. Brutus followed them. Richard was heading towards him, a skip in his step and huge grin on his face, then they were in each other's arms.

"You saw that?" Richard asked.

"I did."

Suddenly he and Richard were alone together in the candlelit space, which seemed infinitely more vast now that it had emptied of performers and guests. Cheeks glowing, Richard extended a sparkling flute in Donnie's direction. "Come on," he said. "You've earned this. We both have."

Donnie accepted the glass. They toasted.

"We've still got a wedding to plan," Donnie said.

"Yes, well, I have considerably more experience with those than I do with receptions at gay porn studios for rich people who've never heard the word no."

There was a knock nearby. They both turned to see Brutus standing right inside the doorway to the main studio. "Everyone's on the bus and I'm about to join them. You boys good to shut everything down?"

"Yeah," Donnie called back. "But lock the front door behind you."

"Who's going to blow out all the candles?" Brutus called back.

"I will," Richard answered, but he was staring into Donnie's eyes.

"When are they coming to get all this stuff?" Brutus called back.

"Tomorrow," Donnie answered. "When there's less traffic."

There was a short pause before Brutus said, "So you all going to fuck in here?"

"*Get out, Brutus!*" Donnie bellowed.

"Thank you for all your help, Brutus," Richard called back. "You were a prince. Make sure nobody table dances at the restaurant. It sounds like a nice place."

Once they were finally alone, Richard stepped into his embrace. "I'd say that was a success."

"You get anything other than a kiss off her? Did she say you're off the hook?"

"Not in so many words, but I've known her long enough to be able to read the signs. They were all very good. Thanks to you."

Their mouths met.

"You deserve a present," Richard said when they parted.

"You're about to pick your fantasy."

"Given how badly you wanted to know it the other day, I'd say that's your present." Still firmly in Donnie's arms, Richard glanced around the space. "And since my cleaning crew came through yesterday…"

"If it's out on the floor, it's been cleaned. We strike the stuff as soon as it's used and stow it in back before wiping it down there."

Richard met his gaze. "Good to know."

"So what do you say?"

"How is this going to work? I pick a set and we improv our way through the rest?"

"I've got a costume room out front that's pretty well stocked. But yeah, basically."

"Well, it turns out I have some role-play experience."

Donnie tightened his embrace. Through gritted teeth, he said, "Pretend you don't. Just for my sake."

Eyebrows arching, Richard laughed gently. "Sex Monster's getting possessive. That's an interesting development."

"Getting?"

Richard smiled, but he'd fallen suddenly silent. Maybe this was as close as they could safely get to Donnie's proclamation on board the *Golden Boy* the night before. Richard broke the ripple of tension with a gentle kiss on the lips. Then he stepped away, turning slowly to survey the space, and suddenly Donnie's heart was hammering. He'd already learned countless things about Richard's body. Now he'd learn his fantasies too. That felt far more intimate.

Richard took a step, and then another, and then it became clear where he was headed.

The doctor's examination room.

Slowly, he took his suit jacket off and draped it over the stool next to the exam table.

"Looks good," Donnie said, trying to restrain his excitement. "Doctors have to ask a lot of questions."

"And patients have to answer honestly."

"Does the patient need a safe word?"

"*No* will do just fine."

"Alright then," Donnie said, nodding. "I'll be with you in a minute." Then he turned and headed for the costume room, doing his best not to break out in an excited run so he could hurry back to the studio before Richard lost his nerve.

43

At the exact moment Richard thought he might have trouble pretending a porn studio was a doctor's office, the exam room became an island of light in a sea of inky black.

He took his seat on the edge of the table, bowed his head, summoning the role of bashful, insecure patient about to make anxiety-producing disclosures to his handsome doctor. A few minutes later, he heard footsteps approaching him through the dark, slower than Donnie's usual bounding. When the former porn star finally stepped into the light, his transformation stopped Richard's breath.

He'd donned the basics—white lab coat, a stethoscope hanging around his neck. But he'd also changed into a collared dress shirt and tie underneath, and he was wearing a pair of thick-framed glasses that made him look both professorial and deliciously intense. There was even some product in his hair too. Sex Monster had coated himself in a shell of conformity and repression, and Richard was determined to make it crack and crumble during the game to come.

The muted sexual thrill of every visit he'd ever had with a male doctor, the knowledge that he was about to be vulnerable at another man's hands in an environment where sex was forbidden, but often discussed, ran through him with shiver inducing force. Then he saw what was tucked underneath the closed laptop computer Donnie was carrying in one arm. A blue and white checked hospital gown Donnie had folded into a neat square. Richard's heart skipped several beats.

"Good morning, Richard." Donnie took a seat on the rolling stool, opened his laptop, and set it atop the white supply cabinet next to the exam bed. "I understand you've got a few issues you'd like to discuss."

"I do, but it's kind of embarrassing, doctor."

"No need in here. It's all on the table." Donnie smiled and began typing, but the look he gave Richard was both cold and expectant. "What seems to be the trouble?" he added.

"It's a sexual issue. With my husband. He's a… Well, he's a top and, um, he says I need to relax more in bed, and I tried to tell him it was psychological and we should try some new things, but he thinks it might be physical. He wants me to get checked out. So here I am."

"Is your husband very large?" Donnie asked the question as if he were asking what type of car the man drove. Which was perfect.

Richard lowered his chin. "I've had bigger," he said as bashfully as he could.

Donnie raised one eyebrow, but that was the only part of him that showed any reaction. That and his intense stare.

"I mean, before him…"

"So you guys are monogamous?" Donnie's voice was drawstring tight, his eyes boring a hole in Richard's face, probing with a curiosity beyond the medical.

Richard nodded.

Donnie nodded in return, but his eyes raked Richard from head to toe before he went back to typing things on his computer. "What else can you tell me about your physical response during sexual activity?" he asked, eyes on the screen.

"Well, we've been married a while. It's kind of routine at this point. I like to try different things but he's kind of stuck in his ways."

Donnie kept typing. It was an unexpected thrill, the idea that Richard's most intimate secrets were being recorded by this fantasy doctor. "What does that mean? Stuck in his ways?"

"Well, it means he usually likes to take me from behind. Which isn't my favorite position, to be frank."

Still typing, Donnie looked at him. "What is?"

"What is what?"

"Your favorite position." Donnie stopped typing and turned his stool toward Richard. "How do you like to get fucked?" Not even the slightest deviation from the clipped, professional tone with which he'd started the scene.

Richard went painfully hard inside his briefs, grateful for the heat that rushed to his face because it would allow him to play the part of the embarrassed patient more convincingly. "Well, I'm kinda traditional, I guess…"

Donnie stood abruptly and closed the distance between them. "I'm just going to check some vitals while we talk."

Richard nodded.

"Unbutton your shirt for me."

Richard followed his doctor's instruction, and the next thing he knew Donnie's fingers were digging in between the flaps and pressing the cold stethoscope to his chest. "What do you mean by traditional?" he asked as he listened to Richard's heartbeat.

"You know…missionary, I guess."

Donnie moved the stethoscope further down his chest, pressing it to Richard's side. "Breathe in for me."

Richard complied.

"Breath out."

Richard complied again.

"So he fucks you from behind and what you'd really like is to get fucked on your back?"

Like he was sliding the question in as an afterthought. Richard nodded, and Donnie removed an otoscope from inside of his lab coat pocket and shined it into his right eye. It was perfect, so perfect, Donnie's pretense of proximity, the cold, clinical but increasingly personal questions coupled with the ordinary examination rituals. It was the invasion Richard had craved from the second he'd walked toward the set.

"Look at me for a sec," Donnie said. He transferred the light from Richard's right eye to his left. "Are there any other ways you like to get fucked?" he asked calmly.

"Sometimes I like to…you know, ride him."

Donnie's grunt had the barest hint of desire in it.

As he peered inside Richard's ears, he absently rested one hand on Richard's thigh. "You know, I'm not hearing anything that's suggesting a major issue on your part. I mean, one of those positions you like is quite strenuous, so if your husband's not satisfied with what you're bringing to the bedroom, it's sounding like the issue's with him and not you." Donnie slowly removed his hand from Richard's thigh and stepped back a few inches. "It's very common, by the way, for one partner who's not up to the task to blame the other. Could you be a bit more specific about his complaints?"

Richard met Donnie's eyes. "He says I don't open up…*fast enough* for him."

He saw the faint flicker of a satisfied smile—Donnie's true smile—fight to break through the medical pose. Which had been exactly Richard's intention, to let Donnie know he'd never opened up for any man, Mark included, as quickly and fully as he had the night before.

Regaining control of himself in the blink of an eye, Donnie nodded. "I see. Well, a lot of that is psychological, as I'm sure you know. But what we can do is conduct a very thorough examination to rule out anything physical. Then maybe we can get your husband off your back and he can take a look at what *he's* not bringing to the equation."

Trying to sound hesitant, Richard said, "So what is the exam going to involve?"

"We're going to test your responsiveness. Make sure everything's in good working order." Donnie turned and handed Richard the hospital gown. "I'll need you to change into this. Would you like me to step out?"

Richard stared down at the hospital gown in his hands as if seriously debating the decision. "I guess not. I mean, you're probably going to have to look at everything anyway, right?"

"That's correct."

Richard stood up, finished unbuttoning his half-open shirt and draped it across the top of the supply cabinet behind the laptop. Then he unbuttoned his suit pants, and that's when he realized Donnie was brazenly staring at him in a way that would have gotten a real doctor called before the medical board. Or thrown in jail. Watching his every move intently, coldly, as he disrobed, as if sizing up all the things he planned to do to Richard's body once this so-called examination commenced. The mingled feelings of exposure and embarrassment thrilled him, set his balls to churning. He pulled his briefs down his legs before primly depositing them atop the pile he'd made of his shirt and slacks. Then it was time to remove his socks. He put a hand out to steady himself as he lifted one foot, and then he felt Donnie's palm come to rest on his bare shoulder, steadying him the way no real professional doctor would.

As he settled onto his back on the exam table, the soft slip of the gown's material transported him even further into the dirty doctor's office of their lustful fantasy.

Donnie rolled the stool closer to the end of the table, then he guided Richard's legs into the stirrups. A rush of cold air swept up into the gown, caressing his balls and already comically hard cock.

Slowly, teasingly, Donnie pushed the gown's hem up over Richard's knees. "Very nice," he said softly, but in that clipped professional tone that was driving Richard wild. "Alright, I'm seeing a lot of responsiveness here already, so that's not the issue."

Donnie's fingers gently caressed Richard's balls, then he grazed one knuckle up the length of Richard's shaft as if he were measuring his hard cock in his mind. It was delicious torture, this middle ground between careful examination and forbidden fondling.

"Okay," Donnie said. He was looking up at Richard now, but he was licking his lips and trying to steady himself with flaring nostrils. "I'm going to need to run a series of tests down here, and I want you to describe for me what you're feeling at all times. More specifically, I want you to tell me if you've ever felt anything you're feeling when you're at home with your husband. Sound good?"

"Yes, doctor," Richard answered, voice thick with the desire he was now having trouble holding at bay. The fantasy was operating on multiple levels now, levels he hadn't anticipated. It tapped into the thrill he got from being vulnerable and exposed in a doctor's office, but it also unleashed a primal desire to get back at his ex for his many betrayals. And then there was Donnie, a man who was dedicated to Richard's desire in ways no other man had ever been. Richard couldn't see where the dirty doctor's hands were going thanks to the gown, so it was a surprise when fingers gently brushed his hole, rubbing a small, teasing circle no real doctor would have tried.

"Can you describe these sensations to me please?" Donnie asked.

"Honestly, mild." It was the truth. And the fact that he could give Donnie accurate instructions about his body's most sensitive spots only made this exercise more delicious. "Right around the hole isn't as sensitive. It's more...up."

"I see." Donnie grazed three knuckles up the length of Richard's ass crack, crossing the hole twice before reaching Richard's most sensitive spot, where his taint met his balls. "I'll need you to stay engaged and describe what you're feeling. Can you do that for me?"

"Down by my...uh...balls. That's...oh, yeah. There. There."

"Here?" With three fingertips Donnie rubbed a gentle circle that sent shimmering waves of bliss through Richard's ass, melting his hips, making his thighs quiver. If the stirrups hadn't been there to hold them up, his legs would have been jelly sliding off the exam table.

"Yes. That's very... Perfect, yeah."

"Does your husband spend enough time right here?" Before Richard could answer, Donnie brought the three fingers to his lips and moistened them with his tongue then returned to his previous motion with slick warmth.

"No, he doesn't," Richard said.

"Alright, well, I'm going to get in a little closer here and..." Before Donnie could finish his own sentence, he'd rolled the stool a few inches forward.

Then suddenly Richard felt a delicious warmth at the base of his ass crack. As Donnie brought his wet tongue up to Richard's hole, lapping at everything he found there, his hands pushed the gown further up Richard's thighs. The fact that he could only see the crown of Donnie's head and the shoulders of his lab coat as he worked his naughty magic drove Richard even more wild. Once again, the forbidden had been made absolutely right by Donnie Bascombe.

Donnie took a breath. "Don't forget to describe what you're feeling," Donnie chided him.

"It's so good. When you go all the way up and down like that. It's so good. The whole length of my... Oh my God. Jesus. Yes."

"Has it ever felt like this with your husband?"

"Never."

"I see." Donnie raised his eyebrow. Those glasses combined with his spit-slick lips made Richard's throbbingly hard cock jerk against his stomach. Donnie's hand seized the base of his shaft, stroking gently. "So we're definitely seeing a lot of openness here. That's good."

"Yes," he said. "It's very good."

"I think for our purposes, however, we're going to need to get this gown off you so I don't miss anything."

Richard nodded, wondering if Donnie wanted him to get down off the table and out of the stirrups. Instead, his dirty doctor pushed the gown up over his body, gathering the paper-thin material in his fists, revealing more of his naked flesh to the cold, teasing air, before bunching it up into a loop around Richard's chest.

Donnie tenderly cupped Richard's chin in one hand, tugging briefly at his bottom lip with his thumb. "You're a very good patient, you know that? Most patients aren't this committed to their treatment."

"Oh, I'm very committed. And you're a very good doctor."

Donnie gave him a paternal pat on the chest and a small, indulgent smile. Jesus Christ, he was good at this. The truth was, he'd done only a handful of role-play scenes with Mark over the years, always of Mark's design. Always about Mark being worshiped, never the other way around. This was something he'd always wanted in his life—to be able to fly off to forbidden places in the arms of someone he could trust.

"For this next part, I'm going to need to watch your face closely while I perform a series of more invasive tests. So I'm going to ask you to maintain eye contact as much as possible. Can you do that for me, Richard?"

Richard nodded. Fully naked now, the cold press of the stirrups added a sharp edge to the currents of pleasure running through him. Donnie walked to the base of the exam table and opened a drawer. What he removed was hardly medical. It looked more like a prostate massager, rubber and solid black. He'd used one a few times, but alone and on himself. The sight of it made Richard's breath stutter and his chest quiver.

"Now this is a very specialized device I only bring out for this sort of exam, but it'll tell us whether there's anything amiss up there."

"Up where?"

Donnie lifted a bottle of lube and slathered the massager with it. "Inside you, of course."

"Oh. I see."

"Is that okay?"

Richard nodded. He was trying to play the part of reluctant, coerced patient, but he was so turned on he doubted there'd be an Oscar in his future.

As Donnie stared into his eyes, Richard felt the hot press of the massager slip inside him on a tide of lube. It hit his G-spot. He was surprised his body didn't physically shimmer from the pleasure of it. When he managed to catch his breath and open his eyes again, Donnie was still gazing at him intently. There were traces of Donnie's wolfish desire there, stamping its paws and baring its teeth behind the dirty doctor's icy composure. Knowing he was reigning himself in, all so he could drag out Richard's fantasy as long as possible, made Richard crave his cock with something that felt like desperation.

"Definitely seeing nice responsiveness here too," Donnie said calmly. "How does it feel?"

"Amazing."

"Great. But we've got one more thing to try here…" He heard the buzzing first, then realized he'd missed the sight of a button on the massager's side because apparently the damn thing had a vibrator setting, and soon its gentle buzz was devoured by stuttering, pleading moans that were ripping from him in a frenzied torrent. "*Excellent,*" Donnie said encouragingly, loud enough to be heard over Richard's unstoppable display. "There we go. That's excellent. Excellent work, Richard." He was trying to think of some line of dialogue that would fit the scene, but he'd been reduced to cursing under his breath and gritting his teeth and gripping the sides of the exam table to keep from bucking himself onto the floor. "Very good responsiveness. Very good."

Suddenly the buzzing stopped. When Richard opened his eyes, he saw a new wildness in Donnie's. "Now I'm very happy with the results of this exam. And I'm pretty confident in my conclusion that all the problems you're experiencing lie with your husband. But in order to be a hundred percent sure, I think I'm going to need to go the full mile here."

"What's the full mile, doctor?" Richard asked as innocently as he could.

Donnie made a show of considering his next words carefully as he chewed his bottom lip, then he nodded abruptly and said, "I'm going to need to fuck you the way your husband can't."

"Okay," Richard said, "well, I mean, we want to be sure, right?"

"We do." Donnie unzipped his jeans, hauling out a cock that had turned roaringly hard by becoming Richard's fantasy. "We absolutely want to be sure." He yanked at the knot of his tie to loosen it, went about slicking himself with lube and rolling a condom on, all without breaking eye contact. His flaring nostrils gave away his desire, and the sight of him, still mostly dressed in such professional garb, with his cock ready to invade, was so damn hot Richard had to close his eyes briefly to keep from blowing across his own stomach.

Gripping Richard's elevated ankles, Donnie pushed gently at his entrance.

Richard opened his eyes, saw Donnie staring into his. He was as miraculously open as he'd been the night before.

When Donnie felt Richard's embrace close around his shaft, his eyes drifted shut briefly and his breath stuttered. He let out a long, satisfied groan that was more Donnie than dirty doctor. "You're a very good patient, Richard," he managed after a few slow strokes.

"You're a very good doctor."

Slowly, Donnie gathered steam. "Am I doing a good job of fucking you, Richard?"

"Yes."

"Am I fucking you better than your husband?"

"You're fucking me better than any other man has ever fucked me, doctor."

Donnie let out a grunt and gritted his teeth, a sign that this last line had almost pushed him out of character entirely. He lifted his head again. "I've wanted to do this since you first walked into my office, you know that?" Donnie reached for Richard's cock with one hand and began to stroke it in time to his thrusts. "So fucking sexy. So unappreciated. So hungry. So in need of my care."

"I'm going to need a lot of visits, doctor. A lot of treatments."

"Yeah? You going to come back and see me?"

"All the time, as much as you want. You've ruined me for other men, doctor."

"Fuck, I'm gonna…" The plea was all Donnie now.

"Do it," Richard commanded. "Do it, doctor."

Donnie bellowed and unleashed, and Richard felt his heat inside the condom, dazzled at the sight of Donnie's liberated desire turning him into a bellowing, shuddering display inside his buttoned-down costume. A second later, Richard followed suit, and then they were gazing at each other, gasping for breath. The stirrups prevented the embrace Donnie seemed inclined to give him, but he was too drained and breathless to move as he held them for support. His grin was big and genuine and purely him, and the sight of it contrasted with the performance he'd just given in a manner Richard found delicious.

After they'd showered together and slipped back into their clothes, they snuggled on one of the love seats Richard had carted in for the reception. Their clean-up routine had felt like a different, added fantasy—different from the doctor's office porn star for a day. Walking in the footsteps of guys so unbidden and liberated they could display their most intimate selves to the world and be wildly lusted after in the process. A fantasy he'd often entertained while knowing full well he wasn't capable of it.

"If it was always that fun, why'd you quit?" Richard finally asked.

"It was *never* that fun."

Richard kissed him gently on the lips. "You know all the right things to say to a scene partner."

"You…" Donnie held him close, lips only inches apart, "are a lot more than a scene partner."

"Good to know."

Here they were again, hovering at the edge of a declaration as inviting as it seemed frightening. And rushed. Hadn't Donnie said as much last night on the boat? That Richard was all he ever wanted. Fine. Maybe he felt that way now. He clearly hadn't dated much. Maybe he was experiencing a grown-up version of puppy love. But there was something about it that was so pure and sincere, Richard was tempted to give himself over to it. But that didn't mean he knew the right thing to say in the face of it.

"It wasn't just mashed potatoes," Donnie finally said. "That night when you asked me why I stopped performing, I told you it was 'cause I loved mashed potatoes. I mean, that's part of it, but it's not all of it."

"Did something bad happen?" Richard asked gently.

"Not terrible. There was a change. I'd always prided myself on my natural erections. Meanwhile the guys around me were popping ED pills or using these crazy pumps and stuff to try to get it up and keep it up. Not me. I loved my job, and part of it was showing up ready to go. Then one day I hit a wall. And it made no sense either. I was totally into my scene partner. Working with a director I trusted. Comfortable set. But it was like I went to reach for something on the shelf and it wasn't there. It scared me. I had to inject Trimix for the first time or we wouldn't get our shoot done. And Trimix had been my hard limit for years."

"What's that?"

"It sounds worse than it is, but it's a needle and it goes in the base of your dick and it gets you, like, instantly hard."

"Ouch."

"I mean, it wasn't the needle. It was this realization that when it came to my…I don't know, *desire*…it was a more limited supply than I realized. And I didn't want to run out. I didn't want to give it *all* to my job. I wanted some of it for…" Donnie reached up and smoothed Richard's hair back from his forehead, and it looked like he wanted to be gazing into Richard's eyes but was suddenly afraid to. "Someone special," he added.

Richard told himself to measure his next words carefully.

He didn't listen. "To be perfectly honest, if you were still performing, I'm not sure I could do...do this."

He let it hang there, wondering if he should try to define what *this* was. Dating. Seeing each other. Seeing where it went. They all seemed like vague terms, too weak to fit their arms around the passion that had exploded between them.

Donnie's eyes met his. "Don't feel like sharing me, do yah?"

No, Richard thought, *not in the slightest, but if I tell you that right out I'm terrified I'll either scare you off or set myself up for disappointment.*

"Maybe not where everyone can see," Richard said.

Donnie held his gaze.

Richard's heart stuttered. Had he declared their arrangement non-exclusive? According to the laws of dating Richard had always lived by—or, more accurately, been subjected to—nothing was exclusive until the people involved agreed it was. Now it seemed like Donnie was waiting for him to say more, and if he hadn't been gently stroking his hair, the moment would have felt entirely tense and awkward.

"Well, you don't have anything to worry about on that front."

With porn scenes. Not with hookups. Not with other men. The desire to ask for clarification burned inside Richard's chest. But he couldn't. It was too soon, far too soon, and this whole thing was too wild. And wonderful.

"Good," Richard finally said, "because I'm crazy about you."

"Excellent. 'Cause I'm, like, completely out of my mind for you."

"Excellent."

Another lingering kiss on the lips and then Richard settled into the man's chest.

44

Cody and Ken's new investor turned out to be a woman of her word and not just a porn fan made temporarily generous by champagne. The Monday after the reception, her lawyer sent along a letter of agreement containing the eye-popping figure she'd mentioned during their brief talk.

A few hours after Donnie gave them the good news, the Apple Pie Twins sent him a barely comprehensible treatment for their dream scene. Donnie put off reading it until Tuesday morning, a day when he had no shoots planned and the coffeemaker all to himself.

The potential cash infusion had his two youngest exclusives thinking big and Donnie reaching for his red pen.

Slayer and dragon fall off cliff together fighting and then dragon turns into human and we realize they're fucking as they fall. They float down to ground while doing each other doggie. Also everything's on fire & we should both have diamonds for eyes. Will be amazing!!!!

"Yeah, we'll see," Donnie said, striking through everything he thought might get someone killed.

Which, it turned out, was most of it.

A text alert made him sit up straight—the first throbbing bars of "Eye of the Tiger," the song he'd assigned to Richard's contact listing on his phone.

> Logan canceled our meeting. Again.

Donnie cursed and pushed back from his desk.

> I'll handle this.

A second later, Logan answered his call.

"Is your dad in the hospital?" Donnie asked.

"No. Why?"

"What about Connor? Did he break an arm or a leg?"

"What it this? Worst Case Scenario Roulette?"

"Sounds like your schedule's clear. You're meeting with Richard this afternoon."

"Look, I already told him. It's not going to work today. I've got—"

"*Make* it work, Murdoch. Richard and I have less than six months now to plan the wedding of the goddamn century, and he's on his last nerve with your bullshit. And you know what? So am I."

"Is there a camera crew there? Are we on a reality show right now?"

"Just for that, I'm coming to the meeting too."

Logan dropped his voice to a growl. "Cool. Then I can tell Connor you're sleeping with our wedding planner."

"We're not just sleeping together. We're dating and we're doing role-play and he's been on my boat and we're having the best fucking sex of our lives. Which is amazing 'cause you know how much sex I've had. And I get to touch his hair whenever I want. And it's the best thing that's ever happened to me, so fuck off."

"Awesome. I'll tell him all of that," Logan snarled. "It should go down great."

"Cool. Then I'll tell him it was *your* idea."

There was a brief pause. "You're playing a dangerous game here, porn star," he whispered.

"See you at four, jarhead."

Donnie ended the call.

A few minutes later, Richard texted again.

> Apparently you handled it. We're on for 4. And apparently you're coming?

Donnie texted back a thumbs-up.

> Show up early. For a special thank you.

Donnie sent back five thumbs-up in a row followed by an eggplant followed by a spray of water. There were many things he'd classed up when Richard entered his life, but his texting game wasn't one of them.

He thought it might be fun to time his arrival so they were only left with about twelve minutes of furtive play in Richard's new office, a callback to the joke they'd shared the night they met. But he was still Sex Monster, so he showed up an hour and a half early. Which was optimistic, but they hadn't seen each other since Sunday, so maybe enough pressure had built up to fire Richard off like a rocket. When he walked into the sparkling new special events office, he saw Gabe had taken over the sitting area as a workspace, and Richard was wrapping up a call. A few seconds later, Richard stood and dismissed his number two with a smile and a nod. Then, once he'd closed and locked the door, he turned and gave Donnie an inviting grin.

"Those are some big windows you got there," Donnie said.

"Wouldn't you know it, they just got drapes." He pulled Donnie close by the open flaps of his leather motocross jacket.

"We'd better close them if we're going to get down to business. Speaking of which, what sort of business are we about to do here?"

"I would think by this point you wouldn't need a menu card."

Donnie cleared his throat and did his best impression of someone trying to sound professional—in a profession that didn't involve sex. "The scope of work will help me determine the best angle of approach given the time I have for the job."

"Oh, I see. Well, I didn't skip lunch, so don't go crazy."

A harsh knock rattled the door.

"Come back later, please," Richard called out without turning around.

"Your mother is here," Jonas said.

Richard's eyes went saucer wide. He spun. Suddenly he'd thrown open the door to a Jonas who looked just as confused as he did.

"I thought you were out on the pool deck, but Gabe said you were in here."

"I haven't been on the pool deck all day."

Jonas seemed startled by this information, but the news he'd come to deliver still held most of his attention.

"Did you just say my mother was here or am I having a stroke?"

Jonas nodded. "I did. And your brother's with her," Jonas added, before swallowing. Richard turned to Donnie, jaw slack, then he looked back at Jonas as if he thought he could offer further explanation.

"I guess you weren't expecting them?" Donnie finally asked.

"My mother has not been to California to visit me since I moved here almost twenty years ago. They're supposed to be in Europe. *What* is going on?"

Nobody said anything for a few moments. Donnie decided to break the silence. "Maybe they got confused and thought this was Europe."

"I would totally laugh at that but I'm starting to think I might be dead. Am I dead? Is this real?"

Jonas said, "I can assure you we are all very much alive."

"Where are they now?" Richard asked him.

"Your brother's at the front desk. Your mother said something about the chandelier being alarming and then she disappeared."

To Donnie, Richard said, "I should go see what's going on. How much time do we have before our meeting?"

"An hour and thirty," Donnie answered.

Richard nodded and departed, leaving Donnie and Jonas staring at each other.

"So I guess this is bad?" Donnie asked.

"Let me put it this way. Even after all the things this place has survived, *this*, the two of them under the same roof might burn it all down."

Donnie swallowed, wondering if he should get a fire extinguisher.

Richard spotted his brother from across the lobby, bent over the front desk in animated conversation with one of the clerks. Behind registration, a giant flat screen television offered a live view of the hotel's beach and sparkling surf. His brother was nothing if not brusquely charming. But in most things they were opposites. For one, Paul had held onto his high school linebacker's frame and, unlike Richard, he hadn't worked to get rid of his Long Island accent. If anything, he played up its rough edges more. Brusque and forceful and good humored was his brother's way, but he'd also worked to adopt the mannerisms of a working-class tough guy, probably in a salute to their father's humble roots.

"Paul?"

Richard's brother threw out his arms and gave him a big bear hug that carried a hint of booze. A champagne flute of the kind the hotel offered all arriving guests sat on the front desk behind him. Paul, not much of a drinker, had emptied it in record time.

"Rich! *Bro!* You look amazing. It's so good to see you."

"This is certainly a surprise."

"Yeah, we thought we'd drop by."

"Sure. It's just a three thousand mile hop, skip, and a jump across country. What happened to Europe?"

"Well, you know the UK decided to basically split off from the rest of the European Union, so now they're their own thing and there was this whole thing with Ireland where it was like—"

"I thought that's where you guys were going, Paul. I know about Brexit, thank you."

Nodding, his brother sighed and looked to the marble floor at his feet, a man growing exhausted with a part he'd been playing for some time now. A part meant to imply—falsely—that everything in his life was just peachy.

The desk clerk leaned forward, holding another champagne flute. "Would your brother like another?"

"Aw, yeah, that'd be great, doll," Paul said quickly, taking it from her hand and downing half of it in three gulps. "Sorry. If you'd spent five days in the car with Mom, you'd need a drink too."

"The *car?*"

The idea of his mother, who thought business class was slumming it, driving clear across the country in a regular automobile was beyond comprehension. Richard needed a stunned moment to collect himself. Paul gave it to him.

"Is this about Susan? Are the kids with her?"

"Susan's the least of it."

If his brother's marriage and children were the least of whatever crisis had brought them clear across the country via interstate, Richard was terrified at the thought of what Paul was poised to reveal. But as the tense silence between them stretched on, he didn't seem all that poised to reveal it. A very bad sign. Whenever one of Paul's business plans or get rich quick schemes failed, he was usually quick to deliver some rosy report about a host of ineffective solutions he'd already started working on. Not this time, apparently.

"Where's Mom?"

"Outside, looking around. She said the restaurant needs drapes."

"Oh, okay. Well, maybe they can hire her to redesign the place given she has absolutely no experience." Richard immediately regretted the anger in his tone.

"We need rooms, brother. And to be honest, I could use a deal."

Quietly, Richard asked the clerk to put a room for each of them on the credit card he'd given them for his incidentals.

Nodding, the clerk started taping keys.

Paul put a hand firmly on Richard's shoulder. "Look, I can fix this, I can. But I'm gonna need a little ground under our feet for a while, okay?"

"Why don't you go grab a table in the restaurant and I'll check in with Mom and we'll come find you?"

He knew better than to ask more questions about the real reason they were both there. If he pressed, his brother would give him a version dripping in varnish and hung with hollow inspirational sayings.

Paul started for the entrance to the restaurant.

Outside, he found his mother at the balustrade, looking out over the sea. Her sunglasses were the size of salad plates and her bob had gone soft and curly, a sign that wherever they'd stayed on their way there, she hadn't had the space or the time to style her hair to its usual perfection. And she was dressed casually, which for her meant a pair of khaki slacks, a lustrous pink silk blouse, and a safari jacket with a dozen useless straps and buckles. As he approached, she stiffened, but she didn't look his way.

"I imagine you're surprised," she finally said.

"I am."

"That makes two of us."

"Well, you apparently had five days on the road to prepare."

"Did you see him?" she asked.

"Yes."

"What did he tell you?"

"That you all need rooms," Richard answered. "And a discount."

His mother let out a huff of breath, then tightened her clasped hands.

"They're on my card, by the way."

"I don't suppose I could get a view? It's better than what I expected for...you know, for the West Coast." She said the last two words with withering contempt.

"We'll see what's available."

"There's that tone I drove all this way for."

"How much?" Richard asked.

His mother didn't answer.

"How much did you lose? How much did *he* lose?" *Of your money,* he didn't need to say.

For a while, she stared down at her shifting fingers. "The house," she finally said.

"Whose?"

"Mine. And his. Both houses."

A pained grunt ripped from him before he could stop it. Both houses. Seven million dollars of Gold Coast history, another three in Greenwich. A legacy gone; an inheritance gone.

"Don't," his mother said quickly, a ragged edge in her voice. "Don't. Don't give me that lecture you gave me when you were in college about how I always loved him more because he was the straight one. I gave him what he wanted because he needed me. And you didn't. You were never even a child. You arrived finished, complete. It sounds good, but it was disturbing, to be frank. When you were four years old, it was like having a board member sitting at the kitchen table. You once told me my agenda for your playdate didn't stand up to *scrutiny*. That's actually a word you used with me. When you were four. Then at seven you began correcting *my* table manners. There was nothing I could do for you, Richard. I spent my days thinking you were either possessed or some genetic experiment they'd foisted on me in the hospital. So between that fact and being ignored by your father, maybe I became too indulgent of your brother's schemes."

"Competent children need love too." The words were out of him before he could stop them. When she didn't lash back with claws bared, he realized how exhausted she was. How beaten. "What was this scheme?"

She waved one hand through the air in front of her. "Oh, I don't know. Something with crypto or pharmaceuticals. There was some pitch deck I barely paid attention to. It was what he wanted, so I did it. And here we are." She sighed and massaged the bridge of her nose with a thumb and forefinger. "I always wanted it to work out. Every time. Not because I wanted to get my money back. I wanted him to succeed at something. Anything."

"What about if you just told him that in his case being a nice guy is enough?"

"Oh, you think he's trying to impress *me*? That's rich."

"What is that supposed to mean?"

"He's trying to impress *you*, Richard. His brother is number one in his field. You want to know the first thing all of his dates ever wanted to talk about, the only thing his wife wanted to talk about? Whatever wedding you'd just thrown that was in *People* magazine. Whether you could get them an audience with Oprah."

"Oprah isn't my client."

"Yet. You just have to face it, Richard. Your sense of alienation from our family is the inevitable result of being the absolute best at what you do. Success mostly inspires jealousy and resentment. Deal with it."

"That's very moving. I'll put it on a pillow and sell it through my website."

A silence settled.

"Is the law involved?" Richard finally asked.

"We're not on the run, if that's what you're asking. We're just...homeless. And Susan's done. She's had it, and I don't blame her."

"I don't either. But she shouldn't spend too long waiting for child support, I take it."

"You know, Richard. You don't have to be such a bitch all the time. The fact is, you're not that good at it. Not as good as me, anyway. And that's a good thing. You've been spared a certain set of circumstances that turned me into this."

"Because of fine parenting?"

"No. Because you left Mark."

Her response stunned him, and he needed a minute to regain his bearings. "You wanted me to get back with him."

She waved a hand through the air as if batting an insect away. "I wanted you to make him *think* you were getting back with him so we could get a bigger check out of that pig."

"Oh, that's much better."

"It wasn't my finest hour, I admit. But we never got to that part of the conversation because you got all huffy and queenie and had to end the call for your mental health or however you put it."

"Queenie? That's right on the line, mother."

"Oh, don't get self-righteous with me. I was there when gay men were invented. You're tame compared to my friends from back then. Their parties went on all weekend, and they called each other things like the Duchess and Lady Fisterly. I went to Fire Island when it was little more than driftwood and cocaine."

"Yes, thank you. I've seen *The Boys in the Band*."

His mother shrugged.

Another silence fell.

"Dad cheated?"

"He paid the bills. A lot of bills. He thought that gave him the right to do whatever he wanted, and I thought having lots of bills paid would make it worth it. Then suddenly I was sixty-five and he was gone, and I was left to wonder what my life would have been like if I had…" For a few seconds, he thought she might not finish the sentence. "Not pretended not to care."

It was a stunningly personal admission for his mother. And maybe a sign that they were entering a new stage in their always strained relationship.

"I'm sorry."

"The truth was, I admired your courage in leaving Mark. But I also resented you for it. And if it's worth anything…" She turned to face him. "On the way here, I was holding out some hope that my humiliation could allow us to have a fresh start."

"Well, it just so happens I have some fairly recent experience with humiliation. Maybe I can share some tips."

She nodded.

"And if it's worth anything, I've spent most of my adult life wondering why we aren't better friends."

"I didn't know that was an option. I thought my failure as a mother disqualified me."

"Perhaps it's time for all three of us to see ourselves more accurately."

She sighed and nodded and looked to her now fidgeting hands.

"I'll speak to Connor Harcourt about a long-term arrangement for you all here. While we figure things out."

"Thank you."

He was tempted to let it remain there, but if they were starting a friendship, he'd need to be more honest with her starting now. "I can't get the houses back, mother. I'm not going to make that much off the divorce and I've made a substantial investment with the new office here."

"I didn't expect you to. Honestly, all we need is a place to stay for a while. And for obvious reasons, I didn't want to be brunching in Oyster Bay when the news broke."

He nodded, relieved. A crunch of grass behind him made him turn.

Smiling sheepishly, Donnie bowed and handed Richard two sets of key cards in the hotel's signature envelopes. Then he turned to go without introducing himself.

"Donnie!"

He turned to Richard, looking wary and nervous.

"Come meet my mother."

The tension around Donnie's mouth evaporated. His shoulders sagged, small signs of how much this introduction meant for him. "It's nice to meet you, ma'am."

She accepted his extended hand. "My. You're a piece. Are you the rebound?"

"He's far more than that, actually," Richard said. "We're seeing each other. But please don't tell anyone. We're trying to plan a wedding. He's the wedding's best man. So it would present some awkwardness if it got out."

"Sure. As long as we can keep the fact that I've destroyed my life pretty close to the vest as well, my lips are sealed. So, what is it you do, Donnie?"

Donnie looked at Richard. "Well, I, uh—"

"He's in adult entertainment," Richard said. "He runs his own studio. It's a very good studio."

His mother went very still, her giant sunglasses hiding whatever shock might have been present in her eyes. Then she nodded and said, "Your father did porn."

"*What*?" Richard bellowed.

"He wasn't *in* it. He ran the books for a small outfit in Times Square when he was putting himself through school. It's very lucrative if you do it right. Do you happen to have a check for ten million lying around, Donnie?"

"Sorry, our *Star Trek* parody didn't bring in the new memberships like we thought," Donnie answered.

"Give us a minute, Mom."

Richard walked Donnie toward the entrance to the conference center.

"Sorry," Donnie said quietly once they were a safe distance away. "I didn't want to intrude. I thought it would be better if you guys could get the keys without having to go back inside." He dropped his voice to a whisper. "Also, we could all kinda hear you, and folks were gathering inside the door over there."

"I appreciate you working crowd control."

"Everything okay?"

"Not for them. Not right now. But it will be, I hope."

"Look, I know we fought hard for this meeting, but if you need to get them settled, maybe I can stall the thing."

"That would be great. If I get her some wine, she might be out in a few minutes. But Paul's another story. Whatever topic people bring up, he recites the Wikipedia page for it."

Donnie nodded, but he was smiling. "You told her what I do."

"Of course I did."

Donnie's smile got bigger.

"What? Like she's in a position to judge? She lost a prime piece of Gold Coast real estate because she can't tell my brother no."

Donnie laughed, but now he was smiling and chewing his bottom lip, like a child who'd been given the greatest present of his life.

"You have nothing to hide. Not from anyone I care about."

It happened so fast he didn't know what had happened until it was over. By the time Donnie was walking away, he realized he'd grabbed him by the lapels and pulled him in for a brief, hard kiss on the lips. Fast enough to evade possibly prying eyes, but forceful enough to convey his happiness and gratitude.

45

After the way he'd stood up for him to Greta Muntz, maybe Donnie should have been prepared for the fearless way Richard had introduced him to his mom. Still, he felt swept off his feet by it. No shame, no embarrassment, no apologies. It had taken all his strength not to wrestle him to the grass for an extended make-out session right there.

So when he pulled his phone from his pocket and saw a longer than usual text from Logan, it took a few seconds for his best friend's terrifying words to wipe the goofy grin from his face.

Connor's office now also say ur goodbyes to ppl you care about cause we might not survive this OMG he's so mad.

In response to Donnie's string of question marks, Logan wrote:

Now. Srsly. No Richard.

A few minutes later, the door to Connor's office flew open before he was finished knocking on it. Connor was so petite that whenever he tried to give Donnie a furious expression, it came across as comical, like a kid on the verge of a tantrum. But in this moment his blue eyes blazed with chill-inducing ferocity, and his mouth was set in a thin, determined line that looked ready to unleash a predatory snarl. Even worse, Logan was sitting on the Chesterfield sofa, head bowed, hands clasped in front of him, looking both crestfallen and ashamed.

He stepped inside.

Connor closed the door behind him firmly. A deadly silence settled.

"What's going on?" Donnie asked.

"You tell me," Connor said. "Start at the beginning."

"Well, I woke up around seven. Didn't have any shoots scheduled so I took my time with breakfast. Gotta try some new coconut milk, though, 'cause the one I bought doesn't really agree with me and—"

Connor shook his head. "Don't be cute right now."

Logan agreed by shaking his head and looking at the floor.

"Maybe it would be better if you guys told *me* what was going on," Donnie said.

"Logan, that's your cue." Connor sank into his desk chair and crossed his arms over his chest. The lovebirds couldn't even look each other in the eye. This was bad, real bad.

Logan cleared his throat. "The night I got you a room down the hall from Richard's—"

"The night you were trying to get him in *bed* with Richard," Connor said through clenched teeth.

Oh, shit, Donnie thought.

Logan sucked in a deep breath. "I made a comment about it in front of one of the security guys, and he in turn made a comment about it today when he saw you go into Richard's office, and Connor overheard."

"*Looks like Logan scored a home run with those two,*" Connor barked. "That's what he said. A *home run.* And then this genius thought his best defense would be to tell me that he wanted you to hook up with Richard so that he would relax about our wedding." To Logan, he said, "*Relax* about our wedding? I have been sitting here from the moment we got engaged trying to get you to *tense up* about our wedding. To pay, perhaps, the slightest bit of attention to it. It took me a year to get you to suggest Oregon, then another to get you to ask Donnie to be your best man. After that, nothing. Every time I brought up an idea, you'd change the subject or shut me down. Or use sex to distract me. And now this. I bring in the best wedding planner in the world and all you can think to do is try to get Donnie to use sex to distract *him.*"

Logan didn't defend himself.

"Do you have any idea how all this makes me feel? The fact that you are being this cavalier about the hotel, about our wedding?"

Logan met his fiancé's eyes. "I'm *not* having second thoughts. Don't even say those words."

"Then act like it. And you." He glared at Donnie. "You, with all your opinions about how a gay wedding shouldn't have traditional gender roles. You know what you did?"

"I feel like you're going to tell me."

"You scared me out of being the bridezilla I knew I should have been all along. If I hadn't let you shame me with all your radical queer lectures, the flowers would be ordered by now and our tuxes would be picked out."

"Okay, maybe, but—"

"No, not maybe—"

"Connor, I get that you're upset but you're kind of being a—"

Connor shot to his feet. "What are you doing with Richard Merriweather?"

"*I'm in love with him!*"

It was like he'd fired a shotgun through the middle of the office.

Logan went straight-backed and rigid.

Connor's jaw fell open, blue eyes wide with shock.

As for Donnie, he was blinking back tears he hadn't known to prepare for, maybe because his words were a shock even to him. "I'm in love with him, okay? And I know it's not the kind of thing anyone expects out of me. And I know you won't think I'll be any good at it. I don't know if I'll be any good at it, to be honest. It's just...it's what I am, okay? And if there was any way to keep myself from going after him, I would have. But I couldn't. I mean, you two are the most important people in my life, and I wouldn't do a damn thing to screw up your wedding. But my world changed direction the minute I saw him, and it has not gone back to its original course.

"And yeah, I hit on him before I knew who he was, and it was awkward and weird and we didn't want to say anything to you guys. And I was going to work with him and that was all. And court him maybe. Even though I didn't really know what that meant. But I wasn't going to lay a hand on him before your wedding. I was just going to care for him, you know. Be good to him. His ex-husband was a shit who cheated on him with all their friends. That's what he needed. For someone to be good to him. So I was. I was good to him. I think. Or that's what he thinks, and that's all that matters to me right now. What he thinks."

For a while, no one said anything, which was good because he needed time to catch his breath and wipe the tears from his eyes. Maybe it was a sympathetic response, or maybe he was still wound up from his previous tirade, but Connor's eyes were moist now too.

"So these are just feelings right now," Connor finally said. "You guys haven't..."

"No. We have. Like a lot. And it's been amazing. And sorry, but I'm not stopping."

Logan shook his head. "You were so close to saving this thing, dude."

Connor turned his chair. "He can't save *you*."

Logan bowed his head.

"Okay," Donnie said, taking a step toward Connor's desk. "Maybe not. But I've got some more to say and it's about you two, so buckle the fuck up and don't interrupt me. Because you guys are literally the most important people in my life, and I can't handle this level of tension between you two. So no one leaves this office until we figure this shit out."

Connor crossed his arms over his chest and sank down into his desk chair again.

Logan sucked in a long, deep breath that made his giant back rise and fall like an ocean swell.

"Connor, you need to accept the fact that stuff like this is hard for guys like us."

"If this is going to be a lecture on how masculine tops can't plan a gay wedding, then you're both getting a letter opener in your eye. I have two."

"No, I'm talking about the fact that we grew up broke. When you grow up like we did, you can't tell the world what you really want. It'll punch you in the face and tell you why you shouldn't want it. Logan's not having second thoughts. It's the opposite. This is the most important day of his life. But it's hard for him to dream about it because...guys with our background, it's just hard for us to dream. Period. You make do instead. You try to live inside the lines. I mean, look at us. All our lives we were like, maybe we'll be a Marine or a porn star."

"I never wanted to do porn, man," Logan grumbled. "That was all you."

Donnie gestured to Connor. "Meanwhile, guys like you wake up one day in college and are like, maybe I'll launch a startup or invent a new medicine."

"I never did either of those things. I gave away my inheritance, remember?" Connor asked.

Donnie nodded. "Which is the kind of crazy shit someone who grew up rich would do."

"Donnie, please tell me your strategy isn't to use my privileged background as a justification for why my fiancé has been deceiving me."

"I'm not justifying anything. I'm trying to tell you there's nothing Logan wants more than you and this wedding." He spun toward Logan. "And you, stop scaring the shit out of the man you love. You know good and well how good he's been to you, so quit it. His heart was in his throat whenever you'd come down to spend the weekend with me on my boat. 'Cause he knew what you and I used to get up to down there. And did he ever complain? Did he ever doubt you? Did he send you five thousand texts to check up on you? Never, not once. Now you do this? Introduce all this doubt in his head by shutting down like some angry kid. Cut it out, man. Enough. You're better than this. *He's* worth more than this."

Logan glared at his feet, but he didn't disagree. For a while, no one said anything.

"Royal wedding under the sea."

The words were spoken so quietly Donnie wasn't sure who'd said them.

Connor sat up in his chair like a dog hearing a strange noise, so it couldn't have been him.

Logan's dark eyes passed nervously between them both, gauging every second of their reactions. "Royal wedding under the sea. That's the theme I want. For the wedding." Jaw quivering, eyes glistening. To Connor, he said, "I want Connor to have a jacket with, you know, embroidery on the shoulders. Because you're my prince, so I want you dressed like one."

Connor rose to his feet as if drawn toward his fiancé suddenly by a string, blinking back tears.

"You know, kind of like that *Red, White, & Royal Blue* movie.

Which I liked way more than I said I did. I was just jealous because you kept talking about how hot the president's son was."

Sinking to the sofa next to him, Connor took one of Logan's hands in his.

"And the under the sea part is because I used to have this dream. After you went to New York, before you came back...I'd have this dream that I was walking rounds down on the beach and you'd wash up on shore and you'd be all glowing and beautiful and I'd rescue you."

"A merman?" Donnie asked. "You used to dream that Connor was a merman?"

"Not a merman. Like...I don't know. An angel in the water. A beautiful creature from another world." Logan swallowed.

Donnie saw a tear slip down the former Marine's cheek.

"A world I didn't belong to."

Connor reached up and turned Logan's chin so their eyes met. "It's your world now too, babe."

"So he had wings but not fins?"

"Please let the merman thing go, Donnie," Connor whispered.

"Did you guys have merman sex?"

Connor's eyes met his with enough force to crack his skull. Donnie nodded and gave him a dual thumbs-up. The truth was, it was a great idea for a scene, and he wished he was taking notes. Maybe Cody and Ken's new investor would fund it.

Logan continued. "Donnie was telling me that Richard can basically transform any room into any place on Earth, and I was thinking maybe...maybe he could, like, recreate the sea caves in there and project water on the ceiling or something... I don't know... It's dumb. I don't..."

"I love that idea." Connor kissed Logan on the cheek. "That's a wonderful idea. I love your ideas, babe. Tell me more."

"I know what our wedding dance should be."

Connor's eyes lit up.

But Donnie, having known Logan for almost a decade, could sense a storm cloud speeding toward them that would darken those eyes in an instant.

"'Enter Sandman,'" Logan said.

Statue still, Connor stared into Logan's eyes like someone who'd just been given a terminal diagnosis but didn't want to show feeling about it in front of their kids.

Donnie, on the other hand, was doing his best not to bust out laughing. But it was hard. Very hard.

"The Metallica song?" Connor's voice was whisper quiet, but it sounded like it required all the breath he'd been struggling to keep in his lungs.

Logan nodded. "I know it's weird, but I've got some ideas and I think it could really work."

Donnie put the back of his hand to his mouth to hold in his laughter. "Power bottoms are always thirsty for a masculine top until he breaks out his music collection."

Connor shot him a menacing look. He sucked in a long, deep breath through his nose before returning his attention to the love of his life. "We'll hire a choreographer to make it work."

"Alright," Donnie said. "This is great. We're back on track. I'll see you guys—"

"You stop right there." Connor closed the distance between them, but he didn't seem anywhere near as angry as he'd been before. "That was a beautiful speech you made about Richard."

"Thanks."

"Has he heard any of it?"

"Not in so many words."

"Go share it with him. Right now." The fear he thought was confined to his gut must have blazed in his eyes because Connor nodded slowly to affirm the order was sincere. "If you're going to risk the most important business relationship I have at this hotel right now, it better be for something real, something worth it. For both of you. And you better be all in, Sex Monster."

Donnie swallowed. "Fine, bridezilla."

"Great. I'll check in with him tomorrow to see how it went."

"So are you guys going to do the make-up sex here or wait till you—"

"Get out," Connor said.

Donnie complied.

Heart pounding, palms sweaty, he headed to the Pacifica Suite first. The thing actually had a doorbell, but there was no answer to his ring or his harsh knock. He could remember the numbers to both rooms the front desk had given Richard's mother and brother. At the first one he visited, the door opened after a single knock. Evelyn Merriweather blinked at him, pulling the tie of her silk robe closed. Her head wrap looked as pricey as his boat.

"Sorry, I thought he might be here."

"He gave me wine because he didn't want to deal with me anymore. If he's not in his room, he's on the pool deck with his brother."

"Thank you. Sorry if I woke you up."

Evelyn called out to him before he made it to the elevator lobby.

Turning, he saw she'd walked several paces out from her open door, clearly struggling for words.

"I just… I want you to know he's not as tough as he thinks he is. So if you're ever in doubt, err on the side of being gentle. He's sensitive, I guess, is what I'm saying. But he's a good person. A better person than me…I think. Anyway, I might not be making sense right now. Like I said. Wine, life ruined. It's been a week. But this feels like something a parent should do, and I'm all he's got now so…"

"I appreciate the advice, Mrs. Merriweather."

"Oh my God. Call me that again and I'll rip out your tongue. Evelyn. Please. I'm going to go back to bed. I look like something Joan Crawford did at the end of her career."

Then she was gone. At least she hadn't threatened his balls. They were starting to feel endangered.

Richard was doing his best to let his brother unload, but the text he'd gotten from Jonas a short while ago was still ringing in his head.

> Screaming coming from
> Connor's office. You okay?

Screaming in Connor's office coupled with no response from Donnie to the last text he'd sent—not good signs. The wind gusts were strong on the pool deck, and a fair amount of other diners had been driven inside. A good thing, since it gave them privacy, and Richard's only sibling needed it.

"She just said *why, why, why* over and over again." Paul gripped his beer bottle with both hands as he detailed the last conversation he'd had with his wife before she'd left. "Why wouldn't you let me be the one to work? You could have stayed with the kids. You're better with the kids. You've always been better with the kids, she kept saying. But you always had to go out and try to be some fucking titan. And I'm sitting there listening to her and thinking, do I not care about my own kids?"

"You love your kids, Paul. You always have."

"So I went out and lost their damn house because I had to be Mr. Big Shot." He took an angry slug of Corona.

"Paul."

His brother looked up from his beer bottle.

"You remember that time in high school when Stu Morrison kept tripping me every morning when I was on my way to my locker? And then one day you shoved him up against the wall and told him if he ever laid a hand on your brother again there'd be hell to pay. You made him apologize to me right there in the hallway. And he did."

Paul nodded, half smile forming.

"I think about that story once a day. I think about it every time I think of you. How you did that for me."

"Still?" he asked. "Is that still what you're going to think about when you think of me? Or are you going to think about how I lost the house?"

"You're a kind man, Paul. That's important."

"Yeah, but it's not extraordinary. You and Dad… Fucking extraordinary, man."

"I beg to differ." Donnie appeared in the entrance to the pool deck, scanning the mostly empty tables for them. "Sometimes a kind man can be an extraordinary thing."

Then he saw the tension in Donnie's expression, the strain in his smile as he walked toward their table. If he hadn't been present for the screaming coming from Connor's office, he seemed to be aware of what had caused it. And he seemed distracted and anxious as Richard introduced him to Paul.

After Paul bid them goodnight, with a bear hug for Richard and a half one for Donnie, Donnie turned to Richard and said, "Can we go for a walk?"

Richard's heart dropped. "Sure," he heard himself say in a thin, reedy voice.

"Cool."

As they left the pool deck, it felt like his feet had stopped making contact with the ground. It felt like he was about to get another dollop of very bad news, and it was important he turn his skin to steel as fast as possible so he didn't fall apart.

He could do this. Even though he'd rather pitch Connor headfirst into a dumpster right now, he could still do it.

What was the worst that could happen? Well, that was easy. Richard might completely flip the fuck out and say he was moving too fast given his divorce wasn't final yet.

They barely said a word to each other as they descended the long wooden staircase to the beach, and the anxiety churning in his gut wasn't anywhere close to the excitement he'd felt the last time they'd made this short trip together.

This time, he was under orders.

They were alone now except for the wind and the footprint-pummeled sand and the row of empty folded wooden loungers. But with their trip to sea level complete, he couldn't remember what he was supposed to say. Whatever he'd told Connor and Logan, that's what. But what *had* he told them? The words had flown from him as if driven by some all-powerful, God-like force.

Love, asshole. The force you're talking about is love, and so what you have to do is tell the man you lo—

"This doesn't seem good." Shivering, Richard folded his arms over his stomach.

"We need to talk."

"Okay, okay. I'll do it. Obviously…"

"Obviously what?"

"You're in trouble, obviously. There was screaming in Connor's office. So I guess we need to dial it back a bit. And cool things down. That's fine."

"It's not fine."

"It is fine. We'll make it fine. Okay, I'm going to go. It's been quite a day and—"

"You're not going anywhere. Shut up."

Richard froze.

"There's ... There's something I need to say."

"I know that. And I'm trying to say it for you."

"I'm not breaking up with you, genius. Stop trying to be tough. Your mom says you try too hard to be tough."

"When did she say that?"

"I have a hypothetical. Okay, what if you had a friend who was really in love with this guy but he was afraid to say so because he wanted to do things with the guy he'd never done with anyone before? And not like fisting or bondage stuff. But, like, relationship stuff. Stuff that was about honesty and trust. Stuff he'd never really had with anyone else. And what if he told you that he wasn't quite ready to say all these things, but it was all tied up in another friend's wedding and that friend said if this whole thing was going to fuck that up, it had to be serious. And the friend needed to tell you. I mean, the guy that—"

"You don't need to use the hypothetical anymore, Donnie."

Donnie swallowed. He felt like he was shaking down to his bones. "It was time for me to tell you that it's real. It was time for me to tell you that I'm in love with you."

Richard's lips parted but the only sound they made was a sigh, and Donnie wasn't sure if it was a good thing because it had been over a decade since he'd told someone he was in love with them and that person had responded by pretending Donnie hadn't said it.

But Richard said, "Donnie."

A whisper. A strained whisper so quiet Donnie almost couldn't hear it over the wind.

"You know what I'm going to say."

"That you're not. That you're still getting divorced. That I'm a porn star."

"No. It's none of those things."

None of those things included an assertion that he didn't love Donnie back.

"Donnie, your nickname is Sex Monster. I lie awake at night wondering whether I should ever ask you to change your ways or if I should just get comfortable with it because I'm so crazy about everything else that you are."

"You're talking about hooking up with other guys?"

Richard nodded.

"Ask me how many times I've done it since I've been to bed with you."

"Donnie, should we *really* go down this road?"

"Just ask me. Please."

"How many?"

"Zero. Now ask me how many times I've tried?"

"How many?" Richard asked quietly.

"Ten. I tried ten times. Because I thought it would help me keep this in perspective, you know. Keep me from getting too obsessive. From rushing you. Each time, I never got past the first swipe. Because I didn't want to. Because they weren't you. Richard, I'm almost forty. I've had every kind of sex there is. A lot. Sometimes for money, sometimes not. And these last couple years I've had to force myself to do it 'cause I thought if I didn't want to that meant I had erectile dysfunction or I was losing my touch or I was getting too old too fast. And now you think I'm going to drop you one day for some new thing. You *are* the new thing. You're so many things. You're all these new and amazing things I never thought I could have."

Richard's nostrils flared as tears streamed down his face. "Promise me this," he said. "Promise me if you change your mind, you'll talk to me first. Because there's one reason you melted my heart, Donnie Bascombe. You are absolutely yourself at all times. And that makes you someone I can trust and count on. And love."

"So you love me back?"

"I love you back really hard."

"As hard as I—"

"Come here and kiss me, jackass, before you say something crude that ruins it."

"*You* brought up my dick."

"How could I not? It's everywhere all the time all at once."

Their kiss made them forget the wind.

46

A week after proclaiming their love for one another, Richard took over one of Sapphire Cove's larger conference rooms to present his complete design for the wedding to Connor, Logan, Naser, Janice Harcourt, and Logan's father, Chip Murdoch, who'd apparently been ordered not to wear one of his usual T-shirts with a marginally offensive saying on it. Sitting a few feet from where Richard stood, Donnie studied the other attendees, delighting in the wonder that filled their eyes. Dazzling projections of Richard's renderings filled the giant screen at the front of the room. Richard's description of the procession sounded almost like poetry. When the presentation was complete, the wedding party rose to its feet, applauding, and Logan stepped forward to give Richard a firm handshake that seemed to forever melt the chill between them in an instant.

Then the real work began. The truth was, the work was now mostly Richard's. Theme established, Donnie could focus on a new and exciting job, being a boyfriend for the first time.

It was new work that brought new discoveries, most of which made him feel like he'd been granted a new and better life. For one, there was no better sex than the kind you had after the man you loved rolled over in bed first thing in the morning, nuzzled himself against you and gave himself to you without preamble, distractions, or obstruction. There was nothing better than waking up with the potential for fulfillment and release lying right there next to you, hungry and ready and absolutely familiar with your body's secrets. Another wonderful discovery, you didn't always need an excuse to text the person you loved. Your life together could be one long conversation, with stops and starts here and there before you picked it up again as if there'd been no pause at all.

Then came their first weekend away.

Four months out from the wedding, Richard took the weekend off to accompany Donnie out to Palm Springs. There, in an isolated desert canyon outside of town, they shot Cody and Ken's high-fantasy porn masterpiece, *Great Balls of Dragon Fire*. Harrison and Matty came along to join Brutus on the crew. But the rest of it was a shoot unlike any other, thanks to the generous funding of Karen Baxter, Cody and Ken's new benefactor, who put them all up for the weekend at the mid-century modern mansion she and her wife had renovated in Old Las Palmas, right down the street from homes that had once belonged to Donna Reed, George Randolph Hearst, and Dean Martin. Aside from their luxurious accommodations, Karen Baxter's funding endowed the shoot with two honest-to-God trailers, the first Donnie had ever used, and a veritable video village like the kind used on large-scale production shoots. Under its shade, he and Richard and Brutus watched the camera feeds on flat-screen monitors. When he looked over and saw the mild grimace on Richard's face as he watched Cody and Ken engaging in strained, performative passion after rutting for fifteen minutes in the hot sun, Donnie smiled.

"I hope those boys have a good chiropractor," Richard muttered.

It was exactly the reaction he'd been hoping for. He'd wanted Richard to see firsthand that his job was a grueling and labor-intensive one, and nothing to be jealous of.

That night, the boys all dined together at Lulu California Bistro, a massive retro diner on the main tourist throughfare in Palm Springs. As they sat surrounded by frosted green glass and strips of pastel neon, Donnie's exclusives asked Richard a series of polite but pointed questions about "his intentions with Porn Daddy." The polite smile with which Richard indulged them warmed Donnie's heart. Clearly, his first ever real boyfriend was charmed by the protectiveness of his crew.

While it didn't arrive with fireworks and declarations, the entire weekend made for a huge leap forward in their relationship. The moment he'd started working in porn, Donnie had known full well he could never have a serious relationship with someone who insisted on a wall of secrecy and shame between their relationship and his job.

Richard hadn't only taken part in a shoot without succumbing to jealousy, he'd taken to Donnie's stable of exclusives like they were family. He didn't discuss his work with arched eyebrows or a sarcastic smirk.

Check, check, check.

Three months out from the wedding, the miraculous happened. After falling out of escrow twice, Richard's old house in Pacific Palisades finally sold. They celebrated by visiting the Parker Hunter studio after hours. It was time to perform one of Donnie's favorite fantasies for a change. The college dorm set was his jam. Having been denied a higher education, his horny imagination had turned leafy college campuses into breeding grounds of dormitory driven lust, and Richard proved more than happy to play the part of the snobby rich kid who agreed to help Donnie with his studies if Donnie let him use his body for sex.

Flush with cash from the sale of the house, Richard decided it was time to start looking for a new place. While Connor was hardly about to push him out the door at Sapphire Cove, he decided to use his business partner's patience as an opportunity to explore parts of Southern California he'd never considered making a home in before—the parts close to Donnie. They visited condos and houses all over Orange County, but each meeting with the real estate agent took them further and further south, in the direction of the *Golden Boy*. Several times, Donnie was tempted to ask him to move in. But it felt too rushed, and the boat, which had been the perfect home for him for years, suddenly seemed inadequate and small for a life he'd never thought he'd have. That said, every time Richard asked his opinion of a house or condo they'd just seen, his heart surged. Because the questions all implied that he wanted Donnie to spend almost as much time inside his new place as he would.

Still, he couldn't decide on a place, and as wedding preparations accelerated toward the big day itself, he abandoned the search altogether. "Maybe LA," he said one night as they lay together in the Pacifica Suite. They'd snuck in an early session before they had to meet Connor and Logan for dinner on the pool deck.

"For what?" Donnie asked, suspecting the meaning of Richard's elliptical statement.

"Like for a new place to live. But that's far, right?" Richard's eyes met Donnie's.

"Way too far," Donnie said, heart drumming.

"I mean...you want me close to you, right?"

"Very," Donnie said, clasping Richard's hand under the sheets. "Very close to me."

Richard smiled, rolled over into him and kissed his neck. "Okay, after the wedding I'll think about it again. But not before. There's too much to do."

They were showering and getting ready for dinner when Donnie's phone buzzed with a text from Logan. He scooped it off the nightstand.

U guys need extra time?

> We're good. Should be down in five.

I thought I saw Richard on the beach.

> Nah, he's right here.

Right here, Donnie thought, *maybe trying to get me to ask him to move in, but I'm not really sure. Or maybe he's going to ask* me *to move in.*

After the wedding, he told himself.

There were questions ahead, for sure. Some of them scary and new. But there was also excitement and potential and more revelations like the ones that had marked the past few months. Once they made Connor and Logan's dreams come true, they'd set about discovering more of their own, he was sure.

"I'm sorry, Tiger," Donnie said once he was finished reading the article.

"It's fine, I guess." Richard sighed.

A month before the big day, they were enjoying a bottle of wine on the *Golden Boy*'s deck as the sun sank behind Point Loma. The interview they'd done with *Coast Magazine* two weeks before had just gone live on the magazine's website, and Connor had forwarded them a link.

They looked great in the accompanying photo even though it was about a quarter of the size of the one featuring the grooms embracing at the hotel's balustrade. Back-to-back, arms crossed over their chests, the camera had captured Donnie and Richard beneath the Dolphin Ballroom's coral-styled chandelier. They were dressed in their wedding attire, navy blue tuxedos picked out for them by Connor. The event wouldn't be black tie, but Connor wanted its architects to stand out from the suit and tie wearing crowd. He'd picked out something formal but distinct for his white one and Logan's black one, both of which would be festooned with custom embroidery the grooms would keep secret from each other until the wedding day.

Giving Donnie such a public role in the wedding's publicity had made everyone a tad skittish, and even though they'd done nothing to hide his profession, the reporter hadn't made hay of it. He was referred to in passing as "an adult entertainment executive" as if it were a career as ordinary as any other.

No, the stinger was at the end, and in an entirely unexpected form.

Sometimes wedding planning can be as romantic as the wedding itself, but you don't have to tell Mr. Merriweather or Mr. Bascombe. Their work on Sapphire Cove's first ever Royal Wedding Under the Sea caused sparks to fly between the pair, and they're now a couple. But this hasn't been happy news for everyone. Particularly Merriweather's ex-husband, wealthy LA hedge fund manager Mark Scottman, who is allegedly still grieving the loss of their marriage. In a written statement to Coast Magazine, Scottman said, "I miss Richard every moment of every day and hope one day we can reconcile." Doubtful given the recently divorced couple finally offloaded their Pacific Palisades mansion earlier this month.

"If I'd known they were going to cover my divorce, I might have let slip that he cheated on me over a hundred times. Still, it's the publicity we were after so…"

Donnie rose from his chair and kneaded Richard's shoulders.

"You look good enough to eat in that tux," Donnie said.

"If memory serves," Richard said, setting his phone aside, "you did a fair bit of that after we took that picture."

Donnie picked him up and carried him into the bedroom so he could do some more.

47

When the limo bus pulled into Sapphire Cove's sun-splashed motor court, Richard was waiting for them next to the valet stand. It was Thursday before the wedding and Donnie was struggling with the fact that he was way more stressed out about the weekend than his boyfriend was. Maybe because weddings were Richard's business. And because he had no inkling of the surprise Donnie had planned for the two of them after the grooms departed on their honeymoon.

He hopped down from the bus, leaving Logan alone in the front row of seats. Richard gave him a coy half smile as they embraced. It was Bachelor Party Day, and they'd done their fair share of jousting about it.

"Look, I just want to be clear," Donnie said. "Nothing sketchy's going to happen tonight, I promise."

"I see. So The Bang Zone is a hands to yourself type strip club?"

"That's all strip clubs if they don't want to get shut down. And I never said The Bang Zone was a strip club."

One of Logan's old Marine Corps buddies came striding out of the lobby. When he spotted Donnie, the giant man's crystal-blue eyes blazed and a pearly white smile appeared in the midst of his thick black beard. On a guy as stoic and calm as him, it was the equivalent of somebody else throwing their arms skyward and squealing. Thomas Simmons, aka Church, had once been Donnie's chief rival for every twink du jour at the San Diego gay bars they used to frequent. Given he was a towering, muscle-bound Navy SEAL who looked like he could withstand a two-by-four being broken across his back without flinching, he'd prevailed over Donnie nine times out of ten. His nickname had been given to him back in his Marine Corps days, by comrades who liked to say, "If you want someone taken to church, call Church."

"How's it going, porn boy?" he said, sliding one powerful arm around Richard's shoulders. "This your new beau? He's pretty."

"He's not that new, Church."

"Yeah, well, that's just 'cause I didn't get to him first."

Donnie's blood pressure spiked so high he could feel a pulse in the crown of his skull. "Make a play now if you want two broken arms."

Laughing under his breath, Church released Richard, then tousled Donnie's hair like he was a little boy, the same thing he used to do when he'd walk past Donnie on his way out of the club with whatever hottie Donnie had just bellyflopped with. "Sad to see you out of the game, my friend. Beating you to the punch used to keep me sharp."

"Yeah, well, for some of us the *game* got really, really *old*. Get on the bus, Church. You've got all night to make me miserable."

Once they were alone together, he noticed Richard was blushing and beaming.

"That was hot," he said.

"Oh, you think Church is hot, huh?"

"No, I think you getting possessive is hot."

Donnie pulled him in close. "Hot enough to tell me where you guys are going tonight?"

"If you don't know, you don't know."

"Seriously, Logan's freaking. He won't get off the bus 'cause he's afraid if he sees Connor, he'll lock him in a storage room."

"Connor's not the one they used to call *twink slayer*."

"Yeah, but that's the thing. Logan says he got it all out of his system years ago, but Connor was such a good boy for so long he's going to explode into all sorts of naughtiness."

"Naughtiness, I see. Well, he should do well to remember the golden rule when you guys are getting lap dances at The Bang Zone."

Just then there was a tap on Donnie's shoulder. Logan's old buddy Sam Corcoran was standing next to him, dressed in a tank top that exposed his lean, muscled arms. The most senior member of Logan's crew, he was an honorably discharged first sergeant who ran his own private security firm now. After having done two deployments under his command, Logan regarded him as a surrogate dad, which made sense. Sam was sweet but firm, always putting the group ahead of himself. But right now those otherwise benevolent tendencies were about to get Donnie busted, he could tell. That and the small translucent bottle Sam was pressing into his hand.

"Best stuff there is right here." Sam's twangy Texas accent never failed to charm him, but right now he wanted him to get lost. "I know everyone says we don't have to worry, but with those rains moving through last month, I hear we've got more mosquitos than ever before. This right here'll keep them all away, I swear it. Don't be put off by the name." He gave them both a beaming smile, winked at Donnie, then boarded the bus, leaving Donnie holding a bottle of Skin So Soft in his hand.

Before Donnie could acknowledge how badly he'd been exposed, Logan's old buddy Edgar Garcia burst from the lobby, fists raised, spinning in circles as he headed for the bus, letting out war whoops like they were getting ready to play a game of football. His cargo shorts and tank top gave away their destination almost as much as Sam's bug spray did. Stocky and baby-faced, Edgar was the youngest member of the group, someone Logan had mentored the way Sam had mentored him. Like Church, he was still on active duty.

Behind him came the last member of their brigade for the evening, Ken Han, the group's token straight friend, arm in arm with his wife Kelly, the wiry and intense Army medic he'd married the year before. Kelly was the epitome of focus at all times, but right now she didn't seem remotely nervous about letting her husband run off with a group of his rowdy buddies for an evening, maybe because she thought they were headed to a gay bar.

Once the rest of their crew had boarded the bus, Donnie pulled Richard in close. "We're not going to a strip club," he whispered.

"I figured that out already," Richard whispered back.

"'Cause you're so smart."

"'Cause there's not a strip club named The Bang Zone in the entire state. But there is a popular ATV trail with that name in Trabuco Canyon. And I imagine bug spray will come in handy there."

Donnie waggled his eyebrows and brought them almost nose to nose. "Okay, well, since I showed you mine, you should show me yours."

"Rest assured, we are not going camping."

"Just make sure he's a good boy, okay?"

"Tell Logan he has nothing to worry about."

"And me?" Donnie kissed him gently on the lips.

"You have absolutely *nothing* to worry about. Ever."

Richard returned the kiss with a harder one of his own, then he patted Donnie on the chest with both hands. "All aboard," he called loud enough for the bus passengers to hear, then he hurried back inside the lobby before Donnie could say anything further.

In the warren of administrative offices, Richard found Naser and his fiancé Mason waiting outside of the closed door to Connor's office. Both men wore jeans and polo shirts and gave off wafts of pricey cologne as he approached. Their expressions, however, looked grave.

"How is he?" he asked.

"He's either got a puppy in there with him or he's freaking out," Mason said. "Lots of whining sounds. We agreed we'd bust in if it sounded like he was having trouble breathing."

Naser added, "Last time we opened the door he told us he was fine and went back to pacing like a zombie."

Richard nodded and sidled up to the door.

Naser touched him gently on the shoulder before he could knock. "Are you sure about this?" he asked quietly.

"Fairly, yes."

Naser nodded. Technically, Connor's bachelor party had been the responsibility of Connor's budget-conscious best man, but Naser had warmed to Richard's idea right away and allowed him to pretty much take over. Months of hearing Connor freak out about the idea of sending his fiancé off on a night of debauchery while simultaneously being expected to enjoy one of his own had primed Naser for Richard's plan.

When Richard knocked, Connor cried out, "It's open!" like he thought he might get arrested if he didn't answer immediately.

Naser on his heels, Richard stepped inside the office. Connor was sprawled out on the Chesterfield sofa, dressed for the evening in white jeans and a cream-colored knit polo, a white rag resting on his forehead. A half empty rocks glass of something strong smelling sat on the coffee table within reach.

"How are we doing this evening?" Richard asked.

Connor groaned. "Can we maybe all go for a walk on the beach and make s'mores or something? I don't want to do anything crazy, I just want to—"

"Sit here and obsess about everything Logan might be doing?" Naser asked.

Connor sat up straight. "You think he's going to *do* something?"

"No, I'm saying I need one of these," Naser said, handing Connor his drink.

Connor took a slug, then he sat up straighter as if struck by a brilliant idea. "Where's my phone? I'm going to text him."

"They left already," Richard said.

Connor darted past Richard toward his desk. "I know. Still, I'm going to give him a hall pass. I'll tell him he can hook up with however many trashy sluts he wants to tonight and get it all out of his system, and then I won't be sitting here thinking about it and we can all have fun. See? Problem solved." Connor found his phone and grabbed it.

Richard gently took it from his hand. "That is not the type of thing we text our fiancé last minute, two days before a wedding."

Connor pouted, eyes shining suddenly. "I know, but what if I'm going out of my mind?"

"You're getting married in front of five hundred guests on Saturday. I'd be worried about you if you weren't out of your mind."

"*Five hundred*? I thought it was three."

"Not after we invited most of the people who worked here over the past decade and almost all of them RSVPd."

"I thought my bachelor party was supposed to be fun."

"Well, technically it hasn't started yet. Give it time." Naser said. "And another drink."

There was a harsh knock on the door before Mason said, "Jaycee and the girls are here."

Jaycee was apparently the college friend who'd given Connor his first event planning gig in New York City, and she'd brought several of their mutual friends with her. Connor sighed, his desire not to disappoint the other guests suddenly outweighing his anxiety.

"Where did you say we were going again?"

Naser locked eyes with Richard, struggling to contain his smirk.

"It's called The Bang Zone," Richard answered.

"What should we do?" Edgar Garcia finally said.

"He'll unclench when we get to the campsite," Sam Corcoran answered.

"Yeah, I don't know about that," Church offered. "This is like we're heloing into Kandahar again."

"I've got edibles. Should we give him one?" Ken Han offered. "Technically they're for my PTSD but I also use them whenever Kelly makes me watch *Vanderpump Rules*."

Donnie wasn't sure what to say. Their stop at the liquor store was supposed to have been their first group bonding activity, but Logan had spent most of it picking stuff off the shelves they'd already added to the cart twice. Things had only gotten worse from there. As the limo bus headed across Inland Orange County toward the mountains, they'd gathered in back while Logan sat by himself up front—reading. Donnie was no psychologist, but he was pretty sure reading a book at your own bachelor party was a sign of profound mental distress. Even if the book was called *Stoic Philosophy For Beginners*.

"Alright, porn boy," Church said quietly. "Go do best man stuff. Give us the all clear when it's safe to come forward."

Logan didn't look up from his book as Donnie took the empty seat next to his. "I hear the twist at the end's killer."

"I've read the same page ten times and all I see in my head is five strippers running a train on my fiancé."

"*Five*? I mean, I've met some power bottoms in my day but that's, like, a *nuclear* powered bottom."

Logan snapped the book shut. "Not helping, dude."

"You really think Richard and Nas are going to let that happen? Nobody's banging strippers tonight. Relax, man. Life is not a porn film. If it was, I wouldn't have to make porn films."

"I should tell him he's got a hall pass."

"A what?"

Logan started pulling his phone from his pocket. "A hall pass, you know. Like he can fool around with whoever he wants tonight. No anal, though. Only oral."

Donnie pulled Logan's phone from his hand and shoved it in his own jeans pocket. "You should shut up and enjoy your time with your friends, which is what tonight is about."

"Distract me then until we can get drunk."

The bus slowed. There was a hiss of brakes. When Donnie looked out the window, he saw an empty parking lot. The landscape on either side of the road had turned hilly and woodsy, and the one building nearby had a faux-frontier façade.

"Where are we?" Donnie asked.

"Isn't this the place?" the driver said back.

Logan shot to his feet. Donnie followed him down the steps. Once their feet hit pavement, they saw a limo bus exactly like their own parked a few paces away.

"Is that Connor's bus?" Logan spun and studied the brightly lit business it was parked in front of. The sign on the front read The Bang Zone. Everyone else stumbled off the bus behind them.

"Driver must have gotten confused," Sam said.

But Donnie was trying not to laugh as he stared up at the sign. Because the sign was actually a canvas banner so spotless and new it could have been hung minutes before their arrival. He sensed the machinations of a certain event planner at work, and it made him smile.

"This is a strip club!" Logan bellowed. "They *did* go to a goddamn strip club!"

"Yeah, buddy, I'm not sure—" But before Donnie could finish the sentence, Logan was striding toward the entrance.

The driver had texted Richard a few minutes before Logan's bus had pulled into the parking lot, so he was several paces from the door when the other groom came barreling in like a man on a mission. Logan was greeted by the sight of his fiancé looking bored out of his mind, seated at a table between Nas and Mason, while his girlfriends from New York availed the dancing boys on stage with dollar bills.

When Connor, now thoroughly buzzed, heard his fiancé call his name, he sprang up from the table, ran to Logan and threw his arms around him. "Babe! You're here! I'm so *bored*!"

Richard approached his boyfriend for the second time that day, enjoying the knowing smirk he gave him before surveying their surroundings some more. He'd transformed the drab banquet hall into an all-male strip club that looked like it had been trucked in from Vegas. The handsome, shirtless bartenders had been recruited from gay clubs in LA and San Diego. The long stage on which four different go-go boys danced—a Marine, a fireman, a shirtless executive in a necktie and tear-away pants, and a football player with no jersey—was draped in gold lamé with matching gold poles for the boys to work. Marine Corps iconography informed the rest of the design. Frenzied light rigs sent kaleidoscopes of neon across every surface. And together he and Naser had worked to fill out the guest list with Connor's old friends from college. Given the highly sexualized environment, Jonas had decided to sit this one out, along with anyone else who was on staff at the hotel.

"Something tells me the driver didn't get confused," Donnie said.

"He didn't," Richard answered.

"And something tells me there's not a gay strip club in Rancho Santa Margarita with the same name as our camp site."

"There wasn't. Until now."

"You made one."

"For both of them." Richard nodded. "You see, a very wise man who also happens to be my boyfriend now once gave me a very compelling speech about how a wedding ceremony should be about the two people getting married, not just a bunch of traditions that don't have any meaning to them. So when I took a step back and realized that the obligation to have separate bachelor parties was making both of our grooms completely miserable, I decided to get inventive."

"With The Bang Zone," Donnie said with a smile.

"If you know, you know," Richard said, granting him a kiss. "And now you know."

Richard pulled him over to the small dance floor and proceeded to bump and grind. "Are you drunk, Mr. Merriweather?"

"Lightly buzzed, I'd say." He drove their hips together as Rhianna belted "Only Girl (In the World)."

For a few minutes, they bumped and ground, and Richard wondered if it was possible for two people to be happier and more turned on at the same time.

"Gonna whip out some of those ballet moves?" Donnie asked.

"Get me another drink and maybe I will. Although it's not the right beat for ballet."

"I'm sure you can make it work."

Whoops and hollers from off to their left drew their attention. At the bar, Logan was guiding Connor's head down so he could do a shot out of a go-go boy's navel. Connor sucked up, turned, and exchanged it with his fiancé in a deep kiss as their friends cheered.

"Woah," Donnie said.

"See. This is what they both needed. A night to let their hair down before the big show. Together."

"Speaking of hair…" Donnie reached up and tugged at Richard's hair tie. Richard reached up and finished the job for him.

"Now what's this about needing the right beat?" Donnie asked. "Should I go make a request?"

Richard sucked in a deep breath and looked at the stage. The dancers were gyrating aggressively. Hands on his hips, he turned to his boyfriend. "I think I can make this work." Then he hopped up on stage as the guests went wild.

Donnie didn't know a damn thing about ballet, so he wasn't sure what to call the moves Richard did on stage. What he understood was that at one point Richard had a foot on one dancer's shoulder, then another, and the gyrating men had been turned into living stripper poles for a far classier routine than the one they'd been performing since Donnie walked in. He was pretty sure the real crowd pleaser, the one that took Richard clear across the stage, was called a *grand jete.* All he knew was the sight of their uptight event planner doing split leaps drove the crowd nuts. Logan even lifted Connor onto a tabletop so he could cheer Richard on.

Then Richard was at the edge of the stage, gasping for breath, eyes wild. "You gonna catch me?"

"There's enough of me to cushion the fall, I guess."

"I like the way you think," Richard said.

"Well, maybe we should—"

Richard leapt. The next thing Donnie knew he was gripping his boyfriend's hips. Richard was briefly, miraculously horizontal in the air above him. Then they both went tumbling. When he looked down, he was staring into the eyes of the guy he loved, taking stock of the length of him to make sure he wasn't injured. Richard was laughing, breathless. And then their mouths met.

If he'd had the ring on him, Donnie would have proposed right there.

48

"You look so hot right now," Donnie said as Richard fastened his bowtie.

"Stop it, Sex Monster," Richard said quietly.

"What? I'm being a sweet boyfriend."

"You're trying to fool around before the wedding, and that's a no."

Late afternoon sunlight drenched the Pacifica Suite, a subtle reminder the ceremony's start time was only hours away. And he was expected in the Penthouse Suite across the hall for a photo shoot with the rest of Logan's wedding party. Still, a hot boyfriend in a tux was a hot boyfriend in a tux.

"I can't help myself, though." Donnie lifted his hands to Richard's shoulders and squeezed.

Fighting a grin and losing, Richard gently pushed them back down to Donnie's sides and went back to work on his bowtie.

"I would never lie about how sexy you are. Sex is my business. It would be a violation of the Smutocratic Oath."

"There's no such thing. Be still please."

Donnie engaged in a performative pout instead.

Cupping his chin and lifting it until they were eye to eye, Richard said, "You love having sex when you're nervous, and you're nervous about officiating. Which you shouldn't be. Your remarks are beautiful, and you have a script to work from."

A script Richard had helped him with. Extensively. The truth was, Donnie was nervous about far more than the ceremony.

He grabbed his boyfriend's hips and pulled him close. "A, I like having sex with you all the time. B, wedding sex is the *best* sex. Everybody looks amazing, and we're all thinking about the same thing. Getting laid. 'Cause deep down that's what a wedding's about. That and love. But C! The tragic irony is that nobody has sex after a wedding 'cause they're usually too drunk or tired."

Richard shook his head. "That is tragic. Remember that speech you gave me about how shooting a scene didn't really turn you on because it's all about the mechanics of getting the shot?"

Donnie nodded.

"Well, that's kind of how weddings are with me when it comes to romance. Everyone else is getting swept off their feet, but I'm running through lighting cues and guest counts and the battle plan for what we need to do if a hundred grand worth of flowers catch fire by accident."

"Hot!"

Laughing, he brought their lips together. "I see what you did there, Donnie Bascombe."

"I can put the romance back in your wedding." They shared a gentle kiss, then Donnie whispered, "Blow me real quick and I promise not to mess up your hair."

Fighting laughter, Richard answered, "*That* is not going to put the romance back into anything, Casanova."

"Fine."

"Don't whine. I'll do the same thing I always do when we stay out late. I'll set an alarm on my watch for five in the morning, make a quick trip to the bathroom, and then start pawing you spontaneously as the sun rises." The air quotes he gave the word *spontaneous* had Donnie lifting one hand to the center of his chest in injured surprise. Richard smothered his reaction with a deep, intense kiss.

"You really do look handsome," Donnie said to him.

"So do you."

"I hope I don't fuck up out there."

"You won't. Now hurry up. Your best friend awaits. I've got to run pre-checks in the command center."

After a passionate kiss goodbye, Donnie headed across the hall to the Penthouse Suite. The other boys were all there looking handsome and photo ready in their dress blues, brass buttons polished and gleaming. They'd had a day to recover from their bachelor party hangovers, and apparently they'd needed it. There were rumors about what Church and Edgar might have gotten up to after they both disappeared for an hour. As he and Logan made their way to the champagne bucket on the dining table, the boys listened attentively while Chip Murdoch told a joke that had Logan shaking his head.

"It's fine if you cry tonight," Donnie said as he poured them both a glass.

"I'm not going to cry. I mean, I'm happy. I'm fucking thrilled. But I won't cry. You know me. I'm not a crier."

"We took bets on when you're going to cry."

"I'm not going to cry. Shut up. Wait. Who's *we*?"

"Me and Gabe. You want a tissue now or you want me to keep it for later?"

"Do you want your nuts down your throat or hanging from your neck?"

A knock on the door silenced everyone and brought Chip and the Marines to their feet. A second later, the photographer and her assistant had entered. By the time they'd finished the photo shoot, the sky outside had started to darken. The big moment was imminent. The suite grew quiet, nerves tightening in anticipation of their call time.

Chip Murdoch, his wiry gray hair plastered down with hair product, looking surprisingly dapper in a black tuxedo given he mostly wore sweats in public, was nodding gravely as someone was saying something to him where he sat on the sofa.

"Dad? You alright?"

His answer was a wet, explosive sob that made everyone jump.

Logan moved to him. "Oh, shit. Really, Dad? You first?"

"If your fucking mother could see you right now..." he managed through hiccupping tears.

Sam and Edgar both let out sounds like a toddler had done something cute, and suddenly Logan was standing over his old man, patting him gently on the back and giving everyone annoyed looks. Ken's wife Kelly went behind the sofa and put her arms around Chip as he sobbed.

"It's alright if you want to join him," Donnie said to Logan. "I'll be out twenty bucks, but it's cool."

"You need to shut up, dude."

"Get it all out, man. You don't want your makeup to run when you're walking down the aisle with your prince."

Still patting his father on the back with one hand, Logan shot Donnie the bird with the other. No sign of tears, but his expression seemed curious. "So what did you bet Gabe about, you know…"

"I said you'd lose it when you saw Connor in his tux for the first time."

"Fuck off," Logan grumbled. But Donnie could hear a slight quiver in his tone.

Chip Murdoch sucked in a deep breath. "We got anything other than champagne up in this joint? Something good? Like Colt 45 or something?"

Ken cleared his throat. "I have some edibles, Mr. Murdoch. Would you like one?"

"That's a little strong for my blood, kid, but thanks."

Another silence fell. Logan made a beeline for the bathroom suddenly.

Donnie tailed him. "Crying in private still counts as crying."

Logan spun to face him. "Maybe you're the one we should be worried about. Why are you so worked up?"

"What do you think? I'm nervous about the wedding too. I gotta read shit. You know I just learned to read."

Logan glared at him.

Donnie shot a glance across the room to make sure no one was eavesdropping.

"I'm going to propose to Richard after the wedding," he finally blurted out.

"*What?*"

"Not, you know, at the wedding. After you guys leave. When we're alone. I don't want to upstage anything."

"Oh my God." Logan was gasping. And blinking. And tearing up. "Holy shit."

"Wait, what? You're crying now. About me? What the fuck?"

"Sex Monster's gonna get hitched." Logan gulped and wiped at his tears with one forearm. "Holy shit."

From the other side of the suite, Church bellowed, "What the hell did you do, porn boy?"

Donnie flipped Church the bird.

"This whole year's been all about me. I kind of forgot you finally found the impossible bitch you've always wanted," Logan said, gulping.

"That's very moving. Thanks, friend."

"I guess I'm more emotional than I thought." Logan enclosed him in a bear hug. "I can't believe this, man. It feels like yesterday I called you to tell you I'd laid eyes on Connor for the first time and you were telling me what a bad fucking idea it was."

Donnie hugged him back. "Yeah. That's a great memory. I should add it to my remarks."

Logan stepped back, holding Donnie by his shoulders. "I'm so excited for you."

"Well, don't get too excited. He might say no."

"That's never—" There was a knock on the door. Everyone went silent and still.

A second later, Jonas opened it with his master key and ducked his head in. "We've got about ten minutes, gentlemen. We should head on down and get you in place for the procession."

Logan nodded, but his eyes were glistening again, and all eyes in the room were on him. "It's really happening," he whispered.

"It is," Donnie said, taking his hand. "I've never been so happy to be wrong about something, dude."

Logan sucked in a deep breath and started for the door. Donnie, feeling both terrified and proud, followed close behind.

It was Richard's first visit to the hotel's Presidential Villa, which was two regular villas combined into a sweeping two-bedroom suite with commanding views south down the coast. A single knock and the door swept open to reveal a stunning Janice Harcourt, her dress a billowing cloud of rose-tinted taffeta. Her salt-and-pepper locks made a thick, artful tumble onto shoulders concealed by a wrap that matched her dress.

"Oh, thank God, you're here," she said, scooping him inside with one arm. "Tell me, wedding expert." She turned him to face the open double doors to the villa's bedroom where Connor was pacing back and forth, lips movingly silently, hands clasped in front of him, nodding slightly at the carpet. "Is this normal? Should we medicate him? He stopped answering questions twenty minutes ago. I'm worried paralysis might be next."

"He's fine, Janice," Naser said from the chaise lounge. He was wearing a white tuxedo jacket and white bowtie. Connor's jacket was the same shade of white. Instead of a tie, however, he sported a high, gold-band collar that matched the embroidery on the jacket's shoulders and its long row of prominent buttons that were fastened all the way to the collar. He'd already donned the sapphire blue sash, and Richard was happy to see he'd pinned it in place perfectly. Logan would wear one that matched.

"I can hear everything." Connor didn't stop his pacing, his nodding, or his rubbing of his hands together. "I haven't lost my hearing, just my ability to feel my fingers. And my feet. And to breathe. Or swallow."

"Seriously," Janice whispered to Richard. "I have Xanax. Should we give him one?"

Richard shook his head. "I once did a wedding where the bride started chewing on the shrubbery and speaking in gibberish because one of her bridesmaids tore the sleeves off her own dress ten minutes before the ceremony. Trust me. He's doing fine. I'll go talk to him."

"Well, if you want something to slip in his drink, my purse is right there."

"*Janice!*" Naser barked.

"What? I already took one."

Richard drew the bedroom doors shut behind him.

Connor stopped pacing. Save for the terror in his big blue eyes, he looked adorable, but Richard kept the thought to himself. He didn't want to infantilize one of the grooms during a moment of stress.

"I feel like Logan had his freak-out months ago, and I saved mine up so I could have all of it right now."

"This is perfectly normal."

"Did you have doubts? You know, before you…"

"Married the bastard who cheated on me? Yes. Because I wasn't in love, I was in lust. But don't worry. You're not having doubts. This is performance anxiety, and it's perfectly normal."

"It's more like performance terror," Connor said. "I'm afraid, Richard. Should I be this afraid?"

"Yes. Because that means it means something. That means it means *everything.*"

Connor nodded, eyes shining with tears, but he looked like he could use some more convincing.

"If you want my advice from a lifetime of doing this, the ones who are calm and relaxed, the ones for whom it's just another day, they're not the ones who last. They're the ones doing it for all the wrong reasons. To impress the guests, to secure their finances, to get their parents off their back, or to role-play some fairy tale even when they know they still haven't found the one who makes their heart sing. But the ones who can't stay still, the ones who can barely breathe, the ones who are terrified, they appreciate the momentousness of the step they're about to take. And I'm not talking about promising someone your future. I'm talking about the courage it takes to stand up in front of God and everyone and say, yes. This is him. This is the one. Especially if you've been told your whole life you're only allowed to love in secret."

Connor's tears slipped free. He threw his arms around Richard in an embrace so tight it felt like he was holding on for dear life.

"Thank you for planning the best wedding in the world," he said through tears.

"Of course."

"And thank you for turning Donnie into someone I can stand to be around for longer than an hour. He was cute in the beginning, but after a few months if he brought up his dick one more time, I was going to push him into traffic."

Fighting laughter, Richard answered, "I do what I can where I can."

Connor pulled back, his face a teary mess.

"I'm also here to tell you we don't have much time."

Connor sucked in a deep breath. The deepest one he'd taken since Richard had entered the room.

Janice, who'd apparently been eavesdropping, opened the bedroom doors and rattled a small pill bottle in her right hand.

"I'm good. Thanks, Mom."

"Suit yourself," she said, then shook one out into her palm and swallowed it without water.

49

Thanks to Richard's brilliance, the Dolphin Ballroom no longer appeared to have walls or a ceiling. Instead, it had undulating waves of flowers threaded with lights that gently pulsed, creating the illusion of rippling water and giving the guests the sense that they'd entered a glittering cave system. Garlands of silver and purple blossoms dangled in some places, resembling the stalactites of a cave ceiling. In others, they embraced the giant blue chandelier—inspired by the glass sculptures of Dale Chihuly, it was already designed to resemble coral—making its sculptured glass look like something alive and still growing. Curvilinear columns of flowers framed the entrances the guests passed through. Nothing about the Dolphin Ballroom seemed static or settled. Everything was plump with beautiful, fragrant potential.

At the head of the ballroom, the windows that usually offered a view of the lawn, balustrade, and Pacific beyond had been filled with projection screens showing images of rippling water, as if the grooms were about to declare their love for each other at the mouth of a cave that opened to a vast undersea world.

From the back of the room, two diagonal aisles emerged from behind a false wall, behind which a divider kept the two wedding parties separate. Both aisles made a *V* through the rear-most section of guest chairs before merging halfway down the ballroom's length, forming a single, traditional aisle. Divided into two wings on either side of the gleaming, golden altar was an orchestra, and as Donnie and Naser started toward each other, the musicians struck up a gentle version of "Part of Your World" from *The Little Mermaid*. When they finally met, Donnie offered Naser his arm and they continued the rest of the way. This modification of a traditional procession would give the grooms the sense of being surrounded Donnie had talked about at their first official wedding meeting months ago. Their families would unite in full view of everyone before continuing down the aisle.

Janice Harcourt and Chip Murdoch followed. By the time Donnie had taken his position in the officiator's spot, the two proud parents had already completed their procession. They turned to face the aisle, and the music changed, from a lilting Disney classic to the more energetic Marine Corps anthem. A duo of Logan's Marines came down both aisles, each pair rolling a matching carriage wheel that was higher than their heads by half. Edgar and Sam were on the right, Church and Ken on the left. Many of the guests gasped, unsure of what they were seeing. Once the wheels were snapped into place on both sides of the raised altar, a murmur went up throughout the crowd. The altar was also a carriage. Their work completed, the Marines moved to the sides until they were flanking the wedding party and standing at attention as if guarding the proceedings.

With a gesture of both hands, Donnie brought the guests to their feet. The orchestra began to play Kelly Clarkson's "Before Your Love," the first slow song Connor and Logan had ever danced to at an LA gay country bar Logan had taken Connor to on their first official date.

Then they appeared, one on each aisle, slowly processing toward their meeting place in the center of the ballroom. When they met up, Connor's jaw quivered as he fought his tears. Logan looked astonished, like he was seeing Connor for the first time. Then, just as they rehearsed, Connor extended his hand and Logan bent forward and gave it a princely kiss before offering him his arm.

Oh shit, Donnie thought.

"Well," Gabe Sanchez said over Richard's shoulder, "I'm not sure if I won my bet or not."

"What do you mean?" Richard asked.

Parked between the entrance to the terraced slope of villas and the hotel's main building, the command center offered multiple views inside the Dolphin Ballroom. While everything had gone perfectly so far, Richard wouldn't breathe easy until the carriage successfully made its exit at the end of the ceremony—and with both grooms on board.

"Donnie and I made a bet that Logan would start crying the minute he saw Connor's outfit for the first time." Gabe pointed to the close shot of the altar. "But Donnie's the one crying."

Richard's heart melted.

"Is the AC crapping out?" Gabe asked. "Or are you heating the place up watching your boyfriend get all soft and gooey?"

"A mix of both, perhaps."

The guests were seated. The grooms were on the altar, both wearing a wicked grin at the sight of their shit-talking officiator blinking back tears.

But Donnie was thrilled. They'd made it. The years of waiting, the months of planning, the stress, the breakdowns, the Come to Jesus meetings. They'd survived them all and now the moment had arrived.

The words came out as if spoken by a power greater than himself. "Tonight we gather to celebrate the marriage of Logan Murdoch and Connor Harcourt. What better temple for this ceremony than the house the Harcourts built. Tonight we gather in the spot where nine years ago a new member of the hotel's security team laid eyes on the man who would become the love of his life for the first time. The road that awaited them was hardly smooth. Its twists and turns brought them to the brink more than once. And some were lost along the way. Tonight we are watched over by the proud spirits of Connor's father and grandfather, and Logan's mother. And so tonight we begin with a reading from Logan's father, Chip. When Logan was only one year old, Chip had to travel out of town for a job. This is the email Logan's mother wrote to him about being alone with their son for the first time."

Chip Murdoch cleared his throat and stepped toward the podium that stood to the left of the altar.

For a second, it seemed like he might not be able to continue. "Hey, babe. I just wanted to let you know how everything's going. Our boy is strong! So strong. You should see the way he pushes his walker around the living room. Such big legs. He's going to either be a basketball player or a football player or all of the above. I don't know. I don't care. He'll win. That's all that matters. He's got strength in him and lots of it. Just like you. And he's got your eyes. But he's got my taste 'cause he stays awake all the way through every episode of *The Wire*. Wish I could say the same for my husband." Laughter rippled throughout the ballroom. "Anyway, he misses you. We both do. But until you come back I put a picture of you next to the sofa, and every night he reaches out and pats it like he's telling you goodnight. Your son loves you, Chip, and so do I."

Chip sucked in a deep breath, folded up the paper, and put it inside his pocket. "You know, um, when these two first met, I'd kind of made a mess of my finances, to put it lightly. And Logan really needed the job here bad. We both needed it. So even though it was a love at first sight kind of thing, my son, always a hero, didn't want to act on it because he didn't want to do anything to endanger the new gig. I didn't know this at the time, and I didn't find out until years after when fate brought them back together. But if I'd known then, if I'd seen the way they looked at each other, I would have sold everything I had left to keep them together."

"You say that now, Pop," Logan said from the altar.

The laughter in response was uproarious.

The laughter was so loud it crackled through the speakers in the command center. Richard kept studying the flowers on the ballroom's ceiling. They'd tested the heat levels a bunch in the LA warehouse, but he wasn't about to let his eye off the ball. Kill switches were programmed on the laptop nearby in case anything started to flicker or smoke.

When Chip concluded his remarks to applause, Donnie introduced Janice, who took to the podium and read a similar letter Connor's father had once written her about him. It looked like there wasn't a dry eye in the house.

"It'll be fine," Gabe said.

"Pray for the carriage, anyway," Richard finally said. "All I can think about is that carriage."

Gabe bowed his head. "Dear Carriage. Please don't fuck up—"

"Gabe, my dear, you're praying *to* the carriage. I need you to pray *for* the carriage."

The door popped open behind them. "Gentlemen. It looks like we're off to an amazing start," Jonas said as he entered.

"No celebrating until the carriage makes its exit," Gabe said. "Bad luck."

Jonas patted him on both shoulders. "I thought you guys took it for a bunch of test drives."

"We did. And it failed the first few," Richard said quietly. "The Marines will need to push it in perfect unison or the carpet creates too much drag. They practiced for hours."

Gabe waggled his eyebrows. "I didn't mind supervising those sessions. Those boys are a *snack*. I'd let that Church guy punch new holes in me."

"Stay professional, young sir."

"Oh, I know," Gabe said softly. "This trailer does seem to have a weird effect on people."

Richard slapped him playfully on the shoulder.

Applause greeted the conclusion of Janice's remarks.

This portion of the ceremony had been one of his riskier ideas, he thought, converting what would have been reception toasts into the text of the ceremony itself. But with the grooms having no attachment to religion, and Donnie arguing for a familial tone, it made sense. Still, he'd worried the intimacy of it might feel out of step with the grandeur of the design, and with a more nervous and hesitant wedding party it might have. But it was coming together beautifully. Maybe because the love these people had for each other was so genuine.

Naser told a story about Connor setting fire to a coffee cake in the microwave of their college apartment because he'd been raised with a personal chef and had started freshman year with no idea how to cook. The crowd laughed as if they were already drunk, which they weren't.

Then it was Donnie's turn. His remarks would take them into the vows. Thanks to his body mic, he didn't have to travel to the podium. Jonas and Gabe stopped their chitchat when they heard him start to speak.

"I'm probably not anyone's idea of a minister or a pastor." A hesitant swell of laughter passed through the crowd. "But I'm proud to call Logan Murdoch my best friend. And I'm proud that he calls me his. To be honest, when they first asked me to play a big role in planning their wedding, I was terrified. But what I've come to realize is that a friend is someone who shows you things about yourself, good things, that you were blind to before. Who gives you an opportunity to reach beyond who you've always been, to live outside the box." More hesitant laughter. "I realized that's what good friends do. They show you that sometimes you're the one who put yourself in the box, and that means you're the only one who can get out of it."

"Oh my God," Gabe said in a sing-song voice, "he's going to say something sweet about you."

"He better not. We scripted this whole thing. We don't want to upstage Logan and Connor."

Jonas said, "He'll improvise something that works, I'm sure."

Richard looked up and saw his old friend smiling. "Well, you've certainly changed your tune on him."

Jonas shrugged. "What can I say? He stepped outside the box."

On screen, Donnie continued. "And by asking me to help plan their wedding, they taught me I was capable of things I'd never thought I was capable of before. They gave me a chance to be the kind of friend I didn't know I could be. And in the process—" He was staring right into one of the cameras now, which made it seem like he was looking into Richard's eyes. "—I got other gifts beyond my imagination. One in particular that's made me as happy as they are."

"Was that in the script?" Gabe asked.

"As happy as *they* are?" Jonas asked. "They're going to be married in thirty seconds."

"Everyone be quiet." Richard sucked in a quick breath through both nostrils to hold back what felt like the threat of tears.

Just then, the trailer door popped open and they were hit by a wave of expensive perfume. Suddenly his mother was struggling into the cramped space, maybe because her purple, billowing gown seemed capable of filling the trailer's interior all by itself. In a suit and tie, Paul held on to one hand she'd thrown out behind her, helping her up the short set of metal steps that met the grass outside like a giant kickstand.

"Mom," Richard said, rising to his feet. "My God. You're all gown."

"Well, I wasn't going to sell everything. I managed to save a few. Christ on his throne!" She turned in place. "This is your office? Do you have your own team of Navy SEALS?"

"What are you doing here?"

"We want to see the show."

"The show's in there. We saved you seats."

"Oh, please." Evelyn waved a hand through the air. "They're both lovely, in a carved cream cheese sort of way. But I barely know them. The show's you. Working. We want to see what you do." She grabbed an empty chair and rolled it toward her. Once she'd managed to settle into a seat, she realized he was still staring at her. "Well, stop staring at me and go back to work. That's why I'm here, for Christ's sake." She clapped her hands twice in quick succession.

Stunned, and more than a little pleased, Richard obeyed.

"Logan?"

There was total silence in the ballroom as Logan and Connor gazed into each other's eyes. "Do you take Connor to be your lawful wedded husband? To have and to hold from this day forward, for better or for worse, for richer or poorer, in sickness and in health, to love and to cherish as long as you both shall live?"

"God, yes," Logan said.

It was one thing to read from a script he'd written, but now that they'd moved into the state's official language for the declaration of marriage, the power of the words coursed through him. He felt a tremble in his bones as he continued. "Connor, do you take Logan to be your lawful wedded husband? To have and to hold from this day forward, for better or for worse, for richer or poorer, in sickness and in health, to love and to cherish as long as you both shall live?"

"Always," Connor croaked, "forever."

There was a silence.

"You have to also say yes. It's the law," Donnie added.

"*Yes!*" Connor croaked through his tears.

"Logan," Donnie said, "repeat after me. I give you this ring in token and pledge of my constant faith and abiding love. With this ring, I thee wed."

Chip stepped forward and presented his son with Connor's ring. Logan slid it onto Connor's finger and repeated the vows. Then Naser stepped forward and handed Connor his ring so he could do the same.

Once the second set of vows was complete, Donnie continued,

"Wildfires couldn't part you and scandals couldn't ruin you. May you join now forever in the bond for which you both fought even as others tried to take it from you for their own selfish reasons. Your love is unstoppable and always has been. Ride it into every sunset and wake with it at every dawn. Because by virtue of the authority vested in me by the State of California, I now pronounce you husbands for life. You may kiss the groom."

A roar went up from the audience. Their mouths met. When they turned to face the crowd, everyone leapt to their feet. Donnie didn't have time to savor the scene. He had work to do, and if he did it wrong, Richard would have his ass. He turned, reached down and pulled the red velvet-lined bench that had been sitting flush with the altar's floor up. It locked into place at waist level with a click.

Both sets of Marines had moved into place next to each wheel. Donnie stepped quickly to the floor. Connor and Logan stepped back and sank to a seat on the newly raised bench. Then Donnie joined the rest of the wedding party as they followed the rolling carriage down the aisle. Waving from their perch like two royals who'd just emerged from Westminster Abbey, Connor and Logan were the happiest he'd ever seen them.

But Donnie's eyes were on the carriage, the security of their wheels, and the pressure they exerted against the carpet. He knew Richard was watching everything just as closely on camera. Then, once it passed through the doors and they'd all emerged into the corridor outside, Donnie felt arms around him, embracing him, congratulating him, then he leapt into the air and let out a war whoop so loud he was sure Richard could hear it in the command center.

50

Across the hall from the vast floral palace in which the ceremony had taken place, the Seahorse Ballroom played host to the reception. It was similarly outfitted, save for the center pieces—the cowboy boots Donnie had suggested to Richard a few nights after they'd first met, a tribute to Connor's disastrous first date gift. After some initial grumbling about how they didn't fit with the overall narrative of Royal Wedding Under the Sea, Richard decided to wrap each one in little sections of fishing net to make them look like a catch that had been dredged up from the bottom of the sea. How they'd surfaced loaded with chocolate and peanut butter cups was an answer best left to the imagination of the guests.

"It wasn't that bad," Donnie said as they slow danced to the wedding band. "Honestly, I thought the choreographer did a pretty good job with it."

"It was a wedding dance to a Metallica song. Alvin Ailey would have struggled with it."

"I'm going to pretend I know who that is."

"The lyrics were terrifying and possibly the least romantic I've ever heard, and the two of them looked like competitive cheerleaders in hell. But please don't tell them I said that. I'm a bitch, but I'm not that big of a bitch."

Donnie nodded and winked at him.

"That was very sweet what you improvised out there."

"About you?"

"Well, I thought it might be, but I didn't want to make any

assumptions."

Donnie smiled. "When are you done tonight?"

"After the grooms depart for the airport, we'll see how many guests are lingering before we start breaking things down."

"I want some alone time with you before we both pass out. Not for sex, don't worry. I know we made an agreement. Spontaneous sunrise groping, or whatever you want to call it."

Richard batted his eyelashes and looked to the floor at their feet. "I don't know. I might have changed my mind about that."

"*Really?*"

Richard affected a bashful look before meeting Donnie's gaze. "It was really sweet. What you said out there. You didn't upstage them but you let me know you were thinking of me. Most of the weddings I do, I'm out of sight and out of mind. It was nice to feel like I was up there with you."

Up there with him.

On a wedding altar.

Was he implying what Donnie thought he was implying, what Donnie *hoped* he was implying? "Well, that was the idea. So…good."

"Good."

"But…you know, whatever happens when we get upstairs, let's talk for a bit. You know, before we tear each other's tuxes off or pass out stone cold on the sofa."

This time their kiss lingered.

"I've gotta get back to the command center," Richard whispered.

"See you soon," Donnie whispered, then gave him another kiss.

Let's talk a bit. Richard's heart raced. Donnie's words, subtle as they seemed, ripped back and forth through his mind. Talk about something more serious than sex, more important than resting after an exhausting night.

He couldn't go there. Couldn't start imagining what Donnie had meant. He put the fantasies out of his head. They were frightening and exhilarating at once.

Instead, he fetched Gabe. The two of them headed over to the motor court to make sure everything was in place for the departure of the grooms. The white Rolls Royce was already parked, the path between it and the lobby doors roped off. A few minutes later, guests started streaming into the motor court in hopes of securing a good view of the wedding's next big event. Someone tapped on his shoulder.

"They're coming out in a few," Jonas said once he turned. "Listen, a woman with the mayor's office is saying she lost her wrap during the cocktail hour. When you were on the pool deck earlier, did you see anything?"

"I wasn't on the pool deck earlier."

Jonas frowned. "You weren't? I could swear I saw you on the cameras."

"Wasn't me. I've gone back and forth from the command center to the reception all night. This is the first time I've been this far from the trailer."

"Weird," Jonas said. Then he was gone. A few seconds later, the spot he'd been standing in filled up with jostling guests. He and Gabe held their ground, but the pushing and shoving became so intense, he almost lost his balance. Gabe reached out to steady him. Was someone about to pull off his jacket? He grabbed the flaps as he righted himself.

"Over here," Gabe said. He was further away than Richard thought. Hadn't he just been tugging on his jacket? He headed over to him, jumping one of the velvet ropes so they could position themselves a few paces behind the parked Rolls and apart from the crowd.

"You okay?" Gabe asked.

"Yeah, that just got intense for a bit there."

Gabe nodded.

"Also, I think Donnie's going to propose tonight."

"*What*?!"

"Don't say anything. I just needed to say it out loud to someone. I might be wrong. It's been a long day."

"How can you be so calm?"

"I'm not calm. I'm completely freaking out. But I'm also working, so let's focus."

A few seconds later, the crowd cheered. Security guided Connor and Logan through the velvet rope lane and toward the curb. Both men had changed into more casual outfits intended for their flight. The sparkler fountains ringing the motor court erupted, gushing white blossoms that sent everything into glittering relief. The grooms turned to the crowd and gave them a huge wave. Then Logan spotted Richard and raced over. He was expecting a handshake. Instead, the giant man pulled him in for a half hug and a kiss on the cheek.

"Thanks for making my dreams come true," he said quickly. "I know I didn't make it easy for you."

"Enjoy your honeymoon."

The Rolls departed. The grooms would spend the night aboard a Gulfstream chartered by Connor's mother. It would stop for refueling in New York before taking them on to Paris. They'd spend a week there, followed by another week in the South of France. When Richard looked back toward the crowd, he saw Donnie standing just inside the lobby doors. He smiled and pointed skyward, no doubt indicating he'd see him upstairs in a bit. Richard nodded enthusiastically and watched Donnie depart, his heart racing.

"I'll go monitor how many guests go back to the ballroom," Gabe said.

Richard nodded as Gabe departed. And suddenly he was on his own, watching the tides of guests move back through the lobby doors.

For a while, he couldn't move. He needed a minute to himself to catch his breath.

He'd just managed to steady himself when he heard footsteps racing toward him.

Two sets of them. Moving with a speed and intention that lit up the hair on the back of his neck. Before he could react, he was thrown to the pavement with such force the wind was knocked out of him. Something covered his face. It smelled like strong medicine. And turned everything black.

Donnie used his key to get into Richard's room. The man had made him one two months before, a sign of their deepening commitment to each other that had filled him with pride.

Ice cubes clinked. The faucet in the wet bar was running. Even though his back was to him, it looked like Richard was preparing drinks.

"Well, you're back early," Donnie said. "I thought there were still some people down in the ballroom."

Donnie slung his tuxedo jacket over the back of a dining room chair. He wanted to make sure the engagement ring was still in its hiding spot, but there was no way to do that without spoiling the proposal. Keeping it on him throughout the night had seemed out of the question. The chances of losing it were too great.

"So I think it goes without saying that tonight was a kick-ass success all around," he turned, "and it was all thanks to—"

"I've missed you, Danger Boy."

The guy who'd just emerged from the wet bar, a drink in each hand, had Richard's height, his poise, his thick, shoulder-length hair. He was even wearing a navy blue tuxedo just like his. But he wasn't Richard. He was the man Donnie had known as Zach Loudon, and he was standing between him and the door.

51

"You need to get the fuck out of here," Donnie said, pulse roaring in his ears.

"Oh, come now. I taught you better than that, sweetie." Greg Raleigh set one of the drinks down on the bar counter beside him. Injections and what looked like expensive plastic surgery had frozen parts of his face, adding to Donnie's sickening sense that he'd just been drop-kicked backward through time. But there was a hard, angry look in his blue eyes that seemed entirely new. "I can only assume someone filled your ear with tall tales about me."

"Yeah, well, my email said it all, so…"

"It sure did. You were quite rude. And given our history I should be allowed to issue some sort of response. At least. That's only fair, right?"

"Get the hell out or you're going to be arrested."

Greg Raleigh laughed. "By who? The cater waiters? Come on. Don't ruin a perfectly lovely evening. Here, have a drink."

Donnie didn't reach for the glass or even acknowledge it.

"How did you get in here?"

"Obviously you have more important questions for me than that. Fire away. I'm listening." He set the drink Donnie had rejected on the counter next to him.

"I got all the answers about you I needed. Now get out. I'm serious." The idea that Richard might come back and find him alone with a man in his room terrified him more than anything. "Why are you dressed like him?"

"Who?"

"Richard. Why are you dressed exactly like Richard?"

"Richard. Your attempt to class up, you mean?"

Memories struck. Months of people asking him if Richard had been in places on the hotel grounds he couldn't have been. Jonas had thought he'd seen him out on the pool deck the day Richard's mother and brother had surprised them all. Logan had thought he'd seen him down on the beach one night when they were supposed to be meeting for dinner on the pool deck. And then of course there'd been Donnie, who on the night they'd first met, had mistaken Richard for the man standing in front of him now. Confusion and anger were turning into dread and rage. Whatever this was, whatever nefarious plan that brought the man formerly known as Zach Loudon to this room, it had been in the works for months.

Donnie lunged at him.

"No, no, no," the intruder said, raising one hand. "This isn't a truck stop, darling. I taught you better." He looked down at his tux as if seeing it for the first time. "I just needed to blend in. The blue's a coincidence. For Christ's sake, it's in the hotel's name. I know how to dress. I'm not a farmer."

A harsh knock exploded against the door. They both jumped.

"Hotel security," Jonas's voice thundered on the other side. "Open the door, please."

"We're having a meeting," Greg Raleigh said. "Could you come back later, please?"

"Open the door immediately. This is a security issue."

Greg Raleigh sighed and turned. He threw the security lock and opened the door the few inches the lock would allow. "What seems to be the problem, sir? I'm sorry, but this is very intrusive."

"Open the door." Jonas's voice was calm and controlled. Did Jonas recognize the man formerly known as Zach Loudon?

"I don't mean to be rude, sir. But I'm not in the habit of taking orders from hotel security so—"

There was a deafening crack. The lock went flying, skittering across the floor to Donnie's feet. The door swung all the way open, and Jonas entered the room holding one of the meanest-looking guns Donnie had ever seen.

Stunned, Greg Raleigh sank to his knees.

"Sit down and shut up or I'll show you the rest of my résumé,"

Jonas told their intruder. "Donnie, shut the door."

Donnie obeyed.

"Get in the chair, Mr. Raleigh."

Not Zach didn't move, his expression a fixed, angry mask.

"Stand up and get in that chair, Mr. Raleigh, or I'll have you drawn and quartered by three different law enforcement agencies in thirty minutes."

Nostrils flaring, Greg Raleigh complied.

"Donnie, there are handcuffs in my jacket pocket. Get them out and put them on our friend here."

"I am not letting anyone *handcuff* me—"

"Or we call Mr. Niro and tell him you're here. You'll be able to settle some old debts."

Their prisoner went very still, eyes glazing over. He looked to the floor.

Donnie fished the handcuffs from Jonas's jacket pocket.

"Hands behind the back of the chair," Jonas said. After a few seconds of resistance, Greg Raleigh followed Jonas's instruction.

Shaking his head at the unreality of the situation, Donnie secured the cuffs around the man's wrists, trying not to think about the number of times those fingers had touched him, stroked him, teased him. He checked their security with a hard tug, then he nodded at Jonas, who slowly pocketed the gun in the holster hidden inside his blazer.

The next knock wasn't as loud. Donnie's heart leapt at the thought it might be Richard, then he realized that was insane. The guy would have used his own key. He opened it a crack, blocking it with one foot.

Evelyn Merriweather smiled back at him. Paul stood behind her. "Let us in, handsome. It won't take long. We just want to tell him what a good job he did."

"He's not here, actually," Donnie said.

"Oh, we'll wait for him then.

"It's not a good time, Evelyn."

"Oh, come on, Donnie. I'm trying to be a more engaged mother here. I need to tell him what a great job he did. He really did do an amazing job, didn't he? I have to say. Wasn't it great, Paul?" She turned and Paul nodded enthusiastically.

"Evelyn. He's not here."

"He's right there. I can see him…" She pointed over Donnie's shoulder, then her face fell when she got a better glimpse of the man in question. "Who is that? Why is he wearing Richard's tux?" She pressed against the door with such force, Donnie wouldn't have been able to hold her back without injuring her, and that was the last thing he wanted to do. "Who are you, queen?" she asked as she approached the chair, then she saw the handcuffs and went still. "What's going on here? Is someone going to tell me what's going on?"

"We're not quite sure ourselves," Jonas said. "But this man is dressed like Richard, and apparently he broke into his room."

Evelyn backed up a step. Paul put one arm protectively around her shoulders.

"Would you like to tell us what you're doing here, Mr. Raleigh?" Jonas asked.

"You're very well trained for hotel security," their captive answered. "I probably shouldn't answer any questions without a lawyer present."

"There's no lawyer who can get you out of the trouble you're in."

Greg Raleigh nodded, as if he was indulging Jonas's decisiveness the way he might stubbornness in a small child.

Just then, there was a shrill chirping from Jonas's waist. He pulled his cell phone out, answered with his first name, then he went suddenly still and turned his back on the room.

Donnie waited for him to turn around again.

"No," he finally said abruptly. "No, don't call anyone. I'll handle it from up here. Send the video to my phone, right now."

"What, Jonas?" Donnie asked.

Jonas walked past the sofa and turned to face them again, but he was distracted by the request he just made, checking his phone as he tried to keep an eye on their prisoner. A second later, whatever it was came through. He tapped buttons, then watched.

Jonas, usually cool as ice, looked stricken. Like he was trying not to shake all over and would only succeed if he stayed statue still.

In what seemed like one motion, he pocketed his phone and charged toward Greg Raleigh. Gun inches from the man's heart now, he dug inside the pockets of Greg Raleigh's tuxedo jacket. The iPhone he pulled out looked familiar—it had Richard's silver case. He set the phone on the table. Then his search turned up a key card and he dropped that on the dining table too.

But he just shook his head as if their captive's audacity astonished and infuriated him at once.

"Where's my son?" Evelyn finally asked.

"Jonas," Donnie said, hating the tremble in his voice. "Tell me what's going on."

Jonas stood up straight. "You switched phones with him. You activated one under an alias, something you knew Niro could track, and you drew them here. Then you dressed like Richard to confuse them. And now they've taken him instead of you. Then you came up here to distract Donnie and keep them apart. You wanted to make sure they weren't together when Niro's men—"

Donnie didn't remember closing the distance between him and the chair. Suddenly he was crouched down in front it and his hand was hurting because he was squeezing Greg Raleigh's jaw hard enough to make his lips spread open in what looked like the threat of a dumb snarl. "*What did you do?*" he roared. "What did you fucking do?" Their captive's eyes went dead. He loosened his grip so the man could speak.

Greg Raleigh made a show of stretching his neck as he sucked in a few strained breaths. "Relax. All of you. Niro will see the potential here. When he realizes it's not me, he'll try to figure out who to make a ransom demand to. And based on what I've read in *Coast Magazine*, your new boyfriend has an ex-husband who will probably pay hefty to get him back. Now the ex might have some conditions—"

The next thing Donnie knew, Jonas was screaming his name. Because Donnie had dragged the back of the chair across the room as if it weighed nothing. He kept dragging it. Out onto the balcony, where he lifted it up and placed its back flat against the rail, grabbing the legs with his other hand to steady it while Greg Raleigh's head dangled backward over the drop. "You'll *fucking pay!*" Donnie roared. "You'll pay that slimeball everything you owe him to get Richard back. Or I swear to God you will not walk out of here."

"Donnie, put him down!" Jonas called.

"Paul, go help Donnie throw that man off the balcony," Evelyn shouted.

Jonas grabbed the legs of the chair and brought them to the floor. Then he quickly drew his gun as he stepped back. Their captive was gasping for breath, eyes wild with terror, snot spackling his upper lip.

"You really believe Niro will issue a ransom demand when he realizes he's got the wrong person?" Jonas asked.

"I gave his guys a little inspiration," Not Zach finally answered. "I printed out that precious article from *Coast Magazine* and put it in his jacket pocket. I even highlighted Mark Scottman's name, just in case the team Niro sends to do the job is a bit dense. Which they often are. Case in point. I'm still alive."

"But now *we* have *you*," Jonas said with a smile.

Greg Raleigh met Jonas's eyes. "You give me to Niro's men and you'll have a murder on your hands."

"I'm fine with that!" Evelyn called out from the living room. She was holding onto her other son for dear life. "His murder. On our hands, I mean. I'm perfectly fine with that in case anyone cares what I think."

"Donnie, can you unlock Richard's phone?"

"I don't know the password," Donnie managed.

"Can you guess?"

Donnie felt like he'd never faced a harder and more important puzzle in his life. "His favorite painter. John Singer Sargent. And I know he used the last two digits of his birth year on a bunch of things."

Jonas tried and shook his head.

"Madame X," Donnie said. "That's his favorite painting by Sargent. Try that with his birth year."

Jonas did and shook his head. Then he started typing again.

"What are you doing?" Donnie asked.

"I'm trying it with *your* birth year," Jonas said.

And it worked. And Donnie told himself not to cry. Not to let this small detail knock the wind out of him when he needed every breath.

"Call Mark," Jonas said, extending the phone to him. "Prepare him. Tell him everything. Because if this actually turns into a ransom demand, he's going to be our only link to the guys who took Richard. Unless Mr. Raleigh, of the many names, coughs up some more information."

A part of him thought Jonas might be assigning him busy work just to keep him from throwing their captive off the balcony. But he needed something to do, so he stepped back inside.

He couldn't find a contact listing for a Mark Scottman, so he started looking for strange entries. Sure enough, he found one where the name had been entered as, **It's Shithead Don't Answer**. His desire to laugh also made him want to convulse with sobs. He walked into the bedroom, phone to his ear. Mark answered after three rings.

"Richard?"

"It's Donnie. There's been an emergency and I need you to listen to me very closely."

The loud music thumping in the background suddenly got fainter. It sounded like Mark was at a bar. "Donnie? What the—I don't have anything to say to you. You shouldn't be calling me on—"

"I need you to get away from the music so you can hear me."

"I don't take orders from you, porn man. Call back when—"

"*Stop fucking talking.*"

There was a stunned silence, but the music got quieter. Mark had followed his suggestion, whether he was on the verge of hanging up or not. "There better be a good reason you're speaking to me in this tone," Mark finally said.

"Richard has been abducted. He was targeted by someone who saw your quote in *Coast Magazine*, and we think they're going to make a ransom demand of you."

"Abducted? Who would abduct—what the hell kind of nightmare have you brought into his life? I mean, what sort of people would— This is ridiculous. I'm hanging up, and if you call back I'm calling my lawyer."

"Mark, if you hang up right now, I'm going to find you and I'm going to hurt you. And I'm going to do it fast. I'm going to use every trick I used to survive on the streets on you in less than a minute. You will never see it coming, and by the time I'm done you will never be the same. And all the lawyers and all the human growth hormone and all the rich friends won't be able to help you then. Because if I lose Richard because of your ego and you're bullshit, I will take away everything you value. *Everything.* Now shut the fuck up and listen to what I have to say."

There was a long silence, but the music didn't get louder and the call didn't end.

"Are you listening?" Donnie asked.

"I guess, yeah. Jesus." He sounded like the wind had been knocked out of him. Good.

"I'm working with someone"—how the hell could he accurately describe Jonas in this moment?—"affiliated with law enforcement. We think they're going to make a ransom demand and they're going to make it of you. When you talk to them agree to everything and then call us on this number right away. Keep your phone on and stay where you can hear it. And take any calls that come in from an unidentified number. You got that?"

Silence.

"*Mark?*"

"I got it. I got it. I'm sorry. I'm just… This is nuts, and I'm kinda drunk right now. I don't…obviously I don't want anything to happen to him."

"Good. Then we're on the same page. Now let's hang up so they can call."

"Okay, sure. Fine."

Donnie hung up. When he went back in the living room, the deck door was closed and the drapes were pulled. A still-handcuffed Greg Raleigh sat with his back facing one end of the dining table. Evelyn and Paul were cowered in one corner of the room, holding on to each other, their tear-stained faces masks of quiet rage.

"Is he going to help us?" Jonas asked.

"Sounds like it. If your gun arm would like a break, I've got some experience with firearms."

Greg Raleigh's eyes flashed to Donnie's with pure fear in them. It looked like Jonas didn't trust him to take over either.

"So we just sit here and wait?" Evelyn finally asked. "I mean, you're clearly some sort of secret agent, Jonas. Can't you torture him or something?"

Another few minutes passed before Donnie turned to Jonas and said, "What's the chance these guys just dump Richard when they realize they got the wrong guy?"

"That sounds like a question for our friend here," Jonas said. "He's got way more experience with Niro than we do."

"Can I be alone with Donnie?" Greg Raleigh asked.

"No," Donnie said.

"That's not going to work, sorry," Jonas said.

"Can we get some privacy? I promise you can keep holding the gun on me if it gives you a hard-on."

"Nothing about you gives me a hard-on. And we're actually about to get some more company," Jonas said. "We've got a full security team on tonight for the wedding, and I'm going to have to get them up here so I can explain why I haven't called the police about that video they just sent me of your scumbag friends abducting Richard off the property."

Greg Raleigh gritted his teeth and tears spilt from his eyes. Donnie had never seen the man cry when they were together, not once. "This was *not* supposed to happen like this."

"How was it supposed to happen?" Jonas asked. "You really thought you'd get your debt paid by the ex-husband of a man who has no interest in getting back with him? Or were you just trying to distract Niro's men so you could cross another border? Maybe hop up to Canada for a different climate?"

"Or were you trying to get back at me for not helping you?" Donnie said quietly.

Laughing silently, their captive stared at the floor with something that looked like defeat. "Nothing is ever all one thing."

"You son of a bitch," Donnie finally managed. He wanted to stay silent, but the emotion rose inside him with too much force and scale. "Fifteen years ago, I would have given you anything. I would have walked through fire for you. I thought I loved you. And you abandoned me for a killer because he could buy you nice things. You made me feel like I wasn't worth being loved. And it was Richard who would teach me how wrong I was. It was Richard who'd teach me that nothing you gave me was actually love. You lied and you gaslit me and you groomed me to be your income stream 'cause you knew the day was coming when you wouldn't be able to turn a trick for anything more than a quarter."

Greg's eyes filled. "You have no idea..." But even now, he wouldn't tell him.

"Everything you told me was a lie. I didn't even know your real name." A shell appeared to be cracking inside Greg Raleigh. "And now, now I find a man I know more than any other, a man I love more than any other, and you take him from me with your fucking underworld bullshit."

"I gave you a life you'd never had before. You would have ended up on the streets again if it wasn't for me."

"You were just another older man who used me for what he wanted. The only difference was, you walked out on the bill."

Was it shame he saw in Greg Raleigh's eyes? Some rising tide of self-awareness. Had being compared to a trick really devastated him?

Jonas watched him closely. When he spoke, his tone was deliberate and steady. "This is a desperate plan, Mr. Raleigh. This is a tired man's plan. A man who's running out of runway. This is the plan of a man who should consider some options he hasn't before."

"I'm not going to start making deals with you if I don't even know who you are."

Jonas turned to Donnie. "Why don't you take Evelyn and Paul into the bedroom and give me a chance to chat with our friend here?"

Donnie gestured to Richard's family to follow him. They rose to their feet as if being ordered to the principal's office.

At the bedroom door, Evelyn turned. "You're going to torture him, right?" When Jonas didn't answer, she added, "I'd just like to put torture back on the table."

Paul gently pulled her the rest of the way into the bedroom.

Donnie remained in the doorway, watching them. He couldn't hear them, but it looked like whatever Jonas was saying, Greg Raleigh was listening. Then, to his amazement, the man started talking. A lot. And Jonas was listening. Meanwhile Richard's phone was buzzing in his hand, a string of frightened texts from *It's Shithead Don't Answer*, all variations on the same thing. No one was calling him. No ransom demands. What should he do? Donnie texted back that he should hold tight, they'd keep him posted.

Jonas rose to his feet, backed a few steps away from Greg's chair, holstered his gun and took out his phone. Who was he calling? Donnie wanted to rush back into the sitting room and find out. But everything about the scene in front of him had shifted and in a direction he desperately wanted to think was positive. Greg was now sagging in his chair as if the cords of tension running through him had been cut, and Jonas was talking fast to whoever was on the other end of the phone, his words too quiet for Donnie to make out. Then he ended the call and gestured for Donnie to come back.

"We've figured something out," Jonas said.

"What?"

"It's probably better if we don't—"

"Yeah, we're way past that now," Donnie said.

Jonas nodded. "Mr. Raleigh here is about to place a call to Mr. Niro to tell him he's going to wire him what he owes him in exchange for Richard's release. He claims his banker's a constantly on call type of guy, what with criminals working odd hours and all."

"It's really going to be that easy?"

"If it's not, we'll have the support of my old friends. They'll be listening in on everything. They've already got plenty of surveillance on Niro and his men. They might be able to swoop in and save the day if Niro's team doesn't cooperate."

"Might?" Donnie asked, struggling for breath.

Jonas nodded. "But before he makes the call, he wants a moment alone with you."

Donnie wanted to protest, but he knew that was stupid. In exchange for Richard's life, he could find a way to endure whatever manipulative lies Greg Raleigh threw his way.

Jonas walked toward their prisoner's chair. "It won't be alone in the literal sense. I'll be over there, watching, but not listening. And if you try anything, I will shoot you."

Jonas took out his gun again and strolled over to the wet bar. It was a short distance, all things considered, but it made Donnie feel as if he and the con artist he'd once known as Zach Loudon were alone on an island together.

"Is that really what you think?" their captive finally said. "That I'm no different than the dirty old men who used you?"

Some of them were a lot less dirty than you, he wanted to say, but if Jonas was right and this guy was actually going to help them get Richard back, he needed to watch his mouth.

"I can't have you thinking you were that worthless to me."

"Please don't do this."

"No, you need to know everything. I loved you too, Danger Boy. It's why I called you that. Because I knew what I felt for you was dangerous. For me. Given who I was. Given who I'd been. You had this spirit about you, this joy. I couldn't understand how given what you'd been through. How you could be so happy all the time. Because I'd been through a lot of the same and I was...so very, very angry. Every john I ever tricked with I thought about closing my hands around their throat when I was done. And I thought if I got your happiness all over me, it would infect me. In a good way. Lift me up, you know? And it did. It really did. For a while, anyway."

Donnie nodded, but being forced to listen was torture. All he wanted was to hold Richard again. To be dancing with him downstairs.

"He threatened you," Greg Raleigh finally said.

"Who?"

"Victor Morozov. The man I left you guys for. He threatened me if I didn't go with him and when I laughed it off, he threatened the two of you. You and Ethan."

Again, Donnie held his tongue. It felt like another lie. If fear of Morozov hurting the two of them had been the only thing keeping him from contacting them, why had he stayed radio silent for over a year after the man had died? He'd only made contact once he'd been desperate for cash. But calling that out wouldn't get Richard back.

"You don't believe me." He sounded more exhausted than angry.

The vaguest lies were always the easiest. "It's like you always used to say. Nothing is ever all one thing."

"Except the way you feel about Richard Merriweather, apparently."

"You got that right."

"I'm happy for you."

"You got a really funny way of showing it."

Greg Raleigh looked into his eyes, and Donnie thought that it was possible he was staring into his actual soul for the first time in his entire life. "Show's not over yet, Danger Boy."

"Maybe we retire the nickname now."

"Still fits. You're still making me do dangerous things."

Donnie rose and walked to the wet bar. He picked up the glass Greg Raleigh had offered him earlier. "What would have happened if I'd taken a drink of this?"

The man looked to the floor. In the silence that followed, Donnie lifted the glass to his lips.

"*Don't!*" Greg cried out. Nobody said anything for several tense seconds. "You just would have had a little nap that's all."

Donnie set the glass back down and turned to Jonas. "If this doesn't work, I'm dumping his ass at sea."

The memories came to him in a jumble, then, gradually, they assumed a kind of chronology. First, the rattle of a fast-moving vehicle beneath him, then the slip and slide of his lifeless feet over dirt as he was carried by both shoulders and all he could think was *Drugged, I've been drugged.* And he had a desire to be angry about it but when he reached for the anger inside himself, his hand went limp.

Then there was the smell. Dry earth with a hint of must. It was a desert smell. He knew it from trips to Palm Springs. And with it came the feel of a mattress beneath him.

Strange tickling sensations on his face and neck, followed by a sudden change in temperature. Some sack or cloth had been removed from his head, and the drugs they'd given him made the sensations of its abrupt removal seem slight. Flurries of speech then. Rapid fire, tinged with alarm. A language he couldn't speak. Italian. Then his world became footsteps departing and approaching. Occasionally he was sat up and fed something. It was soft and sweet. Baby food, which seemed appropriate. Because that's how he felt. Like a baby being occasionally righted in its cradle at the behest of larger, stronger people. He felt a dull sense of relief that whoever was handling him wasn't being rough.

Then came a silence deeper than any he'd ever experienced. A silence so quiet it seemed to rouse him from whatever jumbled mess of half-felt things he'd been lost in before.

He opened his eyes. Nothing covered them. Wood walls all around, pierced with threads of fierce sunlight. And baking heat everywhere. He was in some empty wooden shed. And he was alone. He realized then what had awakened him was the long absence of the footsteps that had tapped out a steady rhythm around him for he had no idea how long. He was still dressed in his tuxedo shirt and pants, but someone had removed his jacket and bow tie and piled them neatly in one corner.

He sat up. His head spun. The headache was terrible. But there was no sign of life anywhere. Slowly, holding the wall next to him for support, he rose to his feet and stumbled out into the light, so blinding it took him several minutes of blinking madly and shielding his eyes with both hands to get his bearings.

Dry, rolling hills dotted with low scrub. A color between brown and blond. California. Dry, desert California. He was in some kind of abandoned shack. A fire lookout with boarded up windows. Tire tracks crisscrossed the dirt at his feet, but there was no sign of a car anywhere, except for the rooster tail of dust far downhill, kicked up by the tires of an approaching car winding its way up the steep hillside dirt road. The grill of Donnie's blue Durango came into view, and he felt his knees start to turn to jelly. Saw Donnie explode from behind the wheel and start running toward him with a speed and determination that frightened him.

He tried to call out to him, but his throat was still too parched.

"*Richard*!" Donnie's voice contained all the power he wanted to put into his.

Suddenly his true love's arms were around him, his lips kissing his cheeks, his hands caressing his face, and this tenderness somehow made the treatment he'd just endured seem even more horrific. Like the last lost hours were a blurry crime scene photo suddenly coming into focus. His legs started to feel weak again.

"What happened?" Richard finally asked. "Did I forget to pay a vendor?"

Donnie's laugh sounded almost hysterical, then it faded as Richard collapsed in the man's arms. There was a roar behind them and a helicopter powered down over the nearest hill. Richard looked skyward, expecting to see the insignia for some law enforcement agency or hospital. But the helicopter was black, anonymous, and when it came in for a landing on the dirt nearby, Jonas emerged from it, accompanied by several men he'd never seen before.

52

The doctor was Jonas's friend. That's all they told him. A friend Richard had never met before. And apparently the guy practiced out of his house. And he was a man of few words. Gray haired and sharp-eyed, with gentle, soft hands. Richard had dozed on the drive there, so he had no real idea where they were. And he didn't care. All he cared about was that Donnie was there, holding his hand whenever he could without getting in the doctor's way.

"Everything looks normal. Feel free to hang out here for a while."

Then the doctor left. They gave him juice and cookies like he was a child, but he didn't mind. They tasted delicious. He was starved. Jonas entered.

The story they told him would have boggled his mind even if he hadn't been exhausted.

Kidnapped. The word somehow didn't seem real, but it was the only description that made sense. He'd been kidnapped. And the men had let him go once they'd gotten their money back.

"So Niro's men just fled the country as soon as they got the money?" Donnie asked.

"Niro panicked. They'd had an exit plan to get Greg Raleigh out of the country once they snatched him. But they weren't about to use it on some high-profile U.S. citizen everyone would be looking for. They were paralyzed while Niro was trying to figure out what to do. Then our offer came in and they were more than ready to deal. Honestly, they probably would have let you go anyway at some point. And punished Mr. Raleigh all the harder for it once they caught up with him."

"But they never will, apparently," Donnie said. "What happens to him?"

Jonas stood. "I'm afraid that answer is not one I can share. But you can rest assured he will never enter your lives again."

Another silence fell. "Alright," Donnie finally said. "Who are they? Your old friends? FBI? CIA? NSA?"

Jonas stood. "I'm afraid I can't answer that either."

Richard cleared his throat, then took a sip of juice to clear it further. "Do Connor and Logan know?" he asked. "I hope this didn't screw up their honeymoon."

"I'm afraid the circle of people who should know about all this is very small. And both of them are outside of it. For now."

"Maybe if you told us who you worked for," Donnie grumbled.

"I am the assistant general manager of Sapphire Cove, and proud of it."

Jonas went to leave when Donnie called out to him.

"Thank you," he said. "Thank you for bringing him back to me. I'll owe you forever."

Jonas took a few steps back into the exam room. "I did what I could. I made the calls I needed to make. But what broke him down in that room was you telling him your truth. That was very brave. Everything you did in that room was brave. I judged you far too harshly, Donnie. You are a far better man than I realized. And you are absolutely worthy of my good friend."

Donnie was blinking back tears. Then he realized Jonas wasn't done.

"Provided you never again attempt to throw someone off a balcony before they've given you pivotal information about a kidnapped loved one."

"Well, that feels like a skill set you develop over time."

"It is. Trust me." Jonas smiled and left.

For a while, Richard just held onto Donnie's hand, then he felt the man's sadness pulling on him like a weight, and so he brought his fingers to his lips. "I'm going to be okay," Richard managed. "The doctor said so. And he's a real doctor. Not a porn doctor."

Donnie laughed, but he was still blinking back tears. "I should have told you," he whispered.

"Told me what?"

"I should have told you the whole story. That my ex was out there somewhere and a goddamn criminal." Tears spilled down his cheeks. "But I just thought it would be one too many things to forgive, dating a guy whose ex had shacked up with a cold-blooded killer. I was ashamed. More ashamed than I'd ever been of anything. I sent him that email to keep him away from us, from you, but maybe I was too hard on him. Maybe I just pissed him off and that's why he did what he did."

"Donnie, he's a criminal. That's why he did what he did. A desperate criminal. And you have nothing to be ashamed of with me. Ever. I don't need to forgive who you are. I *love* who you are."

Donnie brought Richard's hand to his mouth and kissed his fingers gently.

"But Donnie?"

He nodded.

"Can we please go back to Sapphire Cove? I really need a shower."

"Absolutely."

About an hour later, they rolled into the hotel's motor court. Donnie watched Richard closely as he blinked at their surroundings like an awakening newborn bird. They were only paces from the scene of his abduction. Would he have a stress reaction? Donnie had brought him a change of clothes, but he'd only bothered with the T-shirt; that's how eager he'd been to get out of the doctor's office. There was a loud bang against the passenger side door window that made them both jump. Then Evelyn Merriweather yanked open the door.

"For Christ's sake, Mother, I was *just* kidnapped."

"I know and apparently we're not supposed to tell anyone. But *Jesus*." She threw her arms around him and pulled him from the car. The hug they shared looked like it was forty years overdue. Paul came racing out of the lobby doors and the hug became a group affair, then they were all walking up to the Pacifica Suite together.

Richard informed them all he needed some bathroom time, and Evelyn turned to Donnie and threw her arms around him. "Thank God for you. If it had just been me here, I totally would have thrown him off the balcony."

"Kind of a heavy chair for that."

"Paul would have helped. Right, Paul?"

"Sure, Ma."

Then they were gone, and Donnie was alone again in the room where the ghost of the past had taken shape before him and changed form. A few minutes later, the shower stopped. Richard walked into the living room in boxers and a T-shirt and spread his hands, gesturing for Donnie to do...something. He wasn't sure what.

"Should we pick up from where we left off?" he said.

"What do you mean?" Donnie asked.

"Last night you said you had something you wanted to talk about before we passed out."

"Tiger, that was two nights ago."

"Really?"

Nodding, Donnie said, "Yeah. We had to wait for the funds to transfer. It was the worst day of my life."

"Jesus Christ. Those guys drugged me for two days. No wonder I feel so weird."

Donnie stood and moved to him. "Are you sure you don't want to lie down?"

"No, no. This is about healing. This is about getting back to normal. I want to pick up from where we left off the night of the wedding. So, ask me what you were going to ask me."

"Tiger, let's get you in bed so you can—"

"*Ask me to marry you, genius.*" When he saw the expression on Donnie's face, he hung his head. "Sorry. I'm still a little off balance, I guess."

"I know. And maybe that's why I don't want to ask you right now."

"But that is what you were going to ask the other night, right?"

Donnie nodded. "But I'm afraid if you say yes now, it'll be the drugs talking."

"Well, I was going to say yes the other night and I wasn't on drugs then."

"Really?" Donnie asked.

Richard nodded.

Donnie walked over to the chest of drawers under the television and opened the one containing his clothes. The ring box was buried in the back. He closed the distance between them and showed Richard the ring.

"Are you sure?" he asked. "Are you sure you're ready?"

"No," Richard said with a smile. "Because nobody's ever ready for a miracle, because a miracle is like nothing that's come before. There's no preparing for it. But also there's no worrying it will be as painful as something in the past because it's entirely new. So no, I'm not ready. But that doesn't mean it's not right. That I don't want it more than anything."

Donnie went to kiss him.

"But I still need you to get down on one knee."

Donnie complied, holding the open ring box.

"Now actually ask me," Richard said.

"Oh my God. You are so lucky you were just kidnapped."

"Ask."

"Richard Merriweather, will you marry me?"

"Yes, but—"

"*But*? Seriously?" Donnie shot to his feet.

"I can't live on a boat."

"I won't make you live on my boat. I mean, I'm not crazy about the idea of selling it but... We can figure it out. We'll get a place. It doesn't have to be a boat. I know how to live on land. You can just say yes, you know."

"I know." Richard took the box out of his hand, slid the ring onto his finger, and brought their mouths together with a hand on the back of Donnie's head. "Maybe I'm just trying to act like my impossibly, bitchy self so you don't think it's the drugs talking when I tell you I want to spend the rest of my life with you."

"But not on a boat."

"Not on a boat," Richard said as they kissed, "but everywhere else and forever."

53

It took thirty minutes of interrogation, but eventually Jonas's captors caved to his initial request for a pot of Earl Grey. With it, they also brought a metal table where he and his former boss could sit like semi-civilized people. Carol spared him a lot of follow-up questions, but occasionally she paused their interview and stepped briefly from the room. She returned each time a little more relaxed, which suggested that not only was Greg Raleigh talking he was saying things that interested them deeply.

Despite the loosening of restrictions, there'd been no apology for the bag they'd thrown over his head as soon as he'd left Donnie and Richard at the good doctor's house.

And within seconds of cutting the Flex Cuffs from his wrists, they'd used a single metal handcuff to secure his left wrist to the back of his chair. He was allowed one free hand to enjoy his tea, and no more. The tea was swill, so he didn't mind. As an added precaution, two of Carol's security goons stood next to the room's single exit.

"Cute story, but don't do this again," Carol finally said.

"You mispronounced *thank you*."

"You used some of my best people for something personal. We don't do personal. And you don't do what we do anymore at all."

Jonas feigned confusion. "What is it you guys do these days?"

"The mission never changed, Jonas."

"Oh, please. It changed while I was there."

"You knew it would be extralegal from day one. We told you when we recruited you."

"Domestic surveillance. Not domestic assassinations."

Carol's glare intensified. "I see. So you would have been fine shooting the terrorist who killed your parents before he left Berlin, but if you'd caught up with him a few hours before the attack in Chicago you would have put your gun away in the interest of domestic security? Is that it?"

"Using the deaths of my parents to manipulate me sounds personal, Carol."

Carol smiled. "There is no manipulating you, Jonas. It's why I loved working with you. It's why I miss you. But this is not how I wanted to see you again."

"Greg Raleigh had a front row seat to the dealings of one of the world's most notorious international criminals for fifteen years, and I brought him to you with a bow on. That should get me out of this room alive, at least. And my friends left alone."

"The civilians now aware of our existence, you mean? Both of whom happen to be famous. In their own, shockingly unique ways." She blinked a few times. Was she was trying to forget the research she'd probably done into Donnie's professional history or engrave it in her memory? Whatever floated her boat.

"They don't know anything about you," he said.

"Be very, *very* clear about what that means."

"They think I did this with a legitimate government agency that wants to keep it all under the table to avoid an international incident."

"We're legitimate. We're just not publicly recognized."

"They don't know that and they never will."

"Keep it that way. Especially if your dear friend Richard Merriweather suddenly decides he wants to press charges against his kidnappers and realizes that none of this will ever be recorded in a court of law."

"I wouldn't have done any of this if I wasn't confident I could do that as well." He was also confident that for the foreseeable future they'd monitor his phones, Internet activity and overall movements to ensure that he did. "And if I wasn't confident that Greg Raleigh, aka Zach Loudon, will be a gold mine for your not publicly recognized but allegedly legitimate agency."

Carol studied the pot of Earl Grey between them with slightly pursed lips, a sign that she was agreeing with him. "How's the tea?" she finally asked.

"Shitty."

"Yes, well, you should go to therapy and resolve your differences with coffee. Be good. I mean it."

As she rose to her feet, her goons approached him, one holding up a black sack that looked just like the one they'd thrown over his head outside of the doctor's house. "Oh, for Christ's sake. Again? Really?"

Carol stopped at the exit, one hand raised to halt her security team in place. "You could have just left us, Jonas. You didn't have to tear the door off its hinges and burn it on the way out. If you'd admitted you were heartbroken, we would have understood. We've all lost people."

"It wasn't about my parents."

"I'm not talking about your parents." Then she was gone and he knew if he fought the sack her security guys were sliding over his head this whole unfortunate ordeal would only last longer. He needed a nap. Maybe he'd grab one in the car. The drive here had taken two hours.

Epilogue

Two Months Later

The day after escrow closed on their new home, Richard and Donnie invited a small group of friends and family to see the place before they gutted its interior down to the studs. It was three stories of Spanish Mission style charm perched in the La Playa neighborhood of San Diego, boasting gorgeous views east toward the city. From its tiled terrace you could even see Donnie's boat, a tiny white blip down in Shelter Island Marina below.

They carted in chivari chairs and folding tables along with some of the more ornate furniture pieces Richard had used for the reception at Donnie's studio. Ethan supplied the food, and Roman helped him dutifully with setup. Ethan's bakery, *Sucre Vérité,* had been greeted by great reviews a few weeks before, and the last time most of them had been together had been at its opening night party. Connor and Logan had returned from their honeymoon with no clue as to the criminal hijinks that had ensued only minutes after their departure for France. At Jonas's insistence, it had stayed that way. Richard marveled at their blissful ignorance now as he watched Donnie give them a tour of their new home, describing all the renovations they were planning. The few they'd agreed on, anyway.

His mother and brother arrived next. Of course his mother brought wine. Her own bottle, a subtle dig at whatever he was planning to serve. Then came Jonas, and it was time to eat. Once everyone had finished at least a plate of food, Richard and Donnie found themselves alone on the terrace, enjoying the sound of friends and loved ones moving about their new home.

"I have to say, San Diego was not on my list of places to live when I was younger," he said.

"Neither was marrying a porn star, I bet."

Richard pulled him close. "Sometimes the best things in life are a surprise."

Donnie's eyes lit up. "Oh my God. Are you pregnant?"

"Not quite, but not for lack of trying," Richard said.

For a while, they held each other. "My mother is working my last nerve. She can never just bring a bottle of wine. It always has to be better than whatever I'm serving. Like, right now, she's only willing to pour someone a glass from her bottle if they sit there and listen to her detail the label's pedigree for twenty minutes."

"And if I told you she was willing to throw a guy off a balcony to save your life?"

"Remind me every now and then. Especially with her moving in down the street."

He'd found his mother and brother a duplex a few blocks away and was helping them with the mortgage. Paul's bottom floor unit would give him plenty of space to host the kids when they flew out for their regular visits. Upstairs, Richard's mother had set up a living room designed for entertaining on a smaller scale more suited to her new, less affluent life. When it had come time to look for a new job, Richard had encouraged Paul to revisit those passions he'd abandoned early in his life in favor of wild schemes designed to impress the family. That's how he'd ended up working at Chip's Kicks Mission Bay, the new San Diego location of the chain of kickboxing gyms owned and operated by Logan's father. His brother, teetering on the edge of middle age, was reclaiming his inner jock. At his current rate, he'd be managing the place soon.

"I'm happy," Donnie said.

"You think we made the right choice on the house? Or are you still flying high because *Great Balls of Dragon Fire* got nominated for a bunch of GAYVD awards."

"They're GayVN Awards, actually. And yeah, it helps. But not as excited as Cody and Ken. They told me they're writing their memoir."

"That might be a tad pre-emptive."

"I know, but sometimes you've got to let your kids skin their knees on their own. But yeah, I think we made the right choice with the house. And I think you made the right choice with me."

"And did you make the right choice with me?"

"Wasn't a choice. It was more like fate. Love at first sight kind of thing."

Their lips met.

Jonas cleared his throat. "Gentlemen, I fear I must depart."

"So soon?" Richard asked. "You and my mother haven't started arguing about opera yet."

Jonas returned Richard's hug. "I'm…" He was clearly debating the specifics of his answer as his eyes passed between them both. "Putting the finishing touches on something."

"Ah," Donnie said, stepping forward and pulling Jonas into a half hug. "A contract killing. Love those."

Jonas smiled. "The house is lovely. You two are lovely. Together. And I can't wait to see what becomes of this place in five years when you finally stop arguing about what to do with it."

"What, me? I'm easy-peasy. I just need some flat surfaces to fuck his brains out on and I'm good."

"Only flat surfaces?" Jonas asked. "Are you losing your touch, Sex Monster?"

"His lower back's aging along with the rest of him," Richard said, then he pulled Donnie in close and kissed him on the cheek. "Which is how it should be. Jonas?" At the sound of his name, their maybe secret agent friend turned from the back door. "Whatever it is, thank you."

He smiled again and stepped back inside. They watched him silently through the large picture windows as he said his goodbyes to the other guests. Finally, Donnie said, "You think it's got something to do with…"

"Absolutely," Richard answered quietly.

"I'm not going to lie. I feel safer with him looking out for us. For all of us."

"Indeed. It makes me wonder how many other people he's saved," Richard said.

"And from what," Donnie added.

They waited until Jonas had walked out the front door before turning to each other.

"Donnie, that joke about me being pregnant…"

"I don't want kids. Like at all."

"Oh, thank God. I got really nervous there for a second."

"Maybe a dog. I could never have a dog on the boat. Like a Frenchie. They're so cute."

"They're a fortune in vet bills when they get older."

"Okay, what about a harbor seal? He could go back and forth between here and the boat. I could teach him tricks and you could rent him out to clients for their parties."

"How about a grizzly bear instead?"

Laughing, Donnie pulled him in close, lips an inch from his. "Honestly, I just want to spend the rest of my life arguing with you about stuff. It turns me on. In fact…" He started pulling Richard toward the back door to the kitchen. "Real quick."

"Donnie, we have guests."

"Not in the bathroom. The bathroom's empty. I swear."

"I don't do bathrooms, remember?"

"Even when it's *our* bathroom?"

As Donnie went to drag him toward the kitchen door, Richard tugged back hard, slapping him on the ass with his other hand. "I'm still Sex Monster even if I'm your Sex Monster now."

"Well, if you're patient, we can head over to the studio later and try out your new health spa set. I've always wanted to get inappropriate during a massage."

"It's a date."

In the meantime, he rewarded Donnie with a deep and passionate kiss, their first in their new home.

Chain link fencing sectioned the hangar at Oxnard Airport into separate holding areas, most of them filled with cargo containers. But in the center, inside a mostly empty square with walls reinforced by plywood, sat a prisoner awaiting transport. His ankles were cuffed to his chair and his wrists to the well in the center of the table in front of him. An empty chair had been placed a safe distance away. That's where Jonas Jacobs took a seat shortly after he arrived.

"I didn't know if I was ever going to see you again," Greg Raleigh said. His shoulder-length hair had been cut. His new side part, along with his drab outfit, made him look like a conservative dad. The haircut had been forced, he figured. Someone's idea of a punishment for what he'd done at Sapphire Cove, a crime for which he'd never be formally charged. Greg Raleigh's punishment, if you could call it that, would be more nuanced and sustained. "Nobody who questions me knows who you are. Or they're just playing dumb when I ask."

"Nothing is ever just one thing," Jonas said with a smile.

"So Sapphire Cove has its own intelligence agency?"

Jonas laughed and looked down at his crossed legs. The silence that fell between them was briefly filled by the drone of idling jet engines and the occasional roar of a plane taking to the skies. How many times in his old life had Jonas listened to sounds like these and felt like they were coming to him from a faraway, ordinary world, so distant from the shadowy one in which he'd worked for years even if technically it was right next door.

The prisoner didn't seem amused. "You promised me witness protection."

"That's a few more steps down the road. Fifteen years married to one of the world's biggest super criminals, you've got a lot of people who want to talk to you first. I suggest you make them happy."

"Oh, don't worry. I've got loads of experience telling old men what they want to hear."

"These people won't be so easily manipulated. And the comfort of your accommodations from this day forward will depend upon your cooperation."

"Charming," he whispered bitterly, then looked around the holding area as if he were suddenly seeing it for the first time. "So is that all? No goodbye gift? Maybe a blue bow tie?"

"I came to tell you one thing."

"I'm all ears."

"Whatever comes next, if you ever go anywhere near Richard Merriweather, Donnie Bascombe, or Sapphire Cove again, I will destroy you. Painfully."

The prisoner's wry smile left his face. Jonas stood and smiled. "Have a nice flight, Mr. Raleigh."

He was halfway out the door when the silence broke again.

"Who *are* you?"

Jonas froze. It wasn't the question that cut through him, so much as the raw tone in which Greg Raleigh had asked it. A tone that summoned all the confusion and alienation the secrets he was forced to carry aroused in the people to whom he tried to get close. Mr. Raleigh wasn't one of those people, but in an instant, he seemed to have channeled all of their voices at once.

Telling himself to focus on the man in front of him and not the past, Jonas turned and faced him again. "Worry less about who I am and more about who I know. Look at what I've already done and worry what I might be able to do to you if you piss me off again." He stared back at him for what felt like an eternity, even though it seemed like Greg Raleigh was searching his face for some clue and allowing him to do so was dangerous business. But Jonas wanted him to see the sincerity of his threats, and for that he had to lay bare whatever truth his eyes revealed of his soul. "This is your last life, Mr. Raleigh. Don't waste it."

Then Jonas Jacobs was walking out into the sun, confident he'd done everything he could to rid Donnie Bascombe of one of the ghosts of his past. He wasn't foolish enough to believe that anyone would ever be able to do the same for him. That hope had died in him years ago. It had been replaced by new ones. By friends, by a job he loved. By the few people in his life who had also known the man he'd loved, the man he'd lost forever.

The man who, unbeknownst to him, was watching him through a set of binoculars as he headed for his parked car.

Acknowledgments from the Author

Once again, endless praise goes to my best friend, producing partner, podcasting co-host and a *New York Times* bestselling author in his own right, Eric Shaw Quinn, who fixed the part of this novel that wasn't working—again! Hear him fix me every week on our podcast *TDPS Presents CHRISTOPHER & ERIC*. New episodes land each Sunday at TheDinnerPartyShow.com. As Liz Berry likes to say, "Eric should edit all books!"

Speaking of Liz, the Blue Box Press crew remains a tournament of romance champions. Endless love and gratitude to M.J. Rose., Liz Berry, and Jillian Stein, the three women who made Sapphire Cove a dream come true and not just a dream I talked about doing some day.

I'm reaching the point where I can't finish a novel without having Kim Guidroz and Stacey Tardif point out that I suddenly de-aged a character by three years and put another character's backstory in the wrong decade. What would I do without either of you? Probably write a time travel story. By accident. Thank you both for your excellent copyediting.

Profound gratitude goes out to the wonderful Imogen Howson for her series bible and enthusiastic support of the series.

I'm indebted to the team at Unreal Creative who helped make our new series website VisitSapphireCove.com a reality. Thank you Cathy Dipierro and Christine Bocchiaro for making the web an easier place to navigate, and for helping to design such fabulous hotel merchandise.

Thanks to Christine Cuddy and Leslie Klinger, my wise and brilliant attorneys.

And thanks to the friends and colleagues who have been cheerleaders and supporters of the Sapphire Cove series since its beginning, specifically Lexi Blake, Xio Axelrod, and Christine Feehan.

About Christopher Rice writing as C. Travis Rice

C. Travis Rice is the pen name *New York Times* Bestselling Author Christopher Rice devotes to steamy tales of passion, intrigue, and romance between men. An executive producer for television, he has published multiple bestselling books in multiple genres and received a Lambda Literary Award. Together with his best friend and producing partner, *New York Times* Bestselling Author Eric Shaw Quinn, he runs the production company Dinner Partners. Among other projects, they produce the podcast and video network, TDPS, which you can find at www.TheDinnerPartyShow.com. Head over to VisitSapphireCove.com to learn about the Sapphire Cove series. Learn more about C. Travis Rice and Christopher Rice at www.christopherricebooks.com.

Discover More Christopher Rice

Sapphire Sunset
Sapphire Cove, Book 1
By Christopher Rice writing as C. Travis Rice

For the first time *New York Times* bestselling author Christopher Rice writes as C. Travis Rice. Under his new pen name, Rice offers tales of passion, intrigue, and steamy romance between men. The first novel, SAPPHIRE SUNSET, transports you to a beautiful luxury resort on the sparkling Southern California coast where strong-willed heroes release the shame that blocks their heart's desires.

Logan Murdoch is a fighter, a survivor, and a provider. When he leaves a distinguished career in the Marine Corps to work security at a luxury beachfront resort, he's got one objective: pay his father's mounting medical bills. That means Connor Harcourt, the irresistibly handsome scion of the wealthy family that owns Sapphire Cove, is strictly off-limits, despite his sassy swagger and beautiful blue eyes. Logan's life is all about sacrifices; Connor is privilege personified. But temptation is a beast that demands to be fed, and a furtive kiss ignites instant passion, forcing Logan to slam the brakes. Hard.

Haunted by their frustrated attraction, the two men find themselves hurled back together when a headline-making scandal threatens to ruin the resort they both love. This time, there's no easy escape from the magnetic pull of their white hot desire. Will saving Sapphire Cove help forge the union they crave, or will it drive them apart once more?

Sapphire Spring
Sapphire Cove, Book 2
By Christopher Rice writing as C. Travis Rice

Under his new pen name, C. Travis Rice, *New York Times* bestselling author Christopher Rice offers tales of passion, intrigue,

and steamy romance between men. The second novel, SAPPHIRE SPRING, once again transports you to a beautiful luxury resort on the sparkling Southern California coast where strong-willed heroes release the shame that blocks their heart's desires.

Naser Kazemi has never met a problem a good spending plan couldn't fix. But working as the chief accountant for his best friend's resort isn't turning out to be the dream job he'd hoped for. It doesn't help that his fashion designer sister is planning an event that just might bring Sapphire Cove crashing down all around them. When the wild party unexpectedly reunites him with Mason Worther, the gorgeous former jock who made his high school experience a living hell, things go from bad to seductive.

The former golden boy's adult life is a mess, and he knows it's time to reform his hard partying ways. But for Mason, cleaning up his act means cleaning up his prior misdeeds. And he plans to start with Naser, by submitting to whatever the man demands of him to make things right. The offer ignites an all-consuming passion both men have denied for years. But can they confront their painful past without losing each other in the process?

Sapphire Storm
Sapphire Cove, Book 3
By Christopher Rice writing as C. Travis Rice

Under his new pen name, C. Travis Rice, *New York Times* bestselling author Christopher Rice offers tales of passion, intrigue, and steamy romance between men. The third novel, SAPPHIRE STORM, once again transports you to a beautiful luxury resort on the sparkling Southern California coast where strong-willed heroes release the shame that blocks their hearts' desires.

Ethan Blake has dedicated his life to satisfying other people's appetites. At forty-three, he's finally landed his dream job—head pastry chef at an exclusive resort. Now he's got a jet-setting career that's taken him to romantic locations all over the world. But years before, after his parents threw him out for being gay, Ethan supported himself in a manner he'd rather keep under the covers today.

Roman Walker is a twenty-five-year-old fitness celebrity awash in thirsty followers. But when he walks through the doors of Sapphire Cove, it's not just to oversee the menu for his celebrity client's wedding. Decades ago, Roman and Ethan crossed paths on a New York street corner during a terrible, life-changing moment that scarred them both. Now Roman's back for revenge.

But when his plan goes wildly off the rails, Roman suddenly finds himself at the center of an even stranger and darker plot concocted by his most famous client. Well-versed in the ways of the wealthy and the entitled, Roman's former target offers to be his strongest ally during a moment that might derail the young man's newfound career. But the experienced older man's offer also ignites an irresistible and forbidden attraction that threatens to consume them both, even as it exposes old secrets and incurs the wrath of the powerful and the famous.

Dance of Desire
By Christopher Rice
Click here to purchase.

When Amber Watson walks in on her husband in the throes of extramarital passion with one of his employees, her comfortable, passion-free life is shattered in an instant. Worse, the fate of the successful country music bar that bears her family's name suddenly hangs in the balance. Her soon to be ex-husband is one of the bar's official owners; his mistress, one of its employees. Will her divorce destroy her late father's legacy?

Not if Amber's adopted brother Caleb has anything to do with it. The wandering cowboy has picked the perfect time for a homecoming. Better yet, he's determined to use his brains and his fists to put Amber's ex in his place and keep the family business intact. But Caleb's long absence has done nothing to dim the forbidden desire between him and the woman the State of Texas considers to be his sister.

Years ago, when they were just teenagers, Caleb and Amber shared a passionate first kiss beside a moonlit lake. But that same night, tragedy claimed the life of Caleb's parents and the handsome young man went from being a family friend to Amber's adopted brother. Has enough time passed for the two of them to throw off the roles Amber's father picked for them all those years ago? Will their desire for each other save the family business or put it in greater danger?

DANCE OF DESIRE is the first contemporary romance from award-winning, *New York Times* bestselling author Christopher Rice, told with the author's trademark humor and heart. It also introduces readers to a quirky and beautiful town in the Texas Hill Country called Chapel Springs.

READER ADVISORY. DANCE OF DESIRE contains fantasies of dubious consent, acted on by consenting adults. Readers with sensitivities to those issues should be advised.

Desire & Ice
by Christopher Rice

Danny Patterson isn't a teenager anymore. He's the newest and youngest sheriff's deputy in Surrender, Montana. A chance encounter with his former schoolteacher on the eve of the biggest snowstorm to hit Surrender in years shows him that some schoolboy crushes never fade. Sometimes they mature into grown-up desire.

It's been years since Eliza Brightwell set foot in Surrender. So why is she back now? And why does she seem like she's running from something? To solve this mystery, Danny disobeys a direct order from Sheriff Cooper MacKenzie and sets out into a fierce blizzard, where his courage and his desire might be the only things capable of saving Eliza from a dark force out of her own past.

The Flame
By Christopher Rice

IT ONLY TAKES A MOMENT...

Cassidy Burke has the best of both worlds, a driven and successful husband and a wild, impulsive best friend. But after a decadent Mardi Gras party, Cassidy finds both men pulling away from her. Did the three of them awaken secret desires during a split-second of alcohol-fueled passion? Or is Mardi Gras a time when rules are meant to be broken without consequence?

Only one thing is for certain—the chill that's descended over her marriage, and her most important friendship, will soon turn into a deep freeze if she doesn't do something. And soon.

LIGHT THIS FLAME AT THE SCENE OF YOUR GREATEST PASSION AND ALL YOUR DESIRES WILL BE YOURS.

The invitation stares out at her from the window of a French Quarter boutique. The store's owner claims to have no knowledge of the strange candle. But Cassidy can't resist its intoxicating scent or the challenge written across its label in elegant cursive. With the strike of a match and one tiny flame, she will call forth a supernatural being with the ultimate power—the power to unchain the heart, the power to remove the fear that stands between a person and their truest desires.

The Surrender Gate
A Desire Exchange Novel
By Christopher Rice

Emily Blaine's life is about to change. Arthur Benoit, the kindly multimillionaire who has acted as her surrogate father for years, has just told her he's leaving her his entire estate, and he only has a few months to live. Soon Emily will go from being a restaurant manager with a useless English degree to the one of the richest and most powerful women in New Orleans. There's just one price. Arthur has written a letter to his estranged son Ryan he hopes will mend the rift between them, and he wants Emily to deliver the letter before it's too late. But finding Ryan won't be easy. He's been missing for years. He was recently linked to a mysterious organization called The Desire Exchange. But is The Desire Exchange just an urban legend? Or are the rumors true? Is it truly a secret club where the wealthy can live out their most private sexual fantasies?

It's a task Emily can't undertake alone. But there's only one man qualified to help her, her gorgeous and confident best friend, Jonathan Claiborne. She's suspected Jonathan of working as a high-priced escort for months now, and she's willing to bet that while giving pleasure to some of the most powerful men in New Orleans, Jonathan has uncovered some possible leads to The Desire Exchange—and to Ryan Benoit. But Emily's attempt to uncover Jonathan's secret life lands the two of them in hot water. Literally. In order to escape the clutches of one of Jonathan's most powerful and dangerous clients, they're forced to act on long buried desires—for each other.

When Emily's mission turns into an undercover operation, Jonathan insists on going with her. He also insists they continue to explore their impossible, reckless passion for each other. Enter Marcus Dylan, the hard-charging ex-Navy SEAL Arthur has hired to keep Emily safe. But Marcus has been hired for another reason. He, too, has a burning passion for Emily, a passion that might keep Emily from being distracted and confused by a best friend who claims he might be able to go straight just for her. But Marcus is as rough and controlling as Jonathan is sensual and reckless. As Emily searches for a place where the rich turn their fantasies into reality, she will be forced to decide which one of her own long-ignored fantasies should become her reality. But as Emily, Jonathan, and Marcus draw closer to The Desire Exchange itself, they find their destination isn't just shrouded in mystery, but in magic as well.

Kiss the Flame
A Desire Exchange Novella
By Christopher Rice

Are some risks worth taking?
Laney Foley is the first woman from her hard working family to attend college. That's why she can't act on her powerful attraction to

one of the gorgeous teaching assistants in her Introduction to Art History course. Getting involved with a man who has control over her final grade is just too risky. But ever since he first laid eyes on her, Michael Brouchard seems to think about little else but the two of them together. And it's become harder for Laney to ignore his intelligence and his charm.

During a walk through the French Quarter, an intoxicating scent that reminds Laney of her not-so-secret admirer draws her into an elegant scented candle shop. The shop's charming and mysterious owner seems to have stepped out of another time, and he offers Laney a gift that could break down the walls of her fear in a way that can only be described as magic. But will she accept it?

Light this flame at the scene of your greatest passion and all your desires will be yours...

Lilliane Williams is a radiant, a supernatural being with the power to make your deepest sexual fantasy take shape around you with just a gentle press of her lips to yours. But her gifts came at a price. Decades ago, she set foot inside what she thought was an ordinary scented candle shop in the French Quarter. When she resisted the magical gift offered to her inside, Lilliane was endowed with eternal youth and startling supernatural powers, but the ability to experience and receive romantic love was removed from her forever. When Lilliane meets a young woman who seems poised to make the same mistake she did years before, she becomes determined to stop her, but that will mean revealing her truth to a stranger. Will Lilliane's story provide Laney with the courage she needs to open her heart to the kind of true love only magic can reveal?

Sign up for the Blue Box Press/1001 Dark Nights Newsletter
and be entered to win a Tiffany Lock necklace.

There's a contest every quarter!

Go to www.1001DarkNights.com to subscribe.

As a bonus, all subscribers can download
FIVE FREE exclusive books!

Discover 1001 Dark Nights Collection Eleven

DRAGON KISS by Donna Grant
A Dragon Kings Novella

THE WILD CARD by Dylan Allen
A Rivers Wilde Novella

ROCK CHICK REMATCH by Kristen Ashley
A Rock Chick Novella

JUST ONE SUMMER by Carly Phillips
A Dirty Dare Series Novella

HAPPILY EVER MAYBE by Carrie Ann Ryan
A Montgomery Ink Legacy Novella

BLUE MOON by Skye Warren
A Cirque des Moroirs Novella

A VAMPIRE'S MATE by Rebecca Zanetti
A Dark Protectors/Rebels Novella

LOVE HAZARD by Rachel Van Dyken

BRODIE by Aurora Rose Reynolds
An Until Her Novella

THE BODYGUARD AND THE BOMBSHELL by Lexi Blake
A Masters and Mercenaries: New Recruits Novella

THE SUBSTITUTE by Kristen Proby
A Single in Seattle Novella

CRAVED BY YOU by J. Kenner
A Stark Security Novella

On Behalf of Blue Box Press,

Liz Berry, M.J. Rose, and Jillian Stein would like to thank ~

Steve Berry
Doug Scofield
Benjamin Stein
Kim Guidroz
Chelle Olson
Tanaka Kangara
Ann-Marie Nieves
Asha Hossain
Chris Graham
Jessica Saunders
Stacey Tardif
Suzy Baldwin
Dylan Stockton
Kate Boggs
Richard Blake
and Simon Lipskar

Made in the USA
Middletown, DE
10 August 2024

58896436R00231